Moses
Against the Gods of Egypt
Chronicles of the Watchers
Book 3

By Brian Godawa

Moses: Against the Gods of Egypt
Chronicles of the Watchers, Book 3
2nd Edition 2.3b

Copyright © 2021 Brian Godawa
All rights reserved. No part of this book may be reproduced in any form or by any electronic or mechanical means, including information storage and retrieval systems, without prior written permission except in the case of brief quotations in critical articles and reviews.

Warrior Poet Publishing
www.warriorpoetpublishing.com

ISBN: 978-1-942858-85-0 (paperback)
ISBN: 9798753965066 (hardback)
ISBN: 978-1-942858-86-7(eBook)

Images of the Tabernacle and Israelite encampment from Logos Bible Software, www.logos.com

The image of the Ark of the Covenant recreated by Pastor Phillip Anthony Missick is used by permission from Dr. Stephen Andrew Missick, pastor of King of Saints Tabernacle, 2228 FM 1725, Cleveland, Texas 77328, www.kingofsaints.net.

Scripture quotations are taken from *The Holy Bible: English Standard Version*. Wheaton: Standard Bible Society, 2001.

Get a Free eBooklet of the Biblical & Historical Research Behind This Novel.
Limited Time Offer

FREE

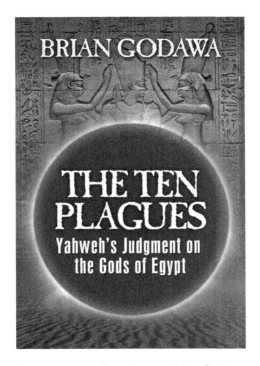

Natural Disasters? Gods at War? De-creation?

Have you heard the claim that the Ten Plagues had natural explanations? Have you wondered what Yahweh meant when he said, "I will execute judgment upon the gods of Egypt"? Did you know that there is a connection between the plagues and Genesis 1? The answers may astonish you. Some of the research behind this novel can be found at the following link:

https://godawa.com/get-ten-plagues/

DEDICATION

This novel is dedicated to Chris Holmes,

a Joshua who spied out the Promised Land: Texas.

You are an intellectual warrior for the kingdom of God.

It is an honor to be your friend.

Before You Read This Novel, Get the Picture Book of its Characters for Visual Reference

Includes Characters from Chronicles of the Apocalypse!

Full-color picture book includes characters for the
Chronicles of the Watchers and Chronicles of the Apocalypse series:

• Jezebel: Harlot Queen of Israel • Qin: Dragon King of China • Moses: Against the Gods of Egypt • Maccabees • Tyrant • Remnant • Resistant • Judgment

These full-color pictures will boost your imagination as you read the novels.

Click Here to Get Now:
(in Paper, Hardcover or Ebook)

www.godawa.com/get-watch-pics/
affiliate link

ACKNOWLEDGMENTS

To Yahweh: You are my law and my grace, my life and resurrection.
To Kimberly: You are my Zipporah, my Eve, my Edna, my Emzara, my Sarah, and every other worthy woman of love in all my stories.
To Jeanette: You are my editor of faithful wounds.

NOTE TO THE READER

Moses: Against the Gods of Egypt is a standalone novel. But it is also part of the *Chronicles of the Watchers* series whose books all share what biblical scholar Michael S. Heiser has called "the Deuteronomy 32 worldview"[1] and what I call "the Watcher paradigm."

Rather than try to re-explain this worldview *within* the story of each novel, I will lay it out here in brief summary. For more detailed biblical support and explanation, I recommend reading my booklet, *[Psalm 82: The Divine Council of the Gods, the Judgment of the Watchers, and the Inheritance of the Nations (affiliate link)](#).* It is the foundation of all three of my novel series: *Chronicles of the Nephilim, Chronicles of the Watchers,* and *Chronicles of the Apocalypse.*

Deuteronomy 32 is well-known as the Song of Moses. In it, Moses sings of Israel's story and how she had come to be God's chosen nation. He begins by glorifying God and then telling them to "remember the days of old":

> *When the Most High gave to the nations their inheritance,*
> *when he divided mankind,*
> *he fixed the borders of the peoples*
> *according to the number of the sons of God.*
> *But the Lord's portion is his people,*
> *Jacob his allotted heritage.*
> *(Deuteronomy 32:8–9)*

The context of this passage is the Tower of Babel incident in Genesis 11 when mankind was divided. Rebellious humanity sought divinity in unified rebellion, so God separated them by confusing their tongues, which divided them into the seventy (Gentile) nations described in Genesis 10 with their

---

[1] Michael S. Heiser, *The Unseen Realm: Recovering the Supernatural Worldview of the Bible*, First Edition (Bellingham, WA: Lexham Press, 2015), 113–114.

ownership of those bordered lands as the allotted "inheritance" of those peoples.

But inheritance works in heaven as it does on earth. The people of Jacob (Israel) would become Yahweh's allotted inheritance while the other Gentile nations were the allotted inheritance of the *Sons of God*.

So who were these Sons of God who ruled over the Gentile nations (Psalm 82:1-8)? Some believe they were human rulers. Others argue for their identities as supernatural principalities and powers. I am in the second camp. In my *Psalm 82* booklet, I prove why they cannot be humans and must be heavenly creatures.

The phrase "Sons of God" is a technical term that means divine beings from God's heavenly court (Job 1:6; 38:7), and they possess many different titles. They are sometimes called "heavenly host" (Isaiah 24:21-22; Deuteronomy 4:19 with Deuteronomy 32:8-9; 1 Kings 22:19-23), "holy ones" (Deuteronomy 33:2-3; Psalm 89:5-7; Hebrews 2:2), "the divine council" (Psalm 82:1; 89:5-7), "Watchers" (Daniel 4:13, 17, 23), and "gods" or *elohim* in Hebrew (Deuteronomy 32: 17, 43; Psalm 82:1; 58:1-2). Yes, you read that last one correctly. God's Word calls these beings *gods*.

But fear not. That isn't polytheism. The word "god" in this biblical sense is a synonym for "heavenly being" or "divine being" whose realm is that of the spiritual.[2] "*Elohim*/gods" does not necessarily mean uncreated beings that are all-powerful and all-knowing. Yahweh alone is that God. Yahweh is the God of gods (Deuteronomy 10:17; Psalm 136:2). He created the other *elohim* ("gods"). These "gods" are created angelic beings who are most precisely referred to as Sons of God.

The biblical narrative is as follows. The Fall in the Garden was not the only source of evil in the world. Before the Flood, some of these heavenly Sons of God rebelled against Yahweh and left their divine dwelling to come to earth (Jude 6), where they violated Yahweh's holy separation and mated with human women (Genesis 6:1-4). This was not a racial separation but a spiritual one. Their corrupt hybrid seed were called *Nephilim* (giants), and their effect on humanity included such corruption and violence on the earth

---

[2] Michael S. Heiser, *The Unseen Realm: Recovering the Supernatural Worldview of the Bible*, First Edition (Bellingham, WA: Lexham Press, 2015), 23-27.

that Yahweh sent the Flood to wipe everyone out and start over again with Noah and his family (Genesis 6:11-13; 2 Peter 2:4-6).

Unfortunately, after the Flood humanity once again united in evil while building the Tower of Babel, a symbol of idolatrous worship of false gods. So Yahweh confused their tongues and divided them into the seventy nations. Since mankind would not stop worshipping false gods, the living God gave them over to their lusts (Romans 1:24, 26, 28) and placed them under the authority of the fallen Sons of God that they worshipped. Fallen spiritual rulers for fallen humanity (Psalm 82:1-7; 58:1-2). It's as if God said to humanity, "Okay, if you refuse to stop worshipping false gods, then I will give you over to them and see how you like them ruling over you."

Deuteronomy 32 hints at a spiritual reality behind the false gods of the nations, calling them "demons" (Deuteronomy 32:17; Psalm 106:37-38). The apostle Paul later ascribes demonic reality to pagan gods as well (1 Corinthians 10:20; 8:4-6). The New Testament continues this ancient notion of spiritual principalities and powers influencing earthly powers "behind the scenes," so to speak (Ephesians 6:12; 3:10). The two were inextricably linked in historic events. As Jesus indicated, whatever happened in heaven also happened on earth (Matthew 6:10). Earthly kingdoms in conflict are intimately connected to heavenly powers in conflict (Daniel 10:12-13, 20-21; 2 Kings 6:17; Judges 5:19-20).

So the Bible says that there is demonic reality to false gods. Just what this looks like is not exactly described in the text of Scripture. But since those Sons of God who were territorial authorities over the nations were spiritually fallen Watchers, that makes them demonic or evil in essence.

So what if they were the actual spiritual beings behind the false gods of the ancient world? What if the fallen Sons of God were masquerading as the gods of the nations to keep humanity enslaved in idolatry to their authority? That would affirm the biblical stories of earthly events occurring in synchronization with heavenly events. It would not have to be a one-to-one correspondence of Watcher with pagan god. Evil angels could put on the disguises of different gods at will to achieve their deceptive purposes.

Psalm 82:8 hints at the final judgment of these fallen gods when it links their disinheritance of the nations to Yahweh "arising" and taking possession of the nations back from them. Through the "arising" of resurrection, the

Messiah would literally assume their territorial rights and power as his own. The messianic connection is explained in more detail in my booklet *Psalm 82*.

That is the biblical premise of the *Chronicles of the Watchers*. The pagan gods like Ra, Horus, Set, Isis, and others are actually fallen Sons of God, Watchers of the nations, crafting identities and narratives as gods of those nations. The ultimate end of these spiritual rebels is depicted in the series *Chronicles of the Apocalypse*. But for now they plan, conspire, and fight to keep their allotted peoples and lands, all while seeking to stop God's messianic goal of inheriting all the nations (Psalm 2:1-9; 82:8) through his seed (Genesis 3:15; Galatians 3:16).

My goal is to use the fantasy genre to show the theological reality of spiritual warfare while remaining faithful to the biblical text.

One other word for those who share my high view of Scripture. In the interest of focusing on the story of Moses, I not only drew from the Bible but from Jewish Second Temple literature as well as Egyptian sources. The purpose of this was not to "add" to Scripture through syncretism, but rather to subvert pagan narratives and fill in the gaps between Scripture in a way that is faithful *to* Scripture.

The reader will notice that there are some strange or shocking differences between this novel and what they are familiar with in their understanding of Moses and his life. Moses is one of the most beloved of Bible heroes. But many of us have preconceptions based on the classic 1956 movie *The Ten Commandments*, starring Charlton Heston as Moses. Fans of that movie will no doubt notice significant differences in this novel. Seti is not the Pharaoh of Moses's youth, and Ramesses is not the Pharaoh of the exodus. And Moses is not like Charlton Heston's superhero portrayal. In this novel, he is much more human and sinful. Rest assured, this author believes the Bible is God's Word, and all proposed interpretations in this novel are based on intense biblical and historical research.

So if you are interested in learning more about the historical, biblical, and religious foundation of this novel and those differences with previous depictions of Moses, I have written a companion booklet explaining the research I've done and the choices I've made. It's called *The Spiritual World of Moses and Egypt: Biblical Background to the Novel Moses: Against the Gods of Egypt*.

Thank you for your understanding of imagination and faith.

Brian Godawa

Author, *Chronicles of the Watchers*

TABLE OF CONTENTS

Free eBooklet iii
Dedication.. iv
Acknowledgments vi
Note to the Reader....................... vii
Table of Contents......................... xii
Map.. xiv
Pronunciation Key xv
Chapter 1.. 1
Chapter 2.. 7
Chapter 3...................................... 13
Chapter 4...................................... 17
Chapter 5...................................... 22
Chapter 6...................................... 26
Chapter 7...................................... 31
Chapter 8...................................... 35
Chapter 9...................................... 42
Chapter 10.................................... 47
Chapter 11.................................... 53
Chapter 12.................................... 66
Chapter 13.................................... 70
Chapter 14.................................... 76
Chapter 15.................................... 81
Chapter 16.................................... 87
Chapter 17.................................... 96
Chapter 18.................................. 100
Chapter 19.................................. 108
Chapter 20.................................. 112
Chapter 21.................................. 117
Chapter 22.................................. 123
Chapter 23.................................. 130
Chapter 24.................................. 136
Chapter 25.................................. 143
Chapter 26.................................. 150
Chapter 27.................................. 154
Chapter 28.................................. 163
Chapter 29.................................. 170
Chapter 30.................................. 176
Chapter 31.................................. 180
Chapter 32.................................. 186
Chapter 33.................................. 193
Chapter 34.................................. 203
Chapter 35.................................. 208
Chapter 36.................................. 217
Chapter 37.................................. 222
Chapter 38.................................. 231

Chapter 39	246
Chapter 40	256
Chapter 41	268
Chapter 42	281
Chapter 43	290
Chapter 44	298
Chapter 45	309
Chapter 46	312
Chapter 47	320
Chapter 48	325
Chapter 49	332
Chapter 50	339
Chapter 51	343
Chapter 52	349
Chapter 53	352
Chapter 54	357
Chapter 55	364
Book of Research This Novel	372
Great Offers By Brian Godawa	373
About the Author	374

MAP

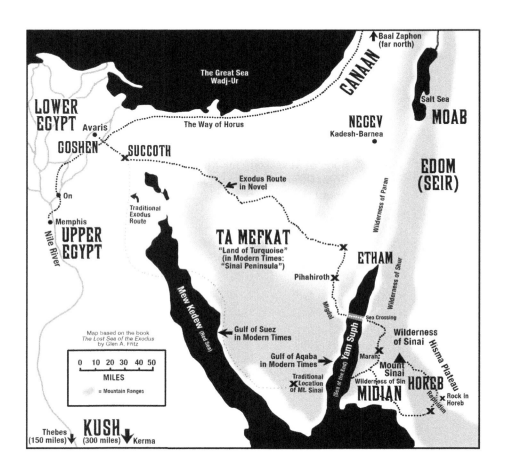

PRONUNCIATION KEY

Foreign Name/Word	English Pronunciation
Amun	Ah-moon
Avaris	Uh-var-iss
Ba, Ka	Bah, Kah
Ba'al	Bale or Bah-awl
Djedneferre Dudimose	Jed-Neffer-uh Dood-ih-mõse
Heka	Heck-uh
Ipuwer	Ip-you-ware
Isis	Eye-sis
Khonsuemwaset	Con-sue-em-wah-set
Khonsu	Con-sue
Ma'at	Mah-ott
Nun	Noon
Nut	Noot
Osiris	Oh-sigh-riss
Ptah	Pe-tah
Ra	Rah
Sobekmose	Sõ-beck-mõse
Ta Mefkat	Tah Meff-cot
Thoth	Tawth
Tjarbit	Char-beet
Yam Suph	Yahm Soof

"On all the gods of Egypt I will execute judgments: I am Yahweh."
Exodus 12:12

CHAPTER 1

The Red Sea

Horus the Great God, Lord of Heaven, faced his nemesis-in-arms on a mountainous ridge near *Mew Kedew* of *Kemet*, the Red Sea of Egypt. Horus had contended for a long time with his uncle Set, lord of chaos and storm, over kingship of the Two Lands. Eighty years of such contention—at least that was how the myth presented it. Set had reigned in the land of upper Egypt in the south highlands and sought to rule over Horus's land of lower Egypt in the north. They tried to settle their dispute like champions.

They assumed their hybrid forms as seven-foot-tall human bodies with zoomorphic heads—Horus with that of a falcon and Set with that of a long-snouted canine creature. Both were bare-chested, wearing light leather battle skirts.

Set swung a gigantic mace that only he, with his massive physique, could lift. Horus dodged and parried with his javelin, drawing blood on Set's arm, enraging him. As immortal Watchers, they could not die, but as created beings, they could suffer the weapons of their warfare.

Horus shouted in fury, "You murdered my father, you sought to murder me, and now you want kingship over all of Egypt?"

Horus thrust his javelin. Set swatted it away.

"You should be thanking me," crowed Set. "Osiris now rules Duat, the underworld, as God of the Dead. If it had not been for me, he would still be stuck married to my nagging witch sister."

Set's words seemed to empower the swing of his mighty mace. Horus sidestepped it, but the weapon's metallic head hit the ground with such force that the earthquake threw Horus off his feet and onto his back.

And Set was upon him.

The story went that Osiris was king of all Egypt and had married Isis, his sister, the goddess of magic. Their brother Set was envious of Osiris's kingship, so he tricked the king and murdered him. Before Isis could recover the body, Set cut the corpse into pieces, sending them to each of the fourteen *nomes*, or provinces, of Egypt. One for each ruler. Isis tracked down all the pieces and reassembled Osiris to resurrect him. The only piece she could not find was his male member, which she recreated with magic. Before Osiris returned to Duat to rule the dead, husband and wife slept together one last time, and Isis gave birth to Horus, the new heir to the throne.

When Set could not find the infant to kill him, he devoted his life to unending chaos to keep the child Horus from taking his rightful throne. At least that's how the Egyptian narrative went. Reality was another story, as told in Enoch's primordial Book of the Watchers.

But now the vengeful Set had Horus on the ground, pinned beneath his mighty strength.

Horus struggled to free his arms. "Let the gods decide."

"Now you appeal to the assembly," complained Set, "when you are losing."

One of Horus's arms was held down by Set's hand. The other was pinned beneath Set's leg.

The canine god snarled maliciously. "If you cannot see things my way, then maybe you should not see anything at all." Set reached down and dug into Horus's right eye.

The warrior screamed in pain as Set gouged out his eye, plucking it from its socket.

He held it aloft in victory, showing it to all the land around them. "Get one last good look at everything you will lose."

But Set's victory was cut short. The sharp edge of Horus's dagger slipped from beneath his opponent's pinning leg and sliced off Set's private parts. Set rolled off Horus with a high-pitched moan, clutching his groin in agony.

No, the gods could not die. But oh, they could suffer pain.

Horus stumbled to his feet, stood victoriously over his wounded rival, and spoke through his own pain. "I think it is time to let the assembly of the gods decide."

"Right rules might! Give the office to Horus! He is the rightful heir!" The argument came from Shu, god of the air. He stood before the gods assembled in court at the temple of Ra in the city of On. Though they currently operated in the unseen spirit realm, the gods used the earthly sacred spaces built by their human subjects whose worship spiritually empowered the deities. Ironic since the deities were supposed to be transcendent of their puny earthlings.

The Ennead—the company of ruling gods—had gathered to resolve this most important of decisions—a question whose answer was also reflected in the earthly realm of authority because heaven and earth were linked: Who would rule the united lands of Upper and Lower Egypt, Horus or Set? So too, the human kings of south and north sought to unify their earthly kingdoms, the Red Land of the desert with the Black Land of the fertile Nile. As above, so below.

Though the Ennead was normally nine in number, others of significance were present as well. All of them manifested their humanoid presence as the covenanted Watchers of Egypt in this divine council of the gods. Ra, a solar deity and king of the gods, presided over the court. Thoth, the scribal god of wisdom and secret knowledge, helped facilitate and record the proceedings.

Isis and Thoth already agreed with Shu that Horus, ruler of the Black Land of the northern delta, should be king of the south as well. No one spoke up for the red-headed Set, ruler of the Red Land of southern desert, so he spoke for himself. "Mighty Ra-Horakhty, the All-Lord, who wears the Red Crown and White Crown of Upper and Lower Egypt, and all the members of this council of shining ones, I am the strongest in this pantheon," Set paused with confidence, "and you know it."

Set turned back to Ra and added with a bow, "With the exception, of course, of your glory. But without me guarding the prow of your solar boat every night, you would not get past the sea serpent Apophis to rise every morning."

That claim was met with silent affirmation. They could not mock the mythology they had crafted for the Egyptians. It was a covenant by which they were bound.

Horus, now wearing an eye patch, guffawed. "You are a brute of strength. I will give you that. But you are also monumentally stupid. I have bested you in all our contests over the years simply through strategy and intelligence. I present my latest evidence of said superiority." Horus raised his trophy of Set's organ taken from their most recent skirmish.

A rumble of laughter rolled through the assembly.

"I disagree," replied Set, raising Horus's gouged eye in the air, "I am not sure that you are seeing things clearly enough." The audience response was not quite as enthusiastic. So Set continued, "As for our contests, before you took from me my manhood, I recall the pleasure of taking yours."

Now the assembly responded with a unanimous gasp of empathy for the violated Horus. The Great God would never forget that horrible experience of rape at the hands of his scheming uncle.

"Enough!" the voice of Ra boomed through the assembly, silencing everyone with his authority. "I have received word from Osiris." He opened the letter from the Lord of the Dead, still abiding in his underworld realm of Duat.

He read the words with deliberation. "Thus saith Osiris, Bull who dwells in On, Son of Ptah. I give my testimony to the Ennead from my dwelling in the West where Duat resides. Horus is my son and therefore benefactor of my throne on earth. There should be no contention. Set killed me, and Ra brought me back to life to be Lord of the Dead. If you defraud Horus, my rightful heir, for the benefit of my brother and murderer Set, I will unleash the horrors of the underworld upon the land of the living. Do what is right. Grant Horus my son the double crown."

The words rang through the hall with fierce solemnity. They had spent millennia building their pantheon of gods, enslaving the Egyptian lands beneath their hands. But internecine squabbles like this threatened their unity. If Osiris made good on his promise of underworld invasion, they could lose their power and become prey to the gods of other nations around them: Kush in the south, Assyria in the north, Babylon in the east.

But Set himself was an unpredictable agent of chaos that also threatened Ma'at, the established order of the cosmos. Placing that agent in control of it all would be more foolish than allowing him to roam free with his disrupting behavior. Set's claim to the throne was empty, and everyone knew it. He was a murderer and a liar and would be banished to the desert where chaos ruled.

Thus, the contendings of Horus and Set were resolved by the assembly unanimously awarding Horus the white crown of Upper Egypt to be worn with his red crown of Lower Egypt, embodying the unity of the Red and Black Lands. The white crown was a bulbous tall pin shape that fit within the wide circular red crown that graced the Great God's head.

Ma'at had been restored. The proper order of the cosmos maintained as Horus was again united with the earthly king of all Egypt, north and south. On earth as it is in heaven.

Thoth, the scribal deity, strode up to Set, held out his hand, and commanded, "The eye of Horus."

Set winced in pain. "Only if he gives me back what is mine."

Thoth replied, "Only if Horus wills it."

Set looked around at the eyes of all upon him, enforcing the will of Horus. He might be the strongest of them all, but he could not stand against them all. He reluctantly reached into his pouch and handed the eye of Horus to Thoth, who walked over to the hawk-headed deity. The humiliation burned Set's soul with the fires of revenge. He was already scheming a new plan.

Thoth reached Horus and gave him the stolen eye. Horus put it back into its socket. Thoth, also a god of healing, spit upon Horus's replaced eye and gave the Great God back his sight. Horus now gleamed with a golden shine as his power and authority returned. He stood to address the assembly, rising to his full height of eight feet.

"Shining ones, Watchers of the Red and Black Lands, listen to me now. Though we have unity, we do not have the security we need for expanding of our pantheon. For as I speak, our perpetual enemy to the south, the land of Kush, still jeopardizes Egypt's dominance. They are led by the rebel god Amun and his allies, Satet, Anuket, and Tawaret."

Those were the names of various deities over the Kushites, a people of dark skin, who thrived several hundred miles south of Egypt down the Nile. Kush was part of a larger area called Nubia that contained similar tribes. Kushites were a distant people but a powerful one that had cost the kings of Egypt many years and many lives in the pursuit of subjugation.

Horus the golden continued, "We must be united to defeat our foes in the south before we can set our eyes on the northern enemy."

He turned to look at Set. "And that is why I will extend the hand of grace to Set, remove his banishment, and return to him what I have taken if he but bends the knee in submission to my rule."

He stared at Set, waiting his response. The entire assembly went deathly quiet. This could turn the tides of war. But Set was an incorrigible self-centered monstrosity. Horus's first act was to gamble his newly gained authority on an offer that would surely be rejected and make him look weak before the assembly. It was as if Set had been given the advantage after all. That the power was in his hands.

But Set knelt to one knee and bowed his head in deference to Horus. He announced, "I pledge my allegiance to the Great God, the Lord of Heaven."

The entire assembly erupted in applause. It was the first moment of unity and hope in a long time for this bickering body of divinities. The feeling of victory was palpable.

And yet Horus watched his kneeling, defeated opponent with a skeptical eye. Set was a murderer, a liar, and a rebel, the very soul of chaos. Though Horus was obligated to accept outward obeisance, he knew that Set was not to be trusted.

CHAPTER 2

Kush

Egyptian overseer General Sobekmose led his army of six thousand soldiers up to the mouth of the Uraeus Valley north of the Kushite capital city of Kerma. It was just before dusk with the sun approaching the horizon. Sobekmose was six feet tall with a muscular frame and skill from years of military training. He wore a *nemes*, the striped cloth headdress that represented the authority of the king, over his tightly cropped dark-brown hair. It could not hide his large bushy eyebrows that gave accent to his unusually bright light-brown eyes.

As eldest son of King Sobekhotep IV of Egypt, Sobekmose represented the sovereign as his general and successor. He was almost forty years old. But as *adopted* son of that ruler, Sobekmose always felt the need to prove himself above and beyond what his station required. So when the Egyptian king called upon Sobekmose to push back the invading forces of Kush, the general did not stop pushing until he reached the Kushite capital city of Kerma three hundred miles south of Upper Egypt.

Sobekmose was both relentless and ruthless toward his enemies. He had first recaptured the old Egyptian capital city of Memphis from the Kushite invaders, enslaving the captives for building projects. He then took back the new urban center of Thebes along with its magnificent temple of Karnak that had been desecrated by the abominable foreigners. But the further Sobekmose went south upriver, further away from the Nile delta, the more he would execute captives rather than enslave them.

After returning the cities and forts along the river back into Egyptian hands, the general kept marching into Kushite territory on his way to Kerma with intentions of retribution. He knew the Kushite king would be expecting him but not from this direction and not this soon. The typical pathway of approach to Kerma was to follow the Nile shoreline and then to cross the water to attack the city on the east bank. But this route was circuitous along the snaking river, taking a week or more, and a riverside attack was perilous for the Egyptian forces.

So Sobekmose took a short cut by crossing the Nile up north at the third cataract where the waters were rough with rocks and boulders. He then came directly south, avoiding the river, and was about to travel through the Uraeus Valley, which led directly to Kerma's north city walls. He would arrive at the capital days before the Kushites anticipated him, thus surprising them. And he would also avoid the disadvantage of attacking from the riverside of the fortress.

But there was a dangerous complication to this strategic surprise route. The valley through which they were about to pass was infested with the winged fiery serpent called the uraeus, which could decimate an army with their venomous bites. It was the reason why the Kushites would never expect their attackers to come this way, a natural threat promising mass casualties into which no informed leader would deliberately march their men.

But Sobekmose was more than informed. He was also prepared. He stood in his chariot looking into the valley before them. His lieutenant and loyal bodyguard Khanethothes rode a chariot beside the general and eyed him for a command. He was the general's physical and mental equal though in some ways his opposite. Khanethothes was bald with white eyebrows and lashes, light-blue eyes, and whitish skin. He was an albino Nubian who had an otherworldly hybrid presence.

Sobekmose gestured, and the trumpeters called forward a special regiment. A hundred wagons carrying large baskets made from papyrus reeds came wheeling to the front of the army. Another command and the baskets were opened.

A flurry of thousands of birds burst out of their baskets and into the valley like a storm cloud. They were ibises, large birds, mostly light-feathered, with hearty bodies, long curved necks, and even longer beaks. Ibises were sacred for their connection to Thoth, the scribal god of wisdom.

And they were snake killers.

Sobekmose smirked at Khanethothes as they watched the flurry of birds descend upon the valley like a regiment of avian mercenaries, hunting and killing a multitude of serpents hidden from the setting sun in the rocks and crevices.

Some of the flying serpents burst out of their hiding places to fight back, their leathery wings allowing them the ability to glide for short distances. They were normally a frightening sight to human victims. But they didn't have the strength or agility of their feathered adversaries, who were swooping and soaring from superior positions. The sounds of ibises screeching echoed against the valley walls like attacking war cries. The soldiers cheered behind Sobekmose.

Khanethothes leaned toward his general with a return grin. "It appears that your tactic worked, General. The soldiers think you are Thoth incarnate. You should have no trouble getting them to storm the impossible fortress of our enemy."

The lieutenant was being a bit ironic. The general was concerned about the Kushites' mighty defenses. Military forces could not fully surround their walled city because of its location on the shore of the Nile, and those walls were tall and deep.

It had taken almost a year for Sobekmose to recapture Upper Egypt. But now they were in the enemy's territory far from home and reinforcements. And it was going to be a long siege.

The standard bearers were the first to step into the cleared valley. They carried the military banners of the king, images of golden winged uraeus serpents on poles just like the serpents that had been killed in this valley. The uraeus was a symbol of the king's own power, thus their presence on many of the headdresses and crowns worn by royalty. But Egyptians believed that the standards were not merely symbols. They were actual repositories of the king's divine power. The attacking soldiers hoped that the divine power of the king contained in his standards would repel any surviving serpents.

As Sobekmose led his army through the cleared Uraeus Valley, his only thought was to pray to the gods that this surprise attack might gain him the upper hand he needed to achieve a most difficult conquest.

His prayers were answered when an Egyptian scout met them just before reaching the end of the valley at dusk. He brought information that the Kushite army, about four thousand strong, was encamped just outside the walls of

Kerma a mere half-mile from the invading forces. And they had no clue what was coming for them.

Sobekmose mused over the relative parity of battle skills between his people and his enemies. Egyptian and Kushite soldiers were similarly dressed and equipped for war. Both wore battle skirts, the Egyptians of white linen with a loin cloth covering, the Kushites of animal skins like panthers or lions. Both tended to be bare-chested with sandals or bare feet, and both used similar weapons of arrows, spears, and swords. Both carried animal skin-covered shields, but the Egyptian version was tall and square with a rounded top while the Kushite version was smaller and round.

Though the Egyptians outnumbered the Kushite forces and had the element of a surprise night attack, his enemies had one advantage in that scenario. They were ebony-skinned, rendering them difficult to see in the dark of evening.

So Sobekmose prayed to Thoth, the moon god of Egypt, to grant them the light to see their enemy as the ibises had seen the serpents in the hidden crevices of the Uraeus Valley. And he planned the attack for the hour just before dawn so that by the time fighting was engaged, the light of day would be their ally.

Sobekmose and Khanethothes led the Egyptian chariots out of the valley and onto the field where the Kushites were quartered. The cloud of dust churned up around them, making Sobekmose think of Set, the storm god, riding on clouds of judgment. Lightning was in his hands and thunder on his lips as his chariot forces crashed into the unsuspecting camp of enemy soldiers in tents.

Most of the Kushites were at ease, sleeping or cleaning up from their dinner meal. They were brutal warriors, but few were able to gather their weapons in time to fight Egypt's mighty swift sword that came down upon their heads.

Chariots first crashed through the camp, trampling everything beneath their war hooves and wooden wheels until chaos led to panic. The Egyptian infantry followed, cutting down the unprepared Kushites trying to muster a fighting force.

Blood ran through the streets as high as a horse's bridle that night. The Kushite army was slaughtered without mercy as the stars fell from the sky and the moon turned to blood. Such was the symbolic language of military destruction. It was swift justice in Sobekmose's mind.

But not swift enough.

About a quarter of the Kushite soldiers had escaped behind the walls of the city and were able to shut the gates before the Egyptians could catch them. Sobekmose led a battery of a hundred Egyptians up to the gates with logs to batter their way in before the Kushites could reinforce the gateway.

The morning sun was rising in the sky at the Egyptians' backs. Ra's rays blinded the eyes of the Kushites facing them. Sobekmose jumped off his chariot in complete disregard for his own safety and engaged in hand-to-hand combat with two Kushite warriors left outside the gates.

He used his *khopesh* sickle sword to hack one warrior to the ground. But when the other tripped over his fallen comrade, Sobekmose allowed him the dignity to stand back up before returning to battle with him. He didn't do so for the sake of fairness. The point, after all, was to win the battle and kill the enemy. But he had a deep-seated sense of pride that wanted all his achievements to be won by superior skill, not from mere luck or favor.

He cut down his opponent with his superior skill.

The Egyptian soldiers began pounding away at the gate's creaking timber with several battering rams, thirty men to a log. But in their haste, they failed to concern themselves with what was going on over their heads. Large cauldrons of boiling pitch came pouring down, scalding many to death. As the survivors sought to rescue their fellow burned, a fiery arrow hit the oily black liquid and caused a firestorm to consume everyone in its fury.

Virtually all the Egyptian warriors involved in the gate offensive perished in the conflagration. Sobekmose tried to drag one of his wounded soldiers to safety, but the heat was unbearable, so he watched in horror, hearing his own men screaming in pain as they were burned alive in the flames.

That moment of dread pause allowed an archer on the precipice to take aim with his bow right at the back of Sobekmose. But the Kushite arrow went askew when an enemy dart hit the archer in the sternum—a dart launched by the bow of Khanethothes, who was guarding his lord and overseer. Sobekmose thanked him with a gesture of his fist over his heart and jumped back onto his chariot. The two rode back to their camp, leaving the Kushites safely behind their impenetrable walls.

Sobekmose and Khanethothes rode their chariots up to a ledge overlooking Kerma with a good vantage point about a hundred yards out. The morning sun illuminated the massacre below.

Sobekmose stared at the main tower. In that rising light, he could see a Kushite woman guarded by warriors standing at the top of the rampart and looking his way. She was dressed in what appeared to be royal garb with gems and golden jewelry sparkling in the sunlight. She stood with a regal posture that betrayed a high status, maybe that of a princess. She turned away quickly and was escorted back into the dark tower.

Khanethothes said, "I saw her watching you at the gates. I trust we sufficiently inspired her with fear."

Sobekmose responded with a shrug. "More importantly, the king."

They returned to their stronghold. Sobekmose did not look forward to the long siege that was sure to follow.

CHAPTER 3

Ra's solar boat began its rising journey across the morning sky. Sobekmose marched his way through camp back to his vast war tent for an appointment he had with the scribe Ipuwer. It had been a week since the siege began. The Egyptians had built their fortified camp on top of the Kushite encampment just out of range of the city walls. They stuck war shields in the ground around the perimeter and placed the general's large tent in the middle of the soldiers' tents. They had sentries keeping watch around the fence of shields to alert the Egyptian forces of any Kushite raids. But there were no raids forthcoming. The Kushites had lost too many of their forces, so they were hunkering down inside for the long haul.

So be it, thought Sobekmose. It would give him time for his messengers to communicate to the Egyptian king of their need for extra supplies and fresh soldiers.

The capture of Kerma would be a significant victory for Egypt. Kush had been a source of much needed trade goods. Ebony, ivory, incense, ostrich eggs, and other exotic commodities were treasured by Egyptians, whose exchange goods of honey, oil, ointments, and woven garments were desired by Kushites. But this southern nation also had an abundance of highly valuable raw materials such as gold, copper, precious stones, and most of all, a large slave workforce for mining those rare earth resources. If King Sobekhotep gained control over this land, he would enrich his kingdom beyond mere trade and increase his own workforce for dynastic expansion.

Sobekmose entered his tent, a large multi-room residence for the royal overseer of the northern army. He had a bedroom, a war room, and another reading compartment for his scrolls that he liked to bring with him. As a royal son, he was trained in all the arts of ruling, including scribal wisdom and multiple languages. He had a love for scrolls. He was fascinated by the learning of the kingdoms of the earth. The laws of Hammurabi of Babylon. The war strategy of Sargon the Great in Akkad. The ancient literature of his own precious Egypt, center of the earth and oldest and wisest of all civilizations.

He made his way to the scroll room where the slender Ipuwer awaited dressed in royal garments that reflected the scribal god Thoth's own dress. A knee-length pleated kilt was wrapped around his waist. His torso was bare except for the wide necklace of turquoise and precious metals that draped his shoulders and upper chest. On his bald head he wore a plain *nemes* headdress, a sign of royal stewardship. The striped version of the headdress was reserved for the king.

"My lord overseer," Ipuwer said. "May we take a seat and begin?"

Sobekmose nodded, and they sat down on wooden stools facing each other.

Ipuwer led. "I am General Sobekmose, crown prince and son of Khaneferre Sobekhotep the Fourth of Egypt's thirteenth dynasty."

Sobekmose repeated the words, "I am General Sobekmose, c-crown prince and son of K-k-khaneferre Sobekhotep the F-f-f-fourth of Egypt's t-t-thirteenth dynasty."

"Very good," said Ipuwer. "Now watch my lips and let us say it together."

Sobekmose focused, trying to concentrate on the smooth pronunciation as he imitated his tutor. "I am General Sobekmose, c-crown prince and son of K-k-haneferre Sobekhotep the Fourth of Egypt's t-thirteenth dynasty."

"Better," said Ipuwer. "Now let us go through our exercises."

Ipuwer was a patient and supportive tutor. Sobekmose had been cursed with a stuttering problem since he was young. It haunted him through the years like an evil spirit. It had gotten better over time, but it seemed he would never fully eliminate it. It was the worst affliction to have as Egypt's crown prince. How could the people believe in the authority of a ruler who spoke with such hesitancy? Rulers needed to be strong and sure. Stuttering was weakness. It was one of the reasons why Sobekmose had striven to excel in both intellectual education and physical prowess. And why he had become a man of few words and a man of action instead.

His military strategy and fighting skills were superior to that of his brother Khahotepre, whose mental capacity was on the level of a baboon as far as the general was concerned. But despite Sobekmose's distinguished traits and status, his origin made his inheritance precarious. Technically, he was firstborn by legal treaty, not by birth. He'd been born in the delta forty years ago after the early death of his birth father to Princess Meryt of Lower Egypt.

In those days, the two kings reigning over Upper and Lower Egypt stressed the nation's unity. Meryt's father, Palmanothes, was king of Lower Egypt in the north, considered "lower" because of its sea level elevation. Sobekhotep IV was the stronger king of Upper Egypt in the southern higher elevation. In the interest of unifying north and south under Sobekhotep, a marriage treaty uniting the young royal widow with Sobekhotep sealed the breach.

One of the covenant's conditions was that the king adopt her son and only living male heir and give the new crown prince the name Sobekmose. He would be removed from royal succession only if Palmanothes's daughter bore Sobekhotep a son, thereby joining in one throne the bloodlines of Upper and Lower Egypt .

All of which did not please Sobekhotep's chief wife at the time, who had just birthed Sobekhotep's own firstborn son Khahotepre. That Sobekhotep had chosen sovereignty over a united, powerful Egypt over securing his own bloodline on the throne rankled both his first wife and his son Khahotepre as he grew into adulthood. Especially when Meryt bore no children to her new husband and king, leaving Sobekmose as heir to the throne.

But if Sobekmose inherited the throne in his current condition, it could plunge the kingdom into chaos. For the king was a god, Horus incarnate on earth. And gods do not stutter. Such a situation could cause a revolution against the Ma'at of Egyptian civilization, its structured peace and orderliness. If the king was manifestly a weak mortal, then eventually the people would believe that they could rule their own lives with every man his own king. And that would truly be chaos, a symbolic return to the formlessness and void of the primeval waters. Sobekmose had to overcome this impediment.

"Think of each word by itself," instructed Ipuwer, "and say it slowly."

It was the last exercise of the day. They now sat before a table where Sobekmose was reading hieroglyphs, the Egyptians' writing system. They were helpful because they were images that typically represented sounds.

Sobekmose read carefully the official titulary of his father: "Khaneferre - Sobekhotep - the - Fourth, - the - living - Horus, - the - Son - of - Ra, - Lord - of - the - Two - Lands – K-k-k-k..." He stopped, his jaw tightened, jutted outward. He howled with pent-up anger, grabbed the table and scroll, and threw them into the shelf of scrolls with a crash.

"Calm, my lord." The scribe was the only one who was allowed to speak frankly to the prince—but only in private. Sobekmose had spent untold hours with him learning languages, writing, and speaking. Ipuwer had earned the prince's trust.

"I cannot command respect if I cannot get through a sentence without stammering!" Sobekmose burst out in anger.

"You just did," said Ipuwer.

Sobekmose paused, off-guard. The scribe was right.

"Because in your anger you were not thinking about your words."

He was right again. The prince had to take his thoughts off himself.

Ipuwer said, "Unfortunately, intemperance will not command respect either."

They had addressed this before. The prince had acquired an explosive temper over the years. His frustration with his inability to conquer this one little impediment to greatness often drove him to rage. He found himself creating excuses to beat any of his subordinates whom he considered a threat to his authority.

But an ill-tempered ruler was not a long-lived ruler.

The scribe added, "Now, if we can only get you to stop thinking about your words—but also without anger."

Sobekmose tried to calm himself down. "I think it is t-t-time to turn that anger against K-k-kush."

"Then by all means," replied Ipuwer. "Our lesson is done."

CHAPTER 4

Sobekmose and Ipuwer entered the holy tent of the lector priests near the prince general's own residence. The priests, Jannes and Jambres, were twin brothers in their twenties who traveled with the army to support their campaign with magic, also called *heka,* the same name of the god of magic. As lector priests, they were bald, shaven of all their hair for the purpose of sacred cleanness. They wore a simple pleated white linen kilt that was knee length with a leopard's skin over their left shoulders to their right hips. Two paws of the leopard remained as part of the pelt's ornament.

The young brothers' handsome foreign faces never seemed to age. Sobekmose had heard rumors that they'd made a deal with the gods for eternal youth. This rumor, coupled with the inability to distinguish between their identical look, added an air of spiritual mystery to their reputation.

But Sobekmose knew they were Asiatics from Avaris, the prince's own home city in Goshen, the fertile Nile delta region. "Asiatic" was the term used of all Semitic-speaking peoples from the north such as Canaan, Syria, and Asia Minor. Some called those people *Habiru,* which meant nomadic migrants, often without a country. The Asiatics in Avaris called themselves Hebrews. But the truth was that the Habiru had migrated from Canaan to the delta of Upper Egypt hundreds of years earlier. They had integrated into their host nation but remained a stubborn lot that sought special privileges for their people.

Jannes and Jambres had rejected their Habiru heritage and had joined the temple of Ra in their youth. Now they were favored priests in the king's entourage and no doubt had their eyes on the high priesthood of Ra as their ambition. That was something Sobekmose could use to his advantage.

Sobekmose and Ipuwer walked past two seven-foot copper pillars at the entrance, symbolic of world trees supporting the roof of heaven.

As they entered the darkened inner sanctuary, they were surrounded by a smokey cloud of incense. The two lector priests appeared out of the smoke and shadows as if materializing out of the spiritual realm, a common ploy of priests to impress their visitors.

Sobekmose felt a little lightheaded from the effects of the incense. He hated not being in complete control of his senses. Though it did lessen his stammering.

The priests spoke in perfect unison. "My lord and overseer Sobekmose, son of Sobekhotep."

"Still looking forever young, I s-see," Sobekmose quipped. "You must tell me your secret some d-day."

One of them, he couldn't tell which one, said, "The secrets of Isis, my lord."

As the mother of Horus, Isis was protector of the king, the living form of Horus. Hers was the most powerful of magic. She was known to be capable of reversing or preventing decay as she had done with Osiris's body. These priests had obvious access to that mysterious mistress of heka.

The other one said, "May we show you what we have done to curse the city of Kerma that it may fall to the king's mighty right hand?"

"You are mind readers as w-well," said the general.

The twins smiled. Sobekmose added, "But w-which one is w-which again?"

"I am Jannes," said the one on the left.

"And I am Jambres," said the other.

What did it matter? Sobekmose still could not see the difference.

The brothers led Sobekmose and Ipuwer to the sanctuary where a small altar stood between two life-sized wooden statues of Ra and his son Horus, signifying the presence and protection of the king himself. There were some figurines and red pots on the altar. As the four approached it, Jannes, the apparent leader of the two, explained to their patrons, "Of course, we speak spells against Kerma every morning, afternoon, and evening."

Spells, charms, and incantations were an integral part of Egyptian heka magic. It was sometimes called "art of the mouth." The creator Ptah spoke forth creation with words. Words could bind and release, seal and destroy if spoken in the right order. Even the right words spoken well by a priest or charmer could compel the gods to respond. The most successful of lector priests were considered eloquent of word.

Jannes arrived at the altar and held up a couple of figurines made of clay with cloth coverings. Sobekmose saw that the figurines, one male, one female, had their hands tied behind their backs. Nails were driven deep into the bodies and heads of both.

"This is the chieftain of Kerma, Shakarra, and his queen, Tannia." The figurines represented a common form of sympathetic magic, the creation of an image that represented a curse's object. The torture and destruction of the image would then translate to real-life pain and suffering in the object it represented.

Sobekmose winced. "Was it necessary for the q-queen?"

"It is a primitive culture, my lord," replied Jannes. "The king and queen rule together." He threw them to the ground and stomped on them. Then Jambres reached for one of the red pots made from unbaked clay and handed it to Sobekmose.

The red color represented the evil of red-haired Set and Apophis the serpent of chaos.

The general read the writing inscribed on the pot. It was an execration text, a curse upon their enemies by name. It read, *Every rebel of this land of Kush, all people in the city of Kerma, all patricians, all commoners, all males, all women, every chieftain and warrior who rebels*. It then listed the names of King Shakarra, Queen Tannia, and other known leaders of the city that would fit on the surface of the pot. Other pots contained more names of rulers elsewhere in Kush.

"They are yours to destroy, my lord," Jannes said.

Sobekmose threw the pot hard onto the ground so that it was smashed into pieces. He continued with the other pots until they were all in broken shards on the floor around them. The heka ritual "breaking of the red pots" was supposed to bring destruction upon those listed on the pots in yet another sympathetic connection of magical curse.

Sobekmose thought he heard a soft breathy sound behind him. "Mio."

It was his pet name. Only the closest in his family called him that. He turned around. Saw nothing.

"My lord?" Ipuwer asked.

"I thought I heard…n-nothing," said the general. "We are done here." He turned to the two lector priests. "C-carry on."

The two of them left the sanctuary.

Jannes and Jambres looked at each other with curiosity.

They turned to face the altar as two large seven-foot-tall figures glided out from the shadows. The priests bowed to the floor and spoke in unison. "My queen, O Isis, who knows all the names. Mighty Heka, he who speaks magic."

"Up with you," Isis said.

The priests raised to their knees and looked upon her beautiful form. It was hazy in the incense, and their senses drugged by sorcery were dulled. But they could see her. They were both seers, capable of seeing beings of the unseen realm with unusual sensitivity.

What they saw was glorious. Isis, pale white of skin, wore a translucent white gown that revealed her sensuous shape beneath. She had a bright shoulder-wide necklace of jewels, black bobbed hair that came down to her shoulders, and an oversized crown that consisted of a circular golden sun surrounded by two curved horns of deity. She moved with smooth elegance, and when she raised her arms, colorful wings could be seen attached along their outer edges.

Though the goddess was female, there was something that seemed masculine beneath her makeup and dress. Jannes had noticed this of all the goddesses he had been allowed to see. But he brushed it aside as a mystery.

Heka was a male with the much simpler dress of a lector priest: white pleated kilt but no leopard skin on his bare chest. He wore a bobbed wig of black hair and sported a tight curved beard of divinity. He carried two snakes in his hands that maintained a stiff statue-like state, making them look like staffs. Both Heka's and Isis's eyes were deep blue like the precious heavenly gem lapis lazuli. All the gods' eyes were this heavenly blue.

Jannes queried, "Why did you not show your glory to my general, O shining ones?"

"Beware that one," warned Isis. "He is not as he appears."

"I do not understand," Jannes admitted.

"He must not become king."

Jannes dared not ask the question. The priests had received a prophesy many years ago of one to come called "The Destroyer of Egypt." Was the god implying a connection? To even consider such a thing about the crown prince would be treason.

Jambres asked, "What should we do, my queen?"

"Stay alert and prepared. We will call upon you when your services are required."

She was referring to the covenant the twins had made with the goddess a generation ago in the days of Neferhotep I. The lector priests had been called upon to persuade the king to perform a massacre of male infants of their own people, the Hebrews. It was a terrible thing to ask of them, so in exchange for their service, they had received eternal youth. But that youth would only last as long as their obedience.

Jannes and Jambres bowed and spoke in unison. "We await your command, O queen, throne goddess, she who knows all the names."

CHAPTER 5

Sobekmose was in his war tent looking over his layout of the siege of Kerma with his trusted Khanethothes and several advisors. He had miners tunneling their way into the city from beneath. That would take a couple more weeks to accomplish. He had tried several times to breach the walls with ladders, the most common tactic, with the most disastrous results. Each time, the ladders were repelled.

Sobekmose had decided to use a strategy that had never been used before.

The general said aloud, "It is time to use the sail attack."

The advisors looked at one another to see who had the courage to speak up. Sobekmose had been working on the sail attack with craftsmen for some time now. He had even tested it in secret. But deploying it in the real world of battle was an entirely different consideration.

Khanethothes was the one to speak. "General, should it not be tested in a minor battle of less consequence? A failure in this context could be ruinous."

The others hummed in support of the challenge.

The sail attack was an approach from the sky using air sails that operated like kites carrying individual soldiers. Sobekmose had learned about it by reading primordial writings about Enoch. The tactic had been used in a secret war on Eden. The forces of evil used similar air sails to try to invade the Garden. Though the evil attackers were repelled by the Cherubim forces in that war, Sobekmose considered the tactic here on behalf of good.

Then later, Sobekmose had been watching children flying kites in the palace yard. They were built in the shape of Khepri, the sacred solar deity, a scarab beetle with wings that brought forth the rising sun and represented creation and rebirth. He had seen how the wind kept the birdlike structures aloft and had wondered if they made similar structures the size of men whether warriors could launch them from elevated buttes and use them to glide into fortresses below. They had tested them and had brought a hundred with them on this campaign.

Sobekmose said, "There are bluffs at our b-b-back."

"But are they close enough?" questioned one of the advisors.

The general replied, "The wind is high in this v-v-valley."

Another spoke up. "High but also erratic." Each objection was fueling the next. The general was getting irritated.

A fourth advisor said, "Archers will be able to shoot them out of the sky."

Khanethothes added, "A few dozen is no match for the multitude that will surely surround them upon landing."

Sobekmose hit the table hard with his fist. Pieces of war games flew all over. He whispered with restrained anger, "They will fly at night, and they will open the gates for the rest of us."

The advisors went quiet. They had pushed the patience of their intemperate general. And he had failed to apply his lesson of wisdom from earlier.

But at least he didn't stammer.

A messenger arrived at the tent entrance. "General! There is a diplomatic entourage from the city approaching."

Sobekmose made his way out of the tent to the entrance of the camp with Khanethothes and the other advisors following.

When he reached the gates, he saw a large royal carriage towed by a herd of thoroughbred horses. It was surrounded by a mere handful of armed guards but was led by a dozen female servants of the city dressed in humble sackcloth. All of them carried olive branches, the accepted symbol of peaceful truce. The walls of the carriage had its curtains pulled back, so Sobekmose could see that it contained a young Kushite woman on a throne chair wearing a multi-colored garment of Kush royalty with gold necklace, bracelets, and crown on her bobbed black wig. She was too young to be queen, so Sobekmose assumed she must be a princess of the royal family sent to communicate the king's will.

His guards approached the entourage and escorted them into the camp.

Sobekmose arranged to meet them in his tent.

The Kushite guards and servants were held outside the general's tent as Khanethothes escorted the princess inside with her two closest consorts.

They approached Sobekmose seated on his throne and dressed in his regal ceremonial uniform. He wore a leather cuirass with the golden wings of Ra crisscrossing his chest as armor. He carried the golden scepter of power and wore the royal striped cloth headdress representing the king, complete with the poised uraeus serpent ready to strike from his forehead. He had wanted them to fear his stature and authority, especially if they were to convey any information back to their king behind the walls of the city.

The princess and her servants knelt with their hands open in vulnerable deference.

Khanethothes stood beside his general.

The princess said, "My lord, we are here on a diplomatic mission."

Staring at the woman, Sobekmose noticed something was off. She did not possess the haughty, confident carriage of royalty. He looked at her two companions, then leaned in to Khanethothes and whispered to him.

The lieutenant spoke for the general. "Which of you is the real diplomat?"

The one on the left stepped forward and pulled down her hood. She looked about eighteen or so, tall and slender. She had the rich black smooth skin of Nubian descent. Here hair was braided in rows and draped down her back and front. When she opened her robe, Sobekmose could see her colorful and elegant royal robe hidden beneath the sackcloth. An animal pelt with golden embroidery and bracelets of precious metal covered her neck and arms.

But her eyes were what captivated him. They drew his attention with their large size and dark intensity.

His face remained stern and disciplined.

She bowed. "My lord, I am Princess Tjarbit, daughter of King Shakarra the Great of the city of Kerma and the land of Kush. Forgive my deception. My intent was caution not malice."

Her companions knelt to the floor in obeisance.

Sobekmose whispered to Khanethothes, who said coldly to her, "What does the king intend with your visit?"

"A marriage alliance."

Sobekmose could barely shield his surprise.

"A treaty between our nations rooted in a marriage of confidence."

Khanethothes was looking straight at his general to see his response.

"If you but wed me as his only daughter, he will open the doors of the city to you—as well as his kingdom."

That certainly struck Sobekmose as odd. The Nubians had only been besieged for a couple weeks now. Was this a trap?

Another whisper. Then Khanethothes demanded, "Why would the king so quickly throw open the doors to a general of whom he knows nothing?"

"But he does know," she protested. "I am the one who told him."

Sobekmose was intrigued by the mystery of this unpredictable woman before him.

"I am the one who advised my father of the offer. Word of your previous victories has convinced the king that the cost of this battle may be too high for Kush. But the question was how would you treat a surrendered enemy? Would you be humane—or cruel? Then I saw you carry yourself in battle at our gate. How you treated your own soldiers as well as your enemies with dignity."

Sobekmose suddenly realized that this was the princess he had seen on the tower, the one Khanethothes had said was watching him.

"When I saw your honorable actions in battle against a Kushite soldier at the gates, and your clear grief that you could not save your men from a fiery death..." She paused, seeming to choke up with emotion. Sobekmose felt his *ka*—his vital energy—drawn to her.

She finished her statement, "Then I knew the reports were true that you are a ruler of integrity and honor. And I knew that the best solution to a continued hostility between our nations would be a marriage alliance. And my father the king agreed."

Sobekmose remained quiet, staring at her, in awe of the moment. He had never experienced anything like it. He did not know how to respond.

CHAPTER 6

Sobekmose pronounced, "I take the hand of Princess Tjarbit of Kush as my wife. So let there be a dynasty of peace for Kush with Egypt as her sovereign protector." The wedding crowd burst out in applause. It was a hurried affair taking place in the Kerma palace of King Shakarra, who now stood with Sobekmose to sign the wedding covenant on his ivory table.

The king was an imposing height, several inches taller than Sobekmose. His black skin was wrinkled with age but without an ounce of fat. He must have been around sixty years old. A golden cap covered his whole head as a crown. Two uraeus cobras perched on his forehead compared to the Egyptian king's single uraeus. Shakarra also wore a rare white lion pelt with more jewels and gold than Egyptian royalty wore. Sobekmose knew the Kushites to have a competitive spirit with their Egyptian neighbors, though both cultures had drawn from each other through much trade over the years.

The king was strong, but Sobekmose could tell the man was weary of the many years of ruling his warrior society. His queen, Tannia, was also a noble and elegant creature, holding her equivalent age much better than her lord. Her full head of black hair was tightly braided and embroidered with beautiful gems and ribbons. She was draped in the finest robe of bright colored silk: yellows, blues, silvers, and golds. The Kushite people were bold in their creativity.

But the queen was more than that. Her presence and elegance rivaled that of Egypt's own queen. Sobekmose could see where her daughter, Tjarbit, got her otherworldly beauty. He considered himself blessed by the gods.

Dressed in similar bright colors and jewelry as her mother, the princess looked into Sobekmose's eyes and into his very *ka*. He felt enchanted by her and kept stealing looks her way as he signed the treaty between their nations and shared the cup of wine with the king.

This union was more than just political. It was also spiritual. Egyptian priests of Ra stood right beside Kushite priests of Amun as rival religious systems seeking unity. Consideration had already begun amongst the high priesthoods of integrating their worship. Plans had been drawn up to construct a life-sized stone statue of the Egyptian king Sobekhotep IV on the isle of Argo in the middle of the Nile. It would be a boundary marker of the Egyptian king's guardianship over the land. The Kushites would protect the image of Sobekhotep as if it were the king himself.

But now there would be a feast. The entire city of Kerma would celebrate with food, dance, and song for the next seven days to honor their new sovereign. Tribute of riches and slaves would come later. For now, there was jubilation. And Sobekmose would enjoy his new bride.

The celebration of sacred union was not restricted to the physical realm of a royal wedding. Outside the city, another celebration was underway in the huge temple complex called the Deffufa. It was not like Egyptian temple complexes, though it did create awe with a similar sense of overwhelming size. The structure was adobe and rose over a hundred feet in height above their heads with a temple at the very top.

Egyptian priests of Ra carried a holy ark past two obelisks marking the gateway of the complex. It was a transportable throne consisting of a small solar barque hoisted by two wooden poles carried by a handful of priests. The barque's central carriage housed Ra's throne and a golden image of the deity in humanoid form with a falcon head and sun crown. At his feet was a footstool, a box that held the scroll of a covenant treaty between the gods of Egypt and Kush.

In the spiritual realm, unseen and unheard by the humans, the god Ra sat within the image of that throne as it approached the temple of Amun. Horus, Isis, Set, and Thoth accompanied the barque on its route, followed by several gods of Kush.

On earth as it is in heaven.

Mastema, the most formidable of the Watchers, had taken on the sun god's identity long ago in the days of Joseph, Egypt's Hebrew vizier, when Jacob's family moved to the delta area of Goshen. Mastema had many names, but his most primeval was Nachash. He had been following Jacob's descendants for a very special reason. As humble and insignificant as they were, they were the promised seed of a king that would eventually rule the world. As Ra, Mastema sought to consolidate the powers of the Two Lands beneath his supremacy so that he would be ready for the rise of that promised seed, whom he planned to crush between his teeth. Uniting Egypt with Kush would help him achieve the supremacy he needed for that victory.

Horus, Ra's son and the patron of Egypt's king, was his most powerful ally to accomplish his plans of absolute power. Horus's real name was Abezethibou of the Watchers, but he embraced playing out the mythology of the great god and lord of heaven, the golden one, Horus.

The priests carried the solar barque throne up many flights of stairs until they arrived at the top, exhausted at having reached their final destination. The temple of Amun was a large structure thirty feet high, thirty feet wide, and thrice as long with two large pillars marking the entrance.

They moved through the entrance and main hall, a hypostyle hall of pillars covered with bright paintings of the stories of the gods from creation to the present.

Past this hall lay the sanctuary of Amun, the Holy of Holies, a chamber watched over by two large sphinxes, throne guardians with lion bodies, eagle's wings, and human heads. Kush had indeed appropriated significant culture from their Egyptian neighbors.

The priests of Amun set down Ra's throne as they moved their god's image from the holy barque that resided in the sanctuary, to be replaced by Ra's image. Amun was a human image with a crown of two vast plumes on his head.

In the unseen realm, Ra and Amun faced each other. Ra said, "Amun, the hidden one, it is good to finally find you, you rascal."

Amun stepped off his throne with a smile and a submissive gesture to his new lord. He bowed as Ra took his place on Amun's throne, his feet on the barque's footstool.

Horus, Isis, and Thoth quietly took their places around the throne as Set stood behind Amun.

Ra sighed with pleasure. "Amun, you have been quite an incorrigible opponent all these years."

Amun replied respectfully, "I take my responsibility seriously as the Watcher of Kush, my lord."

"Of course," said Ra. "I would expect nothing less from any principality or power. But why are you not kneeling?"

Before Amun could respond, Set used his golden scepter to bash the back of Amun's knees. He fell to the ground, grunting in pain.

Ra said, "In fact, why are you not prostrate?"

Set's scepter bashed Amun in the head from behind. The deity's plumed crown flew off his head as it hit the floor with a loud crack and a burst of blood from his broken nose.

Set grabbed Amun's hair and pulled him back up. He spun around and hit the Kushite god in the teeth, breaking them into pieces and throwing him onto his back on the floor.

Amun blacked out for a moment. When he came to, he saw Ra standing over him, shining with glory.

Horus and Set pulled Amun up to his knees, holding him in place to keep him from collapsing again. His four companion deities stood back in fear, not moving an inch.

Through his blurry, unfocused eyes, Amun saw Ra lean in close to him and whisper, "Nevertheless, you have caused much loss and suffering for Egypt all the way up to Memphis. Let me ask you, Amun, what punishment would you expect from me?"

Amun hesitated. The thought was frightening. There were punishments worse than death, especially for immortal beings that could experience suffering without dying. He had enough sense to be honest. He lisped through his broken teeth, "Imprithonment in the earth?"

Since the time of the great flood, captured Watchers could be buried deep into the earth or seas, where they could not dig or swim their way out. There they would consciously await their judgment in a distant future as prophesied by the prophet Enoch.

"Good answer," said Ra with a grin. "And I would do so." He paused. "If we were not facing the most significant threat of our lives."

Amun did not know what his captor was talking about. Horus and Set raised their captive to his feet, steadying him.

"We must all work together or we may find ourselves all imprisoned in Tartarus." Tartarus was the deepest prison of the underworld to which some of the rebellious Watchers had been consigned at the flood. It was said that Tartarus was as far below the earth as heaven was above it.

"So I am not going to punish you. Instead, I am going to partner with you. You see, this man, General Sobekmose, son of the king, is not whom he appears to be. His true identity has the potential to shake the very kingdom of Egypt."

Amun was still in the dark. "How ith that pothible?"

"I will explain it to you later. Tell your pantheon we are now allies. All hostility has ceased. In good faith, I will even offer a binding of our interests. I will allow you to continue to rule in Kush and southern Egypt but as my co-regent. You shall be called Amun-Ra. And when I need you, you will bring all your forces to bear for our purposes. Do I make myself clear?"

Amun nodded. "Yeth."

Ra grinned. "I will tell you the plan. But first, clean yourself up and get those teeth replaced. You sound foolish."

He turned and walked away. Set saw the opportunity to give Amun one more crack on the back of the head, right where his skull had been broken. Amun grunted in pain and collapsed to the floor.

The red god wondered what puny human could possibly jeopardize such a powerful pantheon of gods.

CHAPTER 7

Sobekmose looked up into the night sky from a palace window in the tower of Kerma. The moon and stars shone as gods. Ma'at had been returned to Egypt. Ma'at was at once both the goddess of divine order as well as a description of that order in balance. The king was primarily responsible to maintain that order through right application of the cosmic law of truth, justice, and righteousness. But each individual citizen had the responsibility to live in accordance with it.

Sobekmose felt at one with Ma'at.

"My lord." The soft voice of Tjarbit brought Sobekmose back to earth. He turned to see his new wife standing behind him wearing a translucent gown with titillating nuance that revealed her fully formed figure in the moonlight. She wore an Egyptian-style bobbed wig with large golden earrings and a gold collared necklace. Sobekmose saw she was trembling.

"Are you pleased?" she asked fearfully.

"Pleased?" he replied, staring at her. Her dark-brown eyes looked deeply into his. He could smell the lotus oil on her. The perfume excited his desire. But he did not move to her.

He said, "You are afraid of me. I understand." He was, after all, the conqueror of her people in whose hands their fate now lay. Why would he not do whatever he wanted to them? To her?

"You are a brave and loyal woman," he said. "You have risked your own life for the sake of your people."

"My lord," she said meekly. "May I speak frankly?"

"Yes."

"If your character is consistent with what I observed of you on the field of battle and have heard reported of your character, then my risk has been worth it. We know you could have destroyed this city rather than enter into a treaty that spares our people and allows my parents to keep their throne. This makes you an unusually just and impartial ruler.

He smiled. "*If* my character is consistent. And that is why you t-tremble. B-because you are not certain." He didn't think she was flattering him. He wouldn't blame her if she did. But he thought he could see sincerity in her eyes.

"Now, I will be frank with you," he said. "Believe it or not, I have a fear as well."

She was incredulous. "You, my lord?"

Her moist black skin glistened in the moonlight from the window. He gazed upon her from head to ankle. She could be a goddess. Then he could not look her in the eye.

"I am a v-violent man."

"You are a great man."

"I fear b-beauty."

"Why?"

"I have destroyed so much of it." Memories of war flooded his mind. Conquered men, violated women, enslaved peoples.

"My lord," she whispered. "I entrust myself to you."

He saw in her eyes a noble subject's willing submission. And he felt the desire not to take her but to treat her honorably. He would not destroy this beauty. He would cherish it.

Wearing only a simple night kilt of linen, he approached her slowly.

He reached out and caressed her cheek and neck with the back of his hand. He could not help his slight trembling.

She closed her eyes with surrender.

How could the gods have created such a lovely creature, both inside and out?

He said, "Do you mind my stuttering?"

"I hear no stuttering."

She was right. He realized that he was losing himself in her. He dismissed his concerns.

He turned his hand around and softly held her neck in his palm.

She opened her gown, and it dropped to the floor.

His other hand released the kilt from his waist.

They stood before each other, naked and vulnerable.

He pulled her close and kissed.

He tried to be careful to avoid hurting her with his strength. She was small in his muscular arms. But she was not frail.

He lifted her off the ground and laid her on the satin sheets of the bed, filled with lotus petals. He crawled upon her, and they sealed their unity under the moonlight of Thoth.

The morning sunlight awakened Sobekmose, Tjarbit still in his arms. She must have sensed his awakening. "Good morning," she whispered.

"Good morning," he replied.

He sighed with satisfaction.

"When do we leave for Egypt?" she asked.

"Today."

"To where do we return?"

"Goshen. In the delta."

"I have heard so much about it. What is it like?"

He sighed again with memory. "The smell of cool, salty air flowing in from the sea. A vast, lowland of green, the likes of which you have never seen before. Palm trees, papyrus marshes, and lotus plants everywhere. Tributaries of the Nile creating islands of villages. Planting fields. Large, glorious temples and palaces. I was born there."

"Tell me about your family."

He felt unsure of how much he should reveal to her. He decided to start safely. "My m-mother's name is Meryt. She was the daughter of the king in the delta at a time of much unrest. The T-two Lands had been split apart until marriage united the t-two kings, much like our situation. Sobekhotep IV of Upper Egypt married my m-mother, daughter of the king of Lower Egypt."

She considered his words. "You have told me *about* your mother but not *of* your mother."

He smiled at her sharp insight. "The truth is, the palace's royal children come to know their nursemaids better than their own m-m-mothers. My nursemaid became head of the maidservants."

"What is her name?"

"Jochebed. She is an Asiatic from the north. Habiru. You will like her. She is not very…Egyptian. She is strong, loving, patient. And she spoiled me rotten."

Tjarbit chuckled. "Who are these Habiru?"

"A peculiar people. They pronounce it 'Hebrew.' They migrated from C-canaan to the area of Goshen in the days of Amenemhat III. One of their own had r-risen to the status of vizier of Egypt. His name was Zaphenath Pa'aneah. Ankhu for short. His own people called him Joseph. It is said that Ankhu saved all of Egypt by storing seven years of grains for a famine that arrived just as he had p-predicted. He brought favor upon his people, but over time, he was forgotten, the Habiru became c-conscripted workers, forced to build the royal cities of Avaris and Pithom. So they are not a c-contented people."

She said curiously, "You know this much of your slaves?"

He said, "My mother believed that understanding our servants made us better overseers. I even learned their language."

"Hmm," she wondered. "And what of your father, the king?"

He chuckled. "He wants to be the greatest k-k-king who ever ruled Egypt."

"And you are his heir."

Sobekmose did not respond quickly. He did not need to. The pressure of the expectation was clear in everything he did.

Finally, he said, "He c-cares much for his legacy."

"Surely he is proud of you."

"You have one thing correct. He is a p-proud man."

He felt her hold him tightly, and all his pain melted away in her embrace.

She leaned up on her elbows to look him in the eye. "Well, then let us make him a proud grandfather."

She kissed him.

Sobekmose rolled over on top of her. Kissed her passionately. Gratefully. And gladly performed his duty to provide his own heir to the throne of Egypt with his beautiful black Nubian bride of Kush.

CHAPTER 8

Goshen

It had taken several weeks to return to Egypt from the campaign in Kush. Now Sobekmose rode in a triumphal parade through the streets of Avaris on his chariot toward the royal palace in Goshen. His new Kushite wife Tjarbit stood beside him as he led the horses forward. It was customary in most nations that after conquering enemies, victorious leaders would parade captured rulers through the streets, dead or alive, to humiliate them and elevate the conquering king and his almighty power.

In this case, King Shakarra and his queen had become subject rulers of Egypt, so they followed behind the general's chariot submissively in their own vehicle while retaining dignity by wearing their country's royal dress: rare leopard skin tunics, necks and arms covered with ostentatious amounts of gold, silver, and jewels, as well as bobbed hair wigs with golden crowns.

But the crowd's praise and worship was focusing this triumph more on the general than the king. Sobekmose heard his name yelled out in praise but no glory for Sobekhotep. It was embarrassingly obvious that a large segment of the population considered General Sobekmose as the real victor here when he was supposed to merely represent the king.

As he disembarked his chariot and ascended the steps of the glorious red stone palace, Sobekmose saw his father's face sour from the populace's lack of respect. He noticed his brother Khahotepre scowling as well, his weak eyes, thin body, and wine belly covering for his cunning, deceptive personality.

Sobekmose and Tjarbit knelt to one knee as the herald announced the king's titulary name. "Horus, may the heart of the Two Lands live, Two Ladies of Upper and Lower Egypt, He whose apparitions are flourishing, Golden Horus, He whose *ba*-spirits are powerful, Khaneferre Sobekhotep IV."

Like magic, the title names were supposed to incarnate power in the king and evoke the citizenry's awe. Words embodied power.

The vizier handed the king a golden necklace. Sobekhotep then announced, "I award you, Sobekmose, the Golden Flies of Valor for your bold and courageous victory in Kush."

Sobekmose bowed his head, and the king draped the precious chain on his neck. The crowd exploded with more applause and cheers. Up close, Sobekhotep's grimace revealed a jealousy that the populace could not see from afar.

Then the king noticed Tjarbit beside Sobekmose, and his bitterness melted away. He could not take his eyes off her as she kissed his hand and knelt before him with Sobekmose.

The king gave them a marital blessing to the crowd's approval, then led them inside for a feast of victory, after which the king and queen of Kush would sign a vassal treaty with their new sovereign. The Kushite vassal rulers would be introduced to the palace royalty and shown the glories of Egypt before being sent back to Kerma as loyal subjects of King Sobekhotep.

At the feast, Sobekmose sat on a long couch, below and to the right of his father the king. Khanethothes sat next to his general, eyeing everything for safety. On the other side of the king were Queen Meryt and the king's son Khahotepre.

A servant offered Sobekmose a wine bowl. Others carried food from the table at the center of the room, which overflowed with a freshly killed and cooked ox, roast goose, quail, and duck, all surrounded by bounteous vegetables including leeks, onions, radishes, peppers, chickpeas, and cucumbers. The special dish of the evening was *ferique*, a stew made of chicken, calf's feet, and shelled eggs.

Sobekmose took a deep drink of his wine and watched the celebration's guests, the king and queen of Kush. They sat before Sobekhotep, gaped in awe at the food and gazed around the walls and pillars of the room covered in bright, colorful hieroglyphs telling the stories of Egypt.

Dancing girls in their translucent gowns and bobbed wigs moved to the music of lute, lyre, and flute, focusing on Sobekmose. Everyone seemed to focus on the general for his accomplishment of bringing Egypt victory.

The king took another swig of his own wine and leaned over to Sobekmose. "Mio, you have done well for yourself."

He used that pet name Mio in less formal situations.

"For you, my father, the king," said Sobekmose.

The king was already a bit tipsy, having downed several bowls of wine as he watched the dancers congregate around Sobekmose with their sensuous movements. He said, "Just make sure the people know that, because the way they have been elevating you, it seems they may have forgotten just who is the god of Egypt."

He threw his bowl of wine at the girls before Sobekmose. The cup hit one of them, and wine splashed on several others. It clanked on the floor. They stopped dancing. The king picked up a plate of vegetables and threw it at them. The dancers raised their arms, protecting themselves from the flying food.

The musicians stopped as well, wondering what to do. The whole party had gone quiet.

"Be gone. I am done with you," barked the king to the dancers.

The king stood, a bit wobbly, and yelled angrily toward the musicians in the corner, "I did not say to stop playing music! Continue! Everyone, continue your celebration! I have returned Ma'at to Egypt!"

Nervously, the musicians returned to their music and the guests to their chattering. Sobekmose saw King Shakarra and Queen Tannia staring fearfully wide-eyed at Sobekhotep, who plopped back down on his throne.

Sobekhotep spoke to Sobekmose. "You may have been my mighty right arm in Kush. But ruling a kingdom is not as easy as merely winning military battles. It requires statesmanship and wisdom in governance."

"Yes, of course, father." Sobekmose saw his younger brother Khahotepre leaning in on the other side of the king to listen with a malicious smirk on his face. His mother the queen was trying to stay out of it. She was not allowed to react in public toward the king.

Sobekhotep continued with slurred speech to his son, "When you gain wisdom like mine, then you will understand kingship. Never trust the sentiments of the masses. The people who worship you will turn on you in an instant and kill you as a mob."

Despite the king's jealousy of Sobekmose's glory, his words were true. Khanethothes remained wisely silent beside his general. Sobekmose sought for a statesman-like way to respond. He chose words of adulation, "I seek only to be worthy of you, golden Horus, the son of Ra, Divine of form, King of Upper and Lower Egypt."

As a son, it was all Sobekmose had ever wanted: to make his father proud. To continue the greatness of the family dynasty, of which he longed to feel worthy.

The king replied, "I think I will order you to return to Kush with my new servant king here and oversee the construction of my statue and memorial buildings."

That was a deliberate attempt to punish the victorious general by making him promote the glory of the king far away from the attention of the people. Sobekmose had worked too hard. He had become more beloved by the people than his father, the very one from whom he had sought recognition.

He saw his mother the queen watching him, tears in her eyes, without making a sound.

Sobekmose said, "If that is your will, my father and king."

"Yes, it is my will, indeed," mumbled the drunken ruler, barely able to focus on anything visually. "The will of Horus on earth. I am the good god."

And with that, he fell into a drunken sleep in his chair.

Sobekmose sought to escape his humiliation. He left the celebration early with Tjarbit to retire to their quarters, and to continue exploring their newfound union with pleasure. But when they arrived, they were greeted by one of the household maids, an Asiatic with reddish-brown hair named Miriam, who was kneeling, bowed on the floor with a strange Asiatic man Sobekmose had never seen before. He seemed not much older than Sobekmose, tall, thin, with a large beard and flowing hair. Habiru were a hairy people.

Their kneeling was in deep humility for approaching the prince. Miriam was in tears. Sobekmose had never seen her this distraught.

"What is wrong, Miriam?" asked Sobekmose. He reached for his dagger, looking at the man with distrust as he and Miriam stood up.

Miriam placed her arm around the stranger with acceptance and whimpered, "He is my brother." But she became overwhelmed with grief and collapsed back to the floor. The strange man caught her, though with some difficulty as she was shorter but weightier than most women her age.

Sobekmose said, "Bring her to the couch." He barked to another maid, "And get her a cup of water."

The maid did so, and Miriam took a sip.

Miriam had been a household maid for Sobekmose's entire life. He felt protective of her—as she had been protective of him when he was young. She and Jochebed had been the favorite servants of Sobekmose's mother.

But Sobekmose remained dubious of the man. "What is your name?"

"Aaron," the man said.

Though Sobekmose had never met her brother before, he could see the resemblance.

"He is your brother too," Miriam blurted out.

The words were so alien to Sobekmose it took him a few moments to realize what she had just said. This Habiru was his brother? What kind of nonsense had Miriam gotten herself into?

She added, "And I am your sister."

Sobekmose jerked a confused look at her. "What are you saying, Miriam?"

He searched her eyes for some explanation. But her look seemed determined. She said again, "I am your sister. Aaron is our brother."

He asked, "Where is your mother, Jochebed?"

Miriam began to choke up again. "I am trying to tell you, she's dead. Jochebed has died."

Sobekmose felt his eyes immediately pool with sadness. Jochebed had been his wetnurse and had remained as the head maid who had served him growing up. She was a kind woman and attentive to the young prince. Sobekmose had come to know her as well as his own mother Queen Meryt.

He asked, "How?"

"We do not know," said Miriam. "She just fell to the ground yesterday, and blood came from her nose. She never woke up."

Sobekmose tightened. "What do you mean about…?"

"Jochebed was your mother, Sobekmose. Aaron and I are your siblings."

"What madness is this?" he exclaimed. "Why do you claim such spurious lies?"

"I am not lying to you." She held out a rolled-up piece of papyrus. He took it reluctantly, opening it up.

He looked at the letter, written to him in the Hebrews' language, which his mother had made him learn as part of his education. It was from Jochebed.

"She had written this to give to you if she died. I promised her I would give it to you."

He read the words written in Jochebed's own hand.

> *My dearest Sobekmose, What I have to tell you will no doubt take some time to accept. But I know that in your heart you will know it is true. Let me tell you the story of your birth. When you are done reading this, bring it to your mother the queen, and she will witness to the truth of my testimony. You are not merely the adopted son of Pharaoh. You are also the adopted son of Meryt, your Egyptian mother. You were born a son of Israel, and I am the mother who gave you birth. Your Hebrew name is Moses.*

Sobekmose stopped reading. He could not go on. He felt sick. He had loved Jochebed. She had nursed Sobekmose for the young queen when he was an infant. She had raised him in the royal family until he had been old enough to be schooled. Jochebed had been kind, firm, and determined with him. She had taught him all about her people, the Hebrews. But now she was telling him in her death that they were his people too? That he was not a high-born Egyptian but a low-born slave? Why would she do such a thing? Had she gone mad? Her words were like arrows into his heart.

He felt anger rising in his belly like a fire. Then he crumpled up the papyrus, walked over to the fireplace, and threw it in the flames.

He whispered, "Lies."

"Please, my lord," Miriam said. "The rest of the letter explains why."

Sobekmose looked at Miriam and Aaron and said in a threatening tone, "Get out of my s-s-sight."

The two of them obeyed fearfully and quickly. They left Sobekmose alone with Tjarbit, who remained silent, watching the flames burn up the story of his past in smoke and ash.

Sobekmose walked out to his palatial balcony overlooking the entire area of Goshen.

He saw for miles. The tributaries, the homes, the fields, the temples, and buildings of the delta. Suddenly, they all felt foreign to him. Like he was a stranger in a strange land. His whole cosmos had been turned upside-down in a moment. It couldn't be true. It had to be a lie.

Otherwise, his entire life had been a lie.

He clenched his fist so tightly he felt it go numb. He realized his teeth were clenched, causing a headache. He released his tension and felt vulnerable.

Tjarbit silently slipped up beside him.

She whispered, "If it is true, no one will hear it from my lips. You are a benefit for my people."

"It cannot be true," he said and walked away from her.

CHAPTER 9

The temple of Ra at Avaris stood on the eastern bank of the Pelusiac branch of the Nile, a tributary that split and forked around the city that rose from the waters in a sandy hillock reminiscent of the primeval hillock of creation that rose from the waters of chaos. Many of the Goshen area villages rested atop turtleback mounds of land that protected them from the yearly inundation of the Nile flood.

The gods Ra, Horus, and Sobek had met in the spiritual realm for the arrival of King Sobekhotep to worship with his sons. Horus was the deity whose earthly incarnation was represented in the king as the son of Ra, the exalted one, whose temple this was.

But Sobek, the crocodile god of the Nile, was also patron deity of Sobekhotep, whose name meant "Sobek is praised." His son Sobekmose's name meant "son of the crocodile god." Sobek had the body of a man with the head of a crocodile wearing an Egyptian *atef* crown that looked like Osiris's crown of the underworld, white and long with a bulb at the top. Sobek was considered "the raging one" who rose out of the primeval waters and was lord of the floating islands or hillocks of the delta as well as its ubiquitous marshes. The earthly crocodile was a fearsome predator of the Nile that garnered the respect and worship of Egyptians. Sobek embodied that fearsomeness.

But as the gods convened in the stone sanctuary, unseen and unheard by human senses, they all felt an intuition of danger come upon them. They transformed their presence to that of their warrior animal heads ready for battle and went outside the temple entrance to see if there was anything on the horizon.

In the earthly realm, the Habiru stranger Aaron stood by the large stone pylons of the entrance, shouting to the populace that passed him by. Most of them were Habiru, the descendants of Israel who had assimilated into the Egyptian culture over the past several hundred years. Most of them looked no different than any other Egyptian in their clothes and mannerisms. Aaron's sister Miriam stood by him in support.

"Turn from the idols of Egypt!" pronounced the Hebrew elder. "The God of Abraham, Isaac, and Jacob will send a redeemer who will rescue us from our bondage!"

An angry Sobek spoke to his fellow Watchers. "Should we silence him?" He stepped forward, but Ra held him back. "No, wait."

One of the passersby stopped and shouted back angrily, "We have been afflicted for hundreds of years! Where is this redeemer?"

Another yelled, "You are a false prophet!"

Others began gathering to listen to Aaron. The size of the crowd grew quickly. Aaron cried out, "Our God, El Shaddai, promised to our forefather Abraham that he would make of him a great nation! He told him, 'I will bless those who bless you, and curse those who curse you. And in you all the families of the earth shall be blessed!'"

Though many listened, the hecklers spoke out. "Oh, yes, look how great and blessed the children of Abraham have become! Slaves of Pharaoh are blessing all of Egypt—with our sweat and blood!"

The word *Pharaoh* was Hebrew for the king because it meant "he who ruled from the great house," or palace.

"No, my brethren, listen," replied Aaron, his voice going hoarse. "Our forefather Jacob prophesied on his death bed, 'The scepter shall not depart from Judah, nor the ruler's staff from between his feet, until Shiloh comes, him to whom it belongs. And to him shall be the obedience of the people!'"

Sobek started forward again. He growled, "Prophecy breeds hope. Hope births repentance and faith. We must abort this now."

But as he neared Aaron, an armed warrior figure seemed to rise up from the steps and stood between Sobek and his target. The dark figure was not dressed as an Egyptian soldier. He wore heavenly armor forged in the fires of Eden and brandished a sword of like origin. He was bald with dark skin, Nubian-like, and he glared at Sobek, daring him to take one more step. He too was in the unseen realm.

Sobek backed up to the other gods.

"Gabriel," Horus said in a hushed voice.

"What is an archangel doing protecting this human fool?" Sobek demanded.

Ra knew exactly what the archangel was doing. "Because that fool is onto something."

They all knew the meaning of the prophecy's royal scepter and staff.

Horus spoke the words that all were thinking but feared to say. "The Chosen Seed."

Leaving the human to ramble on, the gods returned to the temple sanctuary. As they approached the Holy of Holies, they stopped in their tracks. Another archangel was waiting for them, sitting on the sacred barque of Ra. He had long blonde hair and was a bit small for an archangel.

It was Uriel.

"Blasphemer!" Sobek blurted out.

Ra tightened. "You dare enter my house like a thief and desecrate my throne?"

"If you think this is desecration," Uriel quipped, "wait till you see what we have in store for *you*."

Horus elbowed Ra, who turned to see two more "thieves" behind them, the bald, black Gabriel and the brown-skinned, beefy warrior Raphael. The gods drew their weapons. They were among the mightiest of the pantheon, so it should have been a battle of equals.

But in actual skill, the gods were outnumbered.

And before they could get their bearings, Raphael had pulled out a bow and launched three arrows in rapid succession right into Ra's heart. He flew back to the floor, paralyzed by the direct hits.

The three angels surrounded the two remaining gods.

Horus and Sobek stood back-to-back. Horus cawed a war cry, and his right eye glowed with a blinding light right into the eyes of the large Raphael. The angel backed up, temporarily blinded. Gabriel used his sword to force the falcon-headed creature up against the stone wall.

Uriel struck first at Sobek with double-handed swords. The angel was small, but he was fast and lethal. The crocodile deity barely kept up defensively with his staff against the rapid, slicing blades.

Horus had picked up Ra's scepter mace and swung it at Gabriel, who used his small shield to absorb the blows.

Raphael was gaining back his vision but not yet able to join Gabriel.

Sobek was no match for Uriel's slicing fury. The crocodile god remained desperately on the defensive as the small angel's aggression wore him down.

One misstep. Uriel's blade cut off Sobek's hand. The staff fell to the floor. But the small dynamo didn't stop. He crisscrossed his two blades, and Sobek's opposite arm fell to the floor. He was defenseless.

But the little warrior kept coming. He was an unrelenting force of aggression, slicing and hacking.

Then suddenly, the sound of a howling jolted them all. The mighty Set came barreling out of the priestly hallway in full tilt, his mace at the ready, canine teeth growling with rage.

Horus's war cry had been heard.

Set hit the partially-blinded Raphael at full force, making him fly ten feet into one of the temple pillars. It knocked the wind out of the angel, and it seemed the very building itself quaked around them.

The chaos deity then went mad, deploying his mace upon Gabriel, whose shield crumpled beneath the force.

Now the odds had evened out.

For but a moment.

Uriel crowed, "Hey dog-face, bite this!"

Set blocked with his mace the storm of blows from the blonde, loud-mouthed angel.

But it was just the time needed for Raphael to get his wind back and Gabriel to throw aside his shield and prepare for double-handed strikes with his broadsword.

Set found himself surrounded by the four angels, all ready to attack.

"Bring it on, godlickers!" Set growled fearlessly. Every muscle in his body tensed in trained preparation. The odds were against him, but he wasn't afraid.

Gabriel quipped, "You are going to regret that demand."

But before anyone could engage, the sound of an angelic trumpet could be heard in the spiritual realm. In the twinkling of an eye, all four of the angels were suddenly gone, leaving Set alone and unharmed. They melted away into the shadows of the pillared hallways of the temple.

"Cowards!" Set yelled after them.

His chest was heaving for breath. He was a mighty warrior, but he had stepped in over his head with this one. It was probably best he had not fought with them after all.

He looked over at his fallen comrades. They were decimated.

He strode to Ra and pulled out the arrows. He noticed that Horus had been disemboweled and the unfortunate Sobek had been hacked to pieces.

If Set had not arrived, they might have been taken and imprisoned in the earth, the most dreaded fate of any Watcher.

But it all made Set realize that the living god Yahweh was on the move. This was no random attack. This was a planned execution. The archangels had targeted the three gods most connected to the human Egyptian ruler. Ra, the king of the gods. Horus, the patron deity of the king. Sobek, the namesake of King Sobekhotep as well as his intended heir.

This could only mean one thing. Yahweh was planning on taking out the king and installing Sobekmose in his place. The gods had known all along that the adopted heir was a dreaded son of Israel. He would be the perfect fit to fulfill the prophesied Destroyer of Egypt.

But was he also the Promised Seed of the Hebrews? The gods had heard rumors amongst the Hebrews of a prophesied king to come.

He couldn't be. The prophecy was clear that the Anointed One would come from the tribe of Judah.

But Sobekmose was a Levite. And if there was one thing Yahweh prided himself on, it was fulfilling his own prophecies. It didn't make sense to Set. What was Yahweh's real plan?

His hatred for that tyrannical despot creator exploded from him with a scream of anger so deep and loud it was sure to be heard throughout the unseen realm of the spirit.

"Plan what you will, Yahweh," he growled. "The revolution grows."

Set replaced Horus's innards and put the pieces of Sobek back together like a macabre puzzle. It would take some time for the heavenly flesh to heal and the gods to return to their full strength. The thought crossed Set's mind to finish the dirty deed that the angels began, burying these comrades in the earth and taking his rightful place as king of the gods.

But he needed the entire pantheon at full strength for what he was planning. He needed them on his side.

CHAPTER 10

Sobekmose waited outside the large oak door of the queen's bed chamber as his mother Meryt was awakened by her chambermaid.

The chambermaid, an older woman, stepped out and announced to Sobekmose, "She is ready to receive you, my lord."

He nodded and stepped inside, closing the door quietly. It was late in the night, the whole household asleep, and the king snoring drunk in his own chambers across the hall.

"Mio? What is wrong?"

Sobekmose approached her. Meryt was standing by one of the pillars around her bed, clutching a night shawl over her gown. Her eyes still blurry from having just awakened, her short hair tussled.

Sobekmose stood staring at her with a scowl on his face. "Is it t-true?"

Her countenance dropped as if she knew exactly what he was asking.

"Is J-Jochebed my birth mother? Am I a Hebrew?"

She paused. "Who told you?"

"She wrote me a letter. M-miriam, who is ap-p-parently my sister, gave it to me. Oh, and I have an older brother as well. Or so the letter at-t-tests."

"Where is the letter?"

"I burned it after I read the f-first few words."

Meryt smiled. "She knew you would. That is why she gave me a copy of the letter as well."

"So it is all t-true."

Meryt sighed reluctantly, "Yes, my son."

"Son? You have been lying to me my entire life."

"I did what I had to do to rescue you from death and give you a future."

"And what f-future is that, stripping me of my royal heritage by telling me I am in truth a slave?"

"My agreement with Jochebed was to wait to tell you until you were old enough to make a difference—or when she died. We had hoped that when you became king, you would treat the Habiru more justly if you knew they were your own people."

He was incredulous, "Why do you care about the Habiru?"

"Ask yourself this," she said. "Why would I bother to adopt a Hebrew boy into my household, one of the very male infants my father was trying to massacre, knowing that child might one day rule over Egypt?"

Sobekmose's eyebrows came together in a puzzled frown. "Are you saying you too are of the Habiru? But that cannot be. You are daughter to a pharaoh."

"It is more complicated than that. Let me read you the letter, tell you your story. Then you can decide what you should do."

Sobekmose considered her words. Meryt left to retrieve the copied letter she had hidden away.

When she returned, she sat across from him near the evening fire and lit an oil lamp for extra light by which to read.

He felt emotion well up within him as she began reading. Jochebed had been a kind and affectionate servant to him. He had treated her with the same favor Meryt had. He could almost hear it in Jochebed's firm yet compassionate voice that she often used with him. He now realized it was a *motherly* voice.

"'I have told you the story of my people the Hebrews over the years when I took care of you in the great house. What I had not told you was that they were your people as well. Now you know. I am sorry to have kept it from you for so long. Please believe me when I say that I did what I did with your best interest at heart. If I was wrong, if I have caused you any pain or suffering, please forgive me, my son. If you cannot, then find some comfort from the fact that loving you from a distance has broken my own heart a thousand times with sorrows.'"

Meryt stopped reading because she could not continue without breaking down into sobs. It moved Sobekmose. Meryt gathered herself and continued.

"'Yet I would do it again, because I believe that you are a special man with a chosen destiny. The god of Israel placed you in the Great House for a reason. For what, I do not know. But you must find out what your purpose is.'"

Jochebed had told Sobekmose some about this god of Israel, El Shaddai. The name meant "mighty god of blessing," but it had never made much sense to him. This god had promised to bless their patriarch Abraham with fruitfulness and blessing to fill the earth, but the children of Abraham had become slaves of Egypt.

"'As I have already taught you, our people first came to Egypt from Canaan in the days of Pharaoh Amenemhat III. They were the sons of Israel, rescued from famine by their own brother Joseph, who had become vizier to the king. Our ancestors were a nomadic people with great flocks and herds, so the king settled them in the richest pastoral region of Goshen near the king's district and put them in charge of his own flocks and herds. They grew prosperous and strong, building the cities of Avaris and Pithom. But the memory of Joseph's heroism faded until one day a pharaoh rose who was taught nothing of Joseph. His name was Sobekhotep III, and he considered the children of Israel to be a threat to his own countrymen. So he seized our properties and wealth with his royal decree and enslaved us.

"'During this time, I met your father Amram, a good man from the tribe of Levi, and we married. I gave birth to your brother Aaron and sister Miriam, and we struggled to stay alive in the midst of this oppression. What I have not yet told you was that you were born in the reign of the next pharaoh, Neferhotep I. Two lector priests of Ra came to Pharaoh and told him of a prophecy of the birth of a Hebrew whose hand will bring destruction to all the land of Egypt. My son, beware the priests Jannes and Jambres. For they serve in your father's court.'"

Sobekmose knew the lector priests of whom she spoke. But Jannes and Jambres were a mere twenty years old. If she was right, they would be over sixty by now. So the rumors of their deal with the gods in return for eternal youth must be real. Was their prophecy of a destroyer just as real?

Meryt continued reading, "'Pharaoh Neferhotep was so frightened by the prophecy that Jannes and Jambres convinced him to exterminate our kind. So he ordered the Hebrew midwives to drown the male infants in the Nile but to keep the females alive to become their slaves. The midwives refused this edict and gave excuses to Pharaoh for their failure to obey. When you were born, I hid you from public view. But after three moons, I could hide you no longer. The Egyptian authorities were going house to house, overturning all our property in search of their prey. They even bribed some of our own people to become informants against us. So I made an infant basket and waterproofed it with bitumen inside and out. I placed it at the edge of the riverbank and placed you in it. It was like the ark of Noah, only with you as its treasure.'"

Sobekmose's learning brought to mind Egyptian comparisons as well. Isis had hidden the infant Horus, son of Osiris, amongst the papyrus marshes of this very delta to hide him from Set's murderous intent. Pharaoh in this analogy was like Set, Sobekmose the true Horus.

"'I put you in the one place of the river we knew they would never search: the bathing area outside the Great House. Young Miriam then watched over you from a distance, hidden.'"

To the prince, Miriam was like the goddess Nephthys watching over baby Horus in his river ark and protecting him.

"'Meryt was the daughter of the king of the delta region at this time. She came down to the bank of the river to bathe and discovered your ark by the edge of the riverbank. She opened it and saw you crying and took you in.'"

Meryt stopped again, tears and a mother's love shimmering in her gaze as she looked up at her son. She said, "This is where I entered your story. There are several things you must know. First, I knew my father's edict was cruel and barbarous, though in the Great House I was removed from the suffering of it all. Second, I was still so young, married less than a year when the prince to whom my father wed me was slain in the endless wars between Upper and Lower Egypt, between my father and Sobekhotep, who is now king.

"Your father—that is, my lord whom you've always believed to be your father—his seed never quickened in me. Then he died, and I did not even have a child in my womb to comfort me.

"When I found you in the river, I will admit at first I saw only a beautiful boy child to fill my empty arms. I knew immediately you must be Habiru and had been hidden there from the king's decree by some desperate mother. I too had hidden myself away in my grief after my husband fell in battle, so it was not difficult to hide away longer and pretend that I had given birth to a son.

"And that is when I met your sister Miriam. She approached me just after I'd drawn you from the water and cradled you in my arms. She was a young girl herself but so aware. She asked if I would like her to find a nursemaid for you. That she immediately returned with a Habiru woman whose breasts overflowed with milk for you told me the girl must be your family and the woman your birth mother."

"But why ad-d-dopt me? Even if the king's decree was cruel, you r-risked much for a Habiru slave child. And if you did ad-d-dopt me, why keep around a woman who could give lie to a successful deception?"

Meryt's generous mouth curved in a sad smile. "That is the other thing you must know. You asked if I, a daughter of Pharaoh, could be Habiru. Well, there were Habiru in my mother's bloodline from the days of Joseph, the Habiru vizier.

"Then a new dynasty arose that forgot all Joseph had done for Egypt. But my mother's family—they did not forget. And they remained powerful in Upper Egypt. My mother made sure that I too did not forget our Habiru heritage—or El Shaddai, the god Joseph served."

Meryt looked at Sobekmose directly, even fiercely. "Understand I could not have claimed you as my own without the help of your true mother Jochebed. We came to be as close as sisters, though outwardly she was careful not to violate her station. We believe that El Shaddai had saved you with a divine purpose as my son. When I was made queen of a united Egypt that was a sign to us that his divine purpose was to make you a prince of Egypt. And one day when you became king, you could undo the terrible crime my father had committed against your people. That you could restore the legacy of Joseph, an alliance profitable to both Habiru and Egypt."

Wild though this story had seemed, Sobekmose could no longer deny its truth. Sincerity burned from his mother's eyes. From the words in his birth mother's letter. Perhaps it was indeed some kind of cosmic justice, being adopted into the very family of the king trying to exterminate him.

"But for this to work," Meryt continued, "your mother and I agreed that she had to allow me to raise you as a son of Egypt and that we would not reveal to you your true identity until you had reached manhood or she had died. We did not want you in a position where you would be torn between two mothers."

She sighed. "Jochebed and I feared that I would have another son that would eliminate your claim to the throne by treaty. But my womb was now barren. When I gave the king no other son, he came to despise me and to blame me.

"I in turn had come to see what a cruel and depraved man Sobekhotep was. And his son is no different. I saw then that a king as just and wise as I knew you to be could become a deliverer to the Egyptians as well as the

Habiru. That this must be the divine purpose for which El Shaddai had given you to me. And though you did not come from my womb, I pray, my son, you do not doubt your place in my heart."

"I have never doubted your love, M-mother, and I hope that you believe me that you have no cause to ever d-doubt mine." Sobekmose paused before adding with some hesitancy, "Jochebed wrote that she named me M-moshe, or Moses, which means in Hebrew I was one drawn out, as of w-water."

Meryt smiled at the subtle wordplay. In Egyptian, "Mose" or "Moses" meant "son of." Sobekmose's name meant "son of Sobek," the fierce crocodile god of the waters of the Nile.

"Yes, our names for you were similar but different. You were not just drawn from the Nile but you were fierce and strong like your namesake, the crocodile god. I even called you my little fierce one."

Sobekmose didn't feel fierce. All he could think of was the irony of the Egyptian equivalent of his Hebrew name "Mose." It was like calling him "son of" without a father reference. And that was how he felt now, like an orphan. A son without a father.

He looked up at her. "Have you met my true father?"

"I am sorry, Mio, no, I have not."

"Where is m-my m-m-m—where is Jochebed buried?"

"In the family plot."

It was a common enough thing amongst the Hebrews. He would visit her grave and find out who his true father was.

Perhaps Sobekmose would be fierce after all.

"Tell me where my mother lived."

CHAPTER 11

The rising sun woke up the inhabitants of Avaris. The three archangels—Gabriel, Raphael, and Uriel—met on a small isle in the Hebrew district just across the river from the Egyptian royal palace and sacred temple precinct. They chose an obscure wheat field for their venue. It was almost harvest, so there was much for which to prepare, but the hard work of the season had not yet begun, which added to the restlessness of the populace.

Gabriel and Uriel discussed their recent battle in the temple.

Uriel argued, "I am merely saying that we should have taken out Set while we had the chance."

"We were not there for Set," Gabriel countered.

"True, but he would have been a bonus victory. And he did keep us from taking the others hostage."

The usually quiet Raphael spoke with authority. "Our purpose was to incapacitate, not kidnap. We performed our duty."

Uriel would not stop talking. "I do not mean to question Yahweh's will, but—"

"Then do not," interrupted Gabriel.

Uriel gave him a look. But he still did not stop talking. "It is not that I am questioning Him. It is just that I am curious."

"So, you are unsatisfied with his orders," said Gabriel.

"No. I would just like to know more."

"That means you are unsatisfied."

"Your problem, Gabriel, is that you are a simple angel. You do not have much curiosity. That is not necessarily faithfulness, you know. It could be ignorance."

"I like simple obedience."

"It does have a ring to it," said Uriel. "Gabriel, the ignorant archangel."

Raphael shushed them both. He heard a sound.

They all drew their weapons. Faced their surroundings.

Four large, armed shadow warriors encircled them in their small clearing near the wheat field.

They were the rest of the archangels: Saraqael, Raguel, Remiel, and Mikael, the host's wiry, wavy-haired, handsome leader.

Mikael spoke out. "Enough bickering, you two. It is happening."

As the Watcher, or Prince, of Israel, Mikael's ready presence often signaled a threat to God's people.

"Where?" Uriel barked out.

"Hebrews are protesting at the temple across the river," Mikael said. "Pharaoh has summoned his army. He is planning to destroy the protestors and then spread his forces out into the Hebrew population."

"Dear Yahweh," said Uriel.

Gabriel finished the prayer. "Empower us."

Though the two of them bickered constantly, they were like brotherly twins when it came to their duty in battle.

"Let us meet them," Mikael said simply.

The seven archangels left on the wings of the wind to the temple of Ra.

When they arrived at the temple across the river branch, the angels assessed the situation. Several thousand Hebrews had congregated around Ra's large stone temple. Its pylons stretched fifty feet over their heads into the sky. The two huge forty-foot statues of Pharaoh Sobekhotep IV and the sun god Ra looked down upon the agitated crowd with solemn, unmoving superiority.

The entrance area was heavily guarded with soldiers. But there was no telling what the mob might do if incited. Such events could lead to occupation of the temple, vandalism, and sacrilege against the gods, against Pharaoh.

Evidently, Aaron's prophesying on the temple grounds had fired the emotions of the Hebrew people. He was an eloquent speaker whose words were like kindling. Aaron's father Amram, a non-descript, balding man of sixty-five years old, stood near his son in support.

There were other prophets standing at the top of the steps who had joined Aaron to pronounce judgment upon Egypt and Pharaoh. The gathering had not been organized as an insurrection. They were merely protesting their slavery, Pharaoh's unjust treatment of their people. It was four hundred years in the coming. The people had had enough. They wanted their voices to be heard.

But it was getting out of control.

Pharaoh had assembled several battalions of infantry just across the riverbank. His soldiers were preparing to cross over and return order to this chaos. Pharaoh was present to lead them because he had felt this was a strike right at the heart of his rule.

But the angels now saw in the spiritual realm the reason for Mikael's urgency. A majority of the pantheon surrounded the temple minus the three incapacitated earlier by the archangels.

Isis and Heka stood with the newly empowered Amun-Ra and the creator god Ptah, guarding the entrance. Around them were the primeval deities of the Ogdoad: Nun, Keku, Hehu, and their counterparts. Beside them were most of the Ennead: the sun god Atum, Shu of air, Tefnut of moisture, Geb of earth, Nut of sky, Nephthys, and many others. Dozens of them, all with weapons drawn, many with animal heads growling for battle.

The protesting humans could neither see nor hear the fire that was about to rain down upon their heads. The archangels would have their hands full protecting the Hebrews from being massacred.

In the earthly realm, Pharaoh was already crossing the river with his armed troops to put down what they were now calling an insurrection.

The crowd of Hebrews shouted their defiance. "No more oppression! Give us Sabbath!" Other agitating words could be heard in their midst, and rocks were thrown at the soldiers standing around the perimeter.

Away from the crowd, Mikael the archangel scanned the line-up of divinities by the gates. "Set is not there. Have any of you seen Set?"

Looking at each other, they shook their heads. None of them had.

Then it hit Mikael with fearful realization. Set had figured out the purpose of their attack on the high gods earlier, to weaken the Egyptian principalities over Pharaoh to benefit Moses. So Set was going straight for that target. The god of chaos had used this threat of Hebrew annihilation as a diversion to draw archangelic protection away from Moses.

"Gabriel, take charge!" Mikael barked. "Stop this slaughter. Protect the sons of Israel. I have to find Moses."

Before Uriel could ask an annoying question, Mikael was gone.

• • • • •

Miriam led Sobekmose and Tjarbit in disguise through the southern Hebrew sector of Avaris to their local cemetery. They wore cloaks with hoods and stayed close to the walls of passing homes to avoid being recognized.

The streets were quite empty because of the masses that had gathered at the temple upriver. In fact, Sobekmose was told that Aaron was one of the instigators and Amram had gone with him. Sobekmose would meet his real father later.

Despite the danger, Tjarbit had come with him, his secret being as important to protecting her people as to protecting his. Sobekmose could only imagine what would happen to the treaty and to the residents of Kush should the king discover his vaunted and prestigious new treaty had actually been sealed by the marriage of the Kushite princess with a Hebrew slave, not a crown prince of Egypt.

Sobekmose held Tjarbit and Miriam back. He looked around them in the surrounding walled yards and down an alley way. As if he was looking for something.

"What is it?" Miriam whispered.

"I think someone is following us," Sobekmose whispered back. But they could see no one. He gestured. "Keep moving."

They continued onward—right past the god Set in the unseen realm perched on a rooftop of the house watching them pass. The canine deity jumped down to the ground and landed in a crouched position, absorbing the jump. He stood to his feet and strolled after his prey with deliberate intent, pulling out his war mace.

• • • • •

The king's northern infantry of several thousand soldiers had crossed the river branch at the temple of Ra and split in two. Half went forward to meet the Hebrew mob on the right side. They waited for their orders as the other half of the soldiers went to the rear of the large temple complex to flank the Hebrews' left side.

In the spiritual realm, the archangels had climbed the temple's fifty-foot walls and located themselves directly over the line of gods backed up against the entrance pylons below.

King Sobekhotep and his son Khahotepre stood in chariots on a ledge overlooking the large open area of the temple entrance. The king figured there must be five thousand Hebrews below.

Good, he thought. *I have been looking for an opportunity to thin the numbers of these multiplying desert rats.*

He alerted his trumpeters. They called out the king's command.

The army attacked. From both sides they hit the Hebrews, crushing them in a pincer move.

But another call to war echoed through the heavenly realm: Gabriel's trumpet. Five of the angels dropped on the unsuspecting line-up of Egyptian gods below them.

• • • • •

The sound of the distant trumpets alerted Set to the battle that was going on at the temple upriver. As he closed in on Sobekmose, he saw them turn a corner to enter the gate of the cemetery.

Set turned the same corner to follow them in. He stopped at the sight of Mikael leaning against the wall with sword in hand as if casually waiting for the god's arrival.

"Why don't you pick on someone your own size?" Mikael quipped.

Set raised his mace and took a defensive stance. "You prove me right, archangel. This Hebrew traitor *is* the chosen Destroyer of Egypt. Otherwise you would not be the one protecting him."

As the Prince of Israel, Mikael was the Watcher and Guardian of Yahweh's seed line of Messiah.

"You are only half right," said Mikael. "You should leave the thinking to wiser superiors like Horus."

That made Set explode with rage. He swung his mighty mace at the despicable angel, who dodged it, setting the Egyptian god off balance.

But Set quickly recovered, and the fight was on.

At the family plot, Sobekmose knelt before his mother's grave. Tjarbit stood loyally behind him with Miriam.

He did not know what he was going to do with this newfound knowledge of his true identity. What could he do? He felt completely out of place with nowhere to turn. He was the crown prince who was to inherit the throne of Egypt. But he was a Hebrew, one of the despised classes of people enslaved by that very throne. If Sobekhotep discovered this truth, he would disinherit his adopted son. Could Sobekmose keep his secret until he was king? Could he ever reveal it without causing upheaval throughout the kingdom? He'd already begun to feel an affinity toward the people of Israel. But what would that mean? That he step down, take off his royal robes, and enter the swamps with the Hebrew slaves? That was surely not about to happen.

He stood back up and embraced Miriam. Could he call this woman his sister after all these years?

Then, out of the corner of his eye, he saw a cloaked figure rise in the bushes. It leapt out at them—a hooded man—with a drawn dagger.

Sobekmose threw Miriam out of the way of the attacker and met him head on. They collided and fell to the ground. Sobekmose was experienced in grappling. He held the attacker's knife hand, rolled back, and threw him off onto the ground.

"Tjarbit! Behind me." Sobekmose yelled. Tjarbit joined Miriam behind her husband.

When the attacker faced Sobekmose, he took off his hooded cloak, and Sobekmose saw who was trying to kill him.

"Khanethothes?" he questioned, stunned. Sobekmose stripped his cloak and drew his own long dagger in defense. They faced off with kilts and bare torsos.

The muscular lieutenant crouched like a panther stalking its prey with dagger pointed at his general.

Staggered from the revelation, Sobekmose demanded, "W-who sent you?"

"Khahotepre." The albino Nubian shifted his own blade from one hand to the other, looking for an opening to attack.

"Khahotepre? You would b-betray me for that fool?" The lieutenant had been so loyal to his general. He had even saved Sobekmose's life more than once. This betrayal was deep.

"That 'fool', as you call him, is the true crown prince of Egypt," Khanethothes said through gritted teeth. "I have always served the throne as my ancestors did before me. But a Habiru can never be Pharaoh. That you—and that traitor you call "Mother"—would plot to place your slave flesh on the throne of Horus himself!"

The lieutenant was almost frothing with rage. How could Khanethothes possibly know what Sobekmose himself had learned just hours earlier?

"How did you—?"

But Sobekmose had no opportunity to finish his query because Khanethothes was already lunging forward, his blade a staccato against Sobekmose's parries as the lieutenant got out between gritted teeth, "How did I learn of your treachery? Do you truly think Khahotepre is as incompetent as you wish to believe? He is no warrior, but he is cunning. And he has always used spies."

Of course, thought Sobekmose. *I have always been his only impediment to power*. But still, his lieutenant's loyalty…

"I could not believe it at first," Khanethothes spat out. "Until the queen's maidservant showed us the scroll she'd retrieved from its hiding place."

The spy. Sobekmose knew few things were ever really hidden from servants.

The albino's pallid features were twisted with contempt. "So now we know why you can barely spit out our language. Because you are a filthy Habiru slave and not an Egyptian. Even now, the crown prince is informing his father of your plans to usurp the throne. Your death will be relief to the king's ears."

His lips curled back from his teeth in a snarl, Khanethothes attacked with even greater ferocity. Sobekmose suddenly realized he might lose this fight. But he was not the only one whose life was in danger here.

He had to save Tjarbit and Miriam.

· · · · ·

In the unseen realm at the temple of Ra, the five archangels crushed five gods beneath their fall from above the walls. Then they jumped into action with their weapons against the rest.

Saraqael had stayed on the wall as a sniper to rain down arrows from above. He made a direct hit through the eyes of Heka and Isis, gods of magic. That would minimize their occultic fire power for a while.

Raphael used his mace to bash in the ram head of Khnum the creator god.

Uriel became a whirlwind with his double blades, spinning through the line of gods like a scythe through ripened wheat. Most of the Ennead—Geb, Nut, Shu, Tefnut—were all cut down.

The ambush of archangels had taken the gods by surprise. They were not prepared for these highest of heavenly host.

Gabriel pulled out a special weapon. It was a whip sword forged in Eden of flexible heavenly metal. Ten feet long and razor-sharp. And Gabriel used it with a skill that was terrifying to his enemies. He took off the heads of Atum, Amun-Ra, and several others with his broad swing. It whisked through the air, slicing through angelic flesh, snapping with the sound of a metallic ring in the ears.

Sekhmet, the goddess of pestilence, was an expert with her bow and arrows of pain and suffering. She had dodged behind a pillar and set her lioness eyes on Saraqael as he picked off gods from above.

She launched a volley of missiles that found their mark. The sniper archangel was taken out of commission.

And that was when the tables turned.

The angels lost their cover. Without a battalion to back them up, they were easily surrounded by the remaining gods, who seemed to multiply like flies around them.

In the earthly realm when the Egyptian soldiers first approached the crowd of Hebrews, they rammed them with their large shields and pushed the masses inward. This created a squeezing effect that inspired panic. The Hebrews pushed back. Some threw rocks. But they were not armed. This was only a protest, not an insurrection.

That's when the Egyptian spears and swords came out. The soldiers began eviscerating and hacking down their targets. The Hebrews were like lambs to the slaughter.

Inside the heart of the crowd, Aaron had pulled his father Amram closer to him in protection. They weren't armed, and they weren't fighting men. But they were praying men, so they prayed on their feet, trying to keep from being trampled by the chaos that ensued.

Before they could finish their prayer, Aaron felt a strong hand on his shoulder. It was a large warrior dressed in armor he had never seen before. Brilliant, shining bronze armor. He wondered why no one around them seemed to notice him. He thought this would be his end.

"Come with me," the warrior said.

Aaron didn't know why, but he trusted this guardian. He followed, pulling his father along with him. Where was this warrior taking them?

The warrior opened a way for them through the crowd and up the steps. When confronted by a handful of Egyptian soldiers with shields up and swords drawn, the guardian cut them down as though they were already ghosts.

Aaron felt his mouth open in awe of their protector's skills. He had never seen anyone fight with such—*elegance* was the only word.

When they were safely around the back of the temple, their rescuer led them to a small boat in the reeds.

"Do not take the river home," he said. "Cross this branch, then take the south road and cross back over the river."

"Why did you save us?" asked Aaron. "Who are you?"

"My name is Gabriel," said the guardian. "No time for explanations. In time, you will understand."

Then he was gone, back to the mayhem above them.

• • • • •

Mikael stood determined not to allow the god Set into the yard where he might empower the assassin against Sobekmose.

His heavenly *khopesh* sickle sword could not last long in a brute clash of weapons with Set's mace. This would have been a perfect situation to deploy Gabriel's whip sword. But he didn't have it, so he used his ancient Karabu training to avoid the mighty blows of his nemesis.

Karabu was a fighting technique that had originated with the mighty cherubim in Eden. It looked like the warrior was flowing with the wind around the enemy.

That wind could become a storm of blows. And Mikael used it to frustrate his red-haired enemy, who could not chase the wind. The more Set became frustrated, the more he made mistakes, and that was when Mikael struck.

Khanethothes swung hard with his dagger at Sobekmose. The general dodged it, but he felt the blade nick his bared chest. First blood. While Sobekmose was a highly trained fighter, his nemesis was younger, stronger, and faster. The general already felt his edge waning. He had to do something quickly or face his end at the hands of his subordinate.

Sobekmose chose his expertise in grappling. He rushed his lieutenant, grabbed the man's knife wrist. Khanethothes grabbed Sobekmose's knife wrist in return. And they went down to the ground.

Sobekmose rolled to gain the upper hand. But Khanethothes overpowered him and ended up on top, his knife blade perilously close to Sobekmose's throat. The general dropped his knife and used both hands to stop the inevitable.

Khanethothes also used both hands to push downward. The tip of his knife touched Sobekmose's throat. The general growled in defiance. But he felt himself losing the battle. He just wasn't as strong as his opponent.

Back out in the street, Mikael used the curved, hooked end of his sickle sword to grab Set's mace in mid-air. He was able to twist the blade and pull the mace from the hands of his foe, launching it down the street a good hundred feet.

Set stood unarmed before the archangel. But he was no hero—or fool. So he turned and bolted after his weapon.

The mace was so heavy that Set was known to be the only god who could lift it. But now he had experienced first-hand the mighty strength of this prince archangel.

Mikael knew his enemy would not return today.

The assassin's blade began to creep toward Sobekmose's neck. He felt his energy drain from him.

But then Khanethothes jerked as he was hit from behind. A large rock fell to the ground after smashing his head.

Then Tjarbit was on his back, clawing at his eyes like a tigress.

Khanethothes pulled his blade away from Sobekmose. He slashed backward. Tjarbit slumped to the ground.

Sobekmose used his moment of release to grab his dagger from the ground in his right hand and plunge it into Khanethothes' temple.

The muscular monster stopped in shock, dropped his knife. He crumpled to the ground dead.

Frantically, Sobekmose rolled the assassin off him and crawled up to Tjarbit, who lay on the ground, blood pooling around her. She had been hit deep in the kidney, and the blade had been pulled forward with fatal severance.

Sobekmose could not help her. He could only hold her gently like a precious broken doll in his hands.

Miriam had joined him, weeping, stroking Tjarbit's head lovingly.

"My wife," Sobekmose whispered.

Tjarbit looked longingly into his eyes and echoed his words. "My husband."

Tears of regret streamed down his face. "I am so sorry. Forgive me."

"Nothing to forgive. Embrace your people as you embraced me."

"I will," he said.

She smiled at him, but her eyes became distant, and she slipped into eternity.

Sobekmose felt her *ka* leave him.

Miriam held them both with empathy and weeping.

Deep down within him, a moan churned in his belly. It started as a painful growl and built to a crescendo of howling sorrow.

He knelt over her for what seemed like a lifetime. He felt as though he was outside his body looking down upon them both.

"What are we going to do?" Miriam's words snapped him back to earth. Back to his predicament.

He could no longer deny who he was. And now that Khahotepre had revealed his true identity to the king, Sobekmose could never return to his family. He was a dead man. It was both a death and a rebirth. But what world was he being born into?

Miriam said, "We must get you out of here before someone responds to the noise of your fight."

He finished her thought, "And discovers an official of Pharaoh dead in the family plot of Amram."

She said, "No one must ever know you were here. I will have the men of our household get rid of the body somewhere not tied to our family. But you must leave now."

Sobekmose was already shaking his head. "No, I will not leave my wife. And I wish to meet my f-f-father." He felt the very mention of the word most difficult to push through his lips. A father he had never known, yet whose existence now haunted him.

"No," Miriam responded firmly. "This will be the first place they will look for you. I will take you to a trustworthy friend's home. Father can find you when things calm down."

Sobekmose was already scooping his still, silent, bloodied wife up into his arms when he stopped, a sudden anguished realization freezing him where he stood. "What am I doing? I am now a fugitive. How am I to give her the proper burial that she deserves?"

Miriam laid a gentle hand on Sobekmose's arm, then brushed it across Tjarbit's intricately-coiled hair. "We will make sure she is buried with honor. Do you want to return her to Kush?"

"No," Sobekmose said stubbornly. "I want my wife b-b-buried with my f-family. With my m-mother. Here."

He'd said it. His family. His mother. His identity as a Hebrew.

But Miriam was shaking her head now. "You cannot do that, brother. They will find the fresh grave and kill our entire family. We will bury her among the friends with whom we will hide you."

"An ignominious grave."

"No," she protested. "She will rest in the midst of our people."

Miriam was right. He had no other choice.

Sobekmose stared off into the night. "Then maybe I will kill b-both the k-king and his treacherous son of a jackal. Since I have n-nothing left to lose."

"My brother, listen to me. You are now with us. What you do will affect us all."

"All my p-p-people." He still had a hard time accepting it.

She replied, "There is still much to lose."

·····

The aftermath of the bloodbath at the temple of Ra left the archangels silent with sorrow. They had become overwhelmed by the pantheon and had to retreat. They'd brought the severely wounded Saraqael with them, and the gods did not give chase. They knew Gabriel could call down a legion of angels to slaughter all the gods and imprison them in Tartarus if they wanted to. The fact that they did not only showed that their intent was more singular: to stop the Egyptian army from spreading into the surrounding villages and committing genocide.

Pharaoh Sobekhotep's original goal had been to use this incident as a pretense to move into the population and smite more Hebrews with the edge of his sword. But when he saw the mass murder in the temple area, he considered the loss of so many more slaves and how it would affect his workforce. He had let his emotions get the better of his ambitions.

No, Pharaoh would not push his army to go any further than this arena of slaughter.

He considered it a victory of suppressing an insurrection and left it at that.

CHAPTER 12

It was the end of the day and the houses cast long shadows on the streets of Avaris. Carrying Tjarbit, Miriam and Sobekmose stood at the door of a humble old house in a lesser-known district of the city. Miriam rapped quietly on the door.

The matron of the home was a sixty-year-old woman with long, white hair and an earthy presence about her.

"Shiphrah," said Miriam.

The old lady let them in. She hugged Miriam and turned empathetically to Sobekmose with tearful eyes.

"I am so sorry for your loss. Please, let me give your beloved a place of honor before you bury her."

Shiphrah led him to her own bedroom, where she had Sobekmose place Tjarbit gently on her bed.

Sobekmose was curious about this woman. Who was she? Why did she act so lovingly toward him? As if she knew him.

"My husband is long dead," Shiphrah said. "But you can find an ax in the shed to bury your wife in our family plot at the back of our compound. The Egyptians will never know."

Not all Hebrews used the cemetery for their burials.

"Who are you?" asked Sobekmose. "Why are you doing this for me?" He couldn't help but be dubious. It was the way of royalty. You could not trust anyone, especially those who acted particularly nice toward you.

Shiphrah chuckled and asked Miriam, "You did not tell him?"

Miriam shook her head. Turning back to Sobekmose, the old woman proclaimed, "I was the midwife who delivered your little baby bottom into this world, Moses."

Surprise washed over him. She opened her arms to him. They embraced.

"Thank you," he muttered into her ears. "Thank you for saving me."

"Oh, I did not save you. Your mother did. I simply stalled the Pharaoh of that day for the sake of her and all the others. He was a wicked one."

"My fath—" Sobekmose paused and tilted his head, "our king is no better."

She smiled at him. "I always knew you were special. And here you are from El Shaddai to my household, Pharaoh-in-waiting, here to save our people."

He soured. "I would not put your faith in me. I no doubt have a royal bounty on my head from the king himself for what I've done."

"So it appears Jochebed's hopes for you becoming Pharaoh are dashed. El Shaddai has other plans," Shiphrah said confidently.

Sobekmose wondered who this god El Shaddai really was. He had heard about him from Jochebed's stories, but those stories were wrapped in mystery, and he had never thought of them applying to his own world.

Shiphrah smiled knowingly at Sobekmose. As if she thought she knew something he did not.

"Just the same," she said, "go prepare your wife's resting place out back. I will tend to your wife. Miriam—"

As she gestured, Miriam moved toward the door. "I must go home to let Aaron and my father know what has happened. We will return as soon as possible."

Then she was gone. As Sobekmose dug the pit next to Shiphrah's husband out in the yard, he was overcome by emotion. Instead of weeping, he redirected it into his digging. Pain turned to anger as he swung the pick-ax into the dirt.

In his mind, he attacked Geb, the earth, for being Tjarbit's prison. He attacked Horus and Ra, the patron deities of king and kingdom. He swung the metal tool into the crocodile head of Sobek, his namesake. He spat on the Nile and cursed the fraud that it all had become for him. The gods of Egypt were demons, principalities of evil masquerading as divinities, who deserved the waterless pit of Duat.

But now a deep sadness overwhelmed him. For he was a man without a country, without his gods, without his wife, a father, or a future. What did he have left?

"Brother." The voice came from the top of the grave. Tall Aaron stood there with his hand out to help Sobekmose out of the pit.

"If you keep going, you will hit Sheol and bury yourself."

Sheol was the Hebrew term for the underworld of Duat.

"Is that not the truth," said Sobekmose. He grabbed his brother's hand and came out of the pit.

As he brushed dirt off his skin and kilt, he looked around. "Where is my father?"

Aaron hesitated. "Actually, I do not know. When we got home, I found Miriam who told me about the dead Egyptian assassin. I had my sons get rid of the body. Crocodiles are good for that."

"Is my father afraid to see me?" asked Sobekmose.

Aaron said, "We all have secrets and flaws, brother."

Sobekmose returned to the dirt pile. What was another failed father to him anyway?

"Let us finish burying my wife."

Sobekmose laid his wife to rest that night beneath the host of heaven in a secret grave in the city of his true people. They laid her in a sleeping position on her side, her legs drawn up and one hand behind her head as if asleep. She was dressed in a beautiful white linen night gown Shiphrah provided. It was a Hebrew burial.

It felt odd to Sobekmose that they were not mummifying her. It was all he knew as a royal. This almost felt like a sacrilege to him. If her body rotted, how would her *ba* return to find its home and resurrect? On the other hand, burying his wife in this manner marked his defiance against Egypt. If this was how his people were returned to the dust, then he would come to understand it.

They spoke over the body of Tjarbit with quiet words of prayer. Miriam had mentioned that god El Shaddai again. Sobekmose could not pray to his gods. They were dead to him.

He and Aaron filled the grave with the dirt that would cover her forever. Then Sobekmose did one more thing before putting his brief marriage behind him. He requested of Aaron a piece of papyrus. Then he wrote a letter addressed to the king and queen of Kush, explaining what had happened, his true identity and the consequences to him and to the life of their daughter. He apologized that he could not give her a formal royal burial because he was now a fugitive from Sobekhotep.

What such information would do to the treaty or whether the Kushite royalty would prefer to accept a daughter's loss if that meant avoiding a rekindled war, he could not guess. But at least they would not be left eternally wondering what had become of their daughter. If he could not assuage their grief, he could at least offer them a closure he himself did not feel.

CHAPTER 13

Sobekmose awoke to the morning crows outside. The sun was just coming up. Shiphrah served him, Miriam, and Aaron a breakfast of bread cakes and some figs with water. A humbler meal than his usual fish, vegetables, and platters of fruit in the palace.

But it was not the standard of cuisine or the equally humble lodgings where he'd spent the night that left Sobekmose uneasy and restless. It was a worry he'd never known until the night before. He'd risked his life often on the field of battle, but he'd never had to consider the safety of his own loved ones. His wife. His mother.

Now his wife was dead. As to his Egyptian mother, what had happened to her when Khahotepre had carried his report to the king? Would the queen deny the story she'd told Sobekmose? Denounce the housemaid as a liar? Whatever his suspicions, surely the king would not dare harm his queen, daughter of the Nile delta and beloved by its people. Killing her would surely cause an uprising.

Sobekmose dared not return openly to the palace. But when he'd asked Aaron to arrange a trustworthy Hebrew messenger to take his scroll to the king and queen of Kush, he'd asked for another to be sent to the palace to inquire among the Hebrew servants there as to the queen's well-being. But it was now full light, and the messenger had not returned.

Rising to his feet, Sobekmose asked Aaron for a change of clothes from the attire of Egyptian royalty he still wore. If he could not storm the palace to demand audience with his mother, he wanted to walk amongst his true people and perhaps understand better their plight.

"It is a perspective that cannot be seen without looking through the eyes of four hundred years of affliction," Aaron responded.

Sobekmose considered his words. "Maybe so. But I must begin somewhere. And I would like to start with the temple of Ra."

"No, my brother," Aaron said. "You must stay away from that area of massacre. If someone should recognize you there, it could inspire another uprising, and you might find yourself at the end of a rope."

"Well then, let us go where I may observe without being observed."

Aaron gave Sobekmose a simple kilt without sandals, and the two of them left for the day.

They walked south along the riverbank, watching the fishermen using their nets in the water.

They passed by barley and wheat fields, observing the farmers just beginning their harvest season. Most of them wore a simple single short kilt. Some of them worked naked in the hot sun. There were three seasons in their world based on their mother, the Nile River. First was Inundation, when the river flooded the entire delta, depositing its black silt onto the land, thus inspiring the name the Black Land. That was when many citizens worked on Pharaoh's building program while they waited for the next season, Emergence. This was when the river receded from the emerging land, leaving the rich fertile soil in which the farmers would sow their crops. And Harvest was of course when they would reap their hard labors and provide an abundance of food envied by the rest of the known world.

The three-season cycle retold their story of creation. As Inundation flooded the land, so the god Nun, the primeval waters of chaos, marked the beginning. All was formless and empty. As one of their myths described it, the god Amun's breath moved over the waters like the winds of the early rising. The Emergence season was reminiscent of the creator god Ptah speaking his word that brought forth the emergence of the primordial hillock of land in the midst of the waters of Nun, separating Geb and Shu—land and sky. The land dried and brought forth plants, birds, animals, and reptiles. Then just as farmers and workers rested from their labors, so Ptah rested from his on his heavenly throne, satisfied with his work. And the sun god Ra ruled over all.

Sobekmose and Aaron came upon one of the government buildings the slaves were building. Most of them had returned to the fields for the season, but others were left to finish the work: foreigners, debt slaves, and those without farms. Egyptian seers watched over them with whips and curses, pushing them to their limits to expedite the king's purpose.

Sobekmose saw how much these were an earthy people. He had always considered himself to be of heaven, Ra's heir. His father the king was Horus on earth. But once he died, the king would become Osiris of the underworld, and Sobekmose would be reborn as the new Horus.

The separation became starker to him. As he saw these people—*his* people—through new eyes, the entire royal mythology of his "heavenly" identity as a prince of Egypt began to unscroll before him as a mere rationalization of power.

An ancient hymn of the Egyptians spoke of Khnum, the potter god with a ram's head, crafting mankind from clay. His consort Heket then breathed the breath of life into their nostrils. So man was of the clay. But the king was god's very image. Like the images in a temple, he embodied the god on earth. It was written that Amun-Ra said to the king, "You are my beloved son who came forth from my body, my image whom I have set up on earth to rule." As the son of Ra, sometimes called "the eye of Ra," the king was god on earth.

As "the great god," the king was supposed to maintain Ma'at, or the right order of things, so he could not act arbitrarily. But he had absolute power over the people to achieve Ma'at. And he often exercised it with a heartless concern for the plight and suffering of those over whom he ruled. All were commoners before the throne except the royal kinsmen of the household. Sobekmose contemplated the revelation that the blood flowing in his veins was not divine as he had thought but rather the blood of a commoner. An enslaved nomad commoner at that.

He had been cut off from those whom he'd thought were his people but felt ironically like an alien observer amongst those whom he'd discovered were his actual people.

Sobekmose was drawn from his troubled thoughts as a man in simple worker's garb hurried up to his brother Aaron, mumbled rapidly for a long moment, then took off at a run. The look on Aaron's face as he stared after the man alerted Sobekmose to trouble at hand.

"What is it?" He drew in his breath sharply. "Is…is it m-my m-mother?"

There was deep compassion in Aaron's gaze as he put a hand on Sobekmose's shoulder. "That was the messenger I sent to the palace."

He swallowed, dropped his gaze to his feet, before continuing. "He says that—that your mother, the queen…she is dead and at least one of her handmaidens."

Already a howl of anguish was building up in Sobekmoses's chest. His head swam with the effort to keep it in. "He k-killed her for claiming me as her s-son. The beast."

But Aaron was shaking his head. "No. It is worse. They are claiming that the king and his son were dining when you attempted by stealth to assassinate the king and take the throne for yourself. The queen sought to prevent her own son from bringing down the wrath of the gods by such a vile act, and your blade killed her instead."

Sobekmose felt sick to his stomach. He knew how the narrative would finish.

Aaron continued, "If it were not for the intervention of the brave Khanethothes, who sacrificed his own life to save the king, you would have prevailed with your assassination attempt."

Sobekmose scoffed, "No doubt, I also killed the maidservant who spied for Khahotepre." Aaron nodded, no doubt.

Sobekmose bit back his words so hard that he tasted blood in his mouth where he'd bit his tongue. The worst was that it all sounded plausible enough if the king himself and his son attested to it.

Sobekmose knew too well how both father and son thought. The king would hate the queen for having deceived him all these decades with no less than a lowly Habiru imposter as crown prince living—and conspiring—under his very roof. It was unforgivable and jeopardized the Ma'at of their dynastic rule. She had to die. But the populace would never know because the key players who might testify to the truth were all dead. All except Sobekmose.

He was now a fugitive for allegedly attempting regicide and murdering his own mother. The life Sobekmose had known was at an end.

"Come, brother. Perhaps it is best we go home."

Sobekmose was too numbed by shock and anger to object. His anguished thoughts beat at him like a hailstorm as he continued at Aaron's heels around a corner into the mouth of a narrow alley between buildings.

A dozen paces into the dark canyon created by tall parallel walls, an Egyptian overseer was beating a Hebrew slave with his staff. The agonized groans of the slave and crack of the staff on his body should have drawn attention, but away from them and outside the alley, the rest of the crew continued working as though they were deaf.

He beat the slave over and over again. The slave's attempts at protecting himself from the blows slackened as he lost strength. It looked like one of his arms was already broken by the attack. His face was a bloody pulp. And the overseer did not show signs of easing down.

Beatings were a common enough occurrence in work for the king. But this scene was particularly brutal. It was apparent that only death would stop the monster from his cruelty. And with all that had been thrown at him over the last day and night, it struck Sobekmose's *ka* like never before. The inhumane treatment he had once accepted as Ma'at, the right order of things, he now saw as oppressive injustice. Grabbing Aaron by the arm, he pulled him to a stop. "Wait here."

"Sobekmose, you will draw attentio—" Sobekmose strode into the alley, ignoring Aaron's plea. The Egyptian overseer was too focused on his victim to even turn his head as Sobekmose slipped stealthily up behind him. But the poor soul the overseer had beaten to the point of near death looked up at Sobekmose with puffed, blurred, and bloody eyes.

Noticing the look, the overseer spun around to face his judge.

"Why don't you p-pick on someone your own size?" Sobekmose challenged

The overseer's eyes squinted with disdain. Grabbing the overseer's staff from him, Sobekmose used his open hand to ram the Egyptian's nose right up into his brain.

The overseer dropped dead at the prince's feet.

Aaron arrived in a huff. Saw the body on the ground. "Are you mad? What have you done?"

"Justice," Sobekmose said simply. He still had the Egyptian's staff in his hand as he stared down at the corpse.

"As a prince of Egypt, you would have the right," Aaron said. "But if Pharaoh now seeks your death, this will only make it worse."

Still staring at the overseer's body, Sobekmose quipped, "Then let us find a crocodile."

Leaving the Hebrew to find his way to a house of healing, Sobekmose and Aaron dragged the Egyptian out of the walkway into a barren patch of sand behind the construction zone. Too far away from the Nile, Sobekmose decided burying the overseer with his staff would have to do for now.

As they made their way back to Shiphrah's house, Aaron had to jog to keep up with his brother's determined march. Sobekmose didn't even bother to try to hide the bloodstains all over the clothing he'd donned just hours earlier. He had lost his mother—both mothers—and the pain of that loss had become a rage that threatened to consume him. If the life he'd known had been ripped away, he now felt a new purpose rising in him to fill that void. He would become the destroyer he'd been prophesied to be. If not of Egypt, then of the corrupt, vile leaders responsible for what this beautiful land had become.

"Sobekmose, you are out of control!" Aaron called out breathlessly to his brother's back.

"Hah! You have not yet seen what I can b-become."

"Will you throw it all away? Pharaoh will have our heads."

"Pharaoh already wants my head."

"You may draw his wrath upon your people as well. Is that what you want?"

Sobekmose stopped. He turned to give Aaron a challenging look. "You have told me yourself our p-p-people have been experiencing the w-wrath of many pharaohs for hundreds of years. It is t-time to end this."

He resumed his march back to the house. Aaron ran after him again.

"What do you mean? What are you planning to do?"

"If Pharaoh wants an uprising, I will g-give him an uprising."

"You cannot be serious. You need an army to stand up to him."

They arrived at the house. Sobekmose stopped again before entering.

"We will start small. F-find leaders first. The king already f-fears our numbers. We just need to t-train enough of them. You send w-word to those you trust most to meet t-tomorrow night here in secret."

Sobekmose may have been the younger brother in the family, but he was a leader. And despite the danger he was leading them into, Aaron was following him step by step.

CHAPTER 14

Twenty or so Hebrew elders had shown up to Shiphrah's home the next evening. The shades were drawn, the lamps burned low, and everyone spoke in hushed tones. Sobekmose waited behind the door, unknown to the others but listening in.

Aaron announced, "I have invited each of you here because I trust you and because I know you want a better life for our people."

Several mumbled in agreement.

"Four hundred years ago, our forefather Abraham entered the land of Canaan. Our God promised him that his seed would be strangers in a strange land and that they would be afflicted for four hundred years by Egypt. Ishmael, the son of an Egyptian handmaid, persecuted Isaac, Abraham's child of promise. And so began the promise of our pain.

"Years later, Jacob's sons sold their brother Joseph into slavery in Egypt, but Joseph rose to become vizier. When a famine arose, Israel's other sons traveled to Egypt and Joseph saved them. So our people stayed. They raised families and sought to make a life in this strange land. But it never became our own. As we grew and brought prosperity and security to the pharaohs, we became feared instead of loved. Instead of rewarding us, they enslaved us. In my youth, Pharaoh sought to crush our strength with a massacre of innocent male infants. And the attack at the temple of Ra by our own pharaoh is only the beginning of worse."

More murmurs of agreement filled the room.

Sobekmose stayed listening from behind the door. He was impressed with his brother's oratory skills. Aaron was a true asset for his plan.

"We showed Pharaoh that we did not have the will to fight back," Aaron continued. "So what will be his next massacre? Will it be of our wives? Our children? It is time we do something. And that is why I have called all of you here because I believe you can be the vanguard of a movement to save our people from annihilation. I believe you are the leaders of our future. It will take time. We are few in number. But we will grow."

The group looked around at each other, questioning. Getting them to acknowledge their oppression was easy. Getting them to do something about it might be a bit more difficult.

"And I have just the man to lead our movement. He is my estranged brother, Moses. You may know him as Sobekmose of the house of Sobekhotep."

Sobekmose stepped out from behind the door. The men gasped in surprise. Some looked around, expecting a trap.

Aaron calmed them down. "Men, you know me. I have earned your trust. So trust me now when I tell you that the man you think an heir to the Egyptian throne is actually one of our own. He was born a Hebrew but adopted at birth by the woman who became Queen Meryt, and he was raised as an Egyptian. But Pharaoh now knows his identity and has turned against him, so he must remain in hiding. Sobekmose has led the Egyptian army as a general, and he knows the inner workings of the kingdom that enslaves us. I believe El Shaddai has given us this man for such a time as this. If anyone can organize us to achieve our ultimate freedom, it will be Moses ben Amram."

As Aaron sat down, Sobekmose stood forward to talk. Rather than applause, he was met with sheer silence.

"I warn you, I have a sp-p-eech imp-pediment. So I may be d-difficult to listen to. B-but I assure you, I will be easy t-to follow in battle."

"Battle?" someone in the group spoke out. "Where are we going to get our army? Our weapons? Our training?"

"Just shut up and listen, will you?" another spoke up. "Let the man explain the plan."

"You are r-right to q-question," Sobekmose answered. "We will start small and b-build—in secret."

The first heckler spoke again. "I have full days of planting, working, and harvesting the fields. I have six mouths to feed. Where am I to get the time, let alone the energy, to train in secret after all that?"

"Then go home, coward," the second heckler responded.

"You dare call me a coward?" The first heckler pushed through the group to reach the second one, and a fight broke out. A few punches were followed by a fall to the floor in a struggle for control.

"Why do you strike each other?" Sobekmose yelled out. "W-we should u-unite against Pharaoh."

The heckling brawlers had stopped. The first one said to Sobekmose, "Who made you prince and judge over us? What are you going to do, kill me like you killed the Egyptian?"

The whole place went quiet. Sobekmose felt like he'd been hit in the gut. He and Aaron had been sure they weren't seen by anyone else.

"How could you know of such a death?"

"Did you think the Hebrew who witnessed your actions had no tongue?" the heckler replied. "Or that he would not recognize the elder whose bellowing on the temple steps brought Pharaoh down on us? If you truly are a Hebrew, you have a lot to learn about our people and our ability to spread word. Maybe you are not ready to lead us."

Another in the group pulled out a piece of papyrus. He lifted it up. "That is not even the worst of it. Pharaoh has sent out a decree to apprehend you for execution for murdering your mother the queen and trying to murder the king."

The crowd of men became agitated. Sobekmose raised his hands to calm them. "It is a lie. The king tried to kill me and killed his own queen to hide the truth that I am indeed Hebrew, born to the house of Amram and brother to Miriam and Aaron, though I did not know so myself until recently."

Someone exclaimed, "It does not matter if it is truth or lies. It is the Pharaoh's word against yours. You cannot win. *We* cannot win."

Sobekmose's gut turned again. The men began to murmur with rising fear.

An elder spoke up. "I know my clan well, and I can tell you they are not willing to fight the Egyptians. Most are farmers and brick-makers, not warriors. Freedom is not a concept they believe is possible."

"The same is true of my clan," said another.

"And ours as well," said a third, gesturing to his friends around him.

A fourth one said, "It would take years of preparation, of secrecy. And that is plenty of time for Pharaoh to find you in our midst and punish us all. On any count, it is suicide."

Sobekmose shared a look of resignation with Aaron. He couldn't blame them. The odds were impossible. Yes, Pharaoh was afraid of the Hebrews for their numbers. But the truth was that despite their numbers, they had no will to resist. Sobekmose was a fool to think he could hide in Egypt. His passion for revenge and revolution had blinded him to the reality of his situation. There was no place for him here.

Someone dared to suggest, "If you want to help us, maybe the best thing you could do would be to leave us."

Just then, Shiphrah opened the door and spoke with hushed fright. "Pharaoh's soldiers are going door to door. They are looking for you, Moses."

The men panicked. They scrambled out of the room, jumping over the back wall of the yard to escape into the night.

Sobekmose ran to the front door of the house and cracked it open enough to see down the street. Several doors down, he saw a troop of Egyptian soldiers banging on doors, breaking in, looking for the fugitive.

He closed the door. "Shiphrah, I have en-d-dangered your life. I m-must leave now."

She smiled and held up a full sack with shoulder straps. "I had already packed this with clothes, food, and other items you will need in case this very thing happened."

Sobekmose smiled. "Saved by the m-midwife again."

She smiled in return. "You must leave Egypt. There is no hope for you here."

"But where should I go?"

She hugged him and whispered in his ear, "You seek a father. But your father is in heaven. Find him in the desert of Midian."

He looked at her, confused. But she smiled again. "Now go."

He turned to Aaron. "I will return, my b-brother."

"Whenever you are ready, my brother," Aaron replied.

They could now hear the pounding and shouting at the front door. Egyptian soldiers were upon them. Sobekmose ran to the backyard where all the others had already escaped. Jumping over the wall, he sprinted down the alleyway with no idea of where to run.

But Shiphrah's words echoed in his memory. *You seek a father. But your father is in heaven. Find him in the desert of Midian.*

What did she mean? Had his father died? Had he fled to Midian? Midian was a distant land far to the east beyond *Yam Suph*, the sea at the end of the world. For the Egyptians, a land of danger and tales of mystery.

But the king's entire attention was now on Sobekmose. It was only a matter of time before he got caught. Where else could he hide? Where would they not find him?

CHAPTER 15

The Great Sea

Jannes and Jambres stood on the port side of a large Egyptian trade ship, part of a convoy of ships sent by King Sobekhotep to retrieve cedar wood from the forests of Lebanon at Byblos, Egypt's main port city of trade with the north. Aboard were various Egyptian valuables that Canaanites and Syrians sought in exchange: Egyptian pottery, wine, art and food, as well as Nubian gold that the north craved.

The two lector priests were sent as ambassadors to protect the king's interests with their magic. It was a windy day. The single sails billowed forward. The sailors kept the land in sight to their starboard, never straying too far since their ships were more suited to the Nile River and could not easily handle the size of storms out in the great sea of the Wadj-Ur that lay to the north of the Nile's delta.

The brothers looked out onto the west horizon. Endless water. The direction of the underworld, Duat. And the territory of Apophis, the sea serpent of chaos. Apophis went by many names: Wanderer, Earth Shaker, the Great Rebel, the Evil One. He was among the most frightful beings of the spiritual realm.

As a chaos monster, he was not easily controlled by the gods. And he always brought destruction in his wake. He was the enemy of Ma'at. He led the forces of chaos against the sun god by threatening Ra's solar barque as it floated across the cosmic ocean of Nun. If successful, he would destroy the cosmic order.

Every night according to Egyptian myths, Set, with the help of a few other gods, defeated the serpent, who would simply arise again the next day to attack Ra all over again. It was a cycle of chaos and order that represented for the Egyptians the unending battle for Ma'at in the cosmos. In earlier days,

Apophis had been understood to be huge with a single head like most serpents. In more recent times, it was reported that he had multiple heads, as many as seven, which multiplied his ferocity.

Apophis was not to be trifled with.

Jannes noticed his brother staring out into the abyss with a troubled frown. Then Jambres said out of the blue, "Have you ever regretted it?"

"Regret what?" Jannes was not as inclined to introspective thoughts.

"The price of our ambition."

Jannes sighed. "You must stop obsessing over such things, brother. It will be your downfall. Look at where we are. Chief priests of the temple of Ra, just as we had hoped. Employing magic for the glory of the king of Egypt, ruler of the world. And lest you forget, we have the youth of gods. I have told you before and I will not change my mind, it was a difficult but necessary choice. Every great achievement requires sacrifice."

Jambres did not appear to be satisfied with the justification.

The price they were talking about, the sacrifice they had made, was their father's murder.

"I do not want to hear you speak of this again," Jannes said sharply. "It is done, and there is no going back or raising the dead."

When the two brothers were young children living in a Hebrew district of Goshen, they had become enthralled with Egypt and its grandeur. They were from the tribe of Dan, but their own traditions had become weak and uninteresting. Over the years of enslavement, the Hebrews had assimilated so deeply into the Egyptian culture that there was very little difference that mattered in the eyes of the boys.

So they'd embraced the spirit of Egypt in full as opposed to the insipid compromise of an Egyptianized Hebrew people. They'd learned the gods and goddesses that brought all the cosmos alive to them with personality and vigor. They worshipped the life-giving Nile, gift of the gods. They had decided they wanted to study to become lector priests with an eye toward ultimately becoming chief priests of Ra.

But when they told their father of their ambition, he flew into a rage and punished them. He forbade them any contact with the temple or their Egyptian friends. Their mother had died years earlier, so there was no one to nurture them or speak on their behalf. And when they were caught disobeying their father's commands, he would beat them. He would often do this to both at the same time regardless of which one had offended because he knew they were inextricably linked to each other.

Their father was right about that one thing. Jannes and Jambres did think alike and scheme together in everything.

So one day the brothers made a pact with the god Set to protect them and fulfill their dreams. Set told them that his favor required a sacrifice, the life of their father.

Even at that young age, they had the ability of seers to peer into the spiritual realm. To see things others could not. One night they ambushed their father at home, beating him to death with clubs, then dragging his body into an alleyway and claiming he was murdered by an unknown robber.

The deed had the results Set had promised. The two boys had become orphans and as such were perfect candidates for temple service. They had become initiates and worked their way up through the years until they'd achieved their dream of becoming chief priests of Ra.

But that was not the only sacrifice they had made. By the time they were in their twenties, their close connection with the gods had led them to the biggest challenge of their lives. Horus and Ra had told them to persuade King Neferhotep I to seek the annihilation of the Hebrews—*their own people*—by killing male infants and enslaving female ones.

Despite their conversion to all things Egypt, they could not completely forget their Hebrew origins. They'd had a difficult time considering the implications of having a part in such drastic measures. But then they'd heard from the gods for the first time about the prophesy of the Destroyer of Egypt. Their very hopes and dreams were jeopardized. And when the gods offered them the gift of eternal youth as a reward for their devotion, the thought of Hebrew genocide sounded much more reasonable.

So they'd persuaded the king. Neferhotep sought to exterminate the Hebrew male infants. And the gods had been good on their word as well because both of the twins had maintained the look of youthful twenty-three-year-olds to this day.

Jambres had confided in Jannes that he was secretly glad the extermination did not work since the Hebrew midwives had sabotaged the effort. The king eventually gave up on it in favor of keeping all the Hebrews alive. It was a simple calculation that more slaves were better than less slaves.

"I am tired," said Jannes. "I am going below deck for a nap. Wake me if Apophis attacks us."

Jambres smiled in return. "If I do not, you will just wake up in Duat. Be sure to say hello to Osiris."

With a smile, Jannes gave him a dirty hand gesture and made his way down the ladder into the hold of the ship, where he lay down and fell fast asleep.

Jannes was jolted awake by the violent sensation of rolling back and forth. He hit his side on one of the main posts holding up the deck above. He tried to get up but had a hard time keeping his footing. The sound of cracking thunder above confirmed that they'd sailed into a storm after he had fallen asleep.

Grabbing hold of the ladder, Jannes made it up two rungs before he was tossed to the floor again. He got back up and slowly climbed the wood until he reached the hatch and opened it.

What he saw was not what he had expected. Apparently, he was not on his trading ship anymore. And his brother was nowhere in sight. What he did see was a divine golden throne in the middle of the ship with the sun god Ra seated upon it, wearing his solar disk crown and uraeus on his hawk-like head. A group of deities stood around Ra, both guarding and seafaring their way: Khepri the scarab-headed deity, Atum the creator sun god, the magical Isis, Heka and Hathor, and the lioness of pestilence Sekhmet. The ibis-headed Thoth navigated using the rear steering oar. Jannes looked to the prow of the ship and saw the canine Set scouting the way with javelin in hand, the sacred Eye of Ra painted on the hull below him.

Jannes knew what this was. He was experiencing a dream vision of the solar barque of Ra, called the Boat of Millions of Years.

But why? Visions always had a purpose.

The first thing he noticed was that the gods apparently did not see or hear their human cargo. The second was that the ship on which Jannes should have been was ahead of this ship on the Wadj-Ur by half a league or so. He and his brother must be physically on the other boat right now. Jannes's presence on this solar boat was his *ba*, or spirit body, separated from his physical body. He was on the cosmic waters of Nun in the unseen realm of the spirit.

Grasping the rail amidst the pounding waves, Jannes made his way closer to the throne, where he overheard the gods deliberating.

"Why now, my lord?" Heka asked Ra.

Ra answered, "I have called a council of the Canaanite gods who are in my service. The king of Egypt is securing trade for his palaces and as king of the gods, I am securing tribute from my subjects."

As above, so below, Jannes thought. The principalities of the nations were interconnected with their assigned human authorities on earth.

Ra continued, "The Hebrew Asiatics in Egypt came from Canaan where the Seed of the Woman is to arise."

"What do we care what happens in that filthy little land?" Sekhmet complained. "It is a mere crossroads for the mighty nations of the compass."

Thoth spoke up. "That filthy little land happens to be the home of the giant sons of Anak and the Rephaim. They come from the Nephilim of Noah's day. And we know how that turned out for our predecessors."

Jannes knew all too well to what predecessors Thoth was referring. They were the Sons of God, the two hundred divine ones who had left their heavenly abode in the days of Jared and had come to earth at Mount Hermon. They had been imprisoned in the earth at the great flood, many of them in Tartarus. Such punishment remained a warning to all the gods of the nations.

"But if we do not engage in the sin of the angels, then what have we to worry?" Set speculated.

The sin he was talking about was the violation of the heaven and earth divide. Those Sons of God had mated with the daughters of men, who had then given birth to the Nephilim, the giants of old. The original plan of the fallen ancient ones had been to corrupt Eve's seedline and therefore crush the promise made to her in Eden that her seed would crush the seed of the Nachash, the divine shining one in the Garden. That promise had come directly from the Creator.

The Hebrews were that seedline.

Thoth answered his fellow god, "Has it ever occurred to you, Set, that the Seed of the Woman resides beneath our watch in Goshen? And from that same seed comes the Destroyer of Egypt?"

Set griped, "That is what we all thought of Sobekmose. And now look where he is. Exiled into godforsaken lands. He is no Destroyer."

"Maybe so," Ra spoke up with final authority. "But there are no neutral territories in this war. Once the enemy conquers Canaan, he will not stop there. He will expand his despotic rule to every nation. Yahweh is a vengeful and avaricious tyrant."

It had the effect of ending the discussion. It was clear that this enmity between the Seed of the Woman and the Seed of Nachash was no mere battle of individual foes. It was a clash of kingdoms. Winner takes all the earth.

A storm was rising.

CHAPTER 16

The Wilderness of Shur

Sobekmose was in Arabia on the east side of Yam Suph walking south through a wilderness. He had been traveling now for twelve days, first on a camel, the last few days on foot. When he'd left Avaris in the delta, he could have taken one of two routes. The first was to pass north of Mew Kedew, the Red Sea gulf, and turn south along the coast of the peninsula of Ta Mefkat, the Land of Turquoise. But that was a route that had mines and stone quarries frequented by thousands of Egyptian workers and their overseers.

The safest bet was the second option that was straight through the northern wilderness of Ta Mefkat. This was a wild wasteland that was rarely traveled. And it led to the land of Midian where Sobekmose was going at Shiphrah's suggestion. He trusted that simple peasant woman more than anyone back in that world of royal lies.

Her whisper still echoed through his memories. *Find your father in the desert of Midian*. Though he wasn't sure what that meant. But Midian was as good a place as any in which to disappear when it came to fleeing Egypt, so he'd escaped the city under cover of night with the bag of supplies that Shiphrah had given him. He'd used the few coins he'd had on him to purchase a camel. Or rather, he'd stolen a camel and left the coins for the owner.

He had made the trek through a couple hundred miles of bitter hot sands and winding wadis. The dried-up riverbeds were helpful in staying the course but no help against a sandstorm that came upon him like a giant tidal wave. He could not help but think that Set, the desert god of storm, was behind it. And why not? It seemed like everything and everyone in Egypt had conspired to destroy him anyway.

He had huddled himself beside the shelter of his kneeling camel as the storm swept over them. These animals were built to survive such extremes.

But hardly as much its human rider. At times Sobekmose had felt he was going to suffocate. But the storm had eventually passed on, and he'd been grateful for his beast of burden, knowing he would probably have perished without it.

Unfortunately, Set killed the camel the next day with the bite of a horned desert viper, and Sobekmose had to continue the trek on his own. He had run low on food and was losing his endurance.

By then, he had found himself in Etham at the northern tip of Yam Suph. The Egyptians called it the Sea at the End of the World. Beyond it lay Midian and Arabia, a world of ungovernable nomads. The entire area was barren save for Midianites, Amalekites, and a few other tribes. The Midianites were a confederation of nomadic tribes that lived pastorally off the land with their herds of goats and other animals. The Egyptian name for nomads was *Shasu*, but they preferred to call Midianites a derogatory term that referred to men copulating with goats. They considered the Shasu filthy, uncivilized barbarians.

So for Sobekmose, this was the best place to get the farthest away from Pharaoh's searching eyes.

But he was becoming weary with walking—and thirsty as well. There was no lifegiving river like the Nile in this godforsaken land. He stuck to a well-worn trail that led from well to well since the nomads, despite their lack of so-called civility, were clever enough to create water stations for their travels to and from their seasonal locations.

And sure enough, Sobekmose was proven right when he happened upon a well within the territory he thought was most likely Midian. It was a little oasis in the wilderness with some palm trees and bushes all around. The stone well had a cover for the elements and a ceramic pot connected to a winch. Lifting the wood cover, Sobekmose dropped the pot down the deep hole. He guessed it was about forty feet.

When he hauled it up, he drank the fresh water with relief. With every gulp, he could feel life returning to his beaten body. But he had to be careful not to drink too much as this could cause his system trauma. Taking a final drink, he put the pot back in its place on the winch.

Suddenly he felt a wave of exhaustion come over him. He had not eaten or drunk much in the past few days, nor had he slept much. Now all he knew was that he needed to sleep.

He didn't want to become the surprise victim of any bandits in the area. So he found a location away from the well against a tree behind a bush. Sitting down out of sight with his back against the tree, he fell quickly asleep.

Sobekmose awoke to the sound of arguing over by the well. He could make out both men's and women's voices. The men were shouting in a Semitic dialect not much different than the language of the Hebrews he'd learned from his wetnurse mother, so Sobekmose was able to understand their words.

"Go! Go! We are here to water our flocks!"

Sobekmose stepped out of his hiding place just in time to see at least a half-dozen angry-looking women and several men facing each other in combative stance at the well. From their shouting and the flocks gathered behind each group, they were all shepherds.

One of the women, Nubian by the rich, black hue of her skin and strong, beautiful features, yelled, "We were here first!"

"It does not matter," shouted the lead male, shaking his shepherd's crook at her, "You are women, and you will take your place after us."

Sobekmose spoke up. "Where I c-come from, we treat our w-women with more respect."

Both groups turned to look at him. The pause gave him time to count a total of seven women and four men. He suddenly felt conspicuous. He knew he must look and sound a strange foreigner here. Though he had grown a beard on the long trek here, he wore a colored Jewish robe and an Egyptian *nemes*, the royal headdress, the cloth of which covered his head and draped down upon his shoulders. And his Semitic language was clearly not his own.

The lead shepherd smirked at Sobekmose. He was a stocky, strong man wearing a long-sleeved tunic that went down to his calves, clearly the leader of this band of thugs.

"W-well, y-you r-respect y-your w-women d-do y-you?"

The leader led the other men in a mocking laugh, then approached Sobekmose menacingly. The three others followed him. Though Sobekmose was hungry and lacking strength, he was thankful he'd at least gotten some sleep.

"W-what are y-you g-going t-to d-do about it, j-just st-stammer there?" the leader jeered. All four laughed again before raising their shepherd's staffs ready to attack.

"No," said Sobekmose with intense focus. "I am going to shove those staffs where your goats can't lick them."

The lead shepherd's face turned from smiling to angry. He swung his staff at Sobekmose—who promptly side-stepped him, dodged the weapon, and spun around, disarming the shepherd of his crook and knocking him flat on his back, unconscious.

The other three attacked. Sobekmose used his first assailant's staff to trip one of them on his face in the sand, blocked the second's staff attack, and dispatched the third with a knockout hit to the jaw.

The assailant who still possessed his staff tried a couple other moves, but Sobekmose blocked each with superior training, putting him in a heap on the ground in mere seconds.

When he turned around to the young women, they pulled back in fear. He threw the borrowed staff to the ground. "Fear not. Let me h-help you w-water your flocks, and I will b-be on my way."

The beautiful black girl spoke. "You are an Egyptian."

He smiled and shrugged. Yes, he could not disguise that oddity. And he could not stop staring at the young woman.

"What are you doing here?" she asked.

He smiled. "Escaping Egypt."

The women muttered amongst themselves. What could he mean? The Nubian spoke again. She was clearly a leader in this group of young women. "What is your name?"

He thought about it, suddenly realizing this was an important moment, a turning point for him. He was in a new world now. No one knew him here.

"Moses," he said. He would from now on use his birth name. It sounded odd at first coming from his own lips. But he was no longer Sobekmose of Egypt.

"Well, we thank you, Moses."

"And you are?"

"Zipporah. These are my shy sisters." They giggled at her remark. "My father has no sons, so we must shepherd the flocks."

Five of the other women looked more Midianite but the youngest-looking, barely into puberty, shared Zipporah's darker hue and features, so

Moses assumed the father must have several wives, a common enough practice.

He helped the seven sisters water their flock and bid them farewell, deciding to stay put for at least one more day to gather his strength and refresh himself with the abundance of water. His plans changed the next morning when he awoke to the arrival of the seven sisters and their flocks along with an invitation for him to break bread with their father.

Accepting the offer, he followed them back to their tents a couple miles away. He found himself stealing glances at the dark-skinned Zipporah the entire way back. Midianite women were modest in their dress compared to Egyptian women. As nomads and shepherds, they wore no make-up or jewelry and covered their bodies with full tunics. But modesty of dress didn't keep Zipporah from boldness of personality—or speech. Moses smiled inwardly at the memory of this young woman confronting four large male opponents.

Zipporah appeared not much older than his deceased wife had been and of similar ethnicity though of a lighter shade of skin. But in every other way, they were very different. Whereas Tjarbit was elegant and poised, Zipporah was earthy and rugged. Tjarbit was royal while Zipporah was rural. Her posture seemed to carry the weight of the world, a maturity beyond her years and those of her sisters. Maybe Moses had a preference for the distinctive beauty of Nubians and Kushites. Or maybe he just wasn't interested in naïve young women to mold or control.

"Who is this Egyptian stranger?"

The words broke Moses out of his musing. A bearded Midianite man approached him. He wore a long robe that reminded Moses of those his lector priests wore in court. It was of deep-blue satin with a hood laid back upon the man's shoulders. A long scarf with embroidered wings on it draped his shoulders as well. The man had a long well-manicured beard and fiery eyebrows.

Behind him stood an older woman, presumably the man's wife. She looked Arabian and wore a full-length simple robe like the other women with dark braids wrapped tightly around her head and a questioning stare at Moses.

The man looked as old as Moses's father the king but with more robust health than the ruler who lived in luxury with slaves for his every need. This one and his people were strong nomads surviving off the land. The man grinned and opened his arms wide to hug Moses, who stood a bit rigid, not knowing how to react to the affectionate unfamiliar custom. "They tell me your name is Moses."

Moses nodded.

"Then welcome, Moses, to my humble tent. My name is Reuel, but my friends call me Jethro. So please call me Jethro." He looked at his daughters. "Anyone who saves my daughters is already my friend for life. Although, the truth be told, I sometimes want to kill them myself!" He laughed heartily, and Moses lightened up.

He turned to the woman. "This is my wife Nabila."

She also carried herself with nomadic heartiness. Bowing, she said with sincere warmth, "Thank you for your kindness to my daughters."

Jethro interrupted, "Come, let us sup together. Daughters, make ready our table."

As they walked to the large family tent, Moses noticed what appeared to be a tabernacle set up nearby for worship of a god. It was a tented structure with a little fence about it, and it looked to have several sections built with various pelts of animals and an altar of stone out front.

The hospitality of these Midianites was impressive. They offered both lamb and goat seasoned with spices Moses had never tasted before. There were some vegetables he knew must have been in short supply for nomads as well as plenty of good wine. They had clearly gone all out with their best for him.

They all sat on the floor in a circle with the food in the center, Moses next to Jethro and Nabila. Zipporah sat straight across from Moses, so he could watch her as much as possible, even out of the corner of his vision when looking at others.

Moses asked Jethro about the tabernacle he had seen earlier.

"I am a priest of Ba'al," Jethro said. "That tabernacle serves several tribes in our vicinity. Of course, the nomadic life is not one of much sustenance, so I have to have my daughters shepherd as well to make ends meet."

"No sons?" asked Moses.

Jethro's countenance dropped. Everyone went quiet. Moses knew he had broached something painful. Sons did not merely shepherd but would carry on the family legacy.

"F-forgive me. I did not m-mean to…"

"Nothing to forgive," said Jethro. "I love my daughters with all my heart. And they are perfectly capable shepherdesses. But I did have a son."

Nabila leaned over and hugged Jethro with silent support.

"His name was Reuel after me. He was a fine young man with promise. He was killed in an Amalekite raid a year ago along with my other wife, Asha." He paused, choked up a little, then continued. "Asha was the mother of Zipporah and Ishtara."

He gestured to the two black-skinned daughters. Moses looked only at Zipporah. She stared back at him.

Jethro continued, "Their mother had been a Kushite slave in Egypt. But she escaped to Midian and became one of us. I am sure the two of you would have had an interesting discussion."

Jethro stopped himself. "I apologize. It is not my intent to put my visitor on the defensive."

"No offense taken," replied Moses. "I am sure there would have been much upon which your wife and I agreed."

Jethro smiled broadly. "Indeed." He looked lovingly at Zipporah. "She left me these two beautiful ones. And of all my daughters, most responsible is my girl Zipporah. But also quite headstrong."

Zipporah gave a groan of complaint. Moses could see she was trying to protect her reputation but unwittingly proving Jethro's point at the same time. Moses didn't care. He liked it.

"Fear not, Zipporah," Moses said. "I know w-what it is like to have a headstrong father."

Everyone laughed, including Jethro. Moses and Zipporah kept their eyes on each other through it all.

Moses turned serious toward Jethro. "Have you any recent trouble with the Amalekites?"

"They are the bane of the Negeb and northern Arabia," said Jethro. "But we have managed to avoid them for some time."

Moses had learned about the Amalekites through Egypt's interaction with Canaan. They were an abominable tribe of nomads, cannibals who ate the flesh of their victims and seemed to be gripped by madness. They engaged in the dark arts and were thought to be possessed by desert demons because they howled like it in battle. Moses could see this topic was a sore one for his host.

"But enough about my insignificant life," Jethro went on with yet another smile. The man had a disarmingly pleasant disposition. "I think you have a fascinating story to tell. You may be Egyptian, but by your garb and demeanor you are clearly no commoner. So tell us your Egyptian secrets, Moses."

Moses chuckled. "You are a w-wise one, Jethro. I c-cannot hide from you, c-can I?"

"Why do you hide? Are you a fugitive?" Jethro spoke as though it were exciting that he should be shielding an escaped criminal. Midianites did hate Pharaoh. But even though Pharaoh wanted Moses dead, Midianites would not believe it. If they knew Moses's true position, they might see him as a hostage for ransom. Or worth a hefty reward if turned over to the king's justice.

Moses said, "Egypt is not what I was raised to believe it was. My f-father, my family, my p-people were not who I th-thought they were. So here I am. F-far away from the lies."

"Well then," said Jethro with another big smile, "I can see not all Egyptians are crocodiles after all." Everyone laughed. It broke the tension.

Moses was not going to admit that his nobility was a sham and that he was really a member of a lowly nation of slaves any more than he would admit he was son of Pharaoh. Mystery was his protection.

Jethro got serious. "Where do you want to go? What do you want to do?"

"I do not know yet."

Jethro nodded his head in understanding. "I can see you do not want to talk about your past. That will be for another day. In the meantime, let me propose that you stay with us as my guest until you can make up your mind. Consider us your new adoptive family. Hopefully, we will not disappoint you."

Moses looked straight at Zipporah, whose face was lit up with hope. "I do not think disappointing me would be possible."

She smiled just enough to make clear she'd interpreted his words as he intended. He added, "But you will have to en-d-dure my s-stammering. It is a c-curse."

"Nonsense. We all have our peculiarities. Take Zipporah for instance." Zipporah's eyes went wide with anxiety. "Zipporah belches like a man."

"Father!"

"Truly, she can match any shepherd I know with her gruff loudness."

Everyone burst out laughing. Nabila's laugh drowned out the rest, punctuated by noisy snorts as mirth overtook her.

Jethro said, "And as you can see, my wife laughs with the sound of a horse. I call her my little horsey—whom I love to ride."

They laughed again, Nabila's snorting even more prominent.

"And lest I leave you with a false notion of my own perfection, I can only say that I have the most obnoxious trait of all. Or should I say, 'noxious.'"

The girls knew what was coming. They all started groaning and calling out to stop. But he would not.

"I have the peculiar curse of an overactive gaseous bowel. With a stench that sometimes kills."

He raised his right thigh and sought to release some gas. "I can clear a tent faster than a saluki can chase down a gazelle." Everyone kept yelling at him to stop, not to do it, not now, and other pleas for mercy.

But he let one loose like a rumbling earthquake.

Nabila and the girls all got up to clean the dinner table and get out of there as soon as possible.

Jethro slapped Moses on the back. "You do not have a father. I do not have a son. Maybe this will be a good deal for both of us."

CHAPTER 17

The Great Sea

Jannes held the mast of the solar barque firmly in his arms as waves of the sea storm threatened to wash him overboard. The gods were skilled in their balance on the heaving ship. They held their places with a preternatural ease in the face of the storm. They were still just off the coast of Canaan on their way to Byblos when the heavens broke loose like a living monster with peals of thunder, arrows of lightning, and pounding rain. Their boat rode waves Jannes did not think were possible this close to shore. Was it an attack of the gods of Canaan? Ba'al the storm god? Lady Asherah of the Sea?

No. The deities of that land were fully submitted to the power and authority of Ra and his son Horus. This was something else.

Suddenly, the thunder, lightning, and rain all stopped. The waves ceased billowing and calmed down. The clouds above dispersed, and the storm ended as though sucked up into heaven—or down into the underworld. Jannes could now see that the sun was setting in the west.

Looking toward the shore, he was horrified to see the human ship his brother was on crashed against the reefs in shallow water. It looked like it had shattered into splinters with pieces of wreckage spreading out all over the bay. No sailors were in sight in the water.

He ran to the rails and screamed out, "Jambres! Jambres!"

The gods on his boat still did not see him or hear him. But then it struck him. Maybe this was not a vision. Maybe he had died in the shipwreck. So he was not his *ka*-spirit separated from his body but his *ba*-spirit created at death to go on a spiritual quest. He felt faint with fear.

Then he noticed that the waves had not merely quieted down but had stopped completely. The water was perfectly still and without motion. Like a flat sea of glass. Dead calm.

He felt a deep chill down his back. This was not good. This was…

The water on his starboard side exploded with a violent convulsion, throwing him on his back to the deck.

A huge serpent with seven heads burst out of the sea with a hideous screeching sound from all seven throats. It sounded like metal scraping bone, and Jannes felt it shudder through his whole body. The creature was twice the size of the ship with armor that looked like potsherds over its bluish-green body.

It was Apophis, the sea dragon of chaos. Jannes remembered from his past that the Hebrews and Canaanites called it Leviathan.

Sekhmet responded with uncanny speed. She had already launched two deadly arrows into the thing before it fell back below the surface in a crash of waves.

"I got a neck and a head!" yelled the goddess.

Set stood at the bow with his large bronze javelin perched in his hand, scanning the water. "It is only stunned!" he yelled.

Thoth barked, "There are six more heads where that one came from!"

"I need to hit its heart," Set concluded.

The gods scrambled. Heka began an enchantment against their monstrous attacker. Hathor and Isis stepped to the bow of the boat beside Set and began empowering him with a spell. Hathor was called the Eye of Ra and mistress of all the gods.

"Isis, why do you not call out its secret name?" Set complained. The secret name of a person or creature was the name by which a magician could control that being. No one knew secret names like Isis did.

"Apophis has no secret name," Isis said. "He is chaos."

"Now you tell me this?"

Isis stopped her spell. "You would rather I not help you?"

"By all means, m'lady, continue. I will take what I can get. But you had better hurry."

Before the two goddesses could finish, the barque was hit from below. Rising a dozen feet above the water, it came crashing down with a huge splash, giving witness to the power of Apophis's tail.

Jannes had almost been thrown from the boat on that one, so he grabbed the mast tightly and prayed for the gods' success.

Then three dragon heads broke out on the starboard side of the boat while four dragon heads broke out on the port side. The creature was directly below the craft.

Set could not get at the body to thrust his spear into the heart.

Khepri, Atum, and Thoth lashed and hacked at the three heads with their swords but to no avail. Its armor was impenetrable.

But not for Sekhmet's missiles. On the port side, she hit one head right in the mouth through the soft part of its gullet. The creature bellowed in pain and gurgled with blood. The arrow had hit its larynx.

The serpent's roar was so loud Jannes had to cup his ears with his hands, which made him lose his footing and roll toward the boat's edge. He hit the rail and had the wind knocked out of him. He tried to grasp the wooden rail to keep from bouncing off the ship into the water.

Cursing his lack of a target, Set jammed the javelin into the deck, rushed toward the monster, and launched into the air at the biggest head. He caught the serpent around the neck. It screeched and tried to shake him off. But Set was too strong.

Isis screamed, "Set! Noooo!!"

From primordial days, being immersed in water would weaken the heavenly fallen ones. If Apophis went under, Set could be subject to permanent burial at the bottom of the sea.

One of the dragon's heads turned to take a chunk out of the clinging god, but it was incapacitated with an arrow from Sekhmet through its eye and brain.

The head waved around in convulsions. Like the gods, the beast could not die. But it could suffer enough from heavenly weapons to require healing.

Set began stabbing furiously at the head he was hanging onto. Which made the creature screech in pain and belch out a fireball from its mouth. Hitting the mast, the fireball burnt it to a crisp and the sail to ashes.

Jannes had just dodged his own death.

The creature then plummeted to the depths with Set still on its neck. For a moment, all was still again.

"Set went down!" Isis cried out.

The gods looked over the side of the barque, trying to see where the serpent had gone. But there was no sign of it and no sign of Set.

Ra ordered with caution, "Be ready. Be ready."

But the moment for which they were readying themselves didn't come. The gods relaxed while still remaining vigilant for any sign of approach from the depths.

There was none.

Suddenly, the water at the front of the boat exploded again. This time it wasn't the heads of Apophis that burst out. It was Set. Flying through the air, the god landed on the boat just a few feet from Jannes, smashing what was left of the starboard rails.

"Get ready for the deep!" he yelled out.

Jannes wondered what that meant exactly. But then all wonder left his mind when he saw the main head of Apophis rise out of the sea at the bow of the boat. It had become huge. Ten times its original size. Did the gods' magic turn against themselves?

Jannes held on for his life as the serpent opened its mouth so large that it swallowed the boat whole.

Jannes screamed as complete darkness enveloped the solar barque.

CHAPTER 18

Horeb

The summer season had arrived. The Midianite tribes moved from the lowlands near Yam Suph eastward through the Sinai Wilderness to the Hisma Plateau on the backside of the mountain range. As part of the region called Horeb, it was a large, arid expanse available for pasture grazing during the hot months because of its elevation several thousand feet above sea level. Jethro had pitched their summer residence in the Sinai Wilderness near the base of the mountain range to the west.

Moses and Zipporah were returning from a hike along the mountain range that they often took together. Moses had spent these weeks helping the family while he stayed with them. Zipporah had taught him a few things about shepherding. She had impressed him with her strength of character and tough resilience in this wilderness. He had fascinated her with his knowledge of the world and other cultures. He would spend hours telling her of the stories of Egypt, Babylonia, Assyria, and even of her mother's land of Kush.

They had stopped just outside a part of the range called Mount Sinai, the main peak of the wilderness area where they were. Moses noticed the stationary storm clouds hovering exclusively above Mount Sinai, its top consisting of blackened rock.

"This mount seems often to have storm clouds above it." He had noticed that when he was with Zipporah, he stuttered less. She had a calming effect on him.

Zipporah said, "Father says they conceal the unknown mountain god."

"What mountain god?"

"If he knew, he would not call it unknown."

Moses smiled. "Has anyone ever scaled its heights?"

"No," Zipporah said sharply. "Father forbids it. We should not even go near its base."

"Why is that?"

"Ask Father. He will tell you."

They made their way back to their tents. She said, "Tell me more about Kush."

She had known so little of the land of her origin, only the stories her mother had told her.

"Well, as I said, they are a p-proud and noble people. Fierce warriors and loyal subjects. I was a soldier, and I traveled deep into their land and saw their many cities. I saw their k-king and queen—and their daughter the princess."

He hoped she would not notice his feelings leaking through. "They have high regard for their r-royalty. But their p-priests are very influential, much like your f-father is."

She interrupted him. "You were a soldier? Did you fight them?"

He wanted to be careful what he told her. "Egypt has had a long and varied history with K-kush. We have done much trading and have generally respected one another's sovereignty. B-but I must tell you, Zipporah, that Kush did seek to take over much of Egypt's territory, so yes, Ph-pharaoh did send his army to fight them. But it was to take back land that was originally Egypt's."

"I see."

"Fortunately, the king and queen of K-kush made a deal with Pharaoh to forestall more bloodshed. So the negotiations ended peacefully with K-kush paying tribute to Pharaoh while retaining a certain amount of autonomy. Rather than enslaving their ch-children, we educated them in Egyptian ways. Ph-pharaoh even took one of their gods as his own and agreed to a m-marriage treaty to seal the peace."

"Marriage treaty?" she asked. He could see her thinking it through.

"So Egyptians do not hate Kushites?"

Looking at her, he noticed she was smiling at him. He returned her smile. "No. They sometimes even marry them."

"Oh?" she teased. "And how do Egyptians treat their Kushite wives?"

"In Egypt, w-women are equal under the law. They can sign contracts and own p-property."

Her eyes went wide with wonder. He knew she was fascinated with the land of the Nile. She had asked him many questions about Egypt over the past few weeks he had been here.

She asked with an impish glint, "But I thought you hated Egypt."

Memories of his past life came back to him. "Yes. But not everything. It is still a part of w-who I am. I suppose it always w-will be."

"Do you think you will ever return?"

"Do you want me to?"

"Yes! I mean, no! Of course not. But I would like to visit one day."

He said, "Be grateful you have a family here."

"You miss yours," she said sympathetically. He had told her weeks ago that he had a brother and sister and that his mother and father had died.

She added softly, "You have never spoken of your father."

He sighed deeply. "There is nothing to say."

She said, "You have become like a son to *my* father."

He looked at her with a smile. "If I married one of his daughters, he would be my father-in-law."

She said, "Oh, I do not know if he would let you. Do you think you are good enough for one of us?"

She hit him and ran ahead, making him chase her back to the tents.

He looked back up at the mysterious Mount Sinai before running after her.

Moses and Zipporah had become attached to one another over these last weeks, but his dark history had kept him from asking Jethro for her hand in marriage. Still, he longed for her.

He caught her, swinging her around in mock play. For a moment, they were pressed so close together he could feel her breath on his face, see the tender light in her large brown-black eyes. Then he set her on her feet and stepped back.

"What is wrong, Moses?" The joy drained from Zipporah's expression.

"There is so much you do not know of my p-past."

"I do not care. You said you wanted to start a new life in this land. That is enough for me."

Moses couldn't look her straight in the eye. He whispered, "I was married before. To a K-kushite woman."

Zipporah paused with surprise. He searched her face closely for a sign of rejection. Instead, she seemed sorrowful. "What happened?"

"She died."

"Did you have children?"

"No."

She stood there for a long moment, then commented thoughtfully, "I expect you treated your Kushite woman well."

"I did."

"Good."

He was stunned. This young lady was so full of grace he didn't understand her.

Her eyes brightened. "But it seems you have forgotten how to chase a Kushite woman!"

With a smile she bolted away again, running for the tents.

Moses followed her—with everything in him desiring everything in her.

Jethro met them upon their arrival, and Moses asked to speak with him. They sat down on some stools outside Jethro's tent that looked out upon the distant Sinai range, its mysterious peak still shrouded in dark clouds, punctuated by flashes of lightning.

Jethro handed him a wineskin. He took a deep drink and wiped off his lip.

"Tell me about this unknown g-god of the m-mountain."

Jethro looked surprised. "What did she tell you?"

"She told me to ask you."

Jethro stared off into the distance, looking at that very mountain.

"All I know is that the god of Sinai is a *sheddim*, a desert demon of slavery and despotism."

"How do you know that?"

"Ba'al told me in a vision. Many years ago. He said to stay away from the mountain. So we stay away from the mountain."

Moses considered the words as he too looked out upon the rock that seemed to burst into the sky with fury.

"I wanted to ask you s-something," said Moses. "I think I have d-decided what I want to do."

He looked at Jethro, who remained silent and approving.

"I want to become a p-priest of Ba'al. I want you to teach me."

He looked to see what Jethro's reaction would be. But the Midianite remained silent, contemplative.

Finally, he spoke, "Let me save you the vain hope. I will not initiate you into the priesthood."

"Why not?"

Jethro sighed. "Because it would be a waste of your life."

"What do you mean? Y-you are a p-priest."

Jethro looked him in the eye. "And I have wasted my life."

Moses was shocked by the revelation. Jethro was such a good-natured fellow. Why would he say such a thing?

"Do you seek to dissuade me because of my s-stuttering? Egyptian p-priests must be masters of words for spells and m-magic."

"That is not my reason. I have served Ba'al all my life. But he mocks me. He destroys my only son so that I have no legacy, no future. He is a god of storm who takes but does not give. I do not trust him. I do not trust any of the gods."

"Then why do you remain a p-priest?"

"I fear him. I fear what he might do to the rest of my family. I am his hostage. So I fulfill my vows as ransom. But I would not wish this on anyone, least of all you. You are like a son to me."

Moses tried to take it all in, to figure out what he had just heard.

"You should not be a priest. You should be a king."

Moses searched Jethro's face for a hint of understanding. Had this Midianite discovered his true identity? Jethro had known Moses had a noble background from the time they'd first met. But had he somehow figured out that Moses was the son of Pharaoh?

"So I will teach you how to shepherd instead," Jethro concluded. "That is one thing we Midianites do very well. I believe Zipporah has already taught you much since you spend so much time with her."

He gave Moses a knowing look. "And do not worry, I will not ask you to copulate with goats. That is an Egyptian rumor of envy."

Moses smiled, then said, "You say I should be a k-king, but you want to t-teach me to shepherd?"

"You are a leader, Moses. That much is clear. I believe the gods have a purpose for you. And your military experience is not enough."

Jethro got up from his stool. "Come here. Let me show you something." He walked toward the flock of goats and sheep herded in their pen a short distance away.

Moses caught up with him. When they arrived at the fold, they stopped and looked out over the herds, baaing and bleating, munching on grass, standing safely within their fenced-in protected area.

"People are like sheep and goats," Jethro said. "They move in herds. They follow their shepherd. If you learn how to lead a flock, you can lead a people. A nation."

What was Jethro implying? That Moses could return to Egypt and become Pharaoh?

"And what if you are wrong? What if the gods have no purpose for me?"

"Then you will be a damn good shepherd and benefit my tribe."

Moses saw a big smile on Jethro's lips as the older man finished his line of thought. "I do not care about your past, Moses. I care about your future. Sometimes when I am in the tabernacle and looking at the image of Ba'al, I think to myself, this is a piece of rock carved by the hands of man. We think our Opening of the Mouth ceremony provides a means for inserting the deity's presence into the image. But what kind of divinity becomes confined to a rock or a piece of wood that can be manipulated by men? Broken into pieces even. If I were a god, I would certainly not do such a foolish thing."

Moses appreciated his honesty.

Jethro glanced around to make sure no one was near to listen. "Tell no one this, but I question Ba'al on other counts as well. I ask myself, if he is the mighty storm god who rides the clouds, then why does he seem afraid of the mountain deity that is often surrounded by storm clouds?"

Jethro seemed to catch his mind going astray. "Well, what do you think? Shall you be a shepherd?"

Moses smiled at him. "I shall."

Jethro embraced him, then pulled away and announced, "Well, if you are going to be a shepherd, you will need a vigorous wife to help you. So I think it is time you stop delaying your intent for my Nubian daughter and just ask me for her hand."

Moses was caught off balance by the frankness of his host. He didn't know what to say. So he said the first thing that came to him. "I guess you know me like a son-in-law already."

Moses's wedding to Zipporah was significantly less opulent than his Egyptian wedding to Princess Tjarbit. Midianites had no king, no royal pomp and circumstance, no trip down the Nile in a marriage barque. But they did have clan loyalty, and they knew how to celebrate.

Hundreds had come from several of the other Midianite tribes on the plateau to see the marriage of the daughter of the high priest of Ba'al. What they lacked in wealth, they made up for in community. And that large community brought much food and drink, everyone from their households. It was a feast worthy of a king, and it went on for several days.

Jethro himself married the two of them before a crowd of at least a thousand clan members and visitors. Moses wore a simple white linen tunic and leather belt. At Zipporah's request, he kept his long, wavy hair but trimmed his beard. She dressed in Nubian finery. A leopard pelt over her shoulder. Gold and silver bracelets and necklaces. Her black hair was braided and arranged in a beautiful flowered adornment above her head. Moses could not take his eyes off her.

And he was determined to never let her out of his sight.

After the betrothed signed their marriage covenant, Jethro turned to the crowd and announced, "Let it never be said again that Reuel the shepherd priest of Ba'al has no son!"

The crowd cheered loudly.

Moses looked over at Zipporah and thought how fortunate he was to be able to find a second good wife in a lifetime. He had thought his love had died with Tjarbit's murder. But the gods had been good to him. Unlike his new father-in-law, who grew increasingly doubtful of the goodness of the very gods he served.

He and Zipporah kissed deeply. And all the world faded away as all he could see, taste, and smell was his new bride in their embrace. He felt her tremble in his arms and was grateful that this strong young woman had surrendered herself to him. He would protect her with his life, never let anything hurt her.

And he could barely wait to get her on the marriage bed where they would consummate their love.

They left the celebration and returned to their own tent, raised close to Jethro's tent. A dozen armed Midianite men stood guard around the area in honor of their tradition. A nomadic tribe was always on the lookout for enemies or invaders, so they could never rest. They always slept with one eye open and a sword or spear by the bedside.

But for this one night, the two new lovers could release all cares of the world and surrender to one another in complete unguarded vulnerability.

CHAPTER 19

Duat

Jannes emerged from total darkness into a new world. The solar barque was now in a river valley between two chains of mountains. It was night, but no moon or stars shone their light above. Yet he could see with a clarity he'd never had in the dark before. The gods were positioned protectively around the throne of Ra, who now manifested his ram's head. The air was tense with anticipation as the gods stood ready.

Jannes knew where he was—on the river Wernes in the underworld of Duat. In olden days, only kings were allowed passage on Ra's trip through the underworld. But now Jannes, an important lector priest, was also experiencing the privilege. He was familiar with the books of the Netherworld: the Amduat, the Book of Gates, the Book of the Dead, also called the Book of Going Forth by Day. All these were written for those on this journey to provide for passage and protect from denizens of this outer darkness. And he knew where this would all lead for him.

His attention was drawn to the sound of birds, thousands upon thousands of them the size of sparrows, descending upon the boat to join them on their journey. These were the *ba*-spirits of the dead. They covered every inch of the barque with loud chirping that caused Jannes to cover his ears. Then they became quiet and dissolved into the wood of the craft.

Jannes looked ahead on either side of the riverbank. He saw gods and goddesses—and baboons—twelve of each, representing the twelve hours the solar boat was about to traverse. The baboons and gods all raised their hands in praise of Ra. Then there were a dozen large snakes on both sides who reared their heads and spat forth fire from their mouths, which lit the way for the solar barque's forward drift.

They came upon a first gate for entry. This was a large stone edifice bridging the riverbanks with hieroglyphic engravings on every inch and two huge wooden doors. The hieroglyphs were spells to honor the blessed dead and curse the wicked. The gates did not stop the water like a dam might but let the water flow beneath its wood while stopping all vessels.

Beside the door were three guardians, a gatekeeper in the shape of a Uraeus serpent, and two mummified humanoids, one a guard, the other a recorder. The mummies carried sharp knives in their hands. The eye of Horus painted on the ship's hull caused the guardians to bow in deference to its captain's magical power. But the gates would not open.

All the gods stood still, frozen in wait. Though they did not acknowledge his presence, Jannes sensed a responsibility in his heart. He had studied the books of the Netherworld and knew what was required of him. The guardians would not open the gates unless the traveler pronounced their secret names. Fortunately, Jannes had memorized them for this very eventuality, when he would have to face this journey.

"Open these doors for Ra-Horakhty, O Eavesdropper, O Loud-Voiced, O He-Whose-Face-is-Inverted."

This would be the standard procedure for each gate. He hoped his memory of the various secret names would serve him well, or he would suffer the punishment of Duat. The large gates opened, and the solar barque sailed through into the first hour of the journey.

The second gate was called "He-Who-Devours-All." It was guarded by a giant coiled serpent whose name was pronounced by Jannes as "He-Who-Guards-the-Desert." But the gates opened onto a fertile land of vegetation and produce. Jannes knew this to be the Field of Reeds, a glorious paradise of food and plenty for the sake of the blessed dead that was worked for the deceased by underworld servants. A spell from the Book of the Dead would secure that food and sustenance in the afterlife, a continuance of the benefits of earthly life. Jannes performed it.

"I have come to the Great God
in order that I may receive the provisions
which his goodwill grants of bread and beer, oxen and fowl,
having strength, having power,

plowing there, reaping and eating,
drinking, copulating,
and doing everything that used to be done on earth."

Four boats now joined the solar barque and led it upstream. These were hosted by various deities of grain and water and abundance. They passed by mummified souls on both banks. On the right were the blessed dead, who sang out in praise. On the left were Ra's enemies, who were forever bound with their hands behind their backs, wailing and mourning for their starving future.

The boat slowed beside the left bank for the first of many demons Jannes would have to face on his journey. This one was a bull-headed monster who swallowed sinners turned into donkeys. Jannes recited the appropriate spell from the Book of the Dead.

"Back, abomination of Osiris.
I know where thou art.
Eat me not, for I am pure.
O swallower of sinners, there are no sins of mine on the
docket of the scribe of evil deeds.
Seize me not. Eat me not!"

This was the first foreshadowing of the future of Ra's enemies. Each bank of the river was represented in the Book of Gates as an upper or lower register. On the lower register where the donkey-swallower resided, souls of the damned were swallowed up into outer darkness, a precursor to the Great Judgment Hall of Osiris where their bodies were destined to be decapitated and their *ba*-spirits annihilated.

The third gate opened to a continuation of Osiris's fertility with many acres of land for harvest given by the Great God to the blessed dead. It was not until the fourth hour at the fourth gate that Jannes experienced a dramatic turn of events. The beautiful world of harvest, growth, and rejuvenation turned into the desert wasteland of the Land of Sokar.

The river suddenly dried up and the solar boat ran aground. The gods had to get out and tow the boat in darkness through miles of sand. Jannes moved to the bow of the ship as they dragged it onward. But it was a useless gesture because all light dissipated as they entered a cavern. The darkness became so intense that Jannes could not see his hand in front of his face.

The only reason they were able to see a bit ahead of their steps was because this was also a land of fire-breathing snakes whose flames barely lit the way through the impenetrable darkness.

But the Land of Sokar was also called the Land of Silence. Jannes could hear nothing. Not the footsteps of the gods, not his own breathing, or even his voice. It was as if the darkness itself swallowed up all sound. He began to feel disoriented as if there was no space in which he existed, as if he was floating in nothingness. Panic seized him.

This was part of the underworld journey that replicated Osiris'sdeath after those fields of the bounty of life. The feeling of awareness of one's self and yet a total lack of senses in a state of absolute aloneness was a horror worse than nothingness. Jannes didn't know if he could make it through this hour without going mad.

CHAPTER 20

Horeb

Moses tended to a herd of goats and some sheep on the Hisma plateau. It was summer again, so the Midianites had transferred their residence up to the elevated area near Sinai.

It had been three years since he married Zipporah. She had birthed their firstborn and named him Gershom, whose name meant "sojourner in a foreign land." As much as Moses loved his wife, his father-in-law, and extended family, he still felt like that sojourner. He'd thought he would easily forget Egypt and his dread Hebrew origins, but he could not. He wondered if revealing his secret to his loved ones would lighten his burdened soul. Or would it just make things worse?

Jethro had taught him the art of shepherding. He had grown to enjoy the new life of solitude. He spent many hours thinking as he watched over his flocks in the wilderness lands of Midian, Sinai, and Horeb. He had just finished grazing the flock in green pasture near the range. He had watered them by the still waters of a pool off the creek that flowed through this area. Keeping a flock fed and watered was crucial for leading them. If their bellies were aching, they were always wandering, looking for something to satisfy them.

Now was the time to return home before evening. To keep the herd together and following, the shepherd had learned to sing a common song. The animals would recognize the voice or the tune and know to follow. Some shepherds used flutes, and if they had stayed out too long and were caught in the dark, they would burn a torch to light the way. The herd could see the torch and hear the shepherd's song to follow.

Moses now steered the flock through a small valley wadi that led back to camp. It was a more direct route but not without its own dangers. Shepherds called these wadis valleys of shadows or valleys of death for several reasons.

First, the shadows of the high ridges could bring darkness sooner than desired. But valleys were also locations from which bandits could ambush a shepherd from above with rocks or arrows and steal the herd.

Lastly, wolves and other predators could easily follow, hidden by the boulders and winding pathway, just waiting for a weak or slower animal to lag too far behind. The wolf would then easily snatch its victim before the shepherd noticed.

An additional shepherd at the back would help keep such tragedies from happening. But one could not always afford a second hand. In this case, Jethro's flocks were far too large and pasture too scarce to graze together, so his remaining unmarried daughters worked in pairs herding the flocks assigned to them for available grazing. Moses was expected to defend his charges from human and animal predators on his own.

To accomplish enough, Moses carried both a rod and a staff. The staff was a large wooden piece of carved wood with a hook at the top for grabbing the animals.

The rod was a kind of mace, a thick wooden handle with a piece of iron rock attached to the top. This was a weapon to be used against more ferocious predators like wolves, lions, or bears.

But Moses had not encountered any predators today as he finished his trip back to the family residence. He gathered the animals into a fenced enclosure for protection from predators during the night, counting each animal as they entered the gated area to make sure he didn't leave any behind. Today he counted only fifty-six goats and eight sheep. There were supposed to be nine sheep.

Closing the gates, Moses grabbed his rod and staff and ran back up the pathway from which he'd come. The sun was already low on the horizon, casting long shadows. He hoped the missing animal would not be too far away.

As he ran, he heard a howl nearby and increased his pace. That was surely the call of a wolf that had found a victim.

Sure enough, he came upon a bushy area of brambles and thicket they had passed just outside the valley. There he saw the missing lamb stuck in a thicket, bleating with fear as a lean, mangy wolf approached it with growling teeth.

Still about twenty feet away, Moses pulled back his rod to launch it at the wolf. But before he could release, he heard a swish from behind him and saw a mace hit the wolf in the ribs. It whined with pain as it rolled in the dust from the impact.

Moses turned to see his father-in-law Jethro behind him, smiling.

"I may be getting old, but I still have my aim."

Moses smiled. "I see that a mace is good for something more than religious ceremony."

Jethro said, "I saw you leaving, and I wanted to talk to you."

They walked over to the thicket. Jethro picked up his mace, and Moses used the hook of his staff to pull the sheep from the prickly thicket.

He handed his staff to Jethro to carry and pushed the sheep over to the ground on its side. It bleated in fear. He grabbed the two front legs with his left hand and the two back legs with his right hand, then swung it up and over his shoulders. He needed both hands to hold the squirming little bag of wool and keep it from falling off his shoulders.

Moses turned to Jethro. "Shall we?"

Suddenly, Moses felt a warm stream of liquid against his neck that poured down his left shoulder and drenched his tunic. Moses crinkled his nose and complained, "So this is the thanks I get for saving your woolen rump."

It bleated as if to apologize. Moses shared a hearty laugh with his father-in-law.

They walked the path back to the sheep pens. Jethro told him, "You are a good shepherd."

Moses smiled silently.

Jethro said, "You are still not at home here, are you?"

Moses sadly shook his head no.

"It pains me to hear that. You have become a son to me to replace the dear son I so cruelly lost."

"And you the f-father I never had."

"Is it your people? Do you miss them?"

"I have not been entirely honest about my people."

"I have told you, Moses. Your past will not change my trust in what you have become."

Moses sighed. "I have not lied to you about being Egyptian bred. But I was not born Egyptian. I was adopted into that life. My origin is in the people they enslaved called Israelites. When my low-born status became known, I lost my rights and I rebelled. That is why I am a fugitive from Egypt."

He noticed Jethro was smiling. "You find that amusing?"

"Israelite, you say? Sons of Abraham ben Terah from Ur?"

"Yes. How do you know this?"

"My dear son-in-law, you and I prove to be more closely related than we realized. You see, the Midianite people are descended from Abraham's second wife Keturah."

Moses arrived at the sheep pen dumbfounded. He placed the sheep into the pen and looked at Jethro for more.

Jethro said, "I have heard many stories of the chosen line of Abraham, Isaac, and Jacob. And how Jacob became Israel. We call you the sons of Sarah." He paused sadly. "We sons of Keturah, the lesser, did not garner such favor. We migrated into Arabia where we now reside—and quarrel amongst ourselves like bickering siblings."

Moses stood quietly, trying to understand the implications of what he had just heard. "So, you kn-know about the god of Israel, El Shaddai?"

"Of course. But because the sons of Keturah did not have his divine favor, we questioned his choice."

Moses said, "That may be another thing we share in common."

Jethro said, "But we turned to Ba'al. And I would not recommend it to you now. We will talk more of this, but first I have news we must address."

Moses leaned in with interest.

"I told you about the Amalekite tribe that killed my wife and son several years ago now. It was led by a giant warlord named Cthul."

He paused. It looked difficult for him to continue.

"One of our scouts has delivered intelligence that Cthul's tribe is currently thirty miles north of here near the edge of the wilderness. I fear they may attack us if they find out we are here."

A flush of rage filled Moses's spirit. He growled, "Then we must attack them first."

"No," said Jethro. "We will defend ourselves if we must, but I do not seek conflict. We have managed to avoid it these past few years, and it has benefited our people."

Moses held back his anger. "Cthul murdered your w-wife and son. It is justice."

"It is revenge," countered Jethro. "I will not deny that I want him to pay for what he did. But I fear the price of revenge upon my tribe."

"But if you do not r-retaliate," said Moses, "then your w-weakness invites more."

"I have not done so for years, and we have lived in peace. If I do so now, they will retaliate. Revenge never ends. It just changes hands until we are all dead. I am getting old, Moses. I have seen too much war and the suffering of innocents that results."

Moses replied, "The p-peace you have also comes at a p-price."

"True. But it is a price I am willing to pay. I will not ask Midianite sons to die for my personal loss."

"Then let me lead a small t-team of stealth mercenaries to assassinate Cthul alone. They will n-not kn-know who we were and will have no r-reason to attack you in response."

Jethro thought it over and said with resignation, "I can see I am not persuading you. If you gain the approval of the council elders, then I suppose I cannot stop you."

CHAPTER 21

Duat

Just as Jannes felt his mind fragmenting from the absolute darkness and silence of the fourth hour, he was brought back from the brink by the recurrence of sound and smell. The faint echo of flames somewhere beneath the ground accompanied the caustic stench of sulfur. He knew what was beneath the ground. It was the Lake of Fire, where the damned were annihilated in the judgment of the Second Death. Then the soothing voice of Isis drew his attention as he heard her pronounce the names of the guardians of the fifth gate, and they continued on. Isis was the source of resurrection for Osiris in the myth, so her shining was the beginning of the return to life for both the sun god and Jannes.

Isis led the way to the shore of what could only be the primeval waters of Nun. A short distance offshore, a mound of land began to slowly rise out of the water. It was reminiscent of the primeval hillock of creation. But Jannes knew this was a burial mound of death for the Lord of the Dead, Osiris. By now, Jannes could see in the dark again as Isis was accompanied by her shadow goddess, Nephthys, by her side.

Isis called out, "Osiris, come forth by day. The sun awaits you."

The burial mound began to stir and crumble as a coffin rose up out of the ground. It was guarded by two sphinxes and Anubis, the jackal-headed god of burial. The sphinxes had bodies of lions and heads of humans. This was the sixth gate. Jannes knew that inside the coffin was Osiris' corpse ready to be united with Ra.

Then he noticed the multi-headed Apophis suddenly circling the burial mound in the water. It was not the gigantic manifestation that had originally swallowed the barque in the overworld. But it was still twice the size of the boat, and it was writhing with fury.

Jannes held on as the gods dragged the boat up to the waters and launched it in with a splash.

They were headed right into the chaos.

Jannes now saw a multi-colored serpent slither up from the boat's interior and protectively encircle Ra's body. This was Mehen, Ra's throne guardian.

Isis cast her spells upon Apophis in the water. The serpent writhed about in attempted defiance of the magic, causing splashing waves that rocked the ship with such fury that Jannes found himself catapulted off the boat and into the water. By the time he got his head above water, he discovered he was many yards from the boat. It was drifting away from him. He prayed that Apophis would not notice him in the water.

But the serpent did. It turned, several of its heads focused on Jannes, and began to approach him. Jannes was closer to shore but not close enough to outswim the monster. It closed in on its prey.

But its diverted attention was enough time for Set at the prow to launch his iron javelin into the back of the beast and apparently through its heart as well. It stopped dead in the water, bumping up against Jannes.

Suddenly, it began to convulse as if coming back to life.

Jannes froze with fear. Then he saw several of the serpent's heads begin vomiting up the contents of its stomach. They were decapitated heads of the dead victims Apophis had consumed.

The water around Jannes filled with rotting human flesh. He swam desperately back to shore to get away from this sea of death. Such a supernatural monster never really died. Its defeat was only temporary until it resurrected. Jannes did not want to wait around to experience that return.

Safely at shore but exhausted and heaving for breath, he looked up and realized he was on Osiris'sburial mound. He turned back and saw four large goddesses arise from the water, each carrying knives. They dragged the corpse of Apophis ashore and began hacking it into pieces. Jannes knew the names of the goddesses from the books of the Netherworld: She-Who-Binds-Together, She-Who-Cuts, She-Who-Punishes, and She-Who-Annihilates. He backed away from them as far as possible, considering them as dangerous as the foe they'd vanquished.

His attention was drawn to the solar barque, now pulled up onto the nearby shore. The eight gods picked up Ra on his throne. Mehen the serpent slithered back into the boat, his guardian task fulfilled. They carried the throne on poles up the mound and past the sphinxes to meet Anubis. His jackal head howled into the expanse, and he led them to Osiris'sgreen body wrapped in white linen, scepter in hand, and wearing his underworld white *atef* crown with two large plumes.

Jannes then saw a host of past Egyptian kings materialize from the darkness to witness Ra's union with Osiris into one being, marking the sun god's resurrection. Each of these kings had also become Osiris in their descent into Duat. But unlike those earthly rulers, Ra would separate from Osiris and return to the overworld in the east with his new life.

There were still five more gates yet to complete for Ra's night journey, so the gods carried him back to the solar barque. There would be five more hours of expedition through the territories of Duat on their way to the east. Five more hours of vanquishing Ra's enemies, including one last battle with a revived Apophis before the sun god would rise anew the next morning.

Jannes needed to return to the boat with them, but he found his legs unable to move and his tongue unable to shout out. The harder he struggled to move, the firmer they felt connected to the ground. He wasn't going anywhere.

The boat launched back off into the river Wernes, and Jannes felt his heart race with fear as he watched the ship dissolve into the distant darkness. He was being abandoned to Duat. So this was his death after all. He must have died in the shipwreck off the coast of Canaan. And now he would have to face Osiris.

He turned to look up at the burial mound where the Lord of the Dead was, but when he did, it appeared to be ten times larger than it was originally. It had grown from a large hill to a small mountain. He suddenly realized how hungry he was. And thirsty. His stomach growled painfully. He sat down on the sand to rest.

He heard the sound of a fluttering of wings and was startled as a black raven landed on his right shoulder from behind. He froze in fear. Was it hostile? Another demon? Or was this a hallucination from lack of food and water?

"Jannes," it whispered in his ear.

He didn't know what to say. "Hello?"

"You must be famished."

"I am."

"How will you ever make it up that mountain to Osiris? You have not eaten a thing since you got here. And you have used up all your strength escaping from Apophis."

"How did you know?"

"I have been watching you. From above."

"Do you know where there's food?"

"I do."

"Will you tell me?"

"Yessssss." The protracted *s* sounded like a snake's hiss. The raven continued, "But you must be willing."

"What does that mean?" Of course he was willing. He was starving.

"Turn back to the mound."

Jannes followed the direction and was startled to see another being standing in his way. It was a ghastly-looking creature. Like an upside-down reversal of a human being. Though it was humanoid in its parts, the parts were all in opposite places. Its arms and hands were where its legs and feet were supposed to be. And its legs and feet were where its arms and hands were supposed to be. Its mouth and tongue were in its groin area and its phallus was where a normal human's mouth would be on its face.

The thing then bent over so its feet would be on the ground and its hands would be available to use like any other human. But now, its head was below and its groin's unseemly mouth was above. It spoke to Jannes with a feminine voice that did not match its horrid body.

"Hello, Jannes. Would you like something to eat and drink?"

The thing picked up the plate and wineskin and held them out to the priest. That was when he could see what was on the plate. It looked like feces. And it smelled like a dead body. Flies buzzed around it, verifying his observations.

Just to be sure, he asked, "What is it?"

The thing replied, "Food of the gods."

"It looks like excrement of the gods."

The thing laughed, then asked, "What is the difference?"

"If you must know," the raven whispered in Jannes's ear, "it is feces from the buttocks of Osiris and urine from his phallus."

Jannes felt sick to his stomach. His dizziness cleared for a moment with his memory coming back to him.

The raven continued, "Do not think of it as shit of the gods. Think of it as food of the gods that has been digested and processed for you through the very belly of Osiris himself, Lord of the Dead, god of the underworld. Think of it instead as fruit. If you eat this fruit, you will be like the gods."

Jannes remembered the offer of eternal youth that he and his brother had received from Ra years ago. That too was a painful ceremony that had resulted in the fulfillment of the promise. Great things often required great sacrifice.

So, he took the plate and wineskin reluctantly. He knew that thinking it over too much would just cause more conflict in him, so he moved quickly. He dug out a piece of the excrement with two fingers. He gagged at the smell. But he steeled his will and ate it.

He was surprised to find it sweet to the taste. It didn't have the horrid flavor to match its putrid smell. It was a pleasant surprise. He gulped some of the urine from the wineskin to wash it down his throat. That was sweet as well like juice. Was it all just a clever disguise to make sure only the faithful would obey?

But then that sweet taste became bitter in his stomach. Nausea overcame him and he fell to the ground retching. But nothing would come out. He could feel his convulsing muscles like punches to his gut but with no relief of expulsion.

"Too late," whispered the raven.

The thing said, "You are like the gods."

In Jannes's desperation, it came to him. He remembered the names of these two demons from the Book of the Dead. He pronounced with authority, "I know your name, Upside-Down-One. You are the demon Iaau, the living world reversed."

The thing dropped the feces and urine on the ground.

Jannes looked sideways at the raven on his shoulder. "And you, you are Gebga, butler of the hostile dead, trying to tempt me from finding Ma'at in the house of Osiris."

The raven cawed, left his shoulder, and fluttered desperately over to the Iaau's shoulder.

Through his nausea, Jannes recited a spell from the Book of the Dead. "What I doubly detest, I will eat no more. What I detest is feces, and I will not eat it. Excrement, I will not consume it. 'What will you live on,' say the gods and spirits to me, 'in this place to which you have been brought?' I will not be subdued by my enemies. I will not depart upside-down for you."

As he finished the spell, he suddenly felt his nausea leave him, and his head stopped spinning. He was able to stand upright. But as he did so, the shore at his feet churned into quicksand.

He was swallowed up into the ground.

Once again, he was surrounded by a thick, confining darkness.

But he was on a floor of some kind. He felt it. Stone, solid. Thank the gods. But where was he?

Torches lighted his location. He recognized it now. He was at the gateway of the Judgment Hall of Osiris.

CHAPTER 22

Horeb

Moses and five mercenaries rode horses north toward the wilderness camp of Cthul's Amalekites. They had received the council of elders' support, but they were under strict orders to avoid having their identity discovered. Moses had a couple of ideas prepared for that purpose.

He had picked the five best warriors he knew and offered them pay for their services. None of them would take the money. They would help Moses achieve vengeance for their holy priest.

They were each adept with swords as well as bows. They were going to fight the Amalekite warlord, a giant, so Moses needed the best. If they got caught and were tortured for information, it would bring down the wrath of Cthul upon the Midianites as Jethro had warned. Moses sought to avoid such a tragedy.

After traveling the thirty miles, they set up camp not far from the tribe hidden away in one of the rocky ravines. One of the men, Jabor, was the best scout Moses knew. After a couple days, he returned to their secret camp with details of Cthul's tribe and their regular activities. Jabor had managed to find out that Cthul was going on a hunting expedition.

"How many in his party?" asked Moses.

"I do not know."

"It cannot be that many. When do they leave?"

"Tomorrow morning."

"Warriors, tonight, we position," said Moses. "Tomorrow, *we* hunt."

• • • • •

Moses and his five assassins found locations near the Amalekite camp to hide out until morning. When morning dawned, they followed the only party of men leaving the camp on their way into the wilderness to hunt. The party had two large donkey-drawn covered wagons, evidently to carry the large amount of game they expected to procure.

There were ten Amalekites, all heavily armed with bows, spears, and swords. Their bodies bore occultic tattoos and body piercings. They wore wolf and bear skin kilts and shaved their heads bald.

Cthul was a giant about seven feet tall. The Amalekites were known to have giants in their ranks. Typically ugly abominations, Cthul was no exception. Elongated skull, a double row of teeth, and six digits on each hand and foot. Like other clans of giants in Canaan, the Anakim and Rephaim, Amalekite giants were mighty warriors whose ancient origins were rooted in the cursed Nephilim before the flood.

But Moses was not afraid of Cthul. He was empowered by hatred for this abomination who had murdered his father-in-law's wife and only son. Moses would be the right hand of Jethro's vengeance.

Moses and his hunters followed Cthul's party to the edge of the wilderness where the Amalekites were no doubt planning to hunt game like deer, gazelle, and ibex. Camping inside the tree line, Cthul and his men set up two lookouts for the night watch.

At about the midnight hour, two of Moses's men slipped up to the first night watch and cut their throats. They dragged the Amalekites out of sight, then set up traps for later and waited for the second watch to come.

When the replacements arrived early in the morning, they saw their comrades up and waiting for them. But these were actually Moses's men in disguise, who turned around and ambushed the replacements.

The next attack would not be so easy. Once the replacements failed to return to camp, the other six Amalekites knew something was wrong. In the dawning light with the morning fog moving in, they approached the lookouts in groups of three, ready for ambush.

What they were not ready for was the large net that Moses released above one company of three Amalekites. It enveloped all three, who tried to lash out and cut through the ropes. But they were constrained by the entanglement, allowing Moses and two of his men—Akaya, a stout, strong warrior, and Yamin, a marksman with the bow—to easily dispatch them with swords and arrows.

On the other side of camp, a similar trap was set. Moses and his two men ran over to see how their comrades had fared. He had ordered that if they found Cthul, they were to keep him alive for Moses's blade alone.

But when they passed through the clearing of the camp, Moses spotted the giant and his two warriors dragging the mangled dead bodies of the other three Midianites into the camp toward the fire. They had become human game for the cannibals.

Both sides froze, facing each other across the large fire.

The Amalekites dropped their bodies and growled. The giant Cthul looked like a menacing monster in the fog and dawning light streaming through the trees. He raised his head and howled like a rabid hyena. His two warriors joined in. It was the war cry of the Amalekites.

The two armies of three ran toward each other with swords drawn. Moses had ordered Akaya, his best swordsman, to face down the giant. Akaya would wear him down and disarm him for Moses to finish off.

Yamin had managed to let loose one arrow that hit his opponent in the shoulder before they clashed by the fire. Yamin dropped his bow and drew his sword just in time to meet his foe with ringing metal. The Amalekite was strong but wounded. He struggled to keep up with Yamin.

Moses fought his warrior with everything in him. He was feeling his age as they exchanged blows with their swords. He was a bit slower and not as strong. A shepherd's life was not that of an active military general.

Akaya met Cthul sword to sword. But despite Akaya's own size and weight, his adversary was bigger and stronger. And he carried a much larger sword. The giant pounded away at Akaya.

Moses started to weaken. He didn't have the endurance he'd once had. He started to defend more than attack.

Then suddenly an arrow pierced his opponent from behind. It poked out through the Amalekite's torso, no doubt piercing a vital organ. The man stopped for a moment, stunned but not dead. Moses used that moment to thrust upward into the heart of his enemy. The body dropped to the ground.

He turned just in time to see Akaya deflect his last blow from the giant as his sword hand was cut off with the blade. Cthul then swung wide and halved Akaya's body at the torso.

Cthul turned to Moses, who took a ready stance. The giant approached him casually as if unconcerned with his puny opponent.

Moses swung his sword in attack. Cthul hit it so hard the blade flew from his hands. Moses tried to shake the pain out of his hand.

Looking up into the ugly face of the Amalekite, he realized he was facing his executioner. He would never have vengeance for his father-in-law but would die at the hands of this abomination.

Cthul dropped the sword. Stepping up to Moses, he shoved him hard. Moses flew a dozen feet to his back on the ground. The wind was knocked out of him.

He saw the hulking mass stand over him, then get down onto his knees over Moses and growl, "Who are you? Why are you here?"

Moses would not speak. Could he withstand torture?

But Cthul did not appear to be planning torture. He raised his arms above his head and clasped his hands into a single hammerlike fist, ready to crush Moses's skull in one downward pound.

Just then Moses heard a swish and saw something flying through the air, hitting the giant's skull with a crunching sound.

Cthul fell to the ground in an unconscious heap.

Moses looked over to see Jethro walking up to him.

His father-in-law said, "Thank Ba'al these abominable creatures gave their godawful war cry. I almost failed to find the camp."

Moses said, "That 'ceremonial' mace is proving to be quite useful."

Jethro held his hand out to Moses to help him up. "It is a good thing for you that is all I had to do. I would not last three seconds with that beast."

Picking up his sword, Moses looked over at the unconscious form of Cthul. He handed the sword to Jethro. "If I were you, I would f-f-finish your vengeance now b-before that beast w-wakes up."

Yamin had just pulled his sword from the chest of his prone enemy. Jethro hacked off the head of the murderer of his wife and son, then lifted his battle skirt to piss on it in the dirt.

Jethro said, "We are not out of the wilderness yet. How are you going to turn the Amalekites away from blaming Midianites?"

"We b-brought scimitars and robes of one of the Arab t-tribes to the east. We will plant them around the camp and d-dress our own casualties in the robes so they will think it was Arabs."

A whistle from Yamin drew their attention. He was standing by a large tent. He waved them over.

When they arrived, he whispered in a secret code dialect they used for situations like this, "You better put those Arab robes on."

"Why?" asked Jethro.

"Trust me."

Moses and Jethro put on the robes, then opened the tent flap. Inside were ten young Amalekite boys with frightened eyes sitting on the tent floor looking up at their captors. Ranging in age from about six to nine years old, they were too young to have received their customary tattoos.

Moses closed the flap.

Yamin continued in their secret dialect, "They must have brought their sons to teach them hunting."

Moses added, "They are so young."

Yamin said, "We cannot enslave them. We are too far from home and not equipped for the trip back. They'll track us."

They stood in silence, not willing to say it aloud.

Jethro did. "We have to kill them all."

"No," said Moses.

"They have seen us," Jethro replied.

Yamin butted in. "But they do not know who we are."

"And if we leave Arab weapons and robes as we planned, they will still think we were Arabs," Moses added.

Jethro asked, "Why are you willing to take such a risk?"

"Because our goal was to kill Cthul, not start a war as you yourself had cautioned against. If we kill these young children, we give the Amalekites reason to hunt us."

"And they will not hunt us for killing their warlord?"

"You did not hunt Cthul for k-killing your Midianite warlord, d-did you?"

Jethro shook his head no.

"We hunted him because he k-killed your children."

Jethro nodded in agreement.

Moses said, "In Egypt, I did not kill children. It was not our way. I will not do so now."

Jethro gave an assenting nod. "We will bind them and leave some water. It will be a few days before they are discovered."

They dressed their dead comrade in an Arabian robe and left scimitars and Arabian daggers behind as deceiving evidence of Arab attack.

Because of their physical exhaustion from battle, they traveled only a half day on their journey back. Building a small fire, they first tended to the wounds they received, then made a quick meal, which they ate in silence around the fire. They stretched out to sleep so as to make an early start in the morning.

Moses was awakened in the night to the sound of a scream. He reached instinctively for the dagger under his thigh. He was disoriented by the presence of a young boy kneeling over him, about to plunge a dagger into his chest. He caught the child's arm, stopping the dagger.

"Jethro!" he yelled out.

Throwing the kid to the ground, he bounded to his feet. A bunch of boys were spread out around the smoking embers, watching them like demons in the dark. They were the Amalekite boys they had spared.

Looking over, Moses saw Yamin wrestling with two kids on top of him, a long dagger thrust into his belly. On Moses's other side, Jethro had caught his own attacker before the boy could drive in his dagger. The boys were so young that it took little to overpower them. But ten Amalekite younglings howling like baby hyenas and mobbing three men was not without challenge.

A child swung a long dagger at Moses. Moses dodged it and disarmed the child, turning the sword upon the little monster. They were all little monsters, juvenile spawn of their demonic fathers. They were so young, and yet they were Amalekites. Moses had been judged wrongly about the risk of sparing their lives.

Moses cut down two more of them, though not without costing him a deep cut in his left arm. Jethro had also confiscated a sword and was hacking down the attackers who surrounded him. Yamin was having a more difficult time because of his wound. He received another slash in his leg. He limped and held his stomach as he defended himself against several of the frenzied Amalekite offspring.

Moses cut down the last against him and helped Jethro dispatch his last two. They turned to see the final two Amalekite boy warriors rushing the wounded Yamin.

Moses threw his long dagger and took one of them out.

Jethro had picked up a bow and took down the final one.

They both ran to Yamin.

He was cut up by the attacks. And choking on blood.

"They were too young for this. They were too young."

Moses held him. "I was wrong, Yamin. This is my fault."

"No," Yamin choked. "This is not on you. They fooled us all." He paused. "Actually, it is my fault. I should not be such a heavy sleeper."

Moses and Jethro smiled at the dark humor. Yamin was a good man. He had always seen the best in situations, never took himself too seriously.

Moses felt Yamin's body relax in his hands. Heard his last breath leave his physical form.

He laid his Midianite brother to the ground.

Moses and Jethro looked out on the carnage around them. All ten of those young Amalekite boys had taken up arms and followed the three men here to kill them. Evil was learned early. The sons had borne the sins of the fathers.

Moses muttered to Jethro, "We should have killed them. We should have k-killed them all."

Jethro placed an assuring hand on Moses's shoulder. "We must return their bodies to their camp before the hunting party is discovered."

CHAPTER 23

Duat

Jannes stood before the mighty gates of the Judgment Hall of Osiris, also called the Hall of Double Justice.

A whispering voice as if from the gates themselves spoke to Jannes.

"To which god shall you be announced?"

Jannes replied, "To Thoth, the Interpreter of the Two Lands."

The huge gates, gold-laden with impressed jewels, creaked open. The ibis-headed Thoth stood waiting at the opening.

His voice was strong, "To whom shall I announce you?"

"To him whose roof is fire, whose walls are living cobras, the floor of whose house is the waters. He is Osiris."

Thoth boomed, "Proceed."

Trembling, Jannes stepped through the gates. As he entered the hall, he noticed he now had on white linen and sandals. He felt the black eyeshadow of Egypt around his eyes, and he smelled the scent of myrrh upon his body.

He looked back up. Thoth was gone. In his place was Anubis, the jackal-headed deity. Beyond him at the end of the hall, the green-skinned Osiris sat on his throne adorned in white mummiform with *atef* crown on his head, kingly tight beard on this chin, holding his scepter crook and flail crossed over his chest.

Jannes knew exactly what to do. He had studied the Book of the Dead for years, committing much of it to memory. Now was his moment of justification, of going forth by day.

First, he sang out a hymn to Osiris from the ancient text.

"Hail to you, Great God, Lord of Justice! I have come to you, my lord, that I may see your beauty, for I know your name, and I know the names of the forty-two gods of those who are with you in this Hall of Justice, who drink the blood of those who cherish evil on that day of reckoning.

"Behold, I have brought you truth, I have no falsehood in me. I have done no evil. I have not done what the gods detest. I am pure, pure, pure! My purity is the purity of the great phoenix who rises out of the ashes of corruption into newness of life."

Though Osiris's lips did not move, his voice echoed throughout the hall. "Come forth by day, Jannes, my faithful servant."

Anubis turned to escort Jannes down the pillared hallway of stone. High above in the cornices of the wall and ceiling, he saw a frieze of Ma'at feathers above a line of living uraei, winged cobras writhing in place as if they could descend at any moment. Symbols of order and judgment.

He knew there were forty-two pillars in this hallway because there were forty-two gods of the tribunal standing beside each one of them on that march up to the throne of Osiris. Each of them a judge. Each of them with knife held ready in hand. Each of them with different heads of animals whose presence made Jannes weak in the knees: crocodile, lion, snake, canines, and felines, all with bared teeth and searching eyes. Despite such intimidation, now was his chance to shine with the gods. He had memorized the Declaration of Innocence the gods required be spoken to assure a mortal's justification of life. As he slowly made his way forward, he would announce the secret name of each of the gods and pronounce his innocence of forty-two sins that compromised every category of sin imaginable.

To the first one, he stopped and declared, "O Far-Strider, I have done no falsehood."

Then he recited to the one across the way, "O Swallower-of-Shades, I have not stolen."

And then onto the next, "O Dangerous-One, I have not killed men."

"O Bone-Breaker, I have not told lies."

"O Backward-Facer, I have not committed homosexuality or copulated with a boy."

"O Serpent-Who-Brings-and-Gives, I have not blasphemed God."

He continued on step by step until he had recited to all forty-two judges, proclaiming innocence of all sins including robbery, fornication, ill-temper, impatience, babbling, theft from orphans, pride, and stolen wealth among the rest.

When he got to the end of the line, he stopped and sighed with satisfied relief. He had done it. He had recited the complete negative confession of his Declaration of Innocence with rigorous memory. He had justified himself.

He now stood before the platform of Osiris on his throne. Behind the Lord of the Dead stood Isis and her shadow sister Nephthys. Thoth stood to the side recording all the proceedings.

Anubis turned and faced Jannes. He held the priest's shoulder with his left hand and with his right hand reached into Jannes's chest and pulled out his heart. Because they were in the netherworld, this resulted in no physical pain for Jannes. He also knew that in the overworld he always wore a necklace with a scarab over his heart, protecting him with a spell: "Witness my heart pure when weighed in the balance."

Then the canine burial guardian stepped over to a pair of scales made of gold. He placed the feather of Ma'at on one of the scales. This was the feather of righteousness and justice against which the heart would be weighed. The heart was the seat of the soul and identity of each person. If it weighed lighter than the feather of Ma'at, then that person would be justified before Osiris and receive the eternal reward of resurrection. If the heart weighed more than the feather, that person would be annihilated, consumed by another creature that stood ready on the platform: Ammut.

Ammut was a fearsome creature that made Jannes tremble. It was a hybrid beast with the head of a crocodile, the body of a lion, and the hindquarters of a hippopotamus. Its purpose was to eat the sinner whose heart weighed more than the feather. This was why it was called Devourer-of-Souls.

Jannes watched as Anubis placed the priest's heart on the balance's other scale.

Jannes muttered the spell of hope. "My heart of my mother! My heart of my being! Make no stand against me when testifying, and make no failure in respect of me before the Master of the Balance."

But as he did so, he saw the heart weigh the balance all the way down.

His heart had outweighed the feather of Ma'at.

In that moment, all time froze for Jannes. He saw his entire life relived before his eyes. He and his brother Jambres as young boys playing in the reed marshes of the Goshen. Lying to his mother and father. Disobeying them. Stealing from neighbors. Falling in love with young Rachel. Despoiling her virginity. The funeral of their mother. Rejecting the traditions of their people to worship the gods of Egypt and pursue the temple priesthood of Ra. Fornicating with prostitutes. Fighting with their father, clubbing him to death. Joining the temple. Receiving eternal youth from Ra. Presiding over the mass slaughter of the male infants of their own people.

Now here he was facing the judgment of his whole life with his heart in the balance.

And his heart was heavy with guilt and condemnation. Heavier than the Feather of Justice. He still couldn't believe what he was seeing. It was like expecting to see the world right-side up but seeing it all upside-down. He was completely disoriented. It didn't seem fair.

Osiris turned his back on Jannes.

Jannes blurted out, "O great god Osiris, Lord of Ma'at, my lord Thoth, the Judge of Truth, O great company of the forty-two gods, I do not understand. I have performed the rites. I have served you faithfully. I have recited the Declaration of Innocence. How can this be? How can my heart not be justified?"

Then he noticed that Osiris had changed. When the god turned back to face Jannes, he saw that the green-skinned Lord of the Dead had transformed into someone else, someone he did not recognize. One like a son of man. He had no form or majesty that Jannes should look at him, no beauty that anyone would desire. He appeared to be a man of sorrows and acquainted with grief. He looked like an Asiatic, probably a Hebrew, with a simple beard, wearing a simple robe, white as snow. But a misty cloud wrapped around him, and a rainbow appeared over his head. His face now glowed like the sun, his eyes became like fire, and his legs like pillars of fire, burnished bronze.

Jannes became more frightened by this god than by anything he had previously seen in the entire Duat. Somehow it seemed more real than any of it.

When the god spoke, it was a firm voice accompanied by the sound of thunders. "Jannes, son of Dan. You have been a serpent in the way, a viper by the path that bites the horse's heels so that my people fall backwards."

Jannes was speechless. The phrase "Son of Dan" referred to his tribe.

"You have declared yourself innocent, yet you are not. Your every claim of sinlessness is a lie that condemns you. You have rejected the god of your fathers and have worshipped false gods. You have treated your Creator in vain.

You have not been holy or honored your father and mother. You are a murderer, an adulterer, a thief, and a liar. You have coveted that which is not yours and broken covenant with your people. You have sought to justify yourself, but your words of magic do not justify you. Your deeds do not justify you. You are a son of Adam. I find you condemned."

The nameless judge turned and grabbed Jannes's heart from the scales, then tossed it to the monster Ammut. He caught it in the air and chomped on it, swallowing it whole. Jannes felt a pain in his chest.

Jannes opened his mouth in surprise. "Are you Osiris, my lord?"

"No. Osiris is a demon."

"Who are you?"

"I am the Alpha and Omega, the Beginning and the End. The King of kings and Lord of lords. I am the Judge of the quick and the dead."

As he was speaking, the entire hall of justice and all the gods with it burned up in pyres of flames as though all had been an illusion, a narrative of lies, burned away by reality. He found himself in the clouds of heaven. Behind the glowing, fiery son of man was a new throne with a second bright being upon it. His clothing was also white as snow, and the hair of his head was like pure wool. His throne was fiery flames. Its wheels were burning fire. A stream of fire issued out from behind him. And around that throne, Jannes saw ten thousand times ten thousands of divine beings at this god's service.

Even at this moment, Jannes thought that he might try to use the magic of Duat as he had used with the other beings. Manipulation through naming.

He asked, "What are your names?"

Both beings spoke in perfect unison as one. "I am Yahweh."

Jannes somehow knew that he would have no power over this god through his name. He remained mute, open-mouthed. How could two be one? Was this one god split into two? Or was it two manifestations of one being? He couldn't be sure.

Then the stench of sulfur reached his nostrils, and he saw below him the Lake of Fire rising up to his feet and engulfing him in its flames.

He felt the heat searing his flesh. He screamed in agony.

So this was his destiny after all. The Second Death.

"Why me?" he bellowed, "Why me?"

Just as he felt his life begin to leave his body, he felt a wave of water hit him in the face. A saltwater wave.

Jannes woke up spitting out the water and coughing, gasping for air. He was on the shore of a beach, and his brother Jambres had pulled him out and pressed on his lungs to expulse the saltwater from them. It appeared to be morning.

Jannes felt disoriented. "W-where am I?"

"On a shore near Byblos," Jambres answered. "Our ship wrecked on the shoals."

"The storm?" said Jannes.

"Yes. I almost lost you."

Jannes coughed up some more water. He was horrified to his core because of his experience. He stared into the horizon as if into the abyss. "I had a dream vision."

"Of what?"

"Duat."

"You saw Duat?"

Jannes didn't answer. Jambres drew near him. "What did you see?"

"I..." Jannes closed his eyes. "I was on the solar barque of Ra passing through the twelve gates of the West."

Jambres smiled. "Ah, you went on the sun god's journey through the underworld from setting to rising."

"That is not all."

"What else did you see?"

Jannes was too disturbed and confused by what he had seen in the Hall of Double Justice. He wasn't even sure what it all meant. But now was not the time to talk about it. He must think it over.

"That is for another time. Where is the rest of the crew? Can we get to Byblos?"

Jambres pointed offshore. "Look. They are searching for survivors."

He stood up and began to wave toward the rescue ship.

"Over here! We are over here!"

CHAPTER 24

Midian

Forty years had passed since Moses had joined Jethro's clan in Midian. He was now eighty years old but still in vigorous health. He had lived a full life with his wife and two sons, Gershom and Eliezer. Zipporah was now sixty, and her sons were in their late thirties. They had taken over Jethro's herds after he had retired from his priestly duties to Ba'al.

Jethro had confided in Moses that his decision was not from age. He remained a healthy ninety to this day. But rather it was from his own lack of desire. His faith in Ba'al had crumbled. All the gods seemed impotent to him or capricious and unconcerned with the lives of their human worshippers.

It was the winter season, so Moses had taken his flock to the east side of the wilderness valley near the base of Sinai. As he looked upon the blackened peak beneath the storm cloud, he made a decision.

The Midianites had avoided the mountain because of the warnings of Ba'al to stay away. But Jethro no longer served Ba'al, and he had become increasingly curious over the decades about the mysterious mountain and its god. He had influenced Moses with that curiosity as well. And Moses was finally going to ascend that mountain to see what he could find.

It had been difficult at first for Moses to feel at home in Midian. But over the years, his Egyptian past faded and made it easier to belong here. The Red and Black Land, its gods and people, his origins, all seemed more distant with memory. Along with his love of reading scrolls, the lifegiving Nile, and the pleasures of Egyptian royalty. He embraced the Midianite culture. He had learned to love the pastoral life, the heartiness of Midianite celebrations, their connection to the earth, the seasons. He felt like he'd finally found his place of belonging in the cosmos. He had found a people and a family—and a father in Jethro. In Moses, Jethro had found a son.

Moses ascended the pathway up the mountain, leaving his flocks in the care of his sons. As he walked, it seemed as if the stormy clouds above were increasing in agitation. He heard some thunder and wondered if the unknown god was mad at Moses for invading his territory. Or was it just a brewing storm? No rain was falling, so he continued.

He wasn't too far up when he stopped to rest in a clearing near the path.

He jumped when he heard a rumble of thunder, then saw lightning strike a large bramble bush near the cliff wall. The bush burst into flames. He watched it, expecting the bush to become blackened cinders in moments. But it didn't. It continued to burn but was not consumed.

What was this magic?

Standing up, Moses approached the bush to get a better look.

When he was within a few yards of it, he heard a voice call to him. "Moses." It was a strange voice. Like that of many waters.

He stepped back, looked around. No one was there.

Then again, "Moses."

This time he realized it was coming from the burning bush!

"Here I am," he said.

He began to step forward, but the voice ordered him, "Do not come near. Take the sandals off your feet for the place on which you are standing is holy ground."

Who was this speaking to him?

Well, thought Moses, *he is impressive enough that I had better do what he says.*

Taking off his sandals, Moses stood in his bare feet on the dirt. And when he did, he saw a figure inside the flames, one like a son of man. His face shone like the sun so that it hurt Moses's eyes to stare too long at him. But what he could make out was that this messenger had hair that was white like lamb's wool. His eyes were like flames of fire. He wore a long robe with a golden sash around his chest. His legs and feet disappeared into the flames.

Moses asked, "Who are you, my lord?"

When the voice spoke, the brightness of the flames seemed to increase in intensity. "I am the god of your father, the god of Abraham, the god of Isaac, and the god of Jacob."

Moses turned away, afraid to keep looking. Dread swept over him. His past flooded back into his mind like a deluge. He had heard about this god El Shaddai from the stories of his true mother Jochebed when she served in Moses's household. When he'd learned that he was a Hebrew, he'd known that this was the god of his people. But this god had seemed so distant, so absent during their centuries of oppression. Had he been living here at this mountain all along?

The voice said, "I have seen the affliction of my people in Egypt. I know their sufferings and their oppression. I will deliver them out of the hand of their oppressors, the Egyptians, and I will bring them into the land I promised, a land flowing with milk and honey."

Moses kept his arm up to shield him a bit from the brightness of the light. "What land is that?"

"The land of the Canaanites, the Hittites, the Amorites, the Perizzites, the Hivites, and the Jebusites."

Moses knew that to be the land from which Abraham had come to Egypt with his family.

"I will send you to Pharaoh that you may bring my people, the children of Israel, out of Egypt."

Moses dropped to his knees in supplication. "Who am I that I should go to Pharaoh and perform this monumental task?"

"They are your people. I will be with you. And you will bring them out of Egypt to serve me on this mountain."

Moses panicked. He had spent the past forty years forgetting about his people so that he could find a new people, a new family, a new father. And now this deity was dredging that past up and destroying the illusion of peace that he had created.

Moses wondered if the Egyptian magic of naming would give him some power over the deity.

He asked, "If I come to this people of Israel and tell them that the god of their fathers has sent me and they ask me your name, what shall I tell them?"

The voice said, "I Am Who I Am. Say this to the people of Israel, 'I Am has sent me to you.' I appeared to Abraham, Isaac, and Jacob as El Shaddai, God Almighty. But by my name, Yahweh, I did not make myself known to them. Tell them Yahweh has sent you to them. This is my name forever, and thus I will be remembered throughout all generations."

Moses stayed bowing on his knees. The name kept burning in his mind like the bush. *Yahweh. I Am Who I Am.* He knew he would have no power over this name. It was as if this god was doing the opposite of Egyptian gods. He was not hiding his secret name as something that wielded magical power over him but using his name explicitly as power over others, over Pharaoh and the gods. His power was in his name.

Yahweh continued, "Then take the elders to Pharaoh and tell him, 'Yahweh, the god of the Hebrews, has met with us. Let us go three day's journey into the wilderness to sacrifice to Yahweh our God.' But I know that Pharaoh will not let you go for he thinks himself a god. So I will stretch out my right hand against him and strike Egypt with signs and wonders. I will execute judgment upon the gods of Egypt until the king is compelled to let you go."

Moses was overwhelmed with the implication of this strategy. Yahweh was telling him that there was to be a cosmic war unlike anything on this earth. The gods of Egypt were many. They controlled the weather, the waters, the land, and the sky. Heaven and earth. And yet Yahweh was saying that he was going to execute judgment upon them? Moses knew they would not go without a fight. There was no way he wanted to be human collateral damage in *that* war of the gods.

He protested, "But the Israelites will not believe me or listen to my voice. They will say, 'Yahweh did not appear to you.'"

Yahweh challenged him. "You know this?"

"I know the people of Israel. They are a nation of little faith. When I was there they barely believed in you as the mighty god of blessing you promised to Abraham. What you promise now is so much more."

Yahweh said to him, "Nevertheless, Israel is my son. I am a father to my people. What is that in your hand?"

Moses had been grasping his shepherd's staff the entire time. His knuckles were white. "A staff."

"Throw it to the ground."

What was Yahweh going to do to him?

He set the staff down close in case he needed to pick it up again.

But when he did, he saw that the staff had turned into a serpent.

Moses stood up and backed away in fear.

Yahweh said, "Pick it up by its tail."

Then Moses understood where Yahweh was going with this. He grasped its tail, and the serpent turned back into a staff.

Yahweh was using the Egyptian's own magical practices to reflect a spiritual truth. Lector priests often used this trick by hypnotizing snakes to go stiff. But they never turned into wooden staffs.

And the power of commandeering snakes by their tails was the prerogative of deity. The gods had holy staffs as did Pharaoh. And Pharaoh received his staff of authority upon his coronation as king over the Two Lands. The gods Heka, Horus, Thoth, and Sekhmet all held stiffened snakes by the tails as visual emblems of their power.

Then Yahweh said, "Now put your hand inside your cloak."

Reluctantly, Moses put his hand inside his cloak. He felt it fill with pain, and he withdrew it. He held his hand out in shock. It had become white and leprous, covered with boils of pus.

Yahweh said, "Now put it back inside your cloak."

Moses did so. When he pulled it out, it was healed and whole again.

"And if they do not believe these signs, then you will take water from the Nile and pour it out on the ground," Yahweh said. "It will become blood on the land."

This was certainly impressive but not all that different from what Moses had seen the Egyptian lector priests do with their magic. Such a contest was still not one Moses was confident would be convincing. He didn't think Pharaoh would allow him to keep his head over it.

So Moses tried another tack. "O my lord, you know that I am not eloquent in words. I am slow of speech and of tongue with my stammering. I am of uncircumcised lips. How will they trust such a weakness to deliver them?"

It suddenly dawned on Moses that he had not stuttered this entire time. How was that possible?

Yahweh said, "Who has made man's mouth? Who makes him mute or deaf, seeing or blind? Is it not I, Yahweh, their Creator? I will be with your mouth and give you the words to speak. And you shall say to Pharaoh, 'Thus says Yahweh, "Israel is my firstborn son. Let my son go that he may serve me. And if you refuse, then behold, I, Yahweh, will kill your firstborn son."'"

Moses was sweating now. He didn't want to give up his life for this return to a painful past he had sought to forget or to face the power of Pharaoh. Sure, the gods had influence on the people, even Pharaoh. But Moses had suspected that the gods simply went along with whatever the rulers of the earth did in their own autonomy. Too many prophets and madmen claimed to have the gods on their sides and were crushed by the thumbs of earthly rulers. Attacking Pharaoh's firstborn would surely draw his wrath upon Moses. Would this god protect him then? Or would Moses end up another dead madman?

Moses remained stubbornly defiant. "O my lord, please send someone else."

The sound of the flames burning hotter drew Moses's gaze. He saw within the fire a warrior with a flaming sword, and he knew he had incited this god's anger.

The Angel of Yahweh spoke with the same voice, "Aaron, your Levite brother, can speak well. I have sent for him. You will give him the words to speak. I will be with both your mouth and his. He shall speak to the people for you. He shall be your mouth, and you shall be to him as I am to you."

Moses was running out of excuses. "One last thing, my lord. I was once a general of an army. But you know those people. You know they have not the will to fight for their own freedom."

"I do not want you to fight. I want you to lead. I will fight for you. I will be your right arm."

Moses bristled. The "right arm" of Pharaoh was a metaphor for his omnipotent power of divinity. Moses had seen the favor of gods upon fighting forces in wars, but he had never seen an army win without fighting.

With that, the fire and the flaming Angel of Yahweh suddenly sucked up into the storm clouds above, leaving the bush as if it had never been struck by lightning. Moses couldn't believe what he had just seen. But it appeared that he didn't have much of a choice anymore.

"Moses!"

The words shocked Moses back to earth. He turned to see his brother Aaron, now eighty-three years old, standing on the path.

"Aaron!" Moses exclaimed. "What are you doing here? How did you get here?" Had Yahweh just miraculously transported his brother here from Egypt?

Aaron shrugged. "I had a vivid vision from the God of our fathers."

Aaron approached him, and they kissed each other's cheeks.

"What did he tell you?" Moses asked.

Aaron smiled. "That you were to be our deliverer but that you would not listen because you are a stubborn camel. So I was sent as a hammer to knock some sense through your thick skull."

"He said that?"

"In so many words," answered Aaron. "You have to admit, he was right. That is how you are. That is how I knew the vision was not a deception."

"What was the god's name?"

"Yahweh."

"When did you have this vision?"

"A full moon ago."

"And you traveled all the way here?"

"It took me over a week."

This Yahweh was so sovereignly in control that he had known how Moses would respond in advance. He had sent Aaron long before he talked to Moses for him to be here at just this concluding moment. Clearly, Yahweh was not a god Moses could outthink.

"Moses, did you notice your stuttering is gone?" Aaron suddenly realized.

"Yes, Aaron, I did, thank you."

"You have to admit that is a pretty significant sign."

Moses quipped, "Unfortunately, I still have to take you to speak for me."

"Oh, well, that makes sense. I am a better preacher than you."

Aaron hit Moses's shoulder affectionately. "Come on, brother, I have to have something on you. You cannot get all the glory."

Moses shook his head with amused agreement.

Aaron got serious. "Moses, it is time you stop running and admit who you really are. Embrace your calling."

Moses remained silent in contemplation the entire way down the mountain and all the way back home.

CHAPTER 25

Aaron enjoyed Jethro's hospitality at his Hisma Plateau encampment. The whole family received him with a welcome feast of goat stew, a slaughtered calf, and the best breads and vegetables they could provide. Moses's older brother from Egypt had come to visit!

Jethro and Moses's sons were there. Three of the six sisters with their husbands and children were there. Nabila and Zipporah and her sisters prepared and served the meal. But Moses had asked to keep it to immediate family because there were important things to discuss.

When Moses had confided in Jethro about his true history, they had kept it from everyone else. Moses did not want to disrupt his present life of peace. He had not wanted to raise the past from the dead.

But Yahweh had raised it for him.

As they sat to eat on the ground in a circle with the spread before them, Moses noticed Zipporah looking curiously at Aaron. He suspected he knew the reason why: Aaron neither looked nor dressed like an Egyptian.

Moses told the family of his experience before the burning bush and this god named Yahweh. He spoke of the Angel in the flames. Of Yahweh taking away his stuttering.

Everyone listened with rapt attention. Aaron explained his vision and how it had all ended in Yahweh calling Moses back to Egypt to deliver the people of Israel out from bondage to Pharaoh.

Silence permeated the dinner party.

Zipporah spoke first to Moses. "So you are not Egyptian. You are Hebrew."

Moses could see her look and her words were filled with a sense of betrayal.

He said, "I am Hebrew by birth, but I was adopted and raised as son of the Pharaoh. I had become his general and was crown prince. When the king discovered my true identity, he sought to kill me. That is why I fled Egypt."

"You were going to be Pharaoh?" Gershom gasped.

"Yes, my son."

Zipporah spoke again, "Why did you hide this from us? Why did you lie to me for so long?"

Everyone looked at Zipporah. It was a bold accusation.

Moses said, "I did not lie to you, Zipporah. I was dead to Egypt, to my people. I wanted to bury my past and create a new life in Midian. You had agreed so yourself. I thought that bringing it up would destroy that new life."

"Yet here you are destroying it," she said.

Her tears were angry, his tears sorrowful.

"For that, I am sorry with all my heart. I can only confess that I was wrong. That I should not have denied who I was, and that I should have shared the truth with you sooner. Can you forgive me, my wife, my family?"

Zipporah got up and left the table, marching back to their tent.

Moses stood up and called to her. "Zipporah!"

She kept walking.

Eliezer asked, "When are we leaving Midian?"

Moses was still watching his wife. "A few days' time," he said and ran after Zipporah.

He arrived at the tent to find her inside, weeping on the floor.

He felt his stomach turn with nausea. He could not imagine hurting her in this way. To think that he had caused her such pain horrified him.

He held her until her sobs calmed down.

"My love," he said, "I will never lie to you again."

"That is not why I grieve," she sniffled. "I cannot talk about it now. I need to be alone. To pray."

He wanted to stay but it would be disrespectful to ignore her request. Releasing her, he stood up. Slowly, he walked out of the tent with a sadness so heavy he felt his legs trembling beneath the weight.

Jethro was waiting for him outside. He said to Moses, "Let us walk."

Together they strolled out into the field beneath the waxing moon. Jethro said, "Give her some time to think it over. She will eventually understand your intent was to protect. She will long for those days of ignorance because now you will be leaving Midian."

Moses sighed. "I would have preferred to die in Midian."

Jethro said, "I know that you will not."

But there was no anger in his voice. He said, "Go in peace, Moses."

Moses said, "There was something that Yahweh said which haunts me."

"Only one thing?"

Moses smiled. "He said that Israel is his son and he is a father to his people."

Jethro hummed with interest. That was something none of the other gods would ever say of their worshippers. Especially not Ba'al. The gods were masters and lords but never fathers. Kings were sons of the gods, but not the commoner, not the people of the king. They existed for the good pleasure of their rulers.

Moses continued, "There is something the midwife Shiphrah told me when I fled Egypt all those years ago that I never understood until now."

"What is that?"

"She said, 'You seek a father. But your father is in heaven. Find him in the desert of Midian.' I used to think it meant that my birth father was dead to me and that you were that father in the desert foe which I was looking."

Jethro hummed interest again.

"But now I know what she meant. Yahweh is the father I have been seeking. It is he who is in heaven, and it was he whom I met in the desert of Midian on that mountain."

Jethro considered the words. Then he said, "I have wanted a son to carry on my legacy since my own son was killed. I have desperately sought to make you that substitute. I had thought that killing the Amalekite who killed my son and wife would bring relief. But it didn't. And now I face the prospect of losing you. I think Yahweh may be trying to tell us both something about family. For you, that God is your true father, and for me, that his people are my true family. I think you need to obey him and return to Egypt. I think it will be the best thing for us both."

Moses put his arm around the man who had been his father figure for so long.

Jethro smiled. "Now I see that I was right to teach you how to shepherd. You will be leading the flock of Israel into a dangerous world of predators. But the stories of our father Abraham are comforting. Yahweh is a shepherd as well."

Moses smiled in return.

· · · · ·

The night was alive with the sound of desert life. Crickets chirping, cicadas buzzing, wolves and coyotes howling. The brush and thicket rustled with a rushing wind. The clouds over Mount Sinai rumbled again with peals of thunder as lightning cracked the sky.

Suddenly, all sound stopped around the mountain. Nothing but the wind was left for any ears should they be listening.

And if those ears were preternatural, they would hear the sound of a war trumpet in the heavenlies. Followed by the stampede of many horses trampling down from the heights.

An army of heavenly host burst out upon the land, riding with fury and bringing judgment in their wake. The Angel of Yahweh led them. He rode a white stallion of victory to judge and make war. His eyes were a flame of fire, and on his head were many diadems. He was clothed in a robe dipped in blood, and he raised the sword of the fury of the wrath of God Almighty.

· · · · ·

Within days, Moses and Zipporah had left their Midianite camp with their sons Gershom and Eliezer as well as Aaron. They packed only what they needed to survive, said their goodbyes to family, and took donkeys for the long road back to Egypt.

On their second night, they sheltered off the road near Yam Suph. Moses and Aaron had gone for a long walk. When they returned, Moses found Zipporah waiting for him by the fire with Gershom and Eliezer already in bed.

Aaron bid them a good night and retired to his tent.

Moses leaned in and whispered to Zipporah, "That night when we were at odds, you said you had to pray. Did you pray to Ba'al?"

"No, my silly husband," she teased. "I prayed to Yahweh. Ba'al was not the one calling you to take your family across the world to Egypt."

She lowered her gaze in shame. "That was why I could not talk to you. I was ashamed of my own vanity."

"What do you mean, my love?"

She took a moment before confessing, "My anger was not from you withholding your family past. It was from the horror of me returning to my family's past. When you said you were a Hebrew and we were returning to your people who are slaves in Egypt, I lost all hope for that would mean a return to the slavery from which my mother had escaped."

Moses felt the weight of her fears. Now he understood her reaction and blamed himself for her unrest. He held her tightly and whispered, "Zipporah, forgive me. I did not know."

She said, "My father has told us tales of Abraham and of his god. He told us of Yahweh's covenant and his choosing of Isaac, the son of Sarah, over the sons of our mother Keturah. We are the rejected—like the sons of Ishmael."

She choked up with emotion. "But now I see that through you I have redemption. I am part of Yahweh's chosen family. I do not know what this trip to Egypt will bring us, but I will follow you, my husband. I trust you, and I trust Yahweh and his covenant with Abraham."

A noise drew their attention to the woods. They saw the flickering light of flames not far away. It was most likely a camp of travelers. But then they saw a horse and rider approach their camp.

"Go to our tent," Moses told Zipporah. "Wake our sons."

She did so, and Moses went out to meet the visitor. He held his sword handle sheathed at his side. At his advanced age, he was not the fighting warrior he used to be. But he would give his life to protect his family from anyone who sought them harm.

He stopped when he saw the rider get off his horse yards away and approach Moses.

The rider was clearly a warrior. His stallion was white. He wore armor that was unfamiliar to Moses. When the two of them were within striking distance, Moses could see that the rider was the messenger he had seen in the burning bush. He wasn't burning bright as in the fire, but it was most definitely the same person.

Moses felt a chill down his spine as the warrior seemed hostile in intent. He had his sword withdrawn and in his hand.

Moses said with a shaky voice, "I am following your command to return to Egypt and free the Hebrews. Are you here to protect us?"

"No," said the warrior. "I am here for the life of your firstborn."

The earlier words of this person from the bush echoed in his mind. He had pronounced taking the firstborn of Egypt in judgment. Now he was to take Moses's firstborn?

"Is this a sacrifice you require?" asked Moses.

"No. It is for violation of the covenant."

Moses did not understand.

The angel continued, "Yahweh is without partiality. He judges the righteous and the wicked with equal justice."

"What covenant have I violated?"

The voice of Zipporah approaching him from behind startled him. "The covenant with Abraham. The covenant requiring all males be circumcised as a sign of being set apart as Yahweh's chosen people."

She arrived and stood beside Moses facing the warrior.

She knelt down and placed two pieces of bloody flesh at the feet of the warrior, then backed away in reverence.

"What is that?" asked a nervous Moses.

"The foreskins of your sons. I circumcised them earlier when you were on a walk."

Moses looked with terror at the bloody foreskins on the ground. He winced in pain, knowing that the act required cutting off the extra sheath of skin that covered the head of the male phallus. He looked back to his tent, wanting to run to his sons to comfort them in their pain.

Zipporah explained, "I've known the stories of Yahweh's covenant with Abraham from my youth. It never applied to me until I married you. A bridegroom of blood you are to me. A covenant relative."

"The covenant is satisfied," said the warrior. He sheathed his sword and walked back to his horse.

Moses was struck dumb by it all. He watched as the warrior got back up on his horse and left in the darkness. Moses had already been circumcised as an infant. But he had never done so with his sons in Midian. He had been neglectful. He knew he had a lot to learn.

And he could tell that this was just an example of the solemnity with which Yahweh took his holy requirements. Not knowing the obligation of a covenant was no excuse for breaking it. Law and consequence was absolute for an absolutely holy God.

Moses muttered, "I need to learn more about Abraham and this covenant."

She said, "Your brother will educate you well."

Moses marched back to their tents. "How are Gershom and Eliezer?"

She followed him. "They are fine. It will take a week or so to heal."

When they arrived at the tent, Moses peeked in on his sons. Both were sleeping. He moved back out by the fire with Zipporah.

Moses said, "This will delay us too long."

"Go ahead," said Zipporah. "We will follow when they are healed."

"No," he said. "I think you and our sons should return to your father in safety. I am walking into a maelstrom of chaos. It is not for you to follow me into it."

He could see the burden of fear lift from her. Then tears of regret pooled in her eyes.

She asked, "When will you return to Midian?"

"I do not know. But Yahweh is our shepherd. And he promises to bring the Hebrews back here to the mountain of God. So I will see you again."

"I will pray for you every day," she said through her tears.

"And I for you."

They went to bed and made love desperately that night, knowing they would not see each other for a long time.

CHAPTER 26

Egypt

The Ennead of the gods met in the temple of Ra at Avaris. It was the beginning of Emergence as the Nile receded. Some of the temple priests had returned to their farms temporarily to plow and plant in preparation for the Harvest. Spiritual activities were slow as select lector priests were paid to perform the basic upkeep of the temple and various sacrifices during this time.

But in the spiritual realm, there was considerable activity.

Ra called the council to quiet. His son Horus sat on one side, the sun god Atum on the other. Isis and Osiris were there as were the gods of the four elements: Shu of air, Tefnut of water, Geb of earth, and Nut of sky.

Set sat unusually quiet, causing none of his usual trouble. Amun-Ra was visiting from the Red Land of Upper Egypt in the south. Thoth recorded the proceedings faithfully as the Distant Goddess gave testimony of her far wanderings in the eastern deserts. Manifesting the head of a lioness, she wore a simple tattered and threadbare tunic. As one of his daughters, she was the eye of Ra.

"My information is certain," she told the tribunal.

"Certain," mimicked Set.

"You doubt my loyalty?" she growled.

"Your loyalty? No. But your lack of discipline and political savvy leaves little to be desired." Everyone knew her as a wild wanderer.

"So says the god of chaos," she hissed at him.

Set ignored her insult. "You tell us of these 'Hyksos,' these shepherd kings aligning against Egypt. Yet I am quite familiar with some of these nomadic desert tribes, and I know them to be incapable of such unity. The Amalekites are cannibals, for god's sake. They don't have allies, they eat them. The Philistines are sea lions of the ocean. They have no aspirations for land expansion."

She protested, "They worship the gods of Canaan. Ba'al is no minor deity. He has a powerful hammer and high ambitions."

"Let us talk of the Canaanite gods," snorted Set. "Yes, Ba'al is a bit of a bull. But his pantheon is still subject to our sovereignty. And their stinking little patch of land is surrounded by Babylon to the east, Assyria to the north, and Egypt to the south. Their only 'ambition' is to clean up after being the toilet of the mighty kingdoms that pass through on their trade routes."

Thoth spoke up. "Distant Goddess, where exactly have you been?"

"The whole of the Land of the Shasu. From the Wilderness of Paran and Sinai all the way up to the Negeb in Canaan."

Thoth was concerned. "There are Anakim in the Negeb."

Set offered, "Now that would be a concern, I grant you."

The Anakim were giant clans of Canaan. Their warring exploits were legendary.

Ra concluded, "Set, you know the desert best amongst us. I want you to go to the Land of the Shasu and investigate the goddess's claims. If her testimony holds, we will prepare to meet this threat."

"If the Great God Ra wills it," said Set. He didn't want to sound too eager. For going to the land of the Anakim was exactly what he wanted to do.

Suddenly the large doors to the sanctuary blew open with the explosive force of a rushing wind.

The gods drew weapons and assumed fighting stances.

Ra stood to his full height of about eight feet, and his skin shone like the rays of the sun. Horus, Atum, and Amun-Ra stood next to him, ready to defend.

A fine cloud of dust was raised by the crashing doors. The gods saw seven beings enter. When the dust settled, they could see the intruders were the seven archangels of Yahweh.

The gods spread out, ready to battle.

Ra saw this was not a challenge. He held his hand out and shouted, "Hold your positions!"

Led by Mikael and Gabriel, the angels stood in line, weapons sheathed but still imposing in their presence: Raphael, Uriel, Raguel, Remiel, and Saraqel. The presence of all seven indicated serious intent.

Ra boomed, "With one call, the entire pantheon can be here in moments."

The angels would be outnumbered ten to one. But Mikael did not flinch.

He announced, "O gods of Egypt, I have come to call upon you to release your grip upon the people of Israel or suffer the consequences."

Set was not impressed. "And I call upon you godlickers to get the hell out of this holy temple. Or your people of Israel will fare far worse than the last time of your insolence." He was referring to the Hebrew protesters under Pharaoh Sobekhotep IV forty years earlier, whose slaughter had stopped just short of genocide.

"Let me cut his tongue out," Set heard the little blonde runt of an angel mutter to Mikael.

The archangels stood silent as if waiting for a response that everyone knew was not forthcoming.

Then Mikael concluded, "Yahweh is coming to Egypt riding a swift cloud. Thus saith the Lord, 'On all the gods of Egypt, I will execute my judgments. I am Yahweh.'"

Before Ra could respond, the angels turned and ran out the door. Set followed to see where they had gone. He saw them mount horses and scatter to the four winds. Looking out onto the horizon, he saw a distant storm cloud in the unseen realm with lightning and peals of thunder.

He turned back to the gods. "They are gone."

"Why would they announce their intentions like that?" Atum demanded. "It is piss-poor strategy, giving away all hope of a surprise attack."

Horus said, "That is because Yahweh always makes a call for repentance before he attacks. It is his condescending sense of superiority."

Set muttered, "He glories in saying, 'I told you so.'"

"And so it begins." Ra sat back down on his throne with a distant look in his eyes. Everyone knew the promise of Yahweh to bring the Hebrews into the land of Canaan as their inheritance. But for them to achieve that goal, they would have to be allowed to leave Egypt.

Isis spat out, "I say let them go if it will get rid of these annoying gadflies of Yahweh. Does anyone really think those pathetic rodents have a chance against the Anakim and Rephaim?"

"We have already discussed this many times," argued Horus. "If they settle in Canaan, then the Anointed One will be born in the land. And that jeopardizes the gods of all nations. Egypt is not exempt. We must not allow the Hebrews to leave."

They were all sober with the realization of the war that was coming.

"Good luck with that," said Set. "It is time for me to leave for the Negeb—as I was ordered." He was rubbing it in.

He left them, whistling a tune of destruction.

CHAPTER 27

For both Moses and Aaron, coming upon the lush fertile delta of Goshen after a two-week trek through the desert wasteland of Ta Mefkat was like arriving in heaven after a journey through the underworld. At their ages, it was particularly difficult, but they had used the time to get to know one another. They had become close on this journey toward danger.

Moses had told of his life as a fugitive of both Egypt and Yahweh. Aaron had told of the people of Israel and the heritage which they were returning to deliver. If Yahweh was true to his word, their exodus from the land of Egypt would be a resurrection of the people from spiritual death. Over the last four hundred years, they had lost their way and drifted so far from their creator that they would hardly recognize him.

The brothers had also prayed much for the impossible task before them. They did not look forward to the war of gods and men that they were bringing with them. Moses had explained to Aaron Yahweh's predictions of pharaonic rejection and the coming plagues. Yahweh had said he was going to harden Pharaoh's heart, make it heavy with injustice. The Egyptians believed that the king's heart ruled over all. But Yahweh would weigh that heart in the scales of his justice rather than Osiris doing so against his feather of Ma'at.

Moses told his brother how Pharaoh would ultimately let them go but not without a fight. And Israel was not to fight with earthly weapons because Yahweh would fight for them. It was all to glorify the God of Israel through signs and wonders that would give Israel the hope of promise that they had lost.

Aaron had also told Moses that all those of King Sobekhotep IV's regime who sought Moses forty years ago were dead. There had been thirteen kings after him of various short reigns, still under the thirteenth dynasty of rule. It was not a time of stability. The current pharaoh, Djedneferre Dudimose, had been crowned nearly a year ago. Though he had ruled from his throne in Thebes, he was currently at his delta palace in Avaris to oversee extensive building projects.

As the brothers entered Avaris just a mile south of the palace, Aaron explained that during the years of Moses's absence, the pharaohs' power had waned. Meanwhile the number of slaves had grown to one-sixth of the Black Land's greater population. Most of those living in the delta were Asiatics, and most of the Asiatics were Hebrew. They were over half the labor force working on state building projects and agriculture. Pharaoh had become too reliant upon this slave class. An exodus of the Hebrews out of Egypt would be a traumatic hit to the entire land.

Aaron went on to explain that Pharaoh would not be Moses's only nemesis. The king's successor, his firstborn son Khonsuemwaset, was also a force of darkness in the land. His name meant *the moon god Khonsu is in Thebes*, but the crown prince publicly used a shortened version of his name, Khonsu, because he fancied bearing the explicit name of a god.

Khonsu was the Master of the Horse, a general of the chariot divisions just as Moses had been. But unlike Moses, Khonsu was an indulgent young pleasure-seeker in his twenties with a cruel temper. He would beat an entire Hebrew work crew for the failure of one elderly worker to meet his daily brickmaking quota.

There were also rumors that Khonsu preferred the company of other men.

As the two brothers crossed the river branches between the various islands in the delta, Moses noticed that much had changed since he had left forty years ago. But not for the better. Hebrew housing divisions seemed rundown and out of repair. Apparently, Pharaoh was benefiting from their labors, whereas the people were not.

When they entered the old neighborhood of his Hebrew family, Moses felt his stomach churn. His first stop was to Shiphrah's home to visit his beloved Tjarbit's grave. Though Shiphrah had died several years ago, her family still knew Aaron and let them in.

Painful memories flooded Moses's mind as he stood over the grave of his Kushite princess. He would never forget her dignity, her grace and beauty. But this would be the last time he would visit her. He had a new calling to fulfill.

The two brothers then made their way to their family compound. When they walked in the gate, they were interrupted by a slew of little children greeting the returning family members. These were the household's children, grandchildren, and even great-grandchildren born after Moses had gone into exile. Aaron picked up a little one and hugged her.

"I see the family has been busy," Moses commented.

"My brothers!" came a shout from the entrance into the home.

Miriam stepped out wearing a woolen tunic and robe. Now eighty-six-years old, she was white-haired but still holding up well for her age.

Pushing through the children, she hugged Aaron. Then she paused to look at Moses and burst out crying. They embraced.

"It has been a long time again, my brother."

"Too long," Moses said.

She pulled apart to look into his eyes. "I knew you would be back. I told Aaron so, but he said no for many years."

"Miriam!" Aaron protested.

Moses smiled. "Well, I said no as well. So my brother and I were both wrong. It took a vision from our God to change my mind."

"See?" Miriam said. "Your eldest sister knows the mind of the Maker better than the both of you. You need to listen to her more often."

They shared a laugh.

She got serious. "I want to hear everything of your life in Midian. But first I have someone I want you to see."

She led Moses into the house past several of the adults who were no doubt his nieces and nephews.

They entered a small room at the corner of the house. Moses saw a very old man surely over a hundred years old lying in a bed. He immediately guessed this was Amram, his earthly father. The old man was very thin, totally bald, bleary-eyed, and holding his hand out toward Moses as if reaching for him. His voice came out scratchy and weak. "Moses."

It was hard to feel anything for this man whom he had never met. Amram was a stranger to Moses.

"I can barely see you," said the old man.

Taking the oil lamp in his hand, Moses stepped closer and looked down on his frail earthly father.

Amram spoke through tears. "My son. My son. I am dying, but I have been dead in my soul for these eighty years."

They shared a long silence between them before Moses spoke. "I thank you for saving me when I was a child. But when you had the chance to meet me years later, why did you run away? Why did you cower?"

Moses was surprised by the emotion that arose within him. He'd thought this would not be a problem for him. He'd virtually forgotten about this man.

Amram responded, choking up, "Because I was not worthy of you."

Moses was surprised. "Not worthy?"

"When your mother placed you in that basket in the river, I realized that I could not protect you. I could not protect my own son. What kind of father abandons his son to the rivers of chance?"

Moses knelt down closer to him in pity. Amram's feelings of failure had distorted his view of reality. It had not been rivers of chance but the hands of God.

"When your mother died and you finally discovered your true family all those years later, I could not face you because I was not worthy of the great man you had become. I did not deserve to be called your father. I was nothing."

Moses held his father's hand. It was cold, skeletal. He had always thought his father had rejected him. That he had never cared for his son. They had both suffered for so long under false assumptions.

Amram continued, "I have stopped eating because I no longer want to live. I am a broken man. Can you forgive me, my son? Please forgive me for failing you and not being the father you needed."

Now Moses's own eyes welled up with sorrow. He had ignored the pain of losing both his Hebrew father and his wicked Egyptian one. He had moved on. He had found a father figure in Midian. He had thought it was behind him. But now that pain came surging up into his heart, and he could ignore it no longer. He bowed his head.

Moses wept.

His experience with Yahweh on the mountain came to his mind. Yahweh had been his heavenly father when his earthly fathers had failed him. Even when his Egyptian father had tried to kill him. Yahweh had watched over Moses and had carried him like a lost lamb in a loving shepherd's arms while Moses was unaware of it.

"Father," came the words Moses never thought he would say. He saw Amram's eyes brighten at those same words he never thought he would hear from this son. "I forgive you. Because Yahweh has forgiven me. I too am a broken man. How can I not forgive?"

Amram put out his arms, and Moses leaned in to hug him.

"What more can I do for you?" Moses asked.

Amram said, "There is one thing."

Moses pulled away. "Anything."

"Please get me some food and drink. If I want to see that Promised Land Aaron has told me about, I need to stay alive."

Moses smiled. Turning, he saw Aaron and Miriam at the door, still watching and now laughing.

Aaron said, "Let us hope the rest of the Israelites will be as easy to convince."

• • • • •

Sitting on his throne in his holy house in the unseen realm, Ra mulled over his concerns. He breathed in deep the incense offered by the priests on their altars. Now more than ever, the gods needed the strength they gained from worship.

Horus entered the sanctuary.

"Father," he said, drawing the sun god's attention.

Ra looked up. "Any reports?"

"No. Still no sign of the heavenly host."

Ra was frustrated. "Where is that cursed horde? What is Yahweh planning?"

Horus said, "Maybe we should not have exiled Set to the desert. We may need his might and power."

"No. The desert is deliberate for my purposes. We may need his power there if this does not go as I planned."

"Are you still blinded in your eye, Horus?" came the words from the back of the sanctuary. Isis stepped forward with Heka, god and goddess of magic. "Did you not see the disturbance around Avaris in the spiritual realm?"

"What do you mean?" Ra demanded.

Isis said, "Do you remember, decades ago, there was a man we feared would be the Destroyer of Egypt? A Hebrew who had been adopted by the king?"

"He was proven a fraud," Horus said. "Exiled by the king. He was wanted for murder and disappeared into the desert wasteland."

"Yes," said Isis. "And he's back."

• • • • •

The Hebrews of Avaris may have been slaves, but they maintained their own social order and with it their dignity. Their elders led the local Hebrew communities, and they sought to carry out some of their own governance outside Pharaoh's reach. Aaron was one of the city's most influential elders. He had called together the other elders of the various clans to share Moses's message of deliverance.

They gathered in an open area in the southernmost part of the Hebrew quarter, away from the palace and the Egyptians' prying eyes.

Moses stood before the elders and the people who had come for the meeting. There were several hundred elders from each of the various districts and hundreds of Yahweh's most loyal followers among the Israelites. Though everyone suffered together, few such loyal believers remained.

To be better heard, Aaron stood on a small stone platform. He had introduced his brother and had vouched for him by telling them of Moses's life story until his exile. Aaron's reputation carried much weight with the people. And Moses noticed that Aaron gloried in that. He appeared to be placing himself a little too close to Moses's own calling.

"Elders and people of Israel, let me now tell you of our vision from God. I know that what I am about to say to you will be shocking and difficult to believe. But it is true. *Now* is the time of our deliverance."

The people muttered amongst themselves. There had been much talk of this for years. But how could they trust this claim from such a stranger?

Aaron continued, "The God of our deliverance appeared to Moses on Mount Sinai and revealed that he would lead us out of Egypt into a new land of our own."

One of the elders asked, "Is this El Shaddai who spoke to you?"

Moses answered, "You have known him as El Shaddai. But he has revealed his covenant name to me. It is Yahweh, I Am Who I Am, the eternally existent one. I Am has sent me."

The crowd's mumbling rose. The secret names of gods were known only by the gods. To offer his name to them was to bring them into participation with the god's identity and power. What god would do such a thing?

Some in the crowd mulled doubtfully.

"Why would this Yahweh choose to reveal his name to you?" an elder asked. "Why not to one of Israel's elders?"

Aaron said, "We do not know why Yahweh does what he does. I can only tell you what he has told us. And he said to be prepared. Moses and I are going to Pharaoh to tell him to let us leave Egypt. When he does allow it, you must all be ready to leave quickly."

Another elder said, "Surely you can understand why we would ask for some sign of validation since you claim to be a prophet."

Aaron said, "Moses will show you the signs that Yahweh has given us."

Moses stepped forward, took his staff, and threw it to the ground. It turned into a writhing snake that elicited gasps from the crowd. He grabbed it by the tail, and it became a shepherd's staff again.

Aaron spoke to the people. "Yahweh will protect us with his shepherd's rod and staff."

Then Moses put his hand in his cloak and withdrew it as leprous, allowing the elders to examine it to be real before returning it to its healthy state.

Aaron told the elders, "Yahweh is the one who can make the unclean clean."

Then Moses poured out water from the Nile onto the ground, and it turned to blood.

Aaron commented, "This is the blood of Yahweh's judgment coming upon the land."

The elders conversed amongst themselves about the signs.

But even Moses himself was doubtful. These signs reminded him of the kind of magic that lector priests used to do in his presence. How could that be enough for the people to trust that this God would watch over a large multitude of men, women, and children in the desert until they arrived at Sinai? It lacked a sense of proportion to him.

But maybe that was the point. Aaron had told him of Abraham's faith and how Yahweh had promised him an inheritance of the land. Abraham went out from his father's house neither knowing where he was going nor where he would stay. Would bigger, more sensational miracles threaten to replace trust with entitlement?

"Moses." The voice turned Moses's attention away from the elders.

Before him stood two men. One an older man around forty, bald, stocky, muscular. He spoke first.

"We do not have to wait for the elders' decision. We will follow you. I am Caleb ben Jephunneh, and this is Hoshea ben Nun."

The young one blurted out, "We have been preparing for this moment. We are ready to fight."

This younger man appeared to Moses no older than nineteen. He was wiry and jittery with wild, wavy hair and intense posture. He looked as if he was wound tight and ready to explode.

"So you are not father and son?" Moses asked.

"My father is dead," Hoshea said. "Caleb has trained me in the art of war."

Caleb qualified with a smile, "He still has a lot to learn."

"He worries the student shall surpass the teacher," quipped Hoshea.

Moses smiled at their friendly rapport. He saw a strange object on Caleb's belt. It looked like a sword handle, but instead of being connected to a long blade, the sheath was a bulky leather case that made it appear as if the sword was rolled up like a belt might be.

Strange, he thought. "What is that?"

Caleb sheepishly said, "Well, it is a special weapon I received from…" He paused, searching for the right word. "…an old friend." He patted it. "She's called Rahab. After the sea serpent of chaos."

Moses changed the subject. "Men, I thank you for your zeal. But I am sorry to disappoint you. Yahweh will not deliver us from Egypt through warfare."

"Then how?" asked Hoshea incredulously.

"Yahweh will deliver us with his strong right arm."

The men were both silent with surprise.

Hoshea said, "Well, when you get to the point where you need human soldiers for a human battle, then let us know."

Caleb slapped Hoshea on the back of the head and spoke to Moses. "Forgive my apprentice. I apparently have taught him how to fight but not how to respect his elders."

Moses smiled. There was something special about these two. He couldn't put his finger on it, but he could see that despite their light-hearted bantering, they were deadly serious about their intent.

Everyone's attention was drawn to one of the elders who had been chosen to speak to the crowd of hundreds.

He raised his arms and said, "We, the elders entrusted with the care and justice of our people, do proclaim to you that Aaron is one of our most trusted leaders, and his reputation remains beyond reproach. With the signs of today, we believe that the god Yahweh, whom we once knew as El Shaddai, has visited our people and has seen our affliction. Yahweh will make us a way out of Egypt. Let us bow our heads and worship this Yahweh!"

The crowd obeyed. Some lifted hands to heaven, others knelt, and still others laid prostrate on the ground.

One of the elders quipped to Moses, "Now if you can only perform the greatest miracle of all, getting Pharaoh to let us go, then I guarantee you will get the rest of Israel to follow."

Another elder countered, "I am afraid that when they face the chaos of the desert, they may change their minds and cling to the order of Egypt, as oppressive as it is."

Moses smiled and replied, "Trust me, by the time the people of Israel see what Yahweh is going to do to Pharaoh and this land, they will be running into the desert."

CHAPTER 28

Occasionally throughout the year, Pharaoh would hold court with the principals of the cities and tribal elders to give them an opportunity to bring him gifts of gratitude and petition their concerns. This time, Moses and Aaron showed up.

Hundreds of nobles and elites of the people filled the courtyard. The herald announced Pharaoh's titulary. "Djedneferre Dudimose, the Good God, beloved of Thebes, he who is chosen by Horus, who increases his army, who has appeared like the lightning of Ra, who is acclaimed to the kingship of both lands, the one who belongs to shouting."

The two brothers were next in line as a chieftain before them laid out gifts of gold, frankincense, and myrrh before the king, his queen, and their son seated on their appropriate thrones. Father and son were dressed in similar clothes of royal legacy. They each wore the traditional pleated kilt with a starched ornamented apron in front. It was a hot day, so they sported the more comfortable *nemes* royal headdress of striped cloth that draped onto their shoulders in flat lappets and a golden uraeus cobra on the forehead.

The queen was more formal despite the heat. She was dressed in a pleated white, sheer full gown with a red sash and a collar of gold around her neck and shoulders. Her make-up was exquisite, and her headdress was a wig of gold-braided hair with a vulture cap to cover her head with wings and tail.

Several sparsely-clad servant children fanned king and queen with palm leaves. Pharaoh gently stroked the hair of one of them like a pet. Adult male servants surrounded the crown prince. It all reminded Moses of the family paintings of his youth. Colorful pictures of degeneracy and self-deification—in the tombs of the dead.

Moses carried his staff with him as Yahweh had instructed. He grasped it firmly and glared up at the large stone pillars and walls around them. Egypt was impressive with its huge monuments and buildings of vast scale. It was all made to glorify Pharaoh, to elevate him as a god. And yet in the shadow of the mountain of God, this was all just children's toy blocks. Moses saw the hieroglyphs of stories and spells that used to be his heritage on the stone walls around them. These and others like them had been his hope for eternity. It all looked like gibberish to him now. Self-soothing lies and self-aggrandizing delusions.

A small, stout herald announced, "Next to see the king, please announce your names and present your gifts or petition."

Aaron led Moses up steps to a small stone platform to face the court: Pharaoh Dudimose, Queen Nefret, and Crown Prince Khonsu. Moses could now see the king's features. He was an intense man with furrowed brow and square jaw. He looked to be about forty-five years of age. He nestled his formal shepherd's crook and royal mace to his chest. His son looked around twenty-five, muscular and warrior-like. He appeared disinterested as though daydreaming about chariot racing or dallying with his male servants. The queen looked to be about forty years old and equally uninterested in affairs of state or her husband.

Standing silently beside the family was the vizier, the administrator of the state who executed in practical form all the king's commands. He had much more power than was apparent in his quiet, deferential manner. This one was fat, bald, and sported a haughty look.

The brothers bowed. Aaron said, "My lord and king, I am Aaron son of Amram. This is my brother Moses. We are from the tribe of Levi in the southern quarter of Avaris."

"Moses?" Dudimose perked up as though he recognized the name.

Moses felt his heart suddenly race. How or what could Pharaoh know? Everyone of Sobekhotep's regime was dead. Moses had changed his name from Sobekmose, and he was in a full beard and Hebrew robes.

Dudimose stopped stroking his "pet" child and focused in on Moses. "You Hebrews have the strangest names. Your name Moses means 'son of' in Egyptian. Yet you have no father's name before it. Are you a son in search of a father?"

Pharaoh had no idea how close to the truth he really was.

Dudimose then belted out in laughter at his attempted joke. He grabbed his son's hand affectionately. Khonsu jerked angrily away as if horrified by his touch. Moses noticed Pharaoh did not do the same toward his queen.

Moses bowed humbly. "My king, in Hebrew my name means 'drawn out,' as of water."

"Well, then, if you were Egyptian, we might give you the name Hapimose, son of the Nile god Hapi. Since you mention water." A funny thought crossed the Pharaoh's face. "Or maybe even Khnumose for the guardian god of the Nile." Now he was really getting into it. He seemed to enjoy his own humor. "Or what about Sobekmose for the crocodile god of the Nile!"

The words made Moses freeze in fear. He felt himself sweating. He looked up at the king to see where he was going with this. He saw Dudimose sit back, satisfied in his golden chair, apparently unaware of any connection to Moses's Egyptian family name from forty years ago. Sobekhotep and his successors were just names on an old wall of family lineage. There was no way this humble Hebrew would have any connection to that divine seed.

Dudimose mused, "My name means 'son of the gods.'"

Moses sighed with relief. He saw Aaron do so as well.

Dudimose added, "You Hebrews have your own peculiar god, do you not?"

Aaron said, "Yes, my king."

"Well, what is his name?"

"Yahweh, my lord."

"Yahweh," repeated Dudimose thoughtfully. "Yahweh. Funny name. For a funny people." He looked at Moses. "You should call yourself Yahwehmose." Dudimose paused again with a self-satisfied smile.

"So, Yahwehmose, what request do you bring? You people are fond of burdening me with your multitude of petitions."

Aaron and Moses looked at each other with trepidation. Not a good introduction. Moses decided to get right to the point.

"O, king, thus says Yahweh, 'Let my people go, that they may hold a feast to me in the wilderness three days out.'"

It felt a little abrupt. Maybe Moses should have laid out their history with Pharaoh first. It was the usual custom to do so.

He watched the shocked faces of Pharaoh and his family, quietly turning over in their minds what they had just heard.

It was an uncomfortable silence. "Thus says" was a common Egyptian phrase used by their gods as proclamations of demand.

Dudimose burst out in laughter again. His son followed suit. Even the queen smiled.

Dudimose said, "You really are a funny people."

Moses looked at the floor, discouraged.

And then Pharaoh's countenance turned deadly serious. He growled, "How dare you demand. A couple of shepherds with your staffs and tattered robes. You stand before a god."

The brothers bowed low in deference.

Khonsu stood. "Have them whipped for their insolence."

Dudimose held him back. The prince withdrew from his father's touch again and sat back down.

Dudimose continued, "Who is this Yahweh that I should obey him? I have never heard of this deity until now. Let him receive approval from Ra first. And no, I will not let you people go into the wilderness."

Aaron tried a different tactic. "O king, please reconsider. For the god of the Hebrews has met with us, and he is a jealous god. It is only a mere three days' journey to where we can make sacrifice. For if we do not, we fear he will fall upon us with pestilence and the sword."

"Now that I would like to see," said Khonsu. He was finally paying attention.

Again, Pharaoh thought through his response. He said, "Moses and Aaron, why do you try to take the people away from their responsibilities? You would make them lazy to seek rest."

The brothers remained quiet. They'd known full well this was going to happen.

Pharaoh glanced at his son. "My son. You will be king one day. What do you think we should do with these lazy Hebrews?"

The prince grinned diabolically. "I think we should no longer give the Hebrews straw to make their bricks as we have always done. Now we should let them gather straw for themselves."

A dread came over Moses.

"My king," he said, "that burden will slow their productivity."

"Silence!" shouted Dudimose. He looked at his son to finish.

Khonsu said, "Well, we cannot afford to 'slow their productivity,' can we. So let us retain the quota of bricks they are supposed to make each day."

"Ah, brilliant," said Dudimose.

He looked to his vizier, "Harsekher, what say you?"

The fat bald vizier nodded with a shrug, acknowledging it was doable. He looked like he had never done a moment of physical work his entire life.

"Good," Dudimose concluded. "Then it is decreed. Perhaps if the Hebrews are too busy laboring, they may stop their lazy cries of 'let us go offer sacrifice to our god.'" He said the quote with whining mockery.

He looked at Moses and Aaron. "You have my decision. Now get back to work." He gave a wave of dismissal and turned back to stroking his pet child's hair and skin.

Moses and Aaron bowed and walked backwards until they reached the stairs, where they turned and left the courtyard.

• • • • •

Miriam handed a plate of lamb with leeks and turnips to her father Amram in their kitchen area. He was out of bed with a healthy appetite and had gained back most of his strength. His reconciliation with Moses had been like a resurrection from the dead.

It was dinner after a long day. The adults ate together: Moses, Aaron, and Aaron's four sons Nadab, Abihu, Ithamar, and Eleazar along with Eleazar's oldest son Phineas. The young children ate separately. Miriam, Aaron's wife Elisheba, and Eleazar's wife Rachel served the food.

Miriam asked Moses, "Did Pharaoh know about your Egyptian past?"

"No. The politics of a generation ago are long forgotten."

Aaron added, "A good thing too. If Pharaoh knew about the decree of Sobekhotep, he might execute Moses still."

"The decree of straw and bricks will crush us," said Miriam. "The foremen of the workers are speaking ill of you, Moses. And word is spreading."

"We know that, Miriam," said Aaron.

She added, "They say you have made us stink in the sight of Pharaoh. That you put a sword in his hand to kill us."

Moses said, "We met with the foremen. I know of their concerns. I tried to encourage them to hold fast to their faith. Yahweh will deliver us."

"They think you are delivering them out of the pot and into the flames."

"Miriam," scolded Aaron. "Whose side are you on?"

"I am just worried for your reputation," she said to Moses. "How will the people follow you if they feel you brought this suffering upon us?"

Finally, Amram spoke up, putting his hand reassuringly on Moses's shoulder. "The people need to learn that their hope is in Yahweh, not their physical comfort. I have come to learn that the most valuable things of this life come through suffering. My son will lead us to freedom. But it will be costly, and I for one welcome it."

Moses smiled and placed his arm around his father in gratitude.

Miriam would not be persuaded. "I just feel that people want to love their leaders, not fear them."

"I will say this, Miriam," said Aaron. "It will not be love that will inspire Pharaoh to release us, and it will not be love that motivates this stubborn people to leave their bountiful Egypt for a desert wasteland."

She would not back down. "Could you at least speak to the people, Moses, and assure them that Yahweh loves them?"

Aaron changed the subject as he would often have to do. "Speaking of Yahweh, Moses, why don't you tell the family of your experience on Mount Sinai?"

"First, tell us of your life in Midian," said Miriam. "That leads you to Sinai. I want to hear everything. Do you have a wife?"

Moses chuckled. "I do. A most beautiful and wonderful woman. And two sons with their families."

"What is her name?" asked the eager Miriam.

"Zipporah. Her mother was a Kushite."

Everyone's eyes displayed a curious surprise.

Aaron teased him, "You escaped Egypt, but you could not escape your taste for Kushite women."

Everyone laughed.

Moses smiled and said, "She is everything to me. She is a good mother, a loving wife. And she has a strong mind to speak her piece. You should like her, Miriam."

That brought a few more laughs. Miriam said, "Maybe the two of us can get you to listen to us women more often."

"Trust me," said Moses, "she has earned my ear. And my trust."

"Then tell us everything about her and about your sons."

Moses spent the rest of the evening telling them of Zipporah, his family, and his forty years in Midian.

But when he spoke of Jethro, his father-in-law, he could see his father Amram drop in his countenance. Their recent reconciliation had been healing, but it could not replace the lost opportunity of raising his son into manhood and the companionship as peers in later years. Those years had been filled with another father figure.

Moses sought to give Jethro his honor without overdoing it so as to spare Amram shame. "Father, I know you will like him. He is a shepherd as well."

"But will he like me?" asked Amram. "And can I earn your trust?"

"Give it time, Father," Aaron interjected. "We are all starting out as new with Moses."

"I do not know that I have the time," said Amram. He was already one hundred and six years old. He got up. "Forgive me, my son. I do not wish to draw attention to myself. Please excuse me. I need to rest."

Every new journey began with a first few steps, but Moses knew that this quest with family would be a difficult one.

CHAPTER 29

Jannes and Jambres were busy overseeing the cleaning of the holy place in the temple of Ra when they were alerted to King Dudimose's arrival. They quickly put on their fine robes and met the king at their usual royal meeting hall set aside for such purposes. It had a throne-like chair at the head of a rectangular room big enough for about a hundred people. Now there were just seven: the king, his two bodyguards, and four young servant children, two on the king's lap.

When Jannes and Jambres approached the throne, the king scooted the children off the throne and patted them in the rear to leave. They scurried away obediently.

Dudimose looked curiously at the twin brothers. "Welcome, my most trusted lector priests. Do you ever age?"

Jannes said, "My king, we have been blessed by the gods. Chosen to serve Ra as high priests."

Jannes would not speak in detail of their deal for eternal youth with Ra. They still looked in their twenties though they were well over a hundred years old. But this was not always noticed by kings because of the short reigns during most of the dynasty. Rumors had spread because of all the priests who'd known the brothers but had grown old and feeble themselves.

Dudimose returned to his original subject. "I want to speak with Ra."

The brothers looked at each other.

Jannes said, "My lord, Ra only speaks with his priests and then only under rare circumstances."

"Well then, you ask him."

"What do you want us to ask him?"

"Who is this god Yahweh, and do I have anything to fear from him?"

Jannes stopped breathing. He knew that name. He'd never forgotten his vision of Duat he'd experienced so many years ago. He'd also never told anyone, not even his twin brother. It had been such a frightening experience that he'd sought to push it out of his mind. But here it was, barging back into his life like a terrible night demon.

"We are not familiar with this deity," Jambres said. "Where did you hear about him?"

"Supposedly, he is the god of the Hebrews. Two of their elders came to me today and claimed that this Yahweh had demands of me."

"Did the god threaten you?"

"Not really. He simply demanded that I allow the Hebrews to go three days into the desert to sacrifice to him."

Jambres asked, "Are you going to allow them?"

"Of course not. I am the divine Horus, son of Ra on earth. No foreign god tells me what to do."

"And we concur," said Jambres. "The god of a slave people is a weak and pitiable deity."

Dudimose said, "Still, they are a significant portion of our populace. An unrest in their ranks could cause me problems."

Jannes pleaded, "My lord, perhaps it would be a display of your divine grace to allow the Hebrews their worship. A satisfied army of slaves is a less restless one."

Jambres gave him a look of anger for the suggestion. He turned back to Dudimose. "My brother speaks without thinking. Forgive us, lord. We will inquire of Ra and report back to you."

Jannes felt his body fill with fear. He remembered the ease with which Yahweh had burned up the gods of Egypt in his vision. He could feel impending doom in his *ka*-spirit like a sandstorm on the horizon.

•••••

Moses stood in the shadows of a servant back entrance of the House of Life. He had passed a message and was waiting for a response. The House of Life was a large scriptorium that stood across the way from the temple of Ra. It was the location of all the sacred books of knowledge that the priesthood maintained. A vast library of scrolls that he had frequented when he was raised in the royal household. Here they would compile, copy, and store every piece of literature they could find from Egypt to Babylon to Assyria and the uttermost ends of the earth. It was where Moses had spent many of his days reading and learning about other nations, history, medicine, religion, governments, and laws.

He had missed reading over the years he was away. And he had a plan that he prayed would not be foiled by the one person he was hoping would not reject him.

The wooden door opened to an elderly man not much younger than Moses's own eighty years, a scribe, bald and in a linen robe. He stopped and stared at Moses.

Moses said, "Ipuwer. I knew you would still be alive in this dusty old grave of scrolls."

Ipuwer's eyes opened with revelation. "Sobekmose?"

"I have changed my name. It is now Moses. I am amongst my people the Hebrews now. Are you going to welcome me in or not?"

Ipuwer tilted his head a bit as if he wasn't sure. He narrowed his eyes. "What happened to your tongue?"

The scribe had worked for years with Moses to overcome his speech impediment. Moses said, "It is a long story. But it was a miracle of God."

"Which god?"

"That is another long story. But you will soon hear it."

Still, the scribe hesitated.

"Ipuwer, you know full well the entire household of Sobekmose is long dead as is any warrant for my arrest. I am no longer a fugitive that matters in this country. But I am counting on the fact that our relationship still matters for something."

Ipuwer reluctantly opened the door to let him in. He did not appear sure what to do.

With the fugitive inside, the scribe looked around and whispered, "Are you bringing trouble?"

Moses chuckled. "Any claim to the throne I had died forty years ago, you know that. I am a simple shepherd come to ask a favor of an old friend."

Ipuwer relaxed and waved for Moses to follow him. They walked through the kitchen area and into another hallway that led to the library.

As they entered the scriptorium, the musty odor of papyrus filled Moses's nostrils. Rows of wooden shelves were piled high with rolled manuscripts. He breathed it in with pleasant memory. He'd spent countless hours in here reading and learning with Ipuwer's help from his youth. Only now did he realize how much he'd missed reading during his sojourn in Midian.

Leading him into a small side room, Ipuwer closed the door for privacy. Moses took out a piece of papyrus from his cloak and handed it to Ipuwer, who read it and said, "A list of manuscripts. Babylonian, Assyrian, Egyptian, Canaanite, Sumerian."

"I will pay you to copy them and gather them together to prepare them for travel."

"Why?"

"I can only tell you that I have been commissioned by the god of the Hebrews to lead them out of Egypt. And I want to bring these resources with me."

"You will need a wagon for this amount."

"I know. I have others I am gathering from my own people as well."

"Wait, why would Pharaoh let half his slave force go?"

"He has not yet. But he will. Trust me on this. Even if you do not, I will pay you. And if it never happens, you will be that much wealthier for little trouble."

"So you *are* bringing trouble," said Ipuwer.

"I bring nothing. My god Yahweh is going to judge the gods of Egypt. It is going to be unlike anything before in the history of the Two Lands and unlike anything long after."

Ipuwer sighed. "You never were a man of moderation, Sobekmose. I mean, Moses. So I do not expect it even now."

Moses said, "Keep your quill ready. You are going to want to write about what is coming."

• • • • •

Jannes and Jambres had cleared all the priests out of the holy place of the temple. They had lit incense and had taken some drugs for sorcery as they prayed a hymn to Ra.

They spoke it in perfect unison, their voices as one. "Homage to thee, O Ra. Thou art the lord of heaven and earth and didst create beings celestial and beings terrestrial. Thou art the God One, who came into being in the beginning of time. Thou didst create the earth and man. Thou didst make the sky, and thou didst make the waters and didst give life unto all that therein is."

Jannes had closed his eyes in a cross-legged sitting position next to his brother. But as they spoke, he felt dizzy. He could barely finish the hymn. Jannes opened his eyes to see his brother still beside him, also looking foggy and dizzy.

But when he looked up at the image of Ra on the throne, he saw it come alive. Stone became flesh and feather. The god-man with a hawk's head and a solar disk crown with a coiled uraeus on front stepped down and approached the brothers.

Jannes trembled. The sun god stood mere feet away from them and spoke with a vibrant deep voice. "Why do you raise me from my rest?"

Jambres spoke first. "O king of the gods, we come on behalf of the king of Egypt to ask of your wisdom. We have heard of a new god in the land."

"Yahweh," Ra interrupted. He said the name with animosity.

"Yes. That is his name. He is a god of the Hebrews. King Dudimose is concerned to know what he should do in response to the demands of this deity."

"Tell him he must defy this Yahweh with everything in his being. The magician Moses is his mouthpiece. You must support the king with your magic. I will empower you to perform signs and wonders in defense of Egypt."

Jannes felt himself starting to shake. He asked, "Who is Moses?"

"He is a dark lord from Egypt's past. The one prophesied to be the Destroyer of Egypt."

Jannes felt another pang of desperation. He remembered the prophecy. He remembered persuading the king of that day to kill all the male Hebrew infants to stop the prophecy. But how had the chosen one ever survived that devastation? Who was this Moses?

More importantly, Jannes now found himself and his brother in the middle of a war of gods. And Jannes knew in his heart that Yahweh was a powerful deity. He had seen him wipe out the entire Duat in his vision. But was that a deception?

Jannes's shaking became uncontrollable. He fell backward and jerked in a seizure. He heard voices in his head whispering, then screaming at him that he was in danger. He felt like a hundred spirits were pulling and tearing at his body. He didn't know where he was any longer.

When he finally stopped and came back to consciousness, he saw his brother over him, wiping foamy spit from Jannes's mouth and holding him.

"You are well now, my brother. You had a seizure. But you are well."

Jannes could only think one thing in his fevered mind: *No, we are not well. We are in grave danger.* But he was still too frightened to reveal his vision from a generation ago. Would his brother reject him? Would he consider him unclean from such interaction with a hostile demon?

He would keep his secret to himself and pray that Ra's empowerment of magic would be enough.

CHAPTER 30

Within a week, the effect of Pharaoh's edict on the Hebrew brickmakers was devastating. Because they had to get their own straw from the fields without lessening their brick quota, their workload had almost doubled. Many were dropping sick and even dead from heat exhaustion and lack of sleep. The foremen were whipped for missing their quotas, resulting in them becoming more punishing to their own workers.

Several families who had lost loved ones in the sun had gathered around Moses's home to call for justice. Moses felt the weight of the world upon him. He was having a hard time sleeping. Early in the morning, he took a camel a mile out into the desert area beyond the delta to pray.

He stood watching the rising sun with his shepherd staff in hand, clutching his robe tightly against the desert morning cold. All he could hear were the sound of insects and the desert wind whistling in his ears.

He felt rage rising within him again. He knew Yahweh was almighty in power and sovereign in governance. But he could not help his anger. It seemed as if injustice was growing, evil winning. In fact, it was exactly because of Yahweh's almighty power and sovereign governance that he was angry.

He dropped to his knees and cried out to Yahweh, "Oh, Lord, why have you done evil to this people? Why did you ever send me? Since I came to Pharaoh to speak in your name, he has done evil to your people, and you have not delivered them at all."

He looked up and saw a figure approaching him backlit by the blood-orange glow of the rising sun. It was tall and muscular. He saw the head of a hawk.

Ra the sun god.

But as Ra came near, a strange thing occurred. Six sets of wings sprouted from behind him and covered his whole body. When they opened back up and disappeared behind his back, Moses saw his entire visage transformed into a rather ugly, gangly creature. It looked more like an old serpentine humanoid with lapis lazuli slit eyes and burnished bronze scales for skin. The creature reminded Moses of the seraph snakes in the desert.

Moses heard whispering in his ear, but he knew it came from that creature. It was somehow in his head. "You are right to question Yahweh. What kind of a god does evil to his people? What kind of a god promises deliverance but gives suffering?"

The serpent being stood at a short distance as though it saw something and could come no closer. Moses looked behind himself. He saw nothing but the distant city of Avaris. But he felt something—something heavenly and more frightening than this creature—watching over him.

He looked back to the seraph being. "Who are you?"

It flicked its forked tongue and spoke in a powerful voice without moving its mouth. "I am Mastema. I am Belial. I am Abaddon. And who are you, little shepherd? Are you the Destroyer of Egypt?"

Strange that this supernatural creature did not know him.

"No. I am a servant of Yahweh."

"Pffft," scowled Mastema. "You are a puppet. Who is finally asking himself the most important question of all. What kind of puppet master do you serve who claims to be almighty and all-loving yet does not eliminate evil? If he can stop evil but does not, then he is cruel. If he cannot stop evil, then he is impotent. Which is worse?"

It paused, and Moses felt its serpentine eyes pierce his soul. Then it continued. "Do you really want to serve a god like that?"

Moses could not answer.

The whisper became tantalizing. "I made Pharaoh a god. I could turn *you* into a god. I could give you the whole land of Egypt if you but do one thing: fall down and worship me."

Moses heard the sounds of spirits whispering in the winds swirling around him. He heard the sounds of goats, owls, and serpents—the spirit beings of the desert—all telling him to fall down.

Mastema added, "You can still worship Yahweh as well if you would like. He may be jealous, but I am not. I believe in diversity and inclusion. His order is oppression. My chaos is freedom."

In the corner of his eye, Moses saw a bramble bush in the distance. It was burning but not being consumed. Just like the one he had seen on the mountain. He got up off his knees and walked toward it.

The voices in his head became louder, angrier.

The bush seemed to grow more distant as he walked.

He picked up his pace and began to run toward it.

But he never got closer.

The voices and animal sounds faded in his ears.

Finally, he stopped and fell to his knees, this time to catch his wind. He held firmly onto his staff for support.

When he looked up, the burning bush was before him. The serpentine being Mastema was no longer behind him.

A voice came from the bush as it had in Sinai. "Moses."

"Yes, my lord."

"I have seen the affliction of my people. I have heard their groaning of pain and suffering. And I have remembered my covenant that I made with Abraham. Go again and tell them that I will redeem them with my outstretched arm and with a strong hand and with acts of judgment. They will be my people, and I will be their God, and they will know that Yahweh their Elohim has done this."

Moses knew what Yahweh meant with those words. Pharaoh always used the phrases "a strong hand" and "an outstretched arm" as his claim to divine power over the earth.

A confrontation of gods was coming.

Yahweh added, "I will bring my people into the land that I swore to Abraham, Isaac, and Jacob. I will give it to them as a possession, an inheritance. For I am Yahweh."

"I *have* told them," Moses countered. "But they have not listened because their spirit is b-b-broken by their suffering.

"Go and tell Pharaoh again to let the people of Israel go out of his land."

"The people of Israel have not listened to m-m-me. How then shall Ph-pharaoh listen to me?" His stuttering had returned. What was happening to him?

He said with resignation, "I am of un-cir-circumcised lips."

The bush burned brighter than ever. Moses had to shield his eyes.

The voice of Yahweh replied, "I have made you a god to Pharaoh, and your brother shall be your prophet. You shall speak all that I command you, and your brother shall tell Pharaoh to let Israel go out of his land. But I will harden Pharaoh's heart with heaviness. Though I multiply my signs and wonders in the land of Egypt, he will not listen to you. Then I will bring judgment against the gods of Egypt. And the Egyptians shall know that I am Yahweh when I stretch out my hand against them."

Moses noticed that Yahweh was ignoring Moses's weakness. But the more he doubted Yahweh, the more his stuttering returned.

He felt like a failure. "How can you use m-me? I am a man of such little f-faith."

"Obey me with what little faith you have, and you will see skies fall and mountains quake. The heavens and earth shall be created through my covenant."

Moses looked to the ground in shame and said, "Tell me what to do, my lord, and I will do it."

Moses awakened as if from a dream on the desert floor. He looked around. The sun was just rising in the east, and the cool of the desert still chilled him. It felt earlier than when he had arrived. Had he fallen asleep? He couldn't tell if he had just experienced a wakened encounter, or if it had been a dream vision. It was all so real.

But he knew what he had to do. He got up and mounted his camel to race back towards the city.

CHAPTER 31

Moses burst into Aaron's bedroom and shook him.

"Aaron, wake up. We have to meet with Pharaoh. And bring your staff."

The two brothers had used Aaron's elder status to get a meeting with Pharaoh. It was late evening by the time Pharoah received them in the throne room of his palace. When the herald led them through the hallway of pillars toward the throne, Moses noticed that Pharaoh had brought his son and his vizier as well as a dozen of his lector priests from the temple of Ra. And there were the usual handful of servant children that provoked Moses's disgust. God only knew the depraved indecency those poor children suffered at the hand of that beast. It was probably why the queen was not around to subject herself to such humiliation.

The herald announced them. "Aaron and Moses, sons of Amram, elders of Israel, seek audience with the king."

They bowed. As Moses straightened up, he recognized the two lector priests. They were the brothers Jannes and Jambres of his own day, now high priests of Ra, wielders of magic. And in forty years they had not aged a day. They still looked like young men no older than twenty years. Dark sorcery must be behind their appearance.

The expression on Jannes's shocked face suggested the priest recognized Moses despite his white hair, beard, and humble Hebrew tunic. Jambres evidently did not.

Pharaoh said, "My two bold Hebrew shepherds with their staffs come to test my patience again? I hear your lazy people are whining and complaining about their workload."

Aaron said, "My lord the king, thank you for receiving us."

"Well, the only reason why I bothered is because my chief lector priests here warned me about you and your god. For the life of me, I cannot imagine what possible trouble you could cause me with your feeble god and his demands. What was his name?"

Aaron said, "Yahweh, my lord."

"Yes, well, they said a contest of deities might be appropriate. I said I am always game for some entertainment. So entertain me if you can, shepherds. Prove yourselves by working a miracle."

Moses and Aaron looked at each other grimly.

Moses said, "Aaron, take your staff and cast it before Pharaoh."

The four guards on each side of the throne platform stepped forward, drawing their swords to protect Dudimose and his son.

Dudimose raised his hand to stop them, then gestured for them to return to their places. They obeyed.

Aaron lowered his staff and set it gently on the floor near Pharaoh.

When he stepped back, it turned into a uraeus serpent that coiled into a striking position—identical to the one on Pharaoh's crown.

The lector priests backed away in fear.

But Dudimose remained fearless and unimpressed. Khonsu even less so. Pharaoh was supposedly protected by the uraeus as well as Wadjet, the cobra goddess of the delta region. So the irony was not lost on him.

Dudimose broke out in laughter.

Then he clapped his hands. "Wonderful magic!"

Moses and Aaron looked askance at each other again, not knowing how to respond.

"Except it is rather unoriginal. I have seen it plenty of times before."

He turned to Jannes and Jambres. "My priests, show these novice magicians how it is done."

Jannes nodded to the six other lector priests with him. They had prepared for this trick. They all threw their "staffs" upon the ground. The impact broke the stiffened snakes out of their hypnotic state. All seven of them circled Aaron's serpent with hostility.

Moses watched the priests exchange proud looks amongst themselves.

Dudimose gave a self-satisfied smirk. But this quickly turned into shock as Aaron's serpent promptly swallowed all seven of the other staff serpents. With each consumption, it grew a little fatter until it was done. Then Aaron grabbed it by its tail, and the serpent returned to a thin staff.

Dudimose and his son looked dumbstruck. This was no cheap magic. They had never seen anything like it before. Even the lector priests were stunned into silence.

Finally, Dudimose said, "Well, now you have my attention."

Moses sighed with relief until Dudimose added, "But you still do not have my approval. So leave me. I am done with you."

He waved a dismissive hand, and the guards moved to escort Moses and Aaron out of the throne room.

• • • • •

Hapi, the blue god of the Nile River, sat by the water's edge a mile down from the city in a deserted tributary. He was androgynous, a fat male figure with pendulous female breasts that represented the fertility the Nile brought the land. His glory was the Inundation, though now the river had receded.

Khnum, the guardian of the Nile, had called a secret gathering but had told no one why.

Hapi saw Sobek arrive by barque. The crocodile god said, "Where are the others?"

"Patience, reptile, patience," Sobek hissed.

Hapi always tried to claim supremacy with the Nile, but this was not his strong season as Sobek would make a point of later.

Nun, the blue-skinned god of primeval waters, arrived on a barque as well. He was the oldest of the gods and was also glorified at the Inundation when the waters spread like chaos over the land.

How ironic it was that these deities of water were themselves weakened in water from their creation until now. At the great flood, their predecessors, the two hundred ancient ones, had been buried in the earth and sea by the cataclysm of water. Now these gods were appointed over the very element that could incapacitate them all.

Someone had to take the dangerous job.

Nun announced from his barque, "This had better be important, Sobek, because I have things to do, humans to organize."

"How would I know its importance?" complained Sobek.

"Did you not call this meeting?"

"No, I did not. Hapi did."

"What?" demanded Hapi. "I thought Khnum called it."

"What kind of foolishness are you babbling? I did no such thing," said a voice approaching them from the dark. It was Khnum with his ram's head and muscular frame arriving from the desert, one of the main guardians of the Nile.

"It appears we have all been made fools," said Sobek. "Whose trickery is this?"

"Guilty," said another voice from the dark. They all turned to see the small blonde archangel Uriel step out from behind a boulder, his swords drawn.

The four Nile gods drew their weapons, which amounted to daggers and staffs. They were not warrior gods. Still, they could take on one little squirt of an angel.

Then the boats of Nun and Sobek were capsized as three other angels exploded from the water behind them: Gabriel, Raphael, and Saraqel.

The gods rolled off their barques into the river. Taking on his crocodile form, Sobek sought to make it to land. Raphael pulled him by the tail back into the current. Sobek's tail and jaws were mighty, but since he was weakened by the water and angels had no such aqueous flaw, he was no match for Raphael, who subdued him quite easily on the river bottom.

Gabriel subdued Nun and dragged him down to the depths as well.

Khnum and Hapi used their staffs to attack Uriel, who easily defended himself with his two swords.

Saraqel threw a net over the two gods and dragged them into the water with the others.

And so the Nile River, source of life in Egypt, became the prison of its gods.

•••••

Moses and Aaron entered their house in a rush.

"Miriam!" yelled Aaron.

She came running. Amram was close behind.

"Immediately start filling every possible container you can with water from the Nile. Enough for a week of rations."

"Why? What is happening?"

Moses said, "You must trust me. We will be without water for a short time."

"What about the Nile?" she asked incredulously.

"I cannot explain. Just gather as much water as possible before tomorrow. And tell all your friends—today."

"You mean, now?" Miriam asked.

"Yes. Aaron and I are going to the elders. All the Hebrews must do the same all over Goshen."

"What do I tell them?"

"Tell them Yahweh is coming and his judgment will be upon the waters. Tomorrow. But he will not touch the Hebrew districts. There is no time to hesitate."

"That is not enough time to reach everyone," she complained.

He replied, "It is all the time we have."

"Then we had better stop talking and start doing," Amram interjected.

Miriam turned and yelled for all the children in the household to begin their task.

Aaron looked with worry at Moses. "I fear Miriam is right and there will not be enough time."

"Then let us pray for another miracle," said Moses.

They left to spread the news to the elders.

As they made their way through the community, elders split up and passed the word to their families, who passed the word to the clans and tribes. Some of the Hebrews believed. Others did not. There would be a lot of sharing of resources during the next week.

Maybe that will be a good thing for this selfish people, thought Moses.

He could not help but think of his beloved Zipporah and his family in Midian. They would be safely going about their day, tending goats and sheep, drawing water in the valley at the western edge of the Sinai where he had originally met Zipporah and her sisters. He was glad they did not have to face the burdens of what was coming upon Moses's family in Egypt.

But still, his heart ached for them. He missed them dearly. He missed his wife's companionship, the loving brightness in her eyes as she looked at him. He missed her warm embrace, her sweet smell, her soft lips. She had been a soothing balm to his impatient temper. She calmed him with her grace and love.

He missed his two sons and the times they'd shared hunting in the wilderness and shepherding in the fields. He missed his father-in-law whose wisdom had been the heart and soul of Moses's own growth of character.

He prayed that Yahweh would watch over them and prepare them for this new world he was bringing. Moses could not wait to get back to them. But how long would that be? How long would it take to persuade Pharaoh to release the Hebrews? Today would be the beginning. Today would be the first strike in a war against Pharaoh and the gods of Egypt.

CHAPTER 32

One

In the mid-morning hours outside the royal palace in Avaris, Pharaoh marched down to the Nile in his daily processional with his son Prince Khonsu, his vizier Harsekher, and his chief lector priests, among them Jannes and Jambres.

A long stone walkway with pylons led to the river's edge, where a shrine to the gods of the Nile stood. There Pharaoh would pledge his obeisance to graven images of Hapi, Sobek, Khnum, Nun, and others. The priests would then engage in a ritual baptismal ceremony of cleansing Pharaoh followed by a goat sacrifice that would ensure the ongoing fertility of the harvest season.

Citizens lined up along the way to follow the procession, which was watched over by sentinel guards every twenty feet, their bronze *khopesh* sickle swords warning anyone who might consider causing trouble.

When Pharaoh had reached the shrine, his attention was drawn to two Hebrew shepherds who stepped out of the line by the bank of the river, staffs in hand.

Guards surrounded them, ready to strike. But Dudimose yelled out, "Guards! Leave them! Return to your stations!"

He had recognized the brothers Aaron and Moses.

What he did not see was that in the unseen realm Mikael the archangel stood protectively behind Moses. And all around the shrine were the six other archangels from Yahweh's throne: Gabriel, Raphael, Uriel, and the others.

Ra and Horus had been on the side with Pharaoh and his son Khonsu. But when they saw the angels, they'd panicked and sounded an alarm for the pantheon to assemble by the river.

"Where are the Nile gods?" Horus demanded.

"I do not know," said Ra. "They have been unreachable since last night."

"Our strength is diminished," said Horus. "If this is an ambush…"

"If this is an ambush," interrupted Ra, "we will not be taken so easily."

Isis and Heka had arrived. Followed closely by Thoth, Ptah, Sekhmet, and a dozen others. They paused with caution, surrounding the shrine area. The presence of all seven archangels was rare and usually marked a major strategic move on Yahweh's part.

In the human realm, Pharaoh waved the Hebrew brothers forward. They moved within better hearing range but kept their distance.

"Your timing is becoming quite intrusive," said Pharaoh. "My patience is wearing thin. Have you come here to show me another magic trick?"

Moses announced loudly for all to hear, "Hear, O Pharaoh. Yahweh, the god of the Hebrews, sent me to you saying, 'Let my people go that they may serve me in the wilderness.' But so far, you have not obeyed. Thus says Yahweh, 'By this you shall know that I am Yahweh. Behold with the staff that is in my hand I will strike the water of the Nile, and it shall turn to blood. The fish shall die, and the Nile will stink. So this river that you worship as the bringer of life to Egypt shall bring death."

Dudimose raised his brow with doubt. "I see the stakes have risen. You *shepherds* are becoming quite pretentious. But can your performance match your grandiose claims?" He grinned sarcastically, opening his arms up to the river as if to offer them the opportunity.

In the unseen realm, Ra watched the guardian angels with hateful spite. "So that is their strategy. They have taken hostage the Nile gods to lessen our strength so they can curse it."

Moses struck the water with his staff. The crowd gasped in anticipation.

But nothing happened.

Moses announced, "Aaron, stretch out your staff and hand over all the waters of Egypt, the rivers, canals, ponds, pools, and even vessels of wood and stone that hold the Egyptians' water."

Aaron did so. He held his hand and staff out as Moses finished, "They shall all be turned to blood."

Aaron lowered his staff.

Pharaoh was still grinning, amused by it all. The Nile had not changed. Walking down to the edge, Pharaoh knelt with a cup of sacrifice, dipping it in the river. Then he held it up.

"A toast to your worthless god, Yahweh. May he do better next time."

Pharaoh began to drink from the cup.

But after two gulps, he pulled away, coughing and spitting out the water that had turned to blood in the cup. His eyes had widened with shock, rivulets of red running down his mouth and neck.

The crowd became agitated with fear. Some screamed and pointed upriver where a small-capped wave of red pushed its way downriver like a flood.

It passed everyone at the bank, turning the water blood-red in its wake.

People screamed, "Save us, Ra! Save us, Horus!"

Pharaoh leaned over to Jannes and Jambres and whispered, "What can you do?"

Jannes and Jambres conferred with the other priests.

In the unseen realm, Ra called out, "Isis, Heka, empower the lector priests!"

A palace servant broke into the shrine area, winded from running.

"My king! My king! The water in the palace has become blood!"

"All of it?" asked Dudimose.

"The pools, the jugs and storage containers of the household. All have turned to blood."

Dudimose turned to Jannes and muttered angrily under his breath, "Do something, priest. Now."

Jannes pulled away from the others. "We can replicate this magic, my lord. Just give me some time."

He called to a guard, "You there, grab a shovel and dig near the bank to find pure water."

As he did so, Moses and Aaron stood silently watching the cluster of priests desperately trying to call forth Isis and Heka to help them.

In the unseen realm, the gods had backed away in fear from the river of blood. Their strength had diminished with the curse on a main source of their power. The Nile received worship from the people that exceeded even their worship of Pharaoh. This act of drawing first blood was a declaration of war against the gods. But it was also mockery. The Nile was considered to be the bloodstream of Osiris, the original king of Egypt who had become Lord of the Dead. Yahweh was expressing his power over all of Egypt by making it a literal bloodstream of death.

"I have water!" shouted the soldier with the shovel. Ground water was the only water untouched.

Jannes instructed a priest to bring one of the empty jugs from the corner. It would hold a gallon. He dipped it into the water and brought it up to Pharaoh.

Jannes and Jambres said spells over it.

They looked at the king with hope. He stared back with worried brow.

They lifted the jug up and recited a hymn to the Nile in perfect unison.

"Hail to thee, O Nile, that issues from the earth and comes to keep Egypt alive."

In the unseen realm, Isis and Heka cut their own wrists with knives and poured their blood into the jug.

As it was poured out onto the ground, the water appeared to have turned to blood. It splashed out onto the ground, staining the stone red. The crowd applauded.

Dudimose smiled victoriously at Aaron and Moses, who remained unmoved.

But looking back at the stone, Dudimose saw that while the water poured out by the priests looked bloody, it was not as thick and dark as the Nile had become.

He turned back to Jannes.

"Can you undo the curse? Can you turn the Nile back to water?"

"We will try, my king."

"Well, then have your priests stay here and 'try' until they are successful. Meanwhile I will 'try' to restore the Ma'at that I have lost because of your incompetence."

· · · · ·

The first day of the bloody Nile, all the fish died, filling the tributaries with their floating corpses. The stench of the blood was bad enough, but now the rotting fish added to the putrid odor, making many sick throughout the cities. Some amphibian and reptilian life survived, including crocodiles, which now roamed the streets and paths of the cities looking for fresh water and attacking people.

The Hebrews stayed at home and guarded their stored water, rationing it to family and friends.

By the second day, the Egyptians' desperation set in. Without water, the sick and infirm were dying quickly. People began digging all along the Nile for uncontaminated ground water. But they had to do so with scarfs around their mouths and noses because of the stench from the river. Bandits would rob unsuspecting diggers and steal their water jugs, leaving them without the life-sustaining water they needed.

Pharaoh's household slaves were guarded by soldiers, so the Great House did not lack for water.

On the third day, many of the elderly in the cities began dying from dehydration. The sound of wailing could be heard throughout the land. The water was running out for the Egyptians.

By the fourth day, word had gotten out to some Egyptians that the Hebrews had stored water, so gangs of pillagers began showing up in the Hebrew quarters looking for spoils to plunder. The Hebrew elders organized security committees to patrol the neighborhoods to protect their people. Several clashes of bandits and security resulted in dozens of injuries and lost lives.

Jannes and Jambres had led a group of one hundred lector priests at the bank of the river shrine in casting spells and incantations for four days straight. They used every trick at their disposal. Nothing worked.

Jambres took his brother aside and whispered, "Do you recognize who the Hebrew Moses is?"

Jannes decided to not tell the entire truth. "He does look familiar."

Jambres offered, "He is Sobekmose of the house of Sobekhotep IV from forty years ago."

Jannes feigned revelation. "We had thought he might be the Destroyer of Egypt back then."

"The prophecy," agreed Jambres.

"But he disappeared into the desert and was never heard from."

"Until now," Jambres said. "At first I did not recognize him with his beard and the lack of a speech impediment. But the more he talked, the more I began to suspect."

"Do you think he may be the Destroyer?" Jannes asked.

"I do not know. But he may seek to claim the throne."

"No," said Jannes. "Sobekhotep's bloodline was replaced long ago by new families. He has no claim."

"Then why do you think he is maintaining a disguise?"

"I am not sure," said Jannes. "Perhaps it is not a disguise. Perhaps he has truly embraced his Hebrew heritage."

Jambres shook his head doubtfully. "To identify with a nation of slaves?"

Jannes offered, "I think we should keep our knowledge of his true identity a secret. It may become something to use to our advantage later."

"Good idea," said Jambres. "If we can find out why he is keeping it a secret, that may be his weakness for us to exploit at the right moment."

It might also be a way to forestall the confrontation Jannes could see rising between Moses and Pharaoh.

•••••

By the fifth day, unrest in the city was so great that Pharaoh thought an uprising was about to occur. The water that was the lifeblood of their world had become the death knell of civilization. Pharaoh had called his lector priests back into the palace so the failure of their magic to turn the bloody Nile back to water would not ruin their reputation.

Dudimose stood on his palace balcony with several of his servant children, looking out over the city below. Khonsu arrived, radiating the disdain his father was used to seeing in him. But Dudimose had no time to quarrel over family matters right now.

"Prepare the army for an insurrection," said Dudimose. "A desperate and dying populace will not remain obedient. We must find any unrest and crush it immediately or it will spread like wildfire."

"Where shall I begin?" asked his son.

"With the Hebrews. They are the origin of this plague. Let them be the first to experience my strong right arm."

But before the army could be mustered and sent to the Hebrew quarters, a new crested wave of fresh water rolled through the Nile from the south and pushed the river of blood to the sea.

The plague had ended.

And the madness of chaos temporarily left the Egyptians as life-giving water returned.

Courtesy of Yahweh.

CHAPTER 33

Two

The council of the gods, minus the missing Nile gods, met at the temple of Ra. The sun god sat on his throne, Horus and Isis beside him. Thoth kept record.

"So this prophet Moses is the conduit of Yahweh's judgment. Can we stop him?"

"He is guarded by Mikael the archangel," said Thoth. "Any attempt on our part to ambush him could result in a trumpet call to a multitude of the heavenly host."

"Spiritual world war," grumbled Ra.

"And we will lose," added Horus.

Sekhmet stepped forward and bowed. "O Great God, may I suggest you consider calling on Set to return from his chastisement in the desert? We could use his strength and chaos."

Ra knew that Sekhmet had more personal interest in Set than merely strengthening the gods' forces. The two deities often had private liaisons where they carried out perverted fantasies of pain on each other.

"Contrary to your assertion," replied Ra, "Set is not being chastised. I have a very specific purpose for him."

"A backup plan?" asked Sekhmet.

"I will tell you when you need to know," said Ra. "For now, stay alert for any intelligence about our enemies' plans."

• • • • • •

Seven days after Yahweh turned the Nile to blood, Moses and Aaron returned to Pharaoh's court and requested an audience. They met him in his own palace garden, a large atrium fed by a Nile tributary and filled with palm trees and various flora. A small paradise within the royal complex. Pharaoh was apparently avoiding the public humiliation of their previous encounter.

Moses and Aaron were led to Pharaoh and his son by the water's edge. Pharaoh was flanked by two child servants, his vizier, and several lector priests, including Jannes and Jambres. He appeared more serious in disposition than on their previous encounters. Khonsu looked angry.

Pharaoh slowly clapped his hands and said, "I applaud your display of magic. Very impressive. My lector priests tell me that it took them seven days, but they were finally able to return the Nile to fresh water."

Moses saw Jannes and Jambres give each other a guilty look. But he had no need to call out the lie. They would be powerless against what was coming.

Pharaoh added, "I have decided to offer you two Hebrews the position of chief priests over all my kingdom."

Jannes and Jambres looked at each other with shock, then at Dudimose. They had obviously not been made privy to this decision.

Moses shared a look with Aaron. This pharaoh was cunning to try to win his enemies over to avoid a war.

Moses chose to not even dignify the offer with a response. Instead, he simply announced, "Thus says Yahweh, 'Let my people go that they may serve me.'"

Pharaoh mused over the challenge. Khonsu pulled a dagger. Dudimose held him back with a hand. "Put that away."

He turned back to Moses. "And if I refuse again? Will you turn the river back to blood?"

Moses answered, "If you refuse to let them go, behold, I will send a plague of frogs upon all the land. The Nile shall swarm with frogs that shall come up into your house and into your bedroom and into the houses of your servants and into your ovens and your kneading bowls. Frogs shall swarm on all your people over all the land."

Pharaoh considered again. "That is a lot of frogs." He nodded. "This I should like to see."

Khonsu looked angrily at him. "Father!"

Pharaoh shut his son up with a wave of his hand. Moses kept looking at Dudimose as he spoke to his brother.

"Aaron, stretch out your hand with your staff over the rivers, over the canals, and over the pools, and make frogs come up on the land of Egypt."

So Aaron did. He lifted his staff over the tributary as representative of all the waters and prayed, "O, Yahweh, hear the word of your servant Moses and bring forth this plague of judgment upon the land."

Dudimose turned around to look into the water. But nothing happened. He turned back to look at Moses.

The sound of a frog's croak drew their eyes down to a single frog hopping in front of Dudimose on its way from the bush to the water.

Dudimose raised his sandal and stomped on the thing, crushing it with a splatter and a sickening crunch.

He said to Moses, "We are done here."

Moses and Aaron bowed and left Pharaoh's presence.

As Dudimose watched them exit the garden, he heard the sound of frog croaking start to increase. He looked down at his feet and saw one, two, three frogs now hopping in front of him.

The child servants knelt down giggling, trying to catch the frogs.

"Do not touch them!" Dudimose shouted.

The children obeyed and stood fearfully at attention.

Dudimose stomped on two more of the amphibians.

"Go," he commanded sternly. The children scuttled away back to the palace.

"My lord king," said Jannes.

Dudimose turned to see the water of the tributary bubbling with the activity of thousands upon thousands of frogs that began to leave the water and hop out onto land all around them.

It was a plague of frogs.

Dudimose closed his eyes in anger. "Can you replicate this magic, priest?"

"Yes, my lord."

"Then I suggest you do so immediately. I am retiring to my children's quarters to relieve some of my stress—and I do *not* want to be disturbed *unless* you can recreate this infernal magic."

• • • • •

In the temple of Ra, the sun god sensed something was off. He looked around the pantheon of dozens of gods.

"Where is Heket? Where is the Ogdoad?"

Heket was the frog goddess of birth for Egyptians. The Ogdoad were eight primeval deities who according to Egyptian myth embodied the primordial creation. Four male and female pairs represented order and chaos that came together in the formlessness and void of darkness to hover over the watery abyss with a divine wind to create the primeval mound out of the waters from which the sun god emerged.

The gods had humanoid bodies with amphibian and reptilian heads of frogs and snakes representing that creative spawn of sea and land. They were Nun and Nunet, Amun and Amunet, Keku and Keket, Hehu and Hehet.

And they were all missing.

Ra slammed his staff onto the floor with a boom that echoed throughout the sanctuary. "Yahweh has taken more hostages."

Heka entered the throne room. "Great God, I have been with the lector priests of Pharaoh. We have another problem."

Isis and Heka arrived at the palace just in time to help the priests with their spells and magic before Pharaoh. They were back in the palace garden where this had all begun. The priests had servants carve hundreds of wax figurines of frogs and place them at the sandy bank of the stream with the intent of making them come to life.

This was not without precedent in Egyptian magic. As the story went, during olden days a lector priest named Ubaaner had carved a wax crocodile and used magic to make it come to life and eat the adulterous lover of his own wife. So the lector priests now recited Ubaaner's magic spells over the wax frogs to make them come to life.

In the unseen realm, Heka told Isis, "We cannot create frogs from nothing. Only Yahweh can do such a thing."

Isis replied, "But we can move created things from one location to another. Can we not?"

He looked at her, trying to figure out her meaning.

She added, "If we gather frogs from across the river and transport them through the unseen realm to this location, it will look to the humans as if they are being created out of nothing."

"Well planned," said Heka with a grin of understanding. "Let us hurry. These priests are looking more foolish by the minute."

All over the banks of the Nile, frogs had swarmed forth from the waters and were now infesting every nook and cranny of Egyptian lives. People used large brooms to sweep their floor of hundreds of the creatures, only to find them in cupboards and ovens and kneading bowls, just as Moses had proclaimed.

The streets and walkways were full of frogs. Homes and palaces were full of frogs. The temples and holy buildings were full of frogs. They were everywhere. One could not walk without squashing numbers of them beneath one's feet.

The stink of amphibian flesh wafted over everything: food, drink, inside and outside of buildings. Drinking water that had been cleared of the little monsters tasted like dirty fish water and made people gag. The noise of their croaking filled the air from morning until night with an especially loud increase in the evening, keeping the exhausted Egyptians awake.

· · · · ·

"How do they find their way into my bed at night?" yelled Pharaoh to his priests over the croaking mass that filled the garden. "They return to fill my living spaces quicker than servants can get rid of them. Their noise is driving me mad. Their smell is making me sick."

Jannes bowed low and turned to his priests standing over the wax images. They had finished the latest incantation and were waiting for the result.

The sand beneath the wax frogs began to stir. Then thousands of croaking frogs began to burst out of the sand, covering the lifeless wax ones in their wake as if created out of nothing. The priests were surprised by their own success.

"Well," said Dudimose sarcastically. "You have proven your magic. But it does not solve my problem. It makes it worse! I do not want more frogs. I want fewer frogs! Use your magic to kill them or make them leave!"

"We will do so right away, my lord," said Jannes. He turned back to the priests to concoct some kind of spell to do the work.

Dudimose left them, expecting the same lack of results as with the blood Nile.

Moses was awakened in the night by pounding at his house door. He and several of the male family members went to see who it was. Cloaked palace soldiers pushed their way into the courtyard. Moses and the other men backed up in defense.

Stepping inside, two cloaked figures pulled down their hoods. They were revealed to be Queen Nefret and Harsekher, vizier of the king.

Moses and the men bowed the knee.

"My queen."

Aaron arrived and bowed as well.

The queen looked around the yard and home with surprise.

Harsekher waved to the house and behind him. "I noticed on our way here that there are no frogs in the Hebrew quarter. How were you able to rid yourselves of them?"

"Yahweh protects us," said Moses.

"Hmmm. Of course," said Harsekher. "Yahweh."

The queen said to her guards and vizier, "Leave us."

Harsekher hesitated. "Are you sure, m'lady?"

"I said, leave us."

The vizier gave a look of resignation and led the guards outside the gates. Moses and Aaron led their family members back into the house and closed the door.

"We are alone, my queen," said Moses.

Nefret turned to face them. Moses could see her eyes were desperate, without sleep. He could smell wine on her breath.

"As you are aware, I represent the king. I bring you his very words."

Moses remained silent, motionless, listening.

"Thus says Pharaoh, 'Plead with this Yahweh of yours to take away the frogs from me and my people.'" She spoke her next words as if with relief. "'And I will let the people go into the wilderness to sacrifice to your god.'"

Moses and Aaron bowed submissively.

But Moses questioned her, "May I ask why the king did not bid us to the palace?"

She teetered ever so slightly and slowly blinked her eyes. "He does not want to draw the attention he usually craves. And he wanted to see how you lived. So he made me his spy." Chuckling at the half-joke, she gestured to the house. "I can see you live humbly. So apparently you are true prophets."

She stepped closer to Moses so she could whisper. "You must know the king will never give in. He is a jealous god."

"I have gathered as much," said Moses.

"Defying his will means death. There are no exceptions."

He could tell she spoke from experience. She was a hostage of a depraved imperious god.

She added, "I should advise you to beware my son, the crown prince. He is more vindictive than his father. If that were possible."

"Thank you, my queen," said Moses. "Simply command for me when you want the frogs gone, and they will be gone. They shall be left only in the Nile."

"Tomorrow," said Nefret. "Can you have them gone by tomorrow?"

"It will be as you say," said Moses. "So that you may know that there is no one like Yahweh our god."

She sighed with relief. "Thank you."

She used her scepter to hit the gate twice. Harsekher and the guards came back in to escort her away. But Harsekher stepped menacingly close to Moses and whispered to his face. "As vizier, I too speak for the king. Tell no one of this meeting. Or your family will suffer the consequences."

"My lord," said Moses, bowing in acceptance.

After the queen and vizier had left, Moses felt the burden of consequences upon his soul. He went to look in at several of his family members asleep. His own brother and sister, his nieces and nephews, their little children, all sleeping at peace in their beds. And all of them down to the little ones were in danger of their very lives before Pharaoh's threat—because of Moses.

Was this a price he was willing to pay? Yahweh had promised Moses that he would deliver Israel out of Egypt, but he had not promised which ones. Would Moses free his people but lose his entire family by Pharaoh's hand? Would they be the ones to suffer the consequences of this war of gods and men?

He couldn't sleep at first. His mind drifted to Midian and his beloved Zipporah. Before he knew it, he was with her in a memory of a discussion they'd had before he left for Egypt.

It was the winter. They'd been staying at a lodge near Yam Suph. Their decision had been made for Zipporah and her newly circumcised sons to stay behind in Midian.

Moses sat on a rock with Zipporah, and together they watched the sun set over the blue wind-driven waters.

Moses said, "I don't want to leave. I love my life here—with you, our sons and grandchildren, your father. It is the family I always needed but never had. After all these years, I have finally found a land of peace and goodness. Returning to Egypt is like returning to the Abyss. A sea of chaos and evil."

She held him tight. "But you are an instrument of deliverance from that chaos."

"At what price? I bring that world back to my family."

"Is it not Yahweh's will for us as for you?"

"What will happen to you and our sons while I am gone?"

"Do not take this wrong, dear husband, but we will do just fine without you. Our sons and their families do all of the work anyway."

She was teasing him. He played along. "So I am not as necessary here as I have been made to believe?"

"Well, you do eat up quite a lot of food. And you still require a lot of care at night in bed."

"I am beginning to think you may have made a secret deal with Yahweh to get me out of here."

She grabbed him and became serious. "I will miss you, my man of God. I will miss your hearty appetite, your sense of humor, your strength, and most of all our closeness in bed."

"I do not know how long this will take, Zipporah. Months? Years? I do not know if I can do it without you by my side."

"I think that is why you must."

She was right. He had loved his life in Midian so much that he had lost sight of the very One who had granted it all. It was Yahweh who gave, and it was Yahweh who took away. Despite the goodness of all that the Creator would grant in this life, in the end each man faced him alone and made an account for their lives to him alone. Everything Moses cherished the most, the life-giving love of his wife and children, his work, his world—everything good—was only good and meaningful as Yahweh's gifts. Otherwise, they became desert sand sifting through the fingers of death. Risking it all to obey his calling was in the long run not risking anything at all.

·····

The next morning, Pharaoh awoke to the sound of silence. No croaking. The frogs must be gone. He left his two child servants still sleeping and got up to walk to the balcony. He stepped on a dead frog. Lifting his foot from the bloody mess, he realized that the floor was covered with dead frogs. He negotiated his way to the balcony and looked out over the palace.

What he saw was not an encouraging sight. The entire yard was full of dead frogs. Servants were shoveling them into piles and carting them away. Pharaoh wrinkled his nose. The smell was already putrid. As the frogs rotted, the stench would worsen.

His vizier Harsekher arrived. Dudimose asked him, "Is this the scene all over the city?"

"Yes, my king. Dead frogs everywhere. The smell is as bad as the previous plague. We are trying to pile them to burn in bonfires all over the city. I saw one pile as large as a house."

"Bring the crown prince to me."

Harsekher bowed and left him.

Pharaoh knew what this was. This was not just a display of power but an insult to Pharaoh by Yahweh. Rather than returning the frogs to the water or making them disappear back into nothing, Yahweh had struck the frogs dead to make some sort of statement about Egypt's alleged spiritual condition.

Pharaoh mumbled, "The land now stinks like a dead, rotting frog."

His son's voice came from behind him. "It is Moses's flesh that should be rotting in the grave. Why do you not kill him?"

Pharaoh turned to see Khonsu with teeth gritted in anger.

"Because, my son, his magic is not like that of our lector priests. It is different. More powerful."

"So you just let him mock you and curse Egypt?"

"True prophets are protected by the gods. Killing a prophet can bring a greater curse than what we have already seen."

"Then how do you fight him?"

"You do not fight them directly. This Moses seeks to instill fear in me. But I can see that he thrives on attention. So…" Pharaoh smirked. "I will ignore him."

CHAPTER 34

Three

Moses did not hear anything from Pharaoh for a full week after Yahweh had withdrawn his plague of frogs. Walking to the palace, he and Aaron asked for another audience with the king. The servants rejected them at the door.

They retreated a distance away to see if they could see the king on his balcony. But he was nowhere to be seen.

Moses became angry. Marching back to the front entrance of the palace, he stopped at the foot of the steps that led up to the guards with their spears and sickle swords.

"O Pharaoh, try to ignore this!" Moses yelled as loud as he could. "Aaron, stretch out your staff and strike the dust of the earth."

Aaron struck the sandy ground with his staff, stirring up a small cloud of dust.

The two brothers watched as the dust began to swirl and come alive. It became a small swarm of gnats, tiny black insects that were usually more annoying than dangerous.

But Moses knew that this was going to be more than an annoyance.

A rush of wind blew past them, lifting up more sand into the air. That sand also transformed into swarms of gnats.

Within minutes, the entire street was a cloud of gnats covering people, driving them indoors. Every human or animal that did not seek shelter would be overwhelmed and choked to death by the thriving hive around them.

Moses marched angrily through the swarms, which parted for him as he made his way home. Aaron followed quickly behind.

Stepping out onto his balcony, Pharaoh saw the swarms of gnats rising up all over the town. He watched Moses walking through them untouched. He called to his servant, "Fetch me my carriage. I am going to the temple of Ra to speak to my priests."

Pharaoh kept his carriage closed as they drove through the city streets from the palace to the temple. He heard screams of people being overcome by the insects. The carriage drove through several clouds of gnats before they arrived at the temple. The horses were skittish and having difficulty breathing as they had inhaled so many of the little insects on the ride over.

Pharaoh made his way inside the temple complex all the way to the altar outside the holy place.

Jannes, Jambres, and a host of other priests were waiting for him there. They had been briefed of the plague that was currently filling the land. Looking out onto the waterway, they could see huge swarms of the insects moving like large clouds, changing shape as the gnats flew in synchronized fashion. It almost looked as if the insects' unity had created a living, pulsing organism that transcended the individual creatures of which it was comprised. And those cloud entities were hostile.

Out on the Nile, a merchant ship passed through one of the swarms. Sailors jumped off the vessel into the water to escape. Others had their entire bodies covered by the things. The multitude of insects was so large they could lift humans into the air as they sucked the life out of them.

"Can you match this power?" asked Pharaoh, turning to his priests.

Jannes and Jambres glanced at each other darkly. Jannes said to Dudimose, "My lord, we will call upon Isis and Heka, divinities of magic, as well as Geb, the earth god. Surely he will be able to create teeming life from the dust of his own body."

"Well, hurry up, then!" barked an exasperated Dudimose. He began pacing as the priests lit a fire on the altar and sacrificed a goat. They prayed with fervent heart for the help of the gods to bring forth their own swarms for their own benefit.

Nothing happened.

In the spiritual world, Isis and Heka stood with Geb in fear before the priests.

Geb said, "I cannot do this. I cannot bring forth these insects."

Isis replied, "And we have no control over them. They are Yahweh's agents of chaos." Suddenly, they saw a dust cloud arise from the sand around them. It became a massive swarm of gnats that moved toward the gods.

"What are they doing?" Isis asked. "Are they coming for us?"

Geb too was confused. "But we are not in the seen world. How can this be?"

Before they could do anything, the gnat clouds enveloped them, covering the bodies of the gods like a black blanket.

Heka saw what was happening and ran all the way out of the temple. A swarm followed him.

Within seconds, Isis and Geb were covered with so many gnats that their bodily shape was no longer discernible. They became entrapped in the living swarm, which then raised them off the ground and carried them away.

Jannes and Jambres saw it all. They were frozen in terror. Jannes whispered, "Did you see them? Did you see the gods?"

Jambres could only nod.

"What?" barked Pharaoh. "What did you see? What are you talking about?"

Jannes turned to Pharaoh and said, "We cannot produce our own gnats. We have no power to stop them."

The twin priests then spoke in unison. "This is the finger of God."

Down by the river, Heka jumped into the water to escape the giant black cloud that sought him. He would not be carried away tonight.

When he returned to the temple sanctuary, he reported to Ra and the assembly.

"Isis and Geb were taken away by the swarms. They came forth from the earth, but Geb could not thwart them."

Ra sat pensively on his throne, considering their options.

Sekhmet said, "Isis was a powerful deity of magic. How could such earthly creatures have overcome her?"

Horus said, "These are not mere earthly plagues. They are from heaven. Yahweh is taking us out one by one."

"This is more than individual animus," said Ra. "This is de-creation. An attack on us all."

The pantheon of Egyptian gods was not one of individual gods with powers representing individual natural forces. There was not a god of the Nile, a god of frogs, and a god of gnats. It was actually an integrated system of interrelated deities who worked together to maintain the cosmos' order, its Ma'at.

So Hapi may have been the god of the Nile's inundation, but others helped him. Khnum guarded that river along with Sobek the crocodile god. Nun was the god of primeval waters from whence the Nile was separated. The entire river was said to be Osiris's bloodstream. He was lucky to have been absent the day the god's bloodstream became truly blood.

This integrated family of deities involved in every aspect of the creation was also a trait of the Ogdoad that had been kidnapped by Yahweh as well. All eight gods were involved in the creation story of order out of chaos.

Ra concluded, "Yahweh is undoing our power by returning creation to chaos. He turns disease and pestilence against us. He mocks us in his judgments. He proves complete control of all."

"Egyptians will lose all faith in us," said Thoth.

Ra nodded. "And I fear there is much worse to come."

"We must fight," argued Sekhmet. "I will not stand here and be made a fool. Yahweh gave us these lands as our inheritance at Babel. We have legal claim."

"Yes, in his heavenly courtroom," said Ra. "But I've done it before in the days of Enoch and I lost badly. I am not about to rush into another lawsuit until he puts his covenant in stone. Then I will have a hammer strategy."

"What then, O king of the gods, is our strategy?" demanded Sekhmet with a touch of sarcasm. "I am ready and listening."

He glared at her until she backed down.

Then he said simply, "Law is not our only recourse."

Sekhmet raised her brow with feigned surprise.

Ra called out, "Onuris, come forth."

A bearded one came out of the ranks of the gods with a spear in his hand, a rope around his muscular shoulders, and a crown of four high plumes. Onuris was a hunter-god known for capturing the Distant Goddess. He could find anyone anywhere. But he was also a hunter and slayer of all enemies of Ra and Egypt.

"Yes, my king. What is your will?"

"I want you to hunt and kill the Hebrew Chosen One, Moses son of Amram."

A hush went over the pantheon, followed by a flurry of whispers.

"It is time we crush the heel that seeks to crush our heads."

CHAPTER 35

Four

Jannes found himself kneeling before the throne of Ra. Horus stood beside him. Their hawk's heads looked eerily at Jannes, but they did not speak.

In his head, he heard hundreds of voices. Who were they? They built up in a crescendo.

"Moses and Aaron are evil!"
"Yahweh is a demon!"
"Stand up and fight!"
"You are a coward!"
"You are a traitor to Ra, to Egypt, to the king!"
"You are worthless!"
"We will take away your youth!"
"The Devourer-of-Souls will eat you!"
"The Lake of Fire for you!"

The cacophony drove him to his knees. He felt himself going mad. Putting his hands over his ears, he screamed for it to stop.

But the voices did not stop. They just seemed louder, angrier.

Jannes woke up. He was drenched in sweat. Getting up out of his bed, he walked to his brother's room and knocked lightly.

"Come in," said a groggy voice inside.

Jannes slipped in and closed the door quietly.

Jambres rubbed the sleep from his eyes. "Is something wrong?"

"I am not sleeping well," Jannes said.

"Why?"

Jannes sighed as he sat on a small stool by the bed. Priestly compartments were sparse with a simple wooden bed, a small stool, and a small table with personal items. Their garments were provided by the temple, cleaned everyday by servants.

Jannes said, "There is something I never told you."

"Never?" Jambres sounded incredulous. They were so tight in their connection they sometimes shared the same thoughts. Maintaining such a secret for any extended period was completely out of character for them.

"Do you remember when we were in a shipwreck on the way to Byblos forty years ago?" Jannes asked.

"I saved your life."

"Remember when I told you I had a vision of Duat?"

"Oh, yes, I think so."

"I never told you the details."

"You were on the solar barque of Ra in his journey through the underworld to sunrise."

"Yes, but I never told you that I faced the judgment hall of Osiris. I thought I had actually died and was facing the weighing of my heart on the scales of Ma'at."

"The hall of Double Justice? Hmm. Did you recite the Declaration of Innocence?"

"Yes."

"Then you had nothing to worry about."

"Jambres, when my heart was weighed, it was found heavy with injustice."

Jambres looked confused. That was not possible.

"It is true. I was exposed, and the Declaration was a lie. At that very moment, I saw my whole life before me, and I knew that I would be consumed by Ammut, the Devourer-of-Souls."

"So you were warned to live a better life."

"No, Jambres. I was warned that I *cannot* live a better life. But that is not even the worst of the vision."

"What?"

"The weigher of my heart was not Osiris but another god altogether."

"Who? Thoth? Anubis?"

"It was Yahweh. This god of Moses against whom we are now fighting."

Jambres shook his head in confusion. This was bizarre to him. Jannes was talking nonsense.

"What did this god look like?"

"Like a Hebrew son of man."

Jambres remained stunned.

Jannes continued, "Then Yahweh just dissolved Duat and all the gods into nothing, and I found myself before a heavenly throne with one seated on it like an Ancient of Days. It was before him that I found myself judged and burning up in the flames of the Lake of Fire. And then I awoke on the beach."

Jambres was thinking through Jannes's words silently.

"Jambres, we should not fight this Yahweh," Jannes said urgently. "We will lose."

Jambres finally spoke. "Have you told anyone else?"

"Not a soul."

"Good. Tell no one until we can figure this out."

A knock on the door shushed them. Had their conversation been overheard?

A voice came from the other side. "Time for Pharaoh's morning Nile visit."

They both sighed and got ready.

• • • • •

The high priest brothers led the retinue of lector priests behind Pharaoh and his son and vizier down the path to the river to start his morning ritual to the Nile. There were fewer people than before because of the events that had recently unfolded. Many were scared. But some also wanted a sense of reassurance from this ritual of Ma'at.

When they arrived at the shoreline, Jannes saw Moses and Aaron step out again from the crowd to prophesy to Pharaoh. These two Hebrews were getting bolder.

Moses got right to the point. "Thus says Yahweh, 'Let my people go that they may serve me. Or else, behold, I will send swarms of pests on you and your servants and your people and your houses.'"

Oh no! Jannes thought. Gnats were a mild problem compared to the damage that swarms of other insects could do to the land of Egypt.

Moses added, "'But on that day, I will set apart Goshen, where my people dwell, so that no swarms of pests shall affect them. By this you will know that I am Yahweh in the midst of the earth. Thus, I will put a division between your people and my people. Tomorrow, you shall see this happen.'"

With that, Moses and his brother simply turned and walked away. They didn't even stay to hear Pharaoh's response. It was as if all pleading was now over. As if they were just going to call down judgments no matter what.

Jannes could see that Pharaoh looked worried. He was no longer the confident, pompous king with whom Jannes had been familiar. He was now a troubled soul that appeared to be consumed by bitterness and anger.

And Dudimose did not even bother asking his priests to counter the magic. After the previous incidents, he must have assumed they were incapable. He was losing faith in them. Jannes was reminded that Pharaoh had dismissed priests in the past for less failure than this. In those kinds of cases, dismissal involved execution. His heart began to race.

• • • • •

"Tomorrow?" Ra said to his informant Khepri. "Then we will move tonight. Pre-emptive strike upon the enemy. Sekhmet, gather those fleas you told me carry plague and release them into the Hebrew population. They will not even see the fleas coming and fall in droves. If Yahweh will send his pestilence to Egyptians alone, then I will send my pestilence to Hebrews alone. Pestilence for pestilence."

Sekhmet's arrows of pestilence and disease were accurately aimed and powerfully poisoned for the populations she could infect. The myth of Sekhmet's origin lay in the almost complete destruction of humanity in ancient days. Ra had become troubled by the people he'd created, so he'd sent Hathor the goddess as the Eye of Ra to hunt out mankind and kill them. When Hathor arrived in the desert, she was transformed into Sekhmet and proceeded to kill all of mankind with ruthless efficiency. She was stopped short only because a repentant Ra tricked her into getting drunk. Had he not done so, she would have murdered the whole of mankind and bathed in their blood. But her reputation for brutal devastation remained strong and rivaled even that of Yahweh's Destroyer Angel. Only the Canaanite warrior goddess Anat was a close third.

Sekhmet slithered down under cover of night to the Hebrew district in Avaris. She carried jugs filled with infected fleas. They were so small she could fit millions of them into a couple of containers.

When she reached the first mound where the Hebrews resided, she hid herself in the bushes. All around the edge of the riverbank, a heavenly host with flaming swords guarded entrance into the city, creating a wall. They glowed like bronze and appeared to wear the armor of Eden. They looked ferocious. She could see similar hosts surrounding all the other mounds where the Hebrews resided.

There was no way she would be able to slip in and release her disease upon them.

She returned to the temple.

Onuris had been more successful in slipping past the angelic guardians and finding his way to Moses's home. The hunter-god had disguised himself as one of the heavenly host on sentry duty in the streets. He had a gift for camouflage that helped him catch prey and avoid adversaries.

But tonight he discovered his prey surrounded by three predators far more capable than Onuris. The archangels Gabriel, Uriel, and Raphael.

Strange, he thought. *Mikael is the guardian Watcher of Israel and her Chosen One. But Mikael is not here. Where is the prince?*

Moving on before the guardians could discover him, he disappeared into the darkness.

There would be no assassination of the Hebrew deliverer tonight.

•••••

That evening, Jannes had dreams of the spirits taunting him again. It was the same as before. They kept accusing him, warning him, ordering him to fight against Yahweh or else he would lose his eternal youth.

He awoke in the morning to the sound of distant screams. He awakened his brother, and they ran to the steps of the temple to look out upon the city. Other priests had gathered to see what was happening.

All over Goshen there were new swarms. But these were not gnats. They undulated like the gnat swarms and moved like living clouds as well. But they were much larger, much more devastating.

One swarm floated toward the priests with deliberation. They all watched in awe with open mouths until it was upon them. They could hear the buzzing. They began slapping their arms.

Mosquitoes.

"Back inside!" Jannes yelled. The priests ran for the doors. Twenty of them made it.

Jannes watched through a peephole. One of the priests had been outside and down the steps. He quickly became covered with mosquitos. One of the other priests went to help him. They swatted and tried to brush off the pests, but they could not free themselves or get up the steps in time. They were engulfed by the swarm until their bodies looked like black scarecrows waving around. Their screams were quickly stifled by the myriad of mosquitoes filling their lungs.

Within seconds, they fell to the ground lifeless. The only movement was the writhing mass of insects feeding off their blood.

The black cloud finished its feast and moved southward.

Jannes and some of the priests ran out to their fallen comrades.

He stopped in terror at the sight. One of the young priests bent over and vomited.

The two priests' bodies looked like mummified cadavers. All their blood had been sucked out of their bodies. Stretched out over the bones and shrunken organs, their skin was a grotesque gray-blue covered over with millions of tiny, discolored bumps, the bites of the insects. Their mouths were frozen with grimace, their eyes sealed shut behind bulbous puffy flesh.

The sound of more buzzing drew their attention upward. The skies were filled with hundreds of pestilent swarms. More were coming their way, descending upon the towns and villages all around.

Some priests quickly carried the bodies to internment. Jannes and Jambres returned to the temple interior, shutting and locking the doors behind them.

As they walked along the pillared corridor, Jannes whispered to his brother, "Jambres, have you thought about what I told you?"

Jambres kept walking thoughtfully. Then he said, "You are right. We must plan our escape from Egypt."

Jannes sighed with relief. "Where do you think we should go?"

"Should we join the Hebrews?" Jambres queried.

As Jannes looked at him with shock, Jambres added, "They are protected in all this."

"But we would surely be found out, arrested, and executed by Pharaoh."

"We can go south to Kush or north to Byblos."

"We can decide later," Jannes said. "Now we must get to the palace for Pharaoh's call."

In the unseen realm of the temple sanctuary, Ra had already received Onuris's and Sekhmet's reports. The angelic protection of the Hebrews had foiled their plans. This was getting more serious by the day.

Ra asked, "Thoth, does the House of Life contain any of the toledoth scrolls of the Hebrews?" The *toledoth* were records of "generations" of people. They included genealogies and narratives.

"Yes," said Thoth. He knew the scribe Ipuwer had collected the Hebrew documents in his archives.

"Good," said Ra. "Then go and find out what you can about their seedlines. If this Moses is not the Chosen One, then find out who is."

"Yes, my lord."

Ra then ordered, "Khepri, Amun-Ra, Sepa, and Ta-Bitjet, go out and see if you can commandeer any kind of control over some of these swarms. I should think you would have the best luck with scarab beetles."

"Yes, my lord," said Amun-Ra.

Scarab beetles were the iconic representation of Egypt herself. Also known as dung beetles, these insects rolled up balls of dung out of which offspring would spontaneously erupt. They represented the creative power of Amun-Ra, which is why the god had the head of a scarab beetle in some incarnations. So too did Khepri, the creator sun god who took the form of a scarab to represent Egypt as a whole. Sepa was the centipede god while Ta-Bitjet had power against poisonous bites. Together, these gods would seek to summon power to overtake the swarms of pests plaguing the entire land.

Making their way down to the riverside, they began ritual spells to draw their own swarm. Khepri and Amun-Ra manifested themselves as the scarab on their heads and spoke forth the clicking call for the beetle. Within minutes, the distinct sound of the scarab beetle wings could be heard approaching. It sounded like scratchy buzzing.

Amun-Ra and Khepri rose to command the cloud as the others continued their incantations.

A large pulsating cloud of scarab beetles came near the shoreline, then stopped suddenly in mid-air before the gods a few dozen yards out. It was huge. It must have been a hundred feet wide by seventy feet tall, its amorphous shape ever changing with the constant sound of flapping wings.

Amun-Ra and Khepri chanted and waved their hands to the left. The cloud veered to their left. The gods waved to the right, and the cloud veered to the right. They spread their hands wide, and the swarm dispersed to a wider, thinner cloud. The gods brought their hands together, and the swarm condensed into a tight, throbbing sphere.

Amun-Ra and Khepri smiled at each other. They had managed to garner control of their patron insect. But could they do this with other swarms? And could they use this to fight back against Yahweh?

They spread out their arms again. But this time the swarm didn't thin out. It moved a bit closer to the gods.

They waved their hands out again with a stronger gesture. But once again, the swarm moved closer as if it were a questioning pet.

A third arm wave and the swarm moved all the way up to the gods, mere feet away, buzzing, flapping, undulating in a unity of diversity.

"What is going on?" demanded Khepri. "I thought we gained control."

"Perhaps they were mimicking us," replied Amun-Ra. "As a predator does before a kill."

Before Khepri could respond, the black cloud of beetles descended upon the four gods at the riverbank. It swallowed them up into its blackness. It covered their bodies with a hundred thousand mandibles that began to eat the gods.

Normally, scarab beetles only ate dead earthly flesh. But these insects were clearly led and empowered by unearthly forces. It seemed no one was safe from their chaos. The gods screamed in pain as their flesh was pinched off, tiny piece by tiny piece. Their preternatural strength was of no effect against millions of tiny creatures synchronized like a hive mind to swarm and eat.

Within minutes, all four gods were consumed by the horde of insects, which then moved on to the next meal elsewhere.

Flies, mosquitoes, beetles, and swarming pests of all kinds plagued the land of Egypt, killing people and animals, entering homes, even the palace. It was a full three days before Pharaoh finally summoned Moses and Aaron back to the palace.

Moses saw Queen Nefret standing just outside the open door behind the king's throne, watching them discreetly. He lost himself in a moment of thought. How often had he neglected his wife Zipporah? How often had she stood behind him without his knowing? He would never take his worthy queen for granted again.

"Go!" dismissed Dudimose. "Sacrifice to your god, but only within the land of Egypt." Pharaoh had not slept for days. His eyes were bleary, his royal tunic disheveled. He looked as if a swarm of bitterness had devoured his soul.

Moses said, "My king, it would not be right to do so. The offerings that we give to our god would be considered abominations to the Egyptians. They would surely stone us to death."

Aaron added, "We must go three days journey into the wilderness, for that is what Yahweh our god commands us. You would not disobey the commands of Ra to sacrifice in the wilderness, would you?"

Pharaoh sighed and rolled his eyes. He waved impatiently. "Okay, okay. I will let you go into the wilderness. But you must not go so far away."

Moses and Aaron remained steadfast.

Pharaoh added with scolding, "And only after you rid me of these swarms of pests."

Moses became bolder. "O Pharaoh, you said this last time. But then you did not let us go."

Pharaoh yelled, "I will, I will. This time. Just rid me of these swarms of pests before I go mad."

Stealing one more glance behind the throne, Moses saw the queen turn and leave.

The swarms of pests were gone in the morning.

But Pharaoh's heart was made heavy with injustice again. And he would not let the people of Israel go.

CHAPTER 36

Five

For the fifth time, Moses went to Pharaoh to demand that he release the Hebrews to serve Yahweh. For the fifth time, Pharaoh denied the demand. And for the fifth time, Yahweh brought a severe plague. This time it was upon the Egyptians' livestock, specifically those out in the fields such as horses, donkeys, camels, herds, and flocks.

And yet again, Yahweh made a distinction between the livestock of the Egyptians and that of the Hebrews. The livestock of the Israelites were fine, but all the livestock of the Egyptians became diseased and died. Their bloated, stinking bodies filled the land. Because of the disease, they could not be eaten, only buried or burned. And once again, the stench of death permeated everything. The Egyptians began to starve for red meat with only fish, vegetables, and plants to eat.

Even Pharaoh's household suffered the shortage. The crown prince Khonsu had responded quickly when he'd heard of the plague, hiding over a thousand chariot horses down in a caverned stable. Since they were not in the fields, they were not struck down with the disease as the other animals were.

In the unseen realm, Ra sent out various gods to try to save the animals. Sekhmet was sent to counter the disease since she was also a goddess of medicine. Ptah, the creator god whose living image was Apis the sacred bull. Hathor, the cow-headed goddess of regeneration. Haurun, a shepherd god. Banebdjedet, a ram god. Mnevis, the sacred bull of On. All of these banded together to fight this plague with their magic. Other gods connected to these cursed animals like Khnum, the ram-headed god, were already gone.

They had attempted to use sympathetic magic this time. The gods crafted bronze images of each of the diseased livestock. They placed them on standards and walked through the fields with their images to dispel the disease.

But the magic was to no effect. When the gods returned to the temple, they noticed that each of them had pale skin and rashes all over their bodies just like the diseased livestock had experienced. They became nauseous and dizzy.

Amun-Ra fell to his knees. He belted out, "How can this be? How can we divine beings contract this disease?"

Hathor and Mnevis fell to the ground in convulsions.

Ptah choked out, "This is impossible. This is impossible."

True, the divine Watchers could not die by earthly means. But the plague was from heaven. So, they would be eaten up by the disease and become incapacitated for God-only-knows how long.

Their fellow gods dragged their weakened bodies into a pit of fire and burned their angelic flesh so that they could not spread the disease. Their screams echoed throughout the spiritual realm.

· · · · ·

Moses lay in bed, longing for Zipporah. He missed her deeply and wondered how long it would take for Yahweh to finish these plagues. He had never been away from her for forty years. Now he had not seen her for several moons. In some ways, he began to feel himself unraveling without her. If he kept his mind on Yahweh and his calling, it would help.

But part of God's calling was the oneness of man and woman, not merely in flesh but in purpose. Zipporah was everything Moses was not: kind, patient, gracious with others. She was not without her flaws, but their unity was the very thing that made them better people and kept them from falling prey to their worst traits.

He was reminded of the well-known ancient poem:

> *This at last is bone of my bones*
>   *and flesh of my flesh;*
> *She shall be called Woman,*
>   *because she was taken out of Man.*

Zipporah would often tease him of being a spoiled, demanding king because of his temper. He would tease her back of being a rebellious, disobedient queen because of her stubbornness. Laughing together at their weaknesses was a way of addressing them without hurting the other.

It had been so long since Moses had laughed. He could hear Zipporah's sweet voice in his ears. Making her laugh felt like a confirmation of his own worth. For in her, he was truly known and loved. And with her, he truly knew and loved.

And making love to her was a taste of heaven on earth. He even felt a spiritual experience in it as though he was connecting with the divine.

He let his mind drift back to a memory of being in their tent alone, naked, caressing one another. He would touch her smooth, black skin, moving over every curve, treasuring her beauty as no one else could ever do. The warmth of her embrace, the passion growing.

They would kiss, not as mere foreplay but as exploration of one another's souls. Her soft lips, her soft moans of delight and surrender.

As the tension grew, so did their passion for one another. Their desire became like a flame, then like a whirlwind of fire, wrapping them up in its burning without consuming them.

It was as though they entered the throne of the King of Kings together. It was a foretaste of heaven.

Moses caught his breath, feeling spent yet at perfect peace. Shalom.

Zipporah's back was to him. He caressed it with gratitude and pulled on her shoulder to face him.

Then she turned, and he saw that she was not Zipporah but the goddess Hathor! The cow-headed daughter of Ra, mother of Pharaoh.

He recoiled in terror, sick to his stomach.

She spoke in an other-worldly voice through her bovine mouth, "On every high hill and under every green tree."

Moses vomited onto the floor and saw that it looked like molten gold. When he looked back up, Hathor had transformed into a bull-calf, now standing on the ground. It made a hideous agitated lowing that sounded like a calf being slaughtered.

Then he awoke with a gasp, his body covered in sweat. It had been a nightmare.

But it had been so real. Sitting up, Moses ruminated over it all. Yahweh had given him a vision. A warning. This people would not be faithful. He would deliver them, but their hearts would go after other gods. And this is how it would feel to Yahweh. Like a husband betrayed by an unfaithful harlot of a wife.

Moses couldn't even comprehend the pain of that betrayal. For he knew he would not want to live if Zipporah ever did that to him.

Or worse, he might even want to kill her.

It was the lawful punishment for such a crime.

But was this all worth it then? Was this all an exercise in futility? A chasing after the wind? Surviving a series of deadly plagues and facing the wrath of Pharaoh only to have a glorious wedding that ended in the slaughter of the bride?

•••••

Thoth gave a report to Ra in his temple throne room.

"Mighty king of the gods, I have found a possible solution to our dilemma. I found a scribe named Ipuwer who has gathered a small library of scrolls that include the Hebrew toledoth you sought."

"What did you find?"

"Unfortunately, I was kept by some spell from being able to read the Hebrew manuscripts. It must be from Yahweh. But I crafted a way to find out what is in them."

"How?"

"I appeared in a vision to the scribe, and I could see the Hebrew scrolls through his human eyes."

"Excellent, my brilliant Thoth. What did you find?"

"There is a prophecy in their tradition of a mighty ruler coming through the Hebrew tribe of Judah."

"Is Moses that ruler?" Ra asked.

"No. Moses is from the tribe of Levi."

Ra was thrown by the detour from the obvious.

He asked, "Is this Moses then Yahweh's diversion to distract us from his real intent?"

Thoth answered, "They are one and the same. I believe we are being destroyed to make way for their promised king."

Ra asked, "So if we can find this king or his bloodline, we may be able to stop the plagues?"

"Yes," said Thoth. "I have checked the genealogies from the toledoth and compared them against our knowledge of the Hebrew population. I have narrowed down the possibilities to three men."

"Tell me about them."

"Hur son of Caleb is a commander in the Hebrew leadership. But he is too close to Moses. We cannot get to him. But we can get to the other two. One is a different Caleb. Caleb son of Jephunneh. He is thirty-nine and a rising warrior. Word has it that he has been given a heavenly weapon by one of the archangels."

"That is a rare thing."

"Yes. They must have significant plans for him."

"Maybe. But he is a Kenizzite, a convert to Israel from Edom. His tribe joined Judah, but they are still looked upon as dogs by many Israelites."

Ra mused, "Edom does have a long history of enmity with Israel."

Ra was referring to the fact that Edomites were descendants of Esau, whose lineage was perpetually at war with the lineage of his brother Jacob, whom Isaac had chosen.

"Who else is there?"

"The third is Nahshon son of Amminadab. He is the tribal leader of Judah. What better king-in-waiting than the head of the royal bloodline?"

Ra thought it through. "Too obvious. Yahweh likes to use the lowly things of the world for his purposes. The unexpected, the outcast, the rejected. Set our sights on the Kenizzite first."

Thoth said, "He lives in Avaris. Angels are still guarding the habitations of Israel. We could get through, but I doubt we could get very close."

"Hmm. Indeed. So we send human assassins instead. As soon as possible."

"Yes, my lord."

CHAPTER 37

Six

Jannes and Jambres had gone along with their regular duties so as not to draw attention to their plans of escape. They had packed sacks full of survival necessities that included food, tools, weapons, and clothes. Now they were waiting for the right moment to slip away so that they could be long gone before their absence was discovered.

They had decided that moment would be this evening. But their plans were delayed when the next plague hit.

Earlier in the day, Jannes had seen the Hebrew Moses confront Pharaoh again by the river. This time he had brought ash from a kiln. Throwing it into the air, he had declared it to be a fine dust that would spread throughout the land and become boils on man and beast throughout all the land of Egypt.

And boils did break out everywhere. Men, women, and children were stricken with black boils that filled with a green pus. Their skin turned grayish blue. The smell of lanced boils was rancid and could often make others sick.

Thousands were dying.

Nor were the priests of Ra safe in their sanctuary. Over half of them were sick in bed with the plague, and Jambres was one of them.

Jannes brought a jar of clean water to his brother's room. Thank the gods the water was no longer contaminated. Opening the door, he saw his brother in bed with a wool blanket covering him, teeth chattering from fever.

"Shut the door!" croaked Jambres. "The light hurts my eyes."

Jannes closed the door softly as possible. Even sounds were painful for Jambres.

Without warning, Jambres leaned over and vomited into a pot by the bed. The last food he had eaten spewed from his mouth, undigested. Some of it missed the pot, and Jannes had to find a rag to clean off the floor. He had never seen his brother this sick.

He could hear the sounds of moaning and retching throughout the priests' quarters. Just when they'd thought they had seen the worst of these plagues, they'd been hit with this disease of boils on the flesh. Because it was a new sickness, there was no known treatment. But Jannes had done some research and put together a potion and other medicinal tactics to heal his brother.

Pulling out a vial of the potion, he lifted Jambres up to drink it.

Jambres weakly held his hand up to stop the vial from touching his lips. "What is this?"

"A medicine."

"What medicine?" He looked accusingly into Jannes's eyes. "What is in it?"

Jannes patiently described the contents, thinking the disease had also made his brother confused with a slight madness.

"I have mixed juniper, garlic, and sandalwood for your intestinal aches and digestion. I added some thyme for your pain and poppy seeds for your headaches. And, of course, mint for your vomiting. I decided to use the urine from King Dudimose that we had saved for a worthy occasion. I consider your well-being to be that worthy occasion."

Jambres's bleary eyes searched Jannes's for betrayal.

Since the king was a god—Horus on earth—any of the king's bodily fluids were saved as often as possible by priests for their healing properties.

Jambres slowly lowered his hand and allowed Jannes to pour the potion into his mouth. He swallowed with difficulty as his throat was also swollen.

As he poured the liquid, Jannes recited a spell. "This is the elixir of Imhotep, the fluid of Horus, the seeds of Serapis, and the leaves of Sekhmet become a healing. These powers come from the very heart of Thoth."

Jambres lay back in bed and seemed to rest. The Egyptians were the most advanced in the world with their use of both natural physical remedies and spiritual word magic.

But Jannes could not get out of his head the nagging question of why his brother would be afflicted with this disease. They had been given eternal youth from Ra himself. How powerful was this plague that it could overcome the magic of the gods?

He already knew. It was the power of Yahweh.

And this plague was particularly insulting to the priesthood. To serve the gods, one must be pure. So they sought to cleanse their bodies of all impurities. No blemish was allowed in the presence of deity. The priests were clean-shaven of all the hair on their body to pursue that perfect cleanliness. They wore clean linen garments as Jannes did even now. And no disfigurement was allowed on any priest.

So the boils on priests disqualified them for service. No priests meant no offerings in the temples and no spiritual rituals done on behalf of the people. No offerings meant the gods would be dissatisfied. Without this spiritual purification, Egypt was collapsing into chaos.

Jannes pulled out a small figurine he had made of papyrus and wood. It was a human figure. He placed it on the table and began to perform an incantation.

"What are you doing?" came the voice of his brother behind him.

Jannes turned to see Jambres sitting up, glaring at him with wide, fearful eyes. "I said, what are you doing?"

"An incantation of transference."

This was common enough. Priests would seek to transfer a curse or sickness from an individual into a figurine made as a substitute for the sufferer. After which they would destroy the figurine as a cure.

Jambres was acting delirious. He tried to get up out of his bed.

Rushing over, Jannes tried to keep him down safely in his bed. Jambres was too weak to fight back, but he tried.

"Are you cursing me with a figurine?"

"No. Why would you say that? I would never do such a thing to you. You are my brother. It is a transference ritual."

Jambres was apparently confusing this ritual with the figurine curse, a kind of reversal of the transference, in which a curse on a figurine would be projected onto a human enemy.

Jambres mumbled to himself and fell back into a state of delirium.

Jannes wondered why his brother had become so distrustful of him. It must have been a demon that came with the disease.

Taking a clean linen rag, he wrang it out with water. He then laid the rag on his brother's forehead.

He wished he had known what kind of incantation could make Yahweh withdraw this curse. He prayed his brother would survive it. He suspected that he might not.

• • • • •

Amun-Ra, Isis, and Sekhmet, all gods of healing, had already been judged in previous plagues by Yahweh's judgment. So they could not stop the disease of boils that now covered the bodies of mortals and threatened the gods' power in Egypt. Human worship was a source of power for the gods in their ages-old rebellion against Yahweh. Without it, they became powerless.

Ra had charged the three other major gods of healing—Imhotep, Serapis, and Khonsu, all humanoid in form—with the task of fighting this new plague with their healing powers. They were supposed to have assembled at the House of Life to search out any ancient wisdom to help them stop or counter the de-creative chaos.

But in reality, they were already long gone from Goshen and on their way through the desert to find their champion of chaos, Set. He was somewhere to the northeast in the Land of the Shasu on mission from Ra to reconnoiter intelligence about a possible Canaanite threat. But the Land of the Shasu was vast. It went from the Wilderness of Paran and Sinai all the way up to the Negeb in Canaan.

They had run all day with preternatural speed and had made it all the way to the southern Negeb. It would only be a matter of time before they found Set.

"Can we slow down?" complained Khonsu. Despite their divinity, even gods could tire.

Imhotep replied, "When Ra finds out we are gone, we will be punished for insubordination and cowardice."

"We are no cowards," Serapis offered. "Ra will thank us when he realizes we could not do without Set's power."

Imhotep added, "The only way to fight chaos is with chaos."

"But we abandoned our posts," said Khonsu. "We left our comrades in peril." His breathing was labored.

"But we are coming back," said Imhotep. "Frame it any way you want. I have seen the devastation of Yahweh's right arm. We did not stand a chance of survival back there. With Set, we do."

"But what if...?" Khonsu slowed to a stop. He couldn't catch his breath. The others stopped.

"What if we cannot...?" This time he fell to the ground unconscious.

The others ran over to him. They were all exhausted from the run.

When they got to Khonsu, they saw that his naturally green skin had become pale. And he had black boils on his back. When they rolled him over, he vomited up black bile all over his face.

More boils had appeared on his abdomen.

The other gods backed up in fear.

Falling to his knees, Serapis vomited up black bile into the sand. He ripped open his tunic to discover his chest was covered with boils.

Imhotep opened his cloak as well. He too was covered in boils. Some of them popped open, and green pus leaked out with a horrible, fetid smell. They were rotting from the inside out.

"Damn you, Yahweh!" he screamed into the sky. "Damn you to Tartarus!"

Suddenly, the sand around them began to tremble.

The trembling turned into a swirling as if they'd been caught in a large whirlpool of sand.

Then they were sucked down into the earth as in a sinkhole.

It was the jaws of the never-satisfied Canaanite Mot opening wide to consume its Negeb victims.

The healing gods did not find Set in the desert Land of Shasu. Instead, they descended into the depths of Sheol.

・・・・・

Caleb the Kenizzite worked in the smithing shop late at night with his father Jephunneh secretly forging weapons in preparation for Israel's imminent departure from Egypt. They'd stored these all over the cities in the homes of tribal chiefs. Many were buried in the sand in watertight boxes for the right moment when the sons of Israel would be required to fight. They did not know when this would happen or who would lead them, but many believed that the time was at hand and the Deliverer was at the door.

Caleb and his pupil Hoshea were united in devotion to give their lives in service to the Deliverer once he arose—whomever it would be. When they'd met the man Moses and seen his signs, both their spirits were quickened, and they knew that Deliverer was Moses.

And though Moses had told them that Yahweh would be delivering them without an earthly army, they would surely need weapons after their deliverance. So they continued to forge them for the future.

Jephunneh checked the molten mass burning in his stone container. It was bright-red hot. Ready for pour. It was a small amount, enough for a single sword. Jephunneh was a master craftsman, sixty years of age but still going strong. Metalworking kept a man fit though the smoke and heat could be dangerous.

Grabbing the tongs, he locked them on the stone vessel. He pulled it out of the fire and set it on the table by a sickle-shaped mold for a *khopesh* sword, the weapon of choice for many warriors.

Just then Caleb heard a sound. He exchanged a concerned glance with his father. The forge was away from the residential area and on an elevated ridge overlooking the river where the smoke and noise would cause less problems. Blacksmithing was a filthy job.

And no one visited at night.

Caleb and Jephunneh both stiffened to attention as a man and woman approached the shop. The man had long hair and a tattered cloak. The woman was bundled up for the cold and walked devotedly beside her husband.

They seemed harmless enough. But Caleb kept his hammer in his hand as he stepped forward to meet the visitors. Beside the table, Jephunneh watched closely.

"Greetings," said the visitor. "I am looking for a blacksmith by the name of Caleb ben Jephunneh. I hear he does excellent work."

As the man strode closer to the torchlight, Caleb realized his hair looked like a wig. And his wife looked a bit odd in her make-up. A homely woman that looked more like a…

The visitors threw off their disguises, revealing themselves as two bald priests from the temple of Ra armed with long daggers.

Behind Jephunneh, eight other priests of Ra jumped into the shop area from the darkness. They all had shaved heads and the eye of Ra painted on their chests, and all carried an assassin's long dagger.

Seeing his father surrounded by eight shadow warriors, Caleb rushed back into the shop. But Jephunneh was no weak old man. His first impulse was to pick up the molten metal with the tongs and swing it at the nearest attackers.

One of them screamed as the molten hot material hit him in the chest and burned through his body.

The second attacker dodged and moved for Jephunneh. Caleb's thrown metal hammer knocked him out of the way, crushing his skull.

Jephunneh picked up an unfinished short sword on the table just in time to deflect a fourth attacker's thrusts.

Caleb was now without a weapon. He grabbed a leather sharpening strap off a pole just as three assassins rushed him. The first one was the fake woman. Caleb used the strap to wrap around the killer's knife hand, kicked in the knee of the one next to him, and shoved the fake woman into the third killer.

Picking up the dropped dagger, he finished off the one with a broken knee by a downward thrust into the sternum.

He looked across the shop for his special whip sword and saw it hanging in its sheath from another pole.

"Rahab!" he yelled out. And his father knew exactly what to do.

Jephunneh bolted for the ridge.

It looked like he was running away from the shop, but he was actually drawing the assassins out into the open.

Three of them followed.

Caleb had the other four with him.

He ran across the shop for the sword.

He was blocked by an assassin ready to cut him down. Caleb grabbed a mitt that was used for high heat. It was thick enough to protect a hand against a blade.

The attacker slashed downward at Caleb, who reached out and grabbed the blade with the mitt. He kneed the attacker in the groin and kept going until he reached his sword. Whipping it off the pole, he ran for the open after his father.

Jephunneh swung wildly at the three who were closing in on him.

He was buying time for his son.

Caleb made it to the open with his four assassins right behind him.

He watched the swipe of a dagger strike his father in the thigh.

Caleb unfurled Rahab. She was a ten-foot-long whip sword given to him by a mysterious man named Gabriel. The man had also taught Caleb how to use the sword with a special fighting technique that he now used on these hapless unprepared amateur assassins.

He cracked it like a whip, and it took off the arm of Jephunneh's adversary.

"Down!" Caleb yelled.

Jephunneh dove to the ground. The other two assassins were about to jump him from behind. Instead, they experienced the wrath of Rahab cutting through both of their torsos, dropping them like butcher's meat.

Caleb turned to face the other four who now circled him. He was the true target here.

He smiled. Never encircle a man with Rahab in his hand.

He pulled the blade from behind him forward. When it reached its full length outward, he snapped backward and in a circular motion over his head.

The blade spun around like a twirling fan, cutting all four of the men's heads off. One of them was smaller than the others, so it only cut the top of his skull off, leaving half his brain on the ground. The other three lay dead in pools of their own blood.

Caleb paused, listening for any other attackers.

"Well done, my son," came Jephunneh's voice as he limped over to him.

But Jephunneh stopped suddenly with a jolt and a grunt.

He fell forward to the ground, a dagger in his back.

The one-armed assassin had one last attack left in him.

Caleb stepped forward and snapped the whip sword, cutting off the killer's head. Then he dropped his sword and jumped down to where Jephunneh lay on the ground.

"Father!"

He could see the dagger had gone through Jephunneh's back and hit his heart. His father was dying.

"Son, you have made me proud. You have trained well to be a great warrior."

For the first time in his life, Caleb felt tears pouring down his cheeks. "You have made me the man I am."

"Hopefully not with my faults." Jephunneh chuckled and coughed up blood.

Caleb burned like fire within. "I will seek vengeance."

"No. Seek Yahweh. I believe our God has something great in store for you, Caleb."

Caleb wanted to protest, but their time together on earth was over. Jephunneh's last breath slipped from his body. His eyes remained staring at his son.

Caleb gently closed his father's eyes.

• • • • •

Across the river, Horus arose from his hidden location in the reeds and returned to the temple of Ra.

He stood before the king of the gods. The remaining deities of the council awaited anxiously his intelligence.

"Father, from my position I saw no angelic presence protecting the Kenizzite."

"So he is a mere dog," concluded Ra.

"But he used the heavenly weapon with great skill. He killed all ten assassins."

"Never send a man to do a god's job," Ra sighed. "Onuris…"

The hunter-god stepped forward. "Yes, my king."

"Make your way through enemy lines, find the tribal leader of Judah, Nahshon, and kill him."

"Is that wise, my father?" asked Horus.

"Onuris has already gotten past their security once. He can do it again. But just to be sure, I will use the high priest to send more of his assassins. A double force of human and divine should shore up our odds for success."

CHAPTER 38

Seven

Jambres had barely survived the plague of boils. He had his senses back but was still not well enough to perform his priestly duties. Though the boils had left scars on him, he covered them with make-up so that other priests would not question his cleanness for conducting his rituals in sacred space.

Jannes brought him some water to drink and left him for Pharaoh's morning river walk. Just as Jambres was getting better, Jannes was feeling worse, more exhausted from lack of sleep because the dreams of taunting spirits returned every night. He prayed that it would stop. But every night he found himself again in Ra's throne room with the voices assaulting him in his head.

He stumbled his way to the palace in a tired mental fog.

At the river shrine, Moses and Aaron again showed up and demanded of Pharaoh. This was becoming redundant and exhausting to Jannes. But also frightening, not knowing what new destruction would come upon them, as each new plague seemed to raise the stakes.

Moses said, "Thus says Yahweh, the god of the Hebrews, 'Let my people go that they may serve me. For by now, I could have put out my hand and smited you and all your seed forever. But for this purpose I have raised you up, O Pharaoh, to show you my power so that my name may be proclaimed in all the earth.'"

Pharaoh grumbled, "I find your god to be a pompous, arrogant glory hound obsessed with his own self-importance."

Jannes was disgusted with the king. This Hebrew deity had humbled Pharaoh multiple times already, and yet the king remained defiant in his pride. Years of damage had been done to the land, countless Egyptians had died, and still Pharaoh Dudimose would not allow the Hebrew people to sacrifice to their god. It was amazing how much reality mere humans could deny when they considered themselves to be gods.

Yet was it any different from the pride of the common man who remained faithful to that god-king? Was it any different from what he and Jambres had done in their search for eternal life? A few more days and Jambres would be well enough for them both to escape Egypt and all this devastation.

Moses stretched out his staff toward heaven and continued the words of Yahweh. "'Because you continue to exalt yourself against my people and will not let them go, behold, this time tomorrow I will cause heavy hail to fall such as never has been in Egypt from the day of its founding until now. Every man and beast that does not seek shelter will die beneath the storm of my judgment.'"

Everyone's attention was drawn to the east where a distant storm cloud appeared. Lightning lit up the dark skies, followed by the clap of thunder. Sheets of rain could be seen falling like a wall of water. The cloud was advancing toward them.

But Pharaoh turned his back and returned to the palace.

Jannes caught up with him. "My king, shall we alert the populace to take shelter?"

"No," grumbled Dudimose. "I and my household will be safe in our underground tunnels."

From time immemorial, pharaohs cut tunnels beneath their palaces for secret purposes just such as this.

"Let the innocent die at the hands of Yahweh, and they will hate him and worship me even more."

Jannes was horrified. Pharaoh was becoming a genocidal despot to his own people. He would rather his own subjects die if it could aid his agenda.

Jannes had to get the word out without using official means. He knew the queen was not pleased with any of this though she could say nothing without fear of reprisal. But she did have servants who were loyal to her.

•••••

In the unseen realm of the temple of Ra, the creator sun god was becoming as angry and frustrated as Pharaoh Dudimose. Nothing he'd done was able to stop the de-creation of the cosmos. And every god he'd sent to fight had been defeated and eliminated. His power was waning like the moon. He was being eclipsed by Yahweh's judgments. His actions were becoming more defiant and irrational.

Ra sent the gods of sky, wind, and moisture to take control of the coming hailstorm, even though every god sent to counter each plague had been overcome. He was sending his own soldiers to their doom.

He would have even sent Set—also a storm god—into the hopeless tempest, but Set was still in the Negeb somewhere.

• • • • •

Negeb

Ba'al the storm god convened an assembly of Canaanite deities at the request of the visiting Set in the southern reaches of the Negeb. They met at Kiriath-Arba, a city on the top of a large hillside. It was the home of the Sons of Anak, also called Anakim, a tribe of blonde and red-haired, fair-skinned giants with muscular bodies and extra-long necks upon which they wore necklaces of gold and bones. They were one of the most fearsome of a number of giant clans in the land, and they dominated the territory west of the Jordan River.

The Anakim had built a high place for Ba'al at the top of the ridge. It was a Phoenician-style temple with a large courtyard and stone altar of sacrifice out front. The gods met in the Holy of Holies inside the tripartite building. Ba'al led the meeting. He was a huge, muscular warrior who had a mighty mace not unlike Set's. The two storm gods were equals in many ways.

The coastal gods Dagon of the Philistines and Asherah of Tyre were there as well. Chemosh, the Moabite warrior deity, and Ashtart, the violent goddess of sex and war, were the most recent arrivals.

They had all listened patiently to Set's offer of a treaty between the gods of Canaan and Egypt.

"How do we know we can trust you?" Ba'al demanded.

"Because I am offering you the very kingdom of Egypt itself as spoils." Set responded.

"Exactly," said Ashtart. "What Watcher gives up his allotted territory without a fight?"

"There is a fight right now," he answered. "And we are definitely losing to Yahweh. The plagues are not merely devastating our land and people but also eliminating her gods. Yahweh is de-creating Egypt, returning it to primordial chaos. By the time he is done with it, you will be able to send in your human armies and take it over without a fight. It will be like taking a honey stick from a baby's hand."

Ba'al appeared hopeful. "We have a coalition of forces with the Amalekites."

"An unruly lot of cannibals," complained Chemosh.

"Nevertheless," countered Ba'al, "they are an effective army of nomads who traffic in that area."

Ashtart said, "Better to spill their blood than the Anakim's."

Ba'al continued, "The Sons of Arba could help lead the Amalekite forces with a minimum of our own troops."

The Sons of Arba was an honored name given to Kiriath-Arba's three giant Anakim brothers, young rising leaders of the army. Their names were Sheshai, Ahiman, and Talmai. Sheshai was making a name for the three of them with his ruthless battle strategies and tactics. Ahiman was a mighty warrior rumored to be the largest giant in the land at close to fifteen feet in height.

Set explained, "I am worshipped in the delta. If Yahweh succeeds in breaking the Egyptians—and I am confident he will—then you can conquer the Black Land easily. And if the Egyptians let the Hebrews go, your Hyksos invaders can take up residence in the delta where the Hebrews had lived."

"It would be nice to get the Egyptians off our backs," said Dagon.

Ba'al asked Set, "What is in it for you?"

"Look, you and I are both similar storm gods. It will be nothing to switch their worship from me to you. I can take on your identity as Ba'al of the delta, and you will receive the worship without having to leave Canaan. I just want to stay in Egypt."

"You want to rule Egypt," quipped Asherah.

"Of course," he replied. "But I will rule as a client king for Ba'al, the Most High." Set looked straight at Ba'al, unblinking, "Think of yourself as Pharaoh and I as your vizier."

Ba'al considered the offer. He suspected that this was the long-awaited return to Canaan of Abraham's seed. Ba'al had faced Abraham in the battle of nine kings in the Valley of Siddim. He had joined with Ashtart to take over Canaan, knowing that one day they would face their ultimate enemy in combat over that contested land. He suspected that the day had finally arrived.

Ashtart became excited as she always did with the prospect of war. Drawing her sword, she exclaimed, "What are we waiting for?"

"Now is not the time," said Set. "Pharaoh has not yet bowed the knee. If we wait until he does, you can take over Egypt without shedding blood."

"That is no fun," said Ashtart. "I enjoy bathing in the blood of my enemies."

Set said, "When the Hebrews are released, they are coming here because they believe it is their allotment. Then you will have plenty of opportunity to bathe—in Hebrew blood."

"Excellent," said Ba'al. He addressed the others. "I will go with Set to establish my rule in the delta through him and then return here to prepare for a holy war with the Hebrews."

· · · · ·

The Delta

Nut the sky goddess, Shu the god of wind, and Tefnut the goddess of moisture worked with Thoth to prepare their defense against the coming storm. None of these gods had any true power to create or control weather. They were Watchers who had taken on the identities of the various deities to inspire human worship.

But because of their ancient origins, these three deities had accumulated thousands of years of knowledge of the physical world that humans had yet to learn. That knowledge afforded them the ability to act as if they had Yahweh's creative powers even though they only had abilities granted by Yahweh for their *elohim* sphere of existence. Thus their granted powers in the unseen realm and their knowledge of natural elements appeared as signs and wonders to ignorant humans.

They could not create storms from nothing, but they could manipulate earthly elements with other elements to create the natural effect they sought. To "create" a rainstorm, for instance, they might seed the clouds with a chemical element that would stimulate precipitation.

In this case, they sought to *stop* a storm so that it would not produce the prophesied hail. Racing to the east to reach the storm before it arrived in the delta area, the gods brought with them a special powder created by Thoth that consisted of an acidic derivative, a compound that would absorb water like a sponge when seeded in the clouds.

In this case, the powder absorbed two thousand times its weight in water. The result was that the storm would weaken as it required more energy to move the heavier drops of water. The fury would subside, dissipating the storm within hours.

This technique had been used in the past as a way to deceive the Egyptians into thinking that their sacrifices had stopped the wrath of the gods. But it was simply a higher-level manipulation of the natural order.

Since the gods were *elohim* beings of the unseen realm, they could elevate in the sky with these materials. They were perceived as principalities or powers of the air.

The storm was moving swiftly and would reach the delta within the hour. The sun was already dawning in the east. The gods had moved in and out of the thunder, lightning, and rain to pour out their maleficent powder of death.

It began to do its work. The energy of the storm lessened as water drops became heavier. The gods danced and sang together as the rain fell, drenching them in a flood. They would be the first to successfully avert a plague and gain Ra's praise and blessings. No doubt it would also result in more worship from the humans and more power within the pantheon.

But suddenly the storm clouds turned darker. A bolt of lightning larger than any seen before burned like fire from heaven, hitting Nut in the head. Bursting into flames, she fried to a crisp instantly.

A huge updraft sucked the other three into the air, then reversed and slammed them into the ground with crushing force.

Instead of decreasing, the power and energy of the storm increased.

And then the hail began.

At first, they were normal-sized droplets of ice.

But then those heavy droplets of water created by the gods' seeding froze in the upper atmosphere and plummeted to the earth. Some of the droplets consolidated as they froze, creating boulder-sized hailstones. Two-, five-, and twenty-pound chunks rained down with devastation.

A hundred-pound ice rock hit Shu and smashed him like an animal under a chariot wheel.

This was followed by a wave of hail upon the gods that pounded them into the ground, then crushed every inch of their bodies—bones and flesh—into frozen mush.

Yahweh had providentially used the gods to intensify the very storm they sought to deaden. As the hailstones were pulverizing the gods, some of them saw the irony and despaired.

And they had been judged.

Then the deadly hailstorm arrived at the delta.

· · · · ·

Pharaoh and his household were safely hidden away in the tunnels beneath the palace. But the populace had no such protection. With the discreet help of the queen and her servants, Jannes had helped to spread word of mouth throughout the delta, but the plague was so close at hand that many simply did not know about it until it hit them from above.

Some people had sheltered their families and animals in their houses and reinforced their wooden roofs. Others were caught in the fields tending crops or with their herds. Waves of huge crushing hail wiped out everything in its path: human, animal, plants, and trees.

Some Egyptians noticed that the Hebrew districts were once again protected from the hail. The pitch-black storm clouds and rains circled Israelite districts as though each were a separate eye of the storm. The hail stopped at the riverbanks like magic. Lightning lit up the darkness like bolts of fire. One's bones could feel the cracks of thunder.

A multitude of Egyptians ran for the river and jumped in, trying to swim across to safety on the Hebrew isles.

Many of them could not swim across the current and were swept away to drown. Ice chunks hit other swimmers, who bled to death as they drowned. Smelling the blood, crocodiles launched into the water and attacked both living and dead victims. The Nile became an explosion of thrashing and red-foaming splashes.

And hail continued to assault them from the heavens.

But hundreds of Egyptians did make it across to safety on the Hebrew side. Crowds of Israelites felt compassion for their suffering and welcomed them, bringing towels, blankets, and food.

And that provided the cover Onuris and the temple assassins needed to slip past the angelic guardians who kept watch around the cities. Crowds of panicking Egyptians meeting crowds of anxious Hebrews in a confused muddle of humanity. An answered prayer for the predators who walked among them.

On the Hebrew side, Nahshon led his family in bringing assistance to the woeful Egyptian victims. He was the head of the tribe of Judah, as anyone could see from his closely-cropped hair and beard and his expensive garments and sandals. But there was no division of status in an emergency like this. Nobles and commoners alike worked together to rescue those in need.

Nahshon draped a blanket over a woman and her child and offered them some bread. He looked up for the next Egyptian to help and was overwhelmed by the masses of humanity.

He turned around to find himself facing a bald priest of Ra with a dagger raised high for plunging into Nahshon's heart. Nahshon froze like an innocent rabbit before a wolf.

Then out of nowhere from behind, a hand grabbed the priest's dagger, and a foot swept the assassin to the ground. In two swift moves, the priest's dagger was sticking in his own throat.

"Hoshea!" shouted Nahshon.

Hoshea ben Nun looked up and shouted, "They are trying to kill you. Quick, follow me."

He pulled the nobleman by the wrist. Nahshon resisted. "But my family!"

"Caleb is with them. They will be safe."

The nobleman turned to see the bald blacksmith waving at him next to his wife and children.

"It is you they are after."

"Why me?"

"I cannot tell you right now." Hoshea pulled Nahshon through the crush of the noisy crowd. "Just follow me."

"Who are they?" Nahshon shouted.

"Priests of Ra. I saw several others."

Nahshon thought he saw another one bobbing in and out of the crowds following them. "Where are we going?"

"Anywhere away from here."

In the unseen realm, Onuris, disguised as a small, poor Egyptian serf among the masses, had seen the entire incident. He saw the assassin priests trying to follow their target, pushing through the crowds.

There were thirty of them.

Onuris decided to take a less direct route in case Nahshon had angelic protection. He started jogging the opposite direction where his enemies would not be looking.

It wasn't really the opposite direction. He could see the target being led into the forest. He was going to run around the island and intercept the humans on the other side.

But first he had to pick up his weapons that he had secretly floated into the reeds around the back of the isle.

Hoshea led Nahshon to the edge of a ridge and over the river to Caleb's blacksmith shop. Entering, he picked out a short double-sided sword for himself and handed a *khopesh* to the nobleman.

"I am not a warrior," Nahshon protested.

"Do you want to die?"

"Of course not."

Hoshea handed him the handle of the sword. "Just hack at your enemy."

Nahshon took the blade reluctantly. It felt heavy in his hand. Hoshea's family had been close to Nahshon's for years. Nahshon had known Hoshea was training as a warrior, but he had never seen him in action until now.

Picking up some rope, Hoshea draped it around his shoulders, then picked up a folded net and handed it to Nahshon.

"What's this for?"

"I will explain on the way." Hoshea added a bow and quiver of arrows to his load. "Let us go."

They left the shop and entered the small forest at the edge of the isle.

Hoshea whispered to Nahshon as they walked through the brush. "A few nights ago, assassin priests of Ra, just like those who attacked you, attacked Jephunneh, that blacksmith shop's owner, and his son Caleb. They killed Caleb's father, but Caleb was the real target."

"Why would they care about us?"

"We did not know at first. But as we consulted, we realized that you are both from the tribe of Judah. And I remembered the old prophecy about a future king coming from Judah. So we figured that they are trying to kill the ones they think could seed the birth of that savior."

"But what about Moses? He seems to be the Deliverer."

"Moses is a Levite, so he is not the ultimate target."

"How do they know about our lineage?"

"I do not know. Maybe their scribes have our genealogies."

Hoshea began to hook up the net to some rope and tackle that had been attached to some trees.

"What is this?"

"Caleb and I thought to prepare some traps in case something like this happened."

Hoshea moved on to another half-made trap and set it.

Suddenly, he pulled Nahshon down to the ground behind a bush.

He whispered, "Someone is coming."

Within moments, Nahshon too could hear the sound of leaves and plants rustling nearby.

Peeking out, Hoshea could see three shadows approaching from a short distance. He pushed Nahshon into the bush and pulled the leaves over him. "Stay here. If anyone but me finds you, use your sword."

"But wait—"

Before Nahshon could complain, Hoshea ran off into the dark. The younger man was so stealthy Nahshon could not hear a sound of his movements.

The three assassins didn't hear Hoshea either as he slipped up to a tree, waited until they were near, then cut a rope that held a series of iron weights in the trees. The weights fell to the ground, pulling the large net on the ground up into the air.

The three captured assassins yelped for help.

Hoshea drew three swift arrows and silenced them.

But it was too late.

Others were already nearby.

As they arrived in the clearing where the net was, Hoshea used his secret position to launch more missiles. He took down one, two, three more before the remaining assailants dove to the ground or behind trees.

Hoshea ran loudly—in a very specific direction.

Two priest assassins followed him.

But they did not jump where they should have jumped. Instead, they tripped over a hidden rope and tumbled onto one another. Before they could get their bearings, they were pierced through by a log studded with an array of blades that fell from above.

Hoshea hid in the brush until he saw more shadow assassins approaching cautiously. There must have been about twenty of them.

Hoshea didn't care. This was a worthy challenge. He actually thrived on the inner chill of energy that seemed to surge within, giving him heightened awareness and more endurance.

He thrived on killing evil.

Drawing his blade slowly from its leather sheath, Hoshea gripped it with a restrained rage and set off like a ghost into the night.

The assassins traveled in pairs.

One pair heard a sound behind them and turned. Their throats were slashed in one swipe. They fell to the ground, gurgling their blood in death.

Another pair didn't see Hoshea behind a tree until one of their heads was lopped off. The other's followed almost immediately after.

One moron was walking alone in a small clearing, so Hoshea launched out behind him, hacking him down in one swipe.

Then he realized it was a trap.

He suddenly found himself surrounded by six assassins.

"Where is the Judahite?" one of them shouted.

"Come and get him," said Hoshea. He mustered his hatred of the Egyptians that he had built up over all his life. He could feel the four hundred years of oppression surging in his veins.

They came at him.

Hoshea launched into an attack with his sword so furious that none of them could stand. He was pure brute force. He hacked them all to pieces within seconds.

The irony was that Hoshea could feel himself losing his mind in the hatred. He almost did not know what he was doing.

His training had kicked in.

Only when he'd finished, his body drenched in enemy blood and their body parts scattered about, was he finally aware again of where he was. Hyperaware, he heaved deep, shuddering breaths.

Then he heard a new batch of assassins rushing through the brush toward him. He took off to Nahshon's hiding place, running like the wind. He knew this forest, and he knew where he was going. They did not.

He picked up the bow and quiver where he'd left them.

He made it to the bush where Nahshon was hiding.

"Nahshon," he whispered, pulling aside the brush.

But the Judahite elder wasn't there.

Suddenly, Hoshea heard a grunt. A dark figure launched at him, swinging down with a blade. It struck his right arm, and he dropped his sword.

Then he recognized Nahshon. The older man's eyes bulged with fear. "Oh. I am so sorry."

Hoshea jerked left and pushed Nahshon back. A dagger whizzed by and stuck in the tree. "Run!"

Hoshea led Nahshon through the brush. He could hear the assassins not far behind. He held his wounded sword arm to stop the bleeding. He had been planning on training with his left arm for just such a situation but had not gotten around to it.

They came upon a creek bed, and Hoshea halted. Nahshon looked at him for directions.

Hoshea held his finger to his mouth, shushing him.

Then he pointed to the creek bed. It was small tributary from the river, about eight feet wide.

The storm made the sky so dark Nahshon had to squint to recognize glistening scales in the lightning flashes. Filling the entire creek were backs of crocodiles, sleeping or resting. Thousands of them. They must have come here to escape the hailstorm still raging outside the Hebrew isles. The entire creek was full of them, bank to bank all up and down the entire creek bed.

"There is no time," Hoshea whispered quickly. "You must trust me."

Nahshon's eyes went wide with fright.

"They are at rest. They are not expecting us. If we run quickly, we can step over their backs before they realize what is happening. We can be on the other side of the bank in four steps."

"No. You are crazy."

"I am wounded." Hoshea held up his arm Nahshon had cut. "I cannot use my sword anymore."

The noises in the brush were growing louder. A dozen shadows were almost upon them.

Hoshea whispered, "If you go first, you have the best chance."

Nahshon looked down into the dark, roiling creek bed. "What if I miss one of the backs and fall in?"

"Do not miss."

Nahshon rolled his eyes.

"Just see the backs as stones. Do not think about what is beneath the water. Just see the stones. And do not stop."

Hoshea made his last argument. "There is no more time. This way is just four steps. That way is priests who will gut you and pull your intestines out while you watch."

Nahshon nodded okay. The two men slunk down to the bank as quietly as possible.

Hoshea could see Nahshon was trembling. He wanted to keep the older man from thinking anymore about it. He held up three fingers. Then closed his fist and counted: one…two…three.

With a little yelp of fear, Nahshon began stepping across the scaly backs in the water.

Hoshea followed closely behind.

Nahshon made it across and ran like a rabbit up the bank to safety.

Hoshea slipped on the last back because it had started to move. He made it to the bank but fell to the ground. He saw the mouth of a crocodile open wide and hiss at him.

But it did not strike. It was trying to figure out what creature had disturbed its slumber.

Getting up, Hoshea ran up the bank. He found Nahshon sitting in the tall grass.

"I peed my kilt."

Hoshea smiled. "So did I."

He hadn't, but he knew it would make Nahshon feel better.

He moved over to a long log that lay at the top of the ridge, tied up for this very moment.

Just then, the assassins breached the other bank side. There were ten of them. Seeing Hoshea and Nahshon, they started for them.

Hoshea cut the rope holding the log. It rolled down to the water and hit the crocodiles just as the first three assassins were trying to hop off the backs in the water. All three fell into the jaws of the agitated reptiles.

The crocodiles attacked in a bloodbath of teeth, claws, and tail. The water turned as blood-red as the Nile had been.

Hoshea brought up his bow but could not draw back the string.

Taking it from him, Nahshon tried to nock an arrow and shoot it. The arrow flew wide of any mark.

The other assassins backed up. Making a running start, they tried to jump over the crocodiles to the other side.

But the distance was just a bit too far.

A few landed a foot or so away from the bank and were quickly pulled under.

One made it just barely to the other side on land. But a reptilian snout launched out of the water and pulled him into the feeding frenzy.

That was the last one, Hoshea realized.

The assassins had all been taken by the denizens of the Nile.

A fitting end for the servants of Nachash.

Hoshea pulled Nahshon after him to search for a way back.

But both men stopped short at the sight of a bearded seven-foot-tall warrior gleaming like bronze and hold a hunting spear.

An angel? Hoshea wondered.

The unearthly warrior drew back the spear, aiming right at Nahshon.

But before he could heave it, the sound of a tree rustling was followed by another gleaming warrior falling from above and landing right in front of Nahshon, his knees bending like powerful springs to break the fall.

Another angel? This new arrival rose to his full height of seven feet, ready to defend the human.

"Mikael," the first one said. "Thank you for confirming that we had the right one to kill this time."

"You will not be killing anyone this evening, Onuris."

Onuris launched his spear at Mikael.

The archangel side-stepped and caught it with ease.

Hoshea pulled Nahshon aside behind a tree.

Onuris drew a sword. Mikael drew his.

Hoshea then witnessed one of the quickest fights he had ever seen.

As Onuris attacked Mikael, the archangel took down the hunter-god in three swift moves. A defensive block, a disarming, and a thrust through the heart. This Mikael was powerful.

The archangel then used his sword to cut off the hunter's head.

Holding up the head, Mikael said to the humans, "You are safe. Go home to your family."

And he vanished into the night.

Hoshea turned to his ward and said, "Your bloodline must be quite important for the guardian angel of God's people to be protecting you."

Nahshon could only stand with a look of wonder.

Hoshea and Nahshon returned to their families in the Hebrew quarter to tell their story.

The head of Onuris was returned to the temple of Ra.

CHAPTER 39

Eight

Jannes had the taunting spirit dreams again. But this time something was different. The voices laughed at him and told him that today he was going to die.

When he awoke in the morning to meet with Pharaoh, he found himself too sick to get out of bed. His head too dizzy for him to stand. He sat back down, and the urge to vomit rose within him. He stooped over his chamber pot and retched. What came out was black and green bile like he'd never seen before. It looked unnatural.

Entering, Jambres found his brother on his knees on the floor. "What is it? Are you unwell? Is it the plague?" He helped Jannes back into bed.

Jannes felt delirious. "We were going to leave tonight. We must leave."

Jambres settled him down. "Right now, you must rest. You are clearly ill, my brother."

"It does not matter. We cannot wait." Jannes heard the voices again but this time he knew he was awake. They were laughing at him, mocking him. His stomach and throat burned like fire. "We must leave Egypt tonight."

Jambres held Jannes down gently. "You are not going anywhere tonight, my brother. You must rest. As soon as you get well, we will leave."

Slumping back into the bed, Jannes felt himself losing consciousness as Jambres left him.

• • • • •

Nahshon had brought Hoshea to Moses in the early morning. They met in the yard of Aaron's home. Moses looked him over. He was young but lean and strong. He bowed to one knee before Moses.

With a laugh, Moses pulled him to his feet. "Up, young man. I am not a king."

"You are the Deliverer," Hoshea begged to differ.

Moses brushed it off. "Nahshon told me of your exploits last night. Well done. You are a skilled warrior."

"My lord, it is Yahweh who rescued Nahshon last night. I am simply his servant."

Aaron stepped outside to meet the young man. Moses saw Hoshea build up the courage to say something.

Hoshea blurted it out. "I want to be your assistant! I will serve you and protect you with my life."

Moses smiled again. "And you are zealous, indeed."

"I told you so," Nahshon said with a grin. The three elders laughed.

Hoshea bowed his head humbly.

Moses looked at the young man thoughtfully. Then said, "Hoshea ben Nun, I will take you as my assistant."

Hoshea's eyes brightened. He looked like an excited puppy.

Moses added, "And I will give you a new name. From now on, it will be Joshua, which means 'Yahweh saves.'"

Hoshea considered it and quickly said, "Joshua it is. I am Joshua ben Nun. Yahweh is salvation!"

Moses said, "Unfortunately, assistants usually spend most of their time doing mundane tasks, and it is a rare occasion when they are called upon to kill thirty assassins." He smiled. "Are you willing to do boring tasks that no one else wants to do?"

"I will learn, and I will do anything you need. And when we fight the Egyptians, I will lead our men in battle."

Moses shared a serious look with the other two elders. "Joshua, I have already stated clearly: we will not be fighting the Egyptians. Yahweh has told me that *he* will fight for us."

"You mean the plagues?"

"Well, yes. And when Pharaoh finally lets us go, we will leave peacefully for the desert."

"But Pharaoh is not letting us go. He has refused to do so even after seven plagues."

"That is true. And Yahweh has told me there are more yet to come."

"Why?"

"I do not know why. I trust that Yahweh knows what he is doing, and I obey him."

He paused as Joshua nodded thoughtfully, trying to understand and accept his words.

"That is your first lesson of being an assistant. You must subordinate your own desires to your leader's even when it disappoints you."

He saw Joshua smiling with acceptance. The young man dropped down to one knee again. "My lord, you have my blade and my obedience."

Moses pulled him up again, saying light-heartedly, "Joshua, I command you to obey my order to stop kneeling before me."

The others laughed. Joshua smiled though his face flushed red with embarrassment.

Moses turned. "Come, let us go to the river to meet Pharaoh."

Walking through the Hebrew quarter, they took a ferry across the tributary to the Egyptian side. A myriad of bodies of the drowned and half-eaten were piled along the banks for burial. Still unclaimed dead floated in the river.

Moses felt compassion for all the Egyptians still camped on the Hebrew side of the river wondering if the hail would start again though the skies were clear. They had now survived seven plagues and had become a fearful people.

As the ferry arrived at the far bank and they entered the Egyptian district, Moses was overwhelmed by the devastation. Most houses were still standing, their roofs badly damaged or even broken to pieces. But other homes had been pulverized by the large ice boulders, mud brick smashed into piles of rubble. The ice boulders had all melted, leaving the source of the damage invisible. The unseen realm had broken through, wreaked havoc, and closed back up again.

People were caring for the wounded. But many of the dead still lay in the streets, subject to scavenger birds and animals. The sound of women wailing pierced Moses's heart. He could not hate these people. He felt pity for them. Pity that they would have to suffer for the actions of Pharaoh their leader.

And yet Pharaoh was the representative of the people. All peoples and nations rose and fell with their leaders, both earthly and heavenly. So there was a collective responsibility and guilt for cultures that rejected their creator. Yahweh was a just God.

Still, if it had not been for his wife Zipporah back in Midian, Moses might not have cared for these poor souls. He had always been a self-sufficient person who considered most people's suffering to be a deserved part of their station in life. And he'd had little concern for those outside his tribe. But Zipporah's compassionate care for others had moved his heart to see the goodness in treating others the way he would want to be treated. This was not a denial of people's responsibility but an affirmation of their dignity by virtue of their being created in the image of God. One could love the transgressor but hate the transgression.

They walked through the demolished city streets. They passed by fields full of dead animals—cows, goats, sheep, horses—the fruit of those farmers who did not know or heed the warning.

More stench of death with each plague.

Moses noticed that all the crops, the flax and the barley, had also been destroyed by the hail. They had been in the ear and bud. Now they were broken and smashed into the ground. Some could be scavenged, but the bulk of the crops had been lost. He thanked Yahweh that the wheat and emmer were late in coming up this season so that the Egyptians would not all starve to death. But there would be mass shortages and rationing.

When they arrived at the Nile shrine area, it too had been destroyed by the hail. The gateway, the jugs, the images of the gods had all been obliterated. Most of it was just gone, in the river or scattered all around.

Pharaoh and his procession of priests and servants were nowhere to be found. So they marched up to the palace.

When they arrived, Moses saw hundreds of servants cleaning up and trying to repair the massive damage done to the palace grounds. Entire walls of mud brick had been battered back into dirt. Even large portions of stone walls had crumbled.

Moses, Aaron, and Joshua strode over to the wall bordering the grounds below the palace balcony, a mere fifty feet away. Standing along the balcony, Pharaoh and his lector priests stared down at the three men.

Moses spoke the next word from Yahweh to the king.

· · · · ·

Jannes woke up from another fitful sleep. But he was feeling better for the moment. He sat up in his bed to get a drink of water from the jug on the floor. The liquid was like life pouring down his parched throat. Setting the jug back down, he reached beneath the bed to grab the satchel he had packed for their escape. Evidently stuck on something, it gave some resistance.

Jannes yanked harder, and the satchel finally emerged. He looked beneath the satchel for an indication of what had held it fast. To his horror, he found a broken piece of red pottery with his name Jannes written on it in demotic script.

Scrambling out of his bed, he reached beneath it to feel around the dirt floor. Something sharp sticking out of the ground cut into his palm. He pulled it from the dirt and examined it. Another shard of broken pottery.

Horror growing, Jannes used the shard he held in his hand to dig into the dirt beneath his bed. Pulling out several other shards of the same red pottery, he placed them next to each other until he had every piece.

He then placed the pieces together like a puzzle until he could read the inscription.

A dread came over him. The taunting voices in his head returned. They were laughing. The full text was that common to a ritual curse, the breaking of the red pots.

It was a magic technique he and his brother had used many times in the past. The pots were covered with execration texts or names and descriptions of the enemies of the lector priest to be cursed. The pots were then smashed and buried as near to the cursed individual as possible.

These were under *his* bed.

He read the execration text. *Jannes son of Jocham of the tribe of Dan, lector priest of Pharaoh Dudimose, traitor to the king, betrayer of Egypt, demon possessed by the foreign god Yahweh.*

His whole world came crashing in on him. He felt his body shudder. His stomach and throat flamed up again. The laughing voices now accused him, repeating the words he had just read.

He set the pieces on his bed and stared into the abyss of his future.

The sound of the door opening shook him back. He whipped the blanket over the pottery pieces, covering them.

It was Jambres at the door. "Are you feeling better?"

"Not really."

"Well, you missed today's new ranting curse of Moses and his brother. The same thing as before. Thus says Yahweh, 'How long will you refuse to humble yourself before me? Let my people go!'" Jambres rambled through the words with a mocking tone.

"Well, the king would only let them go if they left the women and children behind as a ransom. The king obviously fears Moses has a secret plan to leave for good, so he thought he'd keep some hostages. Only the men would be allowed into the wilderness to sacrifice. An offer Moses immediately refused as he did the king's last seven offers."

Jambres paused dramatically before adding slyly, "Can you guess what the new plague will be tomorrow?"

Jannes was listless, watching his brother without watching him, amazed at how Jambres could act as if he had not just cursed his own blood brother.

"Locusts. Can you believe it? A plague of locusts covering the face of the land like no swarm has ever done in the history of Egypt. We tried to advise the king to reconsider in light of the fact that we just had much of our crops already wiped out by hail. He even brought Moses and Aaron into his court and tried to negotiate. But Moses would not budge, nor would Pharaoh. I think we had better get ready for a temple full of locusts."

Still looking off into the distance, Jannes said, "Maybe we should go tonight before the plague hits."

"You are still not well, my brother. We should wait until you are."

"I am not going to get well."

Jambres looked confused. Then a realization spread across his face.

Jannes pulled back the blanket to reveal the broken red pots. He felt nauseous again.

Now Jambres became cold and calculated. "You betrayed the king. You betrayed Egypt. You betrayed the gods who gave us eternal life."

Jannes felt the voices breaking in again. "My dear brother."

"You are not my brother. I do not know you. I am a servant of Ra and Horus, the incarnation on earth."

Jannes felt dead inside. "I trusted you. I told you the truth. We have both been living a lie. We are serving a false god who is the true Devourer-of-Souls."

Jannes stopped. He lost his balance. The voices blasted in his ears now. He could not hear anything else. He started to tremble. His trembling turned into a seizure. He fell back in bed. His body flopped like a fish out of water, desperately trying to hold onto life.

Then the voices became entities that swirled around his body like ghosts. Dozens of them.

They were evil spirits, and as they left his body, he felt everything in him turn to rot. His hair dropped out. His skin turned aged and thin. His flesh shriveled so that he looked like a living cadaver. His eyes yellowed. His teeth fell out. His body excreted out of every orifice, vomit, excrement, piss, and blood.

All of this occurred within a few moments as Jambres watched in horror.

Jannes died with a look of terror on his shriveled, aged face.

And Jambres finally realized that the eternal youth which they had received from the gods was achieved by spirits possessing their bodies, propping them up with their supernatural presence, but only so long as those spirits remained. When they left his body, Jannes returned to the true state of his age of over a hundred years old.

Jambres made the decision that he would never let that happen to him. He would obey the gods and fight this demon Yahweh to the end.

• • • • •

In the early morning hours, Jambres buried his brother, then led the entire priesthood in sacrifices to the gods of crops: Osiris, Min, Nepri, Renenutet, Sothis, and last of all the god of locusts, Senenhem. They sought to empower the gods with strength to protect their fertile land from the coming plague.

In the unseen realm, those gods were forced by Ra to go out and fight the plague. In truth, Ra was so enraged with his pride and rebellion against Yahweh that he had become irrational with madness. He knew he was sending the gods to their doom.

For he knew that none of these gods had any true control over the crops or locusts. Just as the gods of the Nile had no true control over the Nile and the gods of wind, earth, and sky had no control over wind, earth, or sky and the gods of pests or pestilence had no control over their chaos. These were all fictional narratives crafted to control human beings. The Nile would rise, the crops would grow, and the pests would come because Yahweh, the true creator God, controlled the regularity of seasons and all creation. The gods were rebels with delusions of grandeur.

But they had to try something to fight this next plague. Anything.

The seasonal locusts would come from the south, so the gods went to Memphis, the southernmost city before the delta. They solicited the help of human priests through visions. They warned the priests of what was coming and executed their plan. Since locusts are normally deterred by smoke, the humans built a long line of refuse to burn, creating a huge wall of smoke to repulse the coming insects.

But this was not a seasonal swarm. Yahweh had caused a strong east wind to blow in from the desert of Ta Mefkat and across Mew Kedew, the Red Sea. It lasted all day and night. In the morning, it brought a swarm so large it appeared to be a dust storm covering everything in its wake.

That east wind also blew the line of fire's smoke to the west and out of the way of the locust army coming with the wind.

Osiris, Senenhem, and the other crop gods got caught in the swarm on their way back to the delta. All six of them were enveloped by the cloud. Normally, locusts only ate vegetation, but Yahweh had changed their habits this one time—as he had changed the habits of the scarabs. Within minutes, the gods were consumed by their chomping jaws.

Set was also a god of crops, but he remained safe in the Negeb away from the de-creation tearing apart Egypt and her gods.

·····

Pharaoh Dudimose looked out from his palace heights. It looked like a dark blanket had been thrown over the entire land. He had never seen or heard of a swarm like this in all his life—or the entire dynasty for that matter. Within a day, all the plants and vegetation, crops and trees of the entire land of Egypt had been eaten by the locusts. The vegetation that had not been destroyed by the hail had been consumed by these cursed insects.

He kept swiping away the buzzing little demons. The ringing sound and munching of the ruthless pests caused his head to ache. Covering his ears, he screamed for it to stop. He felt himself losing his sanity. He could not think straight.

He ran back into the palace, the sick sound of crunching locust bodies beneath his every fleeing step.

They were everywhere. Even inside the palace. Servants worked overtime trying to sweep them away and close doors. And this had gone on all day and night. As one of the servants got in his way, Dudimose shoved the man against a wall with a crash.

But the problem was worse than losing his sanity. With the elimination of almost all their food sources, many Egyptians were gathering up locusts to eat for survival. They would dry them out and use them as a source of protein to stay alive. The thought of it made Dudimose gag. He had made sure to secure his own stash of food in closed containers in his tunnels. He and his family would have enough to eat, but he began to consider the possible insurrection that might occur with a starved populace rising up against him. So he had hastily called for Moses and Aaron to meet in his court right away.

As he rushed in, he saw the two Hebrews waiting for him, surrounded by his guards. Jambres, his chief lector priest, was there with some of his subordinate priests.

"Get out!" Dudimose shouted. "Everyone, get out! Except for the Hebrews!"

They all obeyed but not quickly enough.

"Hurry!"

They were gone within seconds.

Once he saw that they were all alone, Dudimose fell to his knees at the feet of Moses and Aaron.

"I have sinned against Yahweh your god and against you. Please, please forgive my sin, only this once, and plead with Yahweh to remove his death from me!"

Dudimose knew that every minute counted. Every minute that the locusts were there meant more loss of food for Egypt.

Moses stared down at him with skeptical eyes.

Dudimose whimpered, "Can you plead right here and now?"

"No," Moses responded, keeping a wary eye upon the king. "But I will indeed plead for you."

Turning, Moses and Aaron left Dudimose in his posture of humiliation. The king quickly got up and brushed off his knees.

And for the ninth time, he felt his heart grow heavy with hardness. The hatred that had momentarily fled from him on his knees returned with vengeance. A river of boiling rage inundated his *ka*-spirit.

•••••

That night, a very strong west wind came upon the land and drove the entire locust swarm eastward toward Yam Suph. Many died in the Red Sea along the way and in the barren lands of Ta Mefkat. Though the land and waters were covered with the carcasses of dead locusts, Yahweh's hand had completely eliminated the voracious swarm.

CHAPTER 40

Nine

Dudimose looked sadly upon the crumpled naked body of the young child with whom he had just spent time. He had gone too far this time. Even he was aware of that. It was too bad. He had liked that one. The boy had given Dudimose much pleasure. He would have to find another boy that looked just like this one to help recreate the sexual experience.

Calling for his servant to dispose of the body, he dressed.

Prince Khonsu arrived at his door with two of his male servants just as the little wrapped body was being carried out.

Khonsu had a sour look on his face.

"Must you be so recklessly indulgent with your compulsion?"

His son's contempt had become more outspoken in recent months. Not even the queen would dare say such words. It hurt Dudimose to realize that he was somehow responsible for the memories that inflicted his firstborn.

Dudimose looked at the two manservants who were with Khonsu. They were the favorites whom his son enjoyed beating into submission for his own gratification.

Dudimose said, "The hippopotamus should be careful of accusing the crocodile in shared waters."

Khonsu replied, "The hippopotamus may share waters with the crocodile, but they do not share natures."

"No?" Dudimose stepped closer to Khonsu. Close enough to make him take a step back in discomfort. "I am a god. Horus on earth. I do as I will." He saw his son swallow nervously.

"And you would do well to remember that I will become Osiris one day and you will be the next Horus." Dudimose paused. "*You* will be the god. And you will do as *you* will. Until that time comes…"

Dropping his firmness, Dudimose felt tears well up in his eyes.

"My son, I never wanted to hurt you. I have only ever loved you."

Khonsu was unmoved. "You and I have different ideas of love."

"Not so different. Nevertheless, we share a common enemy who wars against not just me but against the throne, to which you are the successor."

Khonsu looked away. "That I will not dispute. And I believe I may have discovered the secret name of our enemy."

"You know the secret name of Yahweh?"

"No. Of Moses his servant."

Khonsu had taken Dudimose to the temple of Ra to see the high priests Jannes and Jambres. Because of the king's disgust with the insects, servants had cleared the street of dead locusts in advance of their passage. He didn't want to see them anymore or have to hear their bodies crunching beneath his feet.

As they entered the Holy of Holies, Dudimose gazed up at the high stone walls surrounded by pillars that held up the ceiling in shadows of torchlight. Jambres stood before the images of Ra and Horus, the gods' graven, stolid faces looking down upon their visitors.

Jambres bowed in greeting. "My god and lord the king."

"Where is your brother?" asked Dudimose.

"I killed him."

Dudimose was surprised at the confession's frankness. "Why?"

"Because his heart had been turned toward your enemy, the Hebrews."

"Really. Well, I guess gratitude is in order," said Dudimose.

"No need, my king. I considered it my duty to my Great God the Lord of Heaven."

"Nevertheless, well done," said Dudimose. "So what do you have for me? My son tells me you have the secret name of Moses. You have my attention."

Jambres got right to the point. "His name is Sobekmose son of Khaneferre Sobekhotep IV, previous king of this thirteenth dynasty of Egypt."

"From forty years ago," Khonsu added. "He was the *adopted* firstborn son of the king. When it was discovered he was a Hebrew by birth, he attempted to assassinate the king but failed—and fled into the desert."

Dudimose sobered. "And now he returns to claim my throne."

"No," said Khonsu. "I believe he sees himself as the Deliverer of his people, the Hebrews."

"How do you know this?"

Khonsu gestured to the image of Ra. "Through an oracle, Ra told us where to look." He nodded to Jambres, who pulled out a parchment and handed it to Dudimose. The king opened it but couldn't read the writing. It was some foreign demotic script.

Jambres explained, "That is a written language the Hebrews have developed amongst themselves. I persuaded a scribe from the House of Life to translate it for me. It details Moses's birth origins and his lineage."

Dudimose sought to understand. "So he believes he is *not* the prophesied Destroyer of Egypt but rather the Deliverer of the Hebrews?"

"Perhaps it is both," said Jambres.

Dudimose was now following. "Moses claims to want to take all his people a few days into the wilderness to sacrifice. But he wants to take every man, woman, child, and animal with them. They would never do that unless they were planning on leaving Egypt forever. I have always suspected that was his goal, but I found it hard to believe he would think he could do such a thing. To run away from my outstretched arm? It is madness."

"It is their hope." Khonsu tapped the Hebrew scroll. "This says that they are going to return to the land of Canaan. That is Moses's real goal. And when he leaves, he takes half of Egypt's workforce with him, leaving behind a famine and disease-ridden land without enough slaves to rebuild."

Dudimose mused, "It would destroy Egypt."

Khonsu said, "Deliverer *and* Destroyer."

Jambres said, "I have already begun our cursing ritual against him." He turned and showed Dudimose various wax figures bound and stuck with multiple nails. "These are figurines of Moses, his family, and some of the elders we know about. We will incinerate them in a furnace."

He showed the king broken pottery on the floor. "I have written execration texts using Moses's secret name and the names of his leaders and performed the broken red pots cursing ritual."

He pulled out an amulet and handed it to Dudimose. "The eye of Horus will protect you against Moses's magic."

Dudimose accepted the amulet around his neck. He rubbed it with hope.

Jambres concluded, "And we have priests committed to casting spells and incantations against Moses and his people during all hours of day and night."

Dudimose clenched his jaw with satisfaction. "Well done. This man has wreaked enough havoc in my kingdom. It is time I wreak some havoc in his. Khonsu, take two regiments of soldiers and execute Moses and his entire family. Let us see how his people will do without their Deliverer."

Khonsu protested, "What about your concerns of killing their prophet? They may rise up."

He could see the madness in his father's eyes as Dudimose spoke. "I do not care anymore what they do. If they rise up, I will slaughter them all. If they try to leave, I will slaughter them all. I do not care how their deaths affect Egypt anymore. The longer they remain alive, the greater impact the Hebrews will have on Egypt's future. Once they are all dead, Yahweh will have no one to worship him and he will lose all power. I hate these people. I hate what they are. I hate their god. Bring me the heads of Moses and his brother Aaron."

"Finally, father," said Khonsu, "you and I agree on something."

In the unseen realm of the temple's Holy of Holies, Ra had assembled his pantheon for the very same purpose as the humans. Only a few dozen deities remained whom the archangels had not captured or bound.

Horus returned from reconnoitering the Hebrew areas of Goshen. "They are all gone. The heavenly host are no longer guarding the Hebrew districts."

"I am sure their absence is a clever strategic move," said Ra. "I myself will lead a team to do the work that you cannot seem to accomplish without my help."

Horus protested, "But Father, you know archangels protect Moses. What if it is a trap?"

"That is why I am bringing all the strongest remaining gods with me. We will fight the forces of Yahweh and empower Prince Khonsu in his task." Ra began issuing orders. "Sun gods Aten and Atum. As well as whomever is left of the guardians of my solar barque. Thoth, Serqet, Horakhti, and my protective serpent Mehen." Khepri, Shu, and Sekhmet were already gone. Set, his most victorious protector, had not yet returned from the Negeb.

"What about me?" complained Horus. "I am your strongest and most faithful son."

"Precisely. That is why I want you to stay and guard Pharaoh with the Two Ladies Nekhbet and Wadjet, along with Ma'at, Apis the Bull, and Cobra Goddess Renenutet."

Ra turned to the pantheon. "Let us go quickly. The prince is already mustering his attack force."

• • • • •

Khonsu stepped onto his chariot before five hundred assembled marching soldiers. Putting on his leather gloves, he grabbed the reins. He signaled with his hand and moved forward. A surprise attack on Moses's residence was impossible with so many soldiers, but they would move as quietly as possible to avoid too much of an advance warning. He figured the army would already be on their shores by the time the Hebrews knew what was happening.

Khonsu felt his sword hilt by his side. He was going to personally cut off the heads of the Hebrew prophet brothers and shove them in his father's face with pride. But he was also planning on raping their entire family in front of them first, men, women, and children, saving any of their sons for his own pleasure.

The regiment had made it through the streets down to the water ferry without incident or much attention. Egyptians were told not to sound an alarm.

When they approached the ferry, Khonsu noticed that the sun had been hidden behind some dark clouds, casting a shadow upon them. No lightning or thunder or wind, so not another hailstorm.

He could not help but think of the previous plagues that had arrived with preternatural speed. But he saw no swarms or storms approaching on the horizon. The Nile's waters were still, and all around was calm. Just a few clouds obscuring the sun. He walked his chariot onto the first of several ferries to cross the tributary into the Hebrew quarters of the city of Avaris.

In the unseen realm, the gods Ra, Aten, and Atum boarded the ferry with Khonsu. Thoth and the others boarded a second ferry to follow.

Ra clutched Mehen, who was wrapped around his body and ready for battle. The ferry crossing made Ra think of the myth of his solar boat and the battles he waged nightly with Apophis.

Today would be a different battle. He was certain that they would be facing the most furious combat of this entire sequence of plagues. They and their earthly counterparts sought to kill the Destroyer's entire family. The enemy would certainly be prepared to defend them.

Ra was unprepared however for the sudden darkness that fell upon the land. They were halfway across the river when all light disappeared into complete pitch blackness. The gods had the ability to see in darkness that would normally blind humans. But not this time. He heard Atum scream out.

He thought for a moment they'd been temporarily blinded. But he heard the humans' voices of terror as well, so the humans had also been blinded.

But somehow he knew it was not blindness. The darkness was unlike anything he had seen before. It was a darkness that he could *feel* as though a blanket weighed upon them or a wave engulfed them all.

He felt powerful hands grab his ankles and pull him into the water. Angelic hands. He heard the other gods being pulled in as well. Then he felt the water engulf him in his weakness and those hands wrestle him into submission.

In the earthly realm, Khonsu felt the heaviness of the darkness around them. Had the next plague struck them all blind? He heard soldiers panicking, falling into the water. His own horse whinnied in fear and bolted. Khonsu fell off the chariot just in time as he heard it enter the river, pulling his horse down into the depths.

He clutched onto the barge, determined not to drown in the water around them. He felt the ferry drifting downstream. All around him were screams of soldiers panicking, drowning in the water.

As Khonsu drifted away from the sounds, he collected his thoughts. How had the clouds of the sky so quickly blocked out the sun? How could he get back to land? How far would he drift?

The darkness was so thick he could feel it. Then he heard the crackle and pop of torches burning on the barge. They were still lit. But he could not see them. He crawled toward the sound and followed a pole upward with his fingers until he felt the heat of a torch. He burned his fingers and withdrew his hand. Was this blindness after all?

He could hear screams of Egyptians as he drifted along, which told him this was not a mere localized blindness of his soldiers but an actual plague upon the whole land. Yet he did not hear screams or sounds from the Hebrew side of the river. Why not? He could see nothing in that direction. How could they not also be under this cloak of terror?

Khonsu felt a sense of panic rising from within. This was more than mere darkness. This was a supernatural "outer darkness." The black surrounded his body, suffocated his senses. He could still hear and feel, but even those senses seemed choked by the thick darkness. He could actually feel it as though a cloak clung to his entire body, as if it something sentient tightened its grip on him.

The longer he drifted, the more his mind began to fray. Where was he? Where was everyone else? He could not shake the terror of feeling as if he were drifting away into nothingness. Was this a temporary plague or a permanent strike? If everyone was blind, then everyone would ultimately die. How could he find his way back? Would he drift all the way out to sea? Would he fall in the water now and drown? Where were the gods?

•••••

Ra struggled against his binding at the bottom of the Great Sea. Archangels had dragged him and the other gods down the Nile and deposited them into the black depths, perhaps somewhere off Egypt's coast in a deep undersea trench. He felt the powerful compression of the water upon his body. Because Watchers were weakened in water, they were unable to fight well against the angels and succumbed quickly to their force.

Ra could feel the sting of his bonds pressing tightly against his flesh. He knew exactly what they were made of: hair from the cherubim of the Garden of Eden. It was the only thing that could restrain the gods' supernatural power. And it was often used to permanently bind Watchers in the earth until judgment. Some of the ancient ones were still strangled by this hair since the days of Noah generations ago. Their torment would last for thousands of years until their judgment at Yahweh's final coming.

The thought of such a destiny for himself made Ra rage with anger. He already felt madness coming over him and drowning him in a way that water never could.

• • • • •

Khonsu could not tell how long or how far he had drifted. He thought he might even be to the Great Sea by now. All time and space was lost to him. Until he felt the jolt of his boat hitting something. He heard the lapping water against rocks. He felt the boat stop again.

Shore. He had drifted ashore. Making his way quickly to the bow of the ferry, he felt the rocks below. He dragged himself out of the boat onto the shoreline and fell to his knees in the sand.

He wept with gratitude.

And then he heard some sounds of people nearby. When he looked up, he could see something. A light. Several lights in the distance. His sight had been restored.

But when he looked back toward the barge, he could see nothing but the encroaching thick darkness. It was as if he had entered a part of the darkness that allowed light. He moved toward the lights and the voices.

When he got close enough to hear them, he could tell they were Hebrews. He had landed on the Hebrew side of the river. It became apparent to him that this darkness was another plague from which the Hebrews were spared by their god. They had been allowed light in the midst of darkness. Anger boiled up within him again, and he considered hunting down Moses on his own and killing him.

No. There was no way he could find him now. And no way he could face the dozens of men protecting him. He needed his army to do that. And they were decimated by the darkness, many of them drowned in the river.

Instead, he would survive by hiding out until the plague was over and he could return to the palace and his father.

But how long would this plague last? For that matter, how long could *he* last?

It seemed like three days of darkness had already passed. Khonsu awoke in his hiding place amongst some bushes away from the shoreline. Stepping out, he saw a multitude of torches inland and the sounds of a large gathering. He decided to scout it out and see what he could learn.

Finding a Hebrew robe drying in a yard, he changed clothes in case he got caught. He then made his way through the dark streets toward the lights. When he arrived at a large clearing, he stayed back in the shadows of the walls and watched and listened.

At the center of the clearing was a platform of wood where Hebrew elders stood in a loose semicircle behind two men and a woman. He recognized the latter three as Moses, Aaron, and their sister.

Moses was talking about a ritual sacrifice for the Hebrew families. They were to roast and eat a lamb but first take its blood and slather it over the doorposts and lintels of their houses using hyssop branches as brushes. The blood would be some kind of a sign to a "Destroyer" to pass over the Hebrews so they would not suffer the plague. And they were to stay indoors all night.

What night was Moses talking about? Could this "Destroyer" be the one prophesied by the oracles? And to what plague did Moses refer? Khonsu's mind was reeling.

Moses spoke about this being a day of commemoration that the Hebrews would celebrate forever. And it would be accompanied by another ritual feast of unleavened bread. The Hebrews were to remove leaven out of their houses for seven days and eat no leaven for that month. But what was the point? What did it all mean? The details confused Khonsu.

A messenger approached Moses on the platform, interrupting the gathering. It appeared to be important. When they were done conversing, Moses turned back to the crowd and said, "Go now and select your Passover lambs for the feast. When the darkness lifts, the plague will follow shortly."

Then Moses and several others left with the messenger. The crowd began to split up. Some stayed behind to converse.

Khonsu shadowed Moses and his group of followers toward the river. There were enough of them, about thirty or so elders, for Khonsu to catch up and blend in. The light of the few torches was not enough to reveal the spy in their midst.

He got close enough to the front to hear a young man speaking quite boldly to his lord. "Moses, just give me the word, and Caleb and I will use stealth to find our way into the palace and assassinate Pharaoh. Surely his son would release us after all this."

"No, Joshua," Khonsu heard Moses respond. "I told you, Yahweh is to perform his acts of deliverance through *his* strong arm, not ours."

Poor fool, this Joshua, thought Khonsu. *He does not realize that if they assassinated my father, I would not leave a single Hebrew soul without suffering. In fact, I would order the holocaust of massacre my father is too fearful to order.*

Khonsu had no concern for the consequences to Egypt. He could only think of the satisfaction of revenge. He would burn down the entire land of Goshen if he had to.

As they approached the riverbank, Khonsu heard the sound of another voice speaking loudly in the darkness. "Moses? Moses, are you there?"

It was Khonsu's father Pharaoh calling out from the pitch-black Egyptian side of the water. He had a crack in his voice that Khonsu recognized as fear. The tributary was not wide here, a mere seventy or so feet. The water carried the voice clearly.

How had Pharaoh made it to the river from the palace? It must have been a difficult process of groping through the dark for hours with his train of servants holding hands and cloaks of one another. Khonsu remembered how thick that darkness was, the total blindness, and how helpless he had felt.

"I am here, O king," came the voice of Moses in response.

"Please call back the blanket of darkness upon us," said Khonsu's father. "It is so heavy that no one has moved for these three days."

Moses said nothing.

The king continued with his shaky voice, "You may go serve your god in the wilderness. You may take your wives and your children. Only leave your flocks and herds behind, and all will be well between us."

Again, Moses said nothing.

"Moses?" came the fearful call across the waters.

Then Moses spoke up, and Khonsu heard the hotness of anger rising in the Hebrew leader's voice as he announced, "These nine times have I asked you to let my people go into the desert to sacrifice to Yahweh our god. And these nine times have you gone back on your word. And though the right arm of Yahweh has humbled you each of those times, still you have the gall to withhold full obedience."

"You did not ask of your king, Moses," Pharaoh's voice responded, hardening. "You demanded of him."

"Yahweh demanded of you."

Pharaoh said, "My vizier tells me that bringing your herds and flocks is an operation far too great to accomplish in such a short amount of time. He knows these things. So leave them behind and all your people can go."

Moses's silence seemed like a boiling volcano. His voice was the precursor to the eruption. "Now not only must you let us bring our animals to sacrifice so that not one hoof of our livestock is left behind, but *you* must provide animals for us as well."

Now it was Pharaoh who remained silent. Khonsu could imagine the rage building in his father against this arrogant rebel.

But all of a sudden, the darkness began to lift. Rather, it dissolved like black water turning clear. At first, Khonsu could only see the people around Moses more clearly. Then he could see the water. And then the blurred figures of Pharaoh and his servants across the river. He looked up and saw dark clouds in the sky dissipating and the rays of the sun gleaming down upon them, bathing them in light.

Everyone on both sides of the river shielded their eyes. They had become so accustomed to the dark that it took time for them to adjust to the brightness that currently burned their eyes.

As Khonsu's full vision returned, he could now make out clearly his father standing across the river with Jambres next to him, surrounded by a dozen servants and soldiers. Even the queen had come with them. Khonsu longed to call out to his mother. To tell her he was all right. He dared not. But he could see the sadness of her countenance. She had suffered greatly through all this. She had suffered greatly through his father the king's abusive neglect.

Moses shouted, "Thus says Yahweh, 'By midnight this very day, I will pass through the land of Egypt, and I will smite the firstborn in all the land, both man and beast. From the firstborn of your animals to the firstborn of slaves and even to the firstborn of Pharaoh who sits on his throne, I will execute my judgments upon them and upon all the gods of Egypt. And there will be a cry throughout the land unlike anything that has ever been or ever will be again. But I will make a distinction between Egypt and Israel for I am Yahweh.'"

Khonsu felt panic rising within him. So the next plague would be the death of all firstborn in the land.

Khonsu was firstborn.

Did this god really have the power to do such a thing? Of course he did. He had already sent nine plagues. Why would he not be able to send this tenth?

Khonsu had to get out of there. He had to get back to the other side of the river without being discovered. He saw the terrified look on his mother's face across the river. He had to get back to her and tell her he was okay.

Then Dudimose shouted out, "This darkness has hidden my face from you these three days, Moses. But I say now that the light has returned, take care never to see my face again. For on that day you shall surely die."

"It is true," shouted Moses. "I will not see your face again."

Moses turned with those around him, and they began marching their way back to the Hebrew quarters.

Khonsu got out of their way as if to follow but immediately began looking for a ferry or boat to cross the river back to safety.

CHAPTER 41

Ten

By midday, Hebrew households all over Goshen had chosen or purchased the best unblemished male lambs or goats from their flocks in preparation for the Passover meal Yahweh instructed. Moses and Aaron led their family in prayers and song to calm the fear of the coming tide of death. Moses had shared with them all a poem that he had just started to work on but was unfinished. It looked forward to the land of promise into which Yahweh was going to bring them. Moses led in singing some of the lyrics that brought them hope in the midst of their suffering. These were the very words of Yahweh himself.

> "Give ear, O heavens, and I will speak,
>   and let the earth hear the words of my mouth.
> For I will proclaim the name of Yahweh;
>   ascribe greatness to our God!
> Remember the days of old;
>   consider the years of many generations;
> ask your father, and he will show you,
>   your elders, and they will tell you.
> When the Most High gave to the nations their inheritance,
>   when he divided mankind,
> he fixed the borders of the peoples
>   according to the number of the Sons of God.
> But Yahweh's portion is his people,
>   Jacob his allotted heritage.

· · · · ·

In the house of Pharaoh, Dudimose found all the firstborn child servants and segregated them for the day, placing them under a guard of a hundred soldiers. Though this plague seemed the most outrageous of all, he had seen nine others that had proven themselves true to the word of that deplorable monster Moses. If these of his favorite younglings were taken from his pleasure, he felt he might finally break into full madness.

But now he had to see to his own firstborn son. With a guard of four of his finest warriors, Dudimose went to check on Khonsu, who had called together their entire armed forces to surround the palace. Since Dudimose himself was not firstborn, he felt in no personal danger from Moses's latest proclamation. But he'd felt sick all day at the threat to his son and couldn't even eat with the anticipation of midnight arriving.

While the previous plagues had all been supernatural in origin, they'd often been creatures attacking the Egyptians: frogs, gnats, insects, locusts. So in trying to figure out how the firstborn would be attacked, the king had concluded that this Yahweh or Moses himself might use the Hebrews to assassinate their enemies. Hunt them down with stealth in the night.

But how would they single out the firstborn? Perhaps that was just a diversion. They were a cunning people, these Semite Asiatics. For all Dudimose knew, they had been planning such a stealth attack throughout the entire sequence of previous plagues. And this was their climactic goal. This time, the scourge would not be a swarm of insects but an army of Hebrews.

The sun was just now approaching the horizon at the end of the day. Walking up the steps to the watchtower by the gates of the palace, Dudimose arrived at the top to find his son looking out over the city. They stood silently for a few moments, not knowing what to say to each other.

Dudimose finally broached the subject. "Are you afraid, my son?"

"Are you not?" Khonsu demanded accusingly. "We have just gone through the de-creation of Egypt's cosmos due to the curses of a simpleton Hebrew and his obscure god."

"And that is why I harden my heart against their requests," Dudimose said. "If I give in to such demands from such a worthless people, then I am no longer their god. If it is a war this Moses wants, then let him try. I am out of patience."

"How do you think this Destroyer could possibly know who is a firstborn and who is not?" Khonsu asked.

Dudimose answered, "I think that it is a symbolic threat for a violent rebellion. They want to kill you as my firstborn successor to the throne. They want to destroy our dynasty. And they will perform executions when they are in control."

Khonsu looked over the camp of soldiers below. "No one is getting near the palace tonight. Not without losing their heads."

"If there is an attack by the Hebrews, I will ride through Goshen and hack them all to pieces. Young and old, men, women, and children." Dudimose paused thoughtfully, then added, "I think I will do it regardless."

Looking over the tower ramparts, Dudimose saw hundreds of hacked and bloodied bodies sprawled and rotting in the streets below them. "Who are all those dead?"

Khonsu shrugged. "Egyptians who came to request military protection in the city. Fools. They think we care about them when the very throne of all Egypt is in jeopardy? *They* should be seeking to protect their god-king."

"And his son," added Dudimose. "Khonsu, I do not expect you to ever forgive me, but I want you to know that everything I do, I do to ensure your future reign. You are my son and heir to the throne of all Egypt. And I would slaughter all of Egypt to ensure your ascension to power."

Khonsu looked at him. "I did not tell you what I saw when I crossed the river into the Hebrew quarters that night. I heard Moses relate to them some kind of magical protection for their firstborn. The Hebrews will again supposedly be protected from the plague."

Dudimose replied, "I already have Jambres performing our own magical protection in the palace, though in light of his consistent failures, I confess I have lost faith in his effectiveness."

"Yes," agreed Khonsu. "But then, you are supposed to be the god of Egypt. It is your power that questionable."

Even now, his son was accusing his father instead of allying with him. But he was right. Dudimose's rage over these confrontations had deflated him with defeat verging on madness. He felt helpless against this demon Yahweh. If Dudimose was a god, what could he do to fight this de-creation chaos? How could he restore Ma'at to Egypt? His only hope was that his son would be able to rebuild all that Dudimose had lost.

But he had already lost so much.

In the spiritual realm, the gods Horus, Renenutet, Nekhbet, and Wadjet stood watch over Pharaoh and his son. Ma'at, Apis, and the rest of the surviving minor deities were around the palace walls on watch.

Renenutet asked Horus, "Do we really have to focus our protection on Pharaoh? He is not firstborn like his son."

"I am the firstborn of Osiris," said Horus. "Pharaoh is the incarnation of Horus on earth, so, yes, I think Pharaoh is in danger as much as I."

Wadjet, the cobra goddess, asked, "Has there been any sign of heavenly armies on the horizon?"

"Not yet," said Horus. "And that is why we are focusing our protection on the royal family. Our pantheon has no strength left to protect an entire people. The house of Pharaoh is our last stand."

• • • • •

The Hebrews had been instructed to slay their sacrificial lamb during the time between the two sunsets. At the ninth hour of the day, just around three o'clock in the afternoon, Aaron took a flint knife and cut their unblemished lamb's throat. It was a one-year-old male. For that moment, the skies went dark above Aaron. He looked up to see that clouds had obscured the sun.

Aaron's sons Nadab and Abihu hoisted the poor creature upside-down on a pulley to allow its blood to drain out into the large pot below. In accordance with Yahweh's commands, they were careful not to allow any of its bones to be broken.

This same act was being done simultaneously throughout Goshen as the Hebrews engaged in preparing their first Passover meal on this day, the fourteenth of the month of Abib, a day that would be commemorated forever. It would become the first moon of their sacred calendar. As the land emerged from the waters of creation in this season of Emergence, so Israel was rising to eventually seek her own newly created land.

Miriam had prepared a fire and roasting spit for the animal. They were to roast it all—head, legs, and inner organs—as part of the sacred meal.

As she cooked the animal, Moses and Aaron took the blood to the front entrance of their home. The rest of the household including the children watched Moses take hyssop branches he had tied together to make a large brush and dip it into the pot of blood. He then took the brush and wiped the blood on the two doorposts, then on the lintel overhead.

Aaron then guided everyone back into the house, where they would stay until morning without going outside.

Looking down the street, Moses saw other Hebrews outside performing this same act of blood covering, as Hebrews throughout the delta would be doing this night. Slaughtering male goats and lambs for their blood to be put over their doors and for the meat to be roasted and eaten.

One of the grandchildren was crying as she asked Moses, "Poppa, I am afraid. Will the Destroyer hurt us as well?"

"No, my dear," he replied, stroking her hair lovingly. "If you have faith, if you trust and obey Yahweh, he will protect you from the terror that comes by night."

Inside, the entire family gathered around the feast table. As cued in advance, the children asked in unison, "What do you mean by this service?"

Moses answered, "It is the sacrifice of Yahweh's Passover, for he will pass over the houses of the people of Israel, and he will strike the Egyptians but spare our houses. In this way, Yahweh prepares a sacrificial lamb as a substitute for us just as he did in place of Isaac on Mount Moriah. This innocent lamb from God dies in our place. His blood becomes the covering for our sins to protect us from death."

The children then asked, "And why do we eat the bitter herbs?"

Moses lifted up a plate with parsley, horseradish, and other herbs. "This is to symbolize the bitterness of slavery that we are under in Egypt."

The children asked a final question, "And why do we eat unleavened bread?"

Moses lifted a piece and announced, "Because it reminds us of the haste with which we will leave Egypt, as do these sandals and fastened belts that we wear as we eat."

He raised his staff. "This staff as well. There will be no time for the leaven to rise. So we eat this bread and this lamb in haste."

He broke the bread and said, "These stripes and piercings on the bread are to remind us of the stripes and piercings on Yahweh's Chosen Seed. But Yahweh will deliver us with his outstretched arm."

⋅ ⋅ ⋅ ⋅ ⋅

Horus and the gods stood on the tower's parapet watching over the land. They had been joined by Ma'at and several others. They could see for miles in every direction. As the midnight hour drew near, a faint light on the horizon drew their attention.

The clouds swirled with turmoil. Then flashes of lightning lit up the sky followed by distant thunder. In the spiritual realm, Horus could see a rider on a white horse leading untold thousands of heavenly hosts riding chariots of fire behind him.

And they were approaching Goshen.

Horus gestured to Ma'at, who raised a trumpet and sounded a call to war.

⋅ ⋅ ⋅ ⋅ ⋅

In Moses's household, the meal was done, and everyone had cleaned up. The tension was high. Despite assurances that the lamb's blood would protect them, few could sleep with the thought of what was going to happen tonight through the whole land of Egypt.

Would the blood of a mere lamb really protect them? What if they had not properly adorned their domiciles with the blood? What if it worked but Pharaoh blamed them for the deaths of thousands of his people? Would Pharaoh really let them go, or would Pharaoh change his mind yet again?

These questions ran through Moses's mind as he watched through a window the arrival of an evening fog shrouding everything in its dense wake—a cloud of judgment.

Shuttering the windows, Moses turned back to his family, now gathered with frightened eyes around the fire. The sound of distant screams from Egyptian quarters told him that the Destroyer had arrived. Families howled in pain as the Angel of Yahweh's unseen hand struck dead their firstborn children.

Moses raised his hands and led his family in more song. This part contained the very words of Yahweh. It drowned out the faint sounds of distant terror surrounding them.

> See now that I, even I, am he,
>   and there is no god beside me;

I kill and I make alive;
> I wound and I heal;
> and there is none that can deliver out of my hand.

For I lift up my hand to heaven
> and swear, As I live forever,

if I sharpen my flashing sword
> and my hand takes hold on judgment,

I will take vengeance on my adversaries
> and will repay those who hate me.

I will make my arrows drunk with blood,
> and my sword shall devour flesh—

with the blood of the slain and the captives,
> from the long-haired heads of the enemy.

Rejoice with him, O heavens;
> bow down to him, all gods,

for he avenges the blood of his children
> and takes vengeance on his adversaries.

· · · · ·

In the royal palace, a regiment of a hundred soldiers outside each of their rooms guarded Pharaoh and his son to protect them against gods knew what. But the two men were dealing with their anxiety of this night in different ways. Dudimose got drunk by a fireplace and fell asleep.

Crown Prince Khonsu did not want to believe that he would actually be slain tonight. But he needed something to take his mind off of the specter of the threat hanging over him—something excessive. So he imbibed in an orgy of debauchery.

Khonsu and dozens of his male friends and servants met in the throne room to eat and drink, consume drugs, and engage in acts of perversion. Khonsu lost himself in a mass of writhing flesh and sweat and bodily excretions. He was doing things to his subjects with devices that he had only fancied in his imagination but had never tried before. It was a bacchanal of aggression and submission, pain and pleasure.

It made him feel like a god, doing whatever he willed in the face of doom. It empowered him. It made him feel *alive*.

· · · · ·

In the unseen realm, Horus and his gods guarding the palace walls could see the Angel of Yahweh and his forces enter the city around them and pour through the streets like a river of judgment. The fog could not hide the invasion from their divine vision. Holy ones entered houses with their weapons to smite the firstborn through all the land. Howling screams of both human and animal pain rose like a dirge in the mist.

Yahweh had arrived on the clouds of judgment to Egypt with ten thousand times ten thousand of his holy ones, and they were meting out punishment just as Moses had proclaimed, just as Yahweh had promised. There would be no escape tonight for the children of judgment.

And then Horus felt a chill down his spine as he saw a single rider on a white stallion step through the swirling vapor before the palace walls. The rider stared up at the gods with eyes of fire.

It was him—the Angel of Yahweh. The Destroyer. His head crowned with diadems, his white robe dripping with the blood of the firstborn, and his steed snorting and stomping its feet with readiness.

Horus nodded to Wadjet again, and this time she sounded retreat with her trumpet. The few dozen gods stationed around the palace gripped their weapons and made their way back to Pharaoh and his son to make their last stand.

· · · · ·

Dudimose awoke from his drunken slumber. He was still a bit dizzy, but he was used to it. He would often drink himself to sleep after a session with one of his child servants.

His child servants.

He jumped up and left his room to find out if they were well. His hundred guards followed him until he met the fifty he had set outside the children's room.

He breathed a sigh of relief. They were well. He would go to see his son. What hour of the night was it anyway? He had lost track of the time.

In the unseen realm, Horus, Ma'at, Nekhbet, Wadjet, and Renenutet all followed Pharaoh. A dozen other deities followed close behind for protection. The rest were with Prince Khonsu.

The scream of a woman resonated through the palace halls. Dudimose stopped. The guards looked behind them.

Another scream followed shortly.

The attack had begun.

He shouted, "Protect your god!"

Funny, thought Dudimose. *I don't feel like a god right now.*

The guards surrounded Dudimose on both sides of the hall. They faced outward and drew their weapons—swords, spears, shields. They took a defensive stance toward an unseen opponent.

In the spiritual realm, the gods drew their own weapons as well. They were the first to see what the humans would never see. The Angel of Yahweh walked toward them with a double-sided sword and a large dagger in his hands. His brow was furrowed, and he walked like an unearthly predator, burning eyes focused intently on his prey.

He met the gods first.

In the narrow hallway, they had to come at him one at a time. And one by one, he cut them down without losing stride. He cut off their heads with ease. They had no chance. The last few realized this and turned to run.

"Cowards!" shouted Horus, who encircled Pharaoh with his four other guardians. Horus wished that Set were here. With Set, they might have had a chance.

The Angel walked through the human soldiers, killing discriminately, and only the firstborn at that.

In the earthly realm, the soldiers saw nothing. They looked around in confusion for attackers. But there were none. Yet certain soldiers were falling dead around them. It was as if they were struck dead by an unseen force.

Some of them ran away.

"Cowards!" shouted Dudimose. "Protect your king!"

Others stayed but stood in confusion as they saw no visible foe. Some started swinging their swords in the air as if to hit a ghost. But they only struck each other. It was a madness that was making them kill each other.

In the unseen realm, the Angel met Horus and the four others ready to fight. He paused for just a moment.

"Attack!" Horus shouted.

The gods attacked.

The Angel again moved with ethereal fluidity like a dancer. He spun, ducked, parlayed—and cut off the heads of all four deities with rapid ease. Only Horus was left.

In the earthly realm, Pharaoh Dudimose saw his guardsmen drop dead or kill each other until no one was left. He fell to his knees and wept, his face in his hands, fearful of being smitten as well.

But he was not.

He alone remained alive amidst a hallway of carnage.

Left alive by whatever invisible force had killed them all.

The only thing that mattered now empowered him to run down the hall.

He muttered it to himself as he ran. "Khonsu! My son!"

In the unseen realm, Horus stood staring at the Angel who had stopped his grisly massacre to gaze upon the frightened son of Ra, urine dripping down the god's quivering legs.

Horus knew the end of his story. He would be cut into pieces and imprisoned in the earth.

So he spun around and ran like a coward.

Dudimose tripped and fell to the floor. He looked behind him. Nothing was following. Nothing he could see.

He got back up and continued running through the halls of the palace toward the throne room where his son was.

He didn't know what he could do in such a situation. But he had to be there. He had to defend his son.

Some way. Somehow.

Arriving at the throne room's entrance, Dudimose pushed open the big oak doors.

Inside, another horrifying sight greeted him. Dead naked bodies of Khonsu's male servants and friends sprinkled the floor.

But where was his son? He stepped over the corpses, looking amongst them. He could not find his son.

Until he looked up at the throne.

Sitting upon it was Khonsu, slouched forward as if asleep.

"Dear Horus!" he exclaimed as he ran to his son.

Reaching the throne, he shook him. "Khonsu! Khonsu!"

But Khonsu did not awaken.

He checked the prince's neck pulse.

Nothing.

The Crown Prince of Egypt was dead.

Pharaoh screamed out in agony.

He grabbed Khonsu's body and settled it gently to the floor so he could cradle his son's head in his arms.

"Not my son. Not my son. Khonsuuuuu. Please do not hate me. I never meant to hurt you. It was only my way of showing you love."

His lifeless body weighed heavy in Dudimose's arms.

If only he had not treated his young son the way he treated his servant children.

He whimpered, "I could not help myself."

And then from deep within his *ka*-spirit, Dudimose felt a pain that became a deep guttural sound in his throat. A moan of spiritual pain far greater than any physical wound.

He howled to the sky with misery.

It was a howl that could be heard throughout the entire palace.

As he sat there holding his son, Queen Nefret came running in.

She stopped when she saw the two of them on the floor by the throne.

She walked slowly toward them.

She ascended the steps one at a time.

She stood over them both.

Dudimose looked up at her, his eyes barely able to see her through his tears.

Nefret hauled back and slapped him.

He did nothing in return. He looked into her eyes and saw all the hatred of her entire life focused on him.

"This is your doing!" she cried out. "This is all your doing. He is dead because of you. Because of your pride, you refused to let the Hebrews sacrifice to their god. You are no god. You are a foolish man who does not deserve your own family."

Without any reserve, Nefret took out a knife hidden in her cloak. Dragging it quickly across her neck, she cut her own carotid artery. The knife dropped from her hand, clattering on the floor. Blood spurted out of her neck in throbbing pulses. She stood there glaring at Dudimose with that hatred—until she fainted and fell face first to the floor, her lifeblood draining from her body.

Dudimose could barely look at her.

But her dead open eyes stared at him accusingly.

He wailed. "What have I done? What have I done?"

· · · · ·

The fire was low, and daybreak was not far from dawning. Moses finished his prayer looking to heaven. "Yahweh, you are God of gods. There are none beside you. None comparable to you. So we consecrate to you all our firstborn in all our families. The first to open the womb amongst all Israel, both of man and of beast, is yours. For you have protected your chosen this night with the blood of covering."

When he looked back down, he found that many in the family were asleep. The children nestled in parents' arms, wives in husbands' arms. Every one of them sleeping the peaceful sleep of the righteous.

Moses took his memory back to a time when he and Zipporah were still young and their firstborn son Gershom had recently come into the world. Their life was just beginning together in Midian.

Moses had held the little infant in his arms. Looked into his son's tiny brown face looking back up at him, crying from the shock of entering a new world of danger from a womb of quiet and safety. He was so precious, so fragile and vulnerable. He had no idea of how loved and protected he was in his father's arms.

"My son," said Moses in his memory. "My firstborn son." He smiled and looked at Zipporah, who lay in bed exhausted from giving birth, cared for by the midwife. She smiled despite her pain.

Moses added, "I do not deserve this. I do not deserve you, my precious wife."

"No, you do not, my husband," she teased him with tired eyes. "None of us do."

"Yet here we are." He looked again into the face of his son, now peacefully asleep.

He whispered so as not to wake the little boy, "I do not know what I would do if I ever lost him. If I ever lost either of you."

"You would have to return to Kush to find a replacement," she said, still smiling. He could tell she was happy to see him so happy.

He looked again at his sleeping son's little scrunched face. Gershom had his whole life ahead of him. What kind of man would he become? Who would he marry? Would he be an ordinary man? A great man? Would he carry on Moses's legacy with many children, a tree of life spreading into the future?

Moses came back to the present. Or would his son die early and end the dream, crushed in the grip of the Destroyer? A seed line of thousands ended in an instant.

Still awake, Aaron walked over to join Moses, looking out the window in the night of death all around them.

"You were worried about your family's safety when you first accepted your calling," Aaron said quietly.

Moses nodded.

"If you had run away, Yahweh would have raised up someone else."

Moses could not disagree. "He saves whom he chooses to save. His will be done. Hallelujah."

"Hallelujah," replied Aaron, and he shut his eyes.

Hallelujah was the call to praise Yahweh together. Though it was a terrifying night of judgment for many, those who trusted and obeyed their God praised his mercy shown the elect.

For Yahweh had delivered them this night from the Destroyer.

CHAPTER 42

The next few days after the Destroyer passed over were dark days of mourning throughout all of Egypt. Wailing filled the streets as poor and rich alike prepared the bodies of their firstborn for burial. There was not a household among the Egyptians that had not suffered the Destroyer's hand. Only in the Hebrew districts were the firstborn spared because of the Passover lamb's blood.

In the royal palace, Pharaoh Dudimose wept and mourned for his son Khonsu all day alone in his throne room. It had always been a seat of power for him, but now it felt like an empty, hollow symbol of a broken kingdom. He couldn't find solace in his child servants. They only made him think of his son. At nightfall, he still had not eaten, but he knew what he had to do. He sent messengers to call upon Moses.

The prophet and his brother arrived carrying their shepherd staffs and, as always, dressed in their humble shepherd robes. Dudimose had threatened Moses with death if he would see him again. But all such threats were now worthless. Dudimose had an armed cohort of a hundred soldiers surrounding his throne from fear for his own safety before this prophet of pain.

He had lost everything. He had lost Egypt's wealth, her bounty of food, as well as her gods. And now he had lost all hope for his dynasty in the deaths of his son and his queen. And all of it at the hands of some obscure god from a distant mountain and the god's ill-bred, lowlife lackeys. What kind of god chose slaves and shepherds to serve as his mouthpiece?

Dudimose tore his own royal tunic in emotional agony. He was done. He could no longer fight. Yahweh had won. Moses had won. He was more afraid of Moses than he had been of any world leader. What is more, if Moses and these Hebrew sand rats stayed around any longer, Dudimose thought he might go mad and kill himself in frustration over his own impotence. They had to go. Not just into the wilderness for a sacrifice. He wanted them gone forever.

Never to return to Egypt. Cut out of his body like a cancerous tumor, or he would surely die.

Jambres met Moses and Aaron at the throne room's entrance, blocking their view of the king as he stood across the raised dais from his throne, staring out a window.

Moses didn't speak to the high priest but past him. "My lord king. You called on us."

Still caught up in his pain, Dudimose didn't turn from the window. Yahweh had thoroughly defeated and humiliated him and his gods. Dudimose had no pride left.

But though his voice was low, it was clear enough to be heard throughout the throne room. Rage quivered in every word. "Take your people and go to serve your god wherever he wills. Take your women and children, your flocks and herds, and be gone with you."

"No restrictions?" Moses asked.

"No restrictions. Take everyone and everything. Just please leave as soon as possible. And leave your blessing that there will be no more plagues. I never want to see you or your people again."

The brothers looked at each other. Moses said, "You have my blessing, O king. But are you saying you do *not* want us to return?"

"Yes!" Dudimose shouted. "I do *not* want you to return. Just go. Go!"

He waved a hand above his shoulder in sharp dismissal. He'd steeled himself to maintain his composure and pride until they were gone. But grief again overwhelmed him, and he leaned weakly against the window, nothing left in his soul.

His son was gone forever. The queen he could do without. But not his son. Yes, he had failed him as a father. But that was the worst thing about it all. Yahweh had forever taken away from him the opportunity to reconcile with his son. Khonsuemwaset had gone into the afterlife with a bitterness Dudimose feared would be eternal.

More importantly, Yahweh had taken away his dynasty. Dudimose had no future legacy. His seed, his lineage would die with him.

Behind him, Dudimose heard a slight clearing of the throat. "My lord king."

At the apologetic voice of his high priest, Dudimose wiped his eyes from his tears and looked up.

Beyond the priest, there was no sign of the two unkempt shepherds with their staffs. Moses and Aaron were gone.

······

The next day, Israelites all over Goshen received the word through their elders that they were leaving Egypt. No longer would they be known as Habiru, part of a larger body of Asiatic peoples, as the Egyptians contemptuously termed them. Those leaving Egypt were the descendants of Abraham, Isaac, and Israel, once known as Jacob, and of Israel's sons, now grown into twelve strong tribes. From now on, they would be known as the nation of Israel, the chosen people of Yahweh.

Everyone was to pack as quickly as possible for departure. They were to pack up minimal belongings and prepare all their family members for a long, arduous journey through the desert. Shepherds would bring their flocks and herds. Farmers would bring their animals and seed for growing.

Pharaoh was letting them go. Not just for three days into the wilderness for sacrifices but for good. Excitement and fear filled the Hebrew quarters as the Israelites prepared as quickly as they could to leave.

Meanwhile, Pharaoh had announced his decree to the Egyptians that the Hebrews were allowed to depart Egypt unmolested. Most of the citizenry were as intent as Pharaoh to get rid of them. They gave the Hebrews much silver and gold jewelry and other items, hoping to bribe them for Yahweh's favor upon their exodus. The Israelites took these offerings, considering them a form of plunder for their years of slavery at the hands of the Egyptians.

Aaron reminded his people of the prophecy to Abraham that Yahweh had given in the days of old: "Know for certain that your offspring will be sojourners in a land that is not theirs and will be servants there, and they will be afflicted for four hundred years. But I will bring judgment on the nation that they serve, and afterward they shall come out with great possessions."

One of those great possessions was the mummified body of Joseph their forefather who had saved the Hebrews when he had been vizier of Egypt. In his day, Joseph had made the sons of Israel solemnly swear to take his bones with them when the Israelites left Egypt. Moses made sure that they kept that oath. He had sent Aaron to Joseph's tomb to gather his remains for transport out of Egypt.

Moses brought Joshua with him to the House of Life to retrieve his own greatest possession from Ipuwer the scribe. As he'd done weeks before, he met the scribe at the back door. Ipuwer led them over to the rear stables, where he gave Moses a sturdily reinforced and covered wooden cart packed tight with the scrolls Moses had requested. Ipuwer had copied Egyptian, Babylonian, Canaanite, Assyrian, and other favorite writings of Moses's youth from the original scrolls and tablets onto the lighter, more transportable papyrus of Egypt. Ipuwer had also included transcriptions of Hebrew *toledoth*—stories and genealogies of Israel's past—that Moses had provided from the elders of Israel.

Ipuwer added, "I have also provided you plenty of fresh papyrus and writing utensils."

Moses checked the two mules pulling the cart, then turned back to Ipuwer. He gave the Egyptian scribe a familial hug and kiss, now a common custom to him, though not to Ipuwer.

"Thank you, my old friend. They will come in handy when I finally write that book I have been wanting to write for a long time. The story of my people."

"Knowing you," replied Ipuwer, "I am sure it will be multiple volumes."

They shared a laugh, and Moses and Joshua led the mules back to his home for the trip.

• • • • •

Immediately after their deaths, Pharaoh Dudimose had his son and queen brought on a boat across to the west side of the Nile where embalming tents resided for those who could afford it. He spent several days mourning their deaths along with a dozen paid female mourners, who wailed and played instruments.

Egyptians believed that every person's afterlife journey began with the creation of the *ba*-spirit at death. The *ba* was depicted as a human-faced bird in their art.

Each human body also had a *ka*-spirit—their essential life force. The *ka* was like a spiritual duplicate of the living person that co-existed with one's physical body.

At death, the *ba* would remain around the body while the *ka* began its flight to the western world of Duat. They called it "going west."

Khonsu's body would be mummified as soon as possible to stop the decay of his flesh which was tied to his *ba*. As the flesh decayed, so too would Khonsu's *ba* and spiritual identity. They must maintain that house of flesh for the *ba* so that when the *ka* returned to the body for resurrection, it would have a fit home.

And that maintenance was what was going on in the embalmer's tent across the river. Khonsu's body was being prepared for mummification.

The team consisted of several professional embalmers called Men of Anubis. Jambres the high priest wore a jackal mask of Anubis during the process as a representation of that Lord of the Sacred Land of the necropolis of the dead.

The embalmers placed Khonsu's body face up on an embalmer's board made of slats. The high priest Jambres prayed to Anubis. The embalmers then inserted a long bronze hooked needle up Khonsu's nostrils. The tool broke through a nasal membrane into the brain cavity, where the hook was rotated to whisk the already soft brain tissue into a more liquid form. They turned the body around to let Khonsu's brains ooze out of his nose into a pot. Since the Egyptians believed the brain to be the body's least important organ, they dispensed it to animals for food.

Linen strips were then forced up into the brain cavity to clean and dry it out before using a large syringe to fill the vacant space with resin that hardened to keep the head from collapsing.

The embalmers then drew a red line on the abdomen as a guide to cut a three-inch incision, which they made using a black obsidian glass stone. Its precise sharp edge helped maintain the skin's integrity. From that incision, they removed the moist internal organs that would cause the body to decompose faster. One by one, they pulled out the spleen, liver, intestines, pancreas, kidneys, gall bladder, and stomach.

They left Khonsu's heart in his chest because to the Egyptian the heart was the very center of being. It was the source of all thoughts and feelings. It was the organ that Anubis would weigh on the scales of justice in the Great Hall of Osiris.

The internal organs were stored in one of four canopic jars, each having a lid with the head of one of the four sons of Horus. Mesti, the son with a human head. Duamutef, the jackal. Hapi, the baboon. Qebesenef, the hawk.

Another resin called "the liquid of the children of Horus" was poured into the jars to embalm the organs for eventual use at the resurrection. Jambres prayed to each of the canopic gods to protect and provide for Khonsu's various body parts.

After this, Khonsu's body was ready to be dehydrated. About six hundred pounds of natron powder was shoveled onto the corpse, covering it completely under a mound. Natron was a salt-like substance mined from the western desert that would dry out the body in thirty-five days.

The embalmers would leave Khonsu there in the "place of cleansing" until it was ready for the next step in burial.

Ta Mefkat

It had only taken several days for the Israelites to finish packing up and assemble across the river as a caravan for their long trek into uncertain wilderness. As Moses had forecast, they'd had to bake unleavened loaves of bread for the journey because there was no time to let the dough rise. They had moved with such urgency that Moses considered it a miracle how quickly they were ready.

The number of Israelites was a multitude of many thousands, a majority of whom had come from the surrounding twenty Hebrew towns in Goshen. But they also included thousands more of a mixed multitude of other slaves from conquered enemies like Kush, Canaan, and Syria who were willing to join the Israelites in their quest for freedom. Their Egyptian overlords would barely notice these other peoples' departure amidst their mourning.

There were thousands of livestock, flocks, and herds as well. Stubborn animals, rascally children, and elderly people all conspired to make this journey a most difficult one. A seasoned merchant caravan could travel about fifteen or even twenty miles a day through such terrain. Moses had calculated that ten miles a day would be an impressive accomplishment for this diverse crowd. But he had not figured in their ruggedness born of enduring centuries of hard labor.

Yahweh had told them not to take the northern Way of Horus, also known as the Way of the Philistines, that bypassed the Sea of Reeds and followed the Great Sea before turning south to Sinai. Though this was a more amenable route, Yahweh had warned Moses that the Israelites would probably turn back because of the many Egyptian forts situated along that route, which could lead inevitably to warfare. Instead, they were to take the route Moses had taken, the Way of the Wilderness, a trade route through Ta Mefkat that led directly to Yam Suph, the Sea of the End.

So they launched their exodus east from Avaris toward Succoth, a region in the Wadi Tumilat that was normally two days' journey. The Israelites made it in one long day, and the people rejoiced upon Moses's blessing.

But they were fresh on their journey, and Moses knew that subsequent miles would slow them down. Their first target on their itinerary was the region called Etham on the outer edge of the Yam Suph wilderness. That was less than two hundred miles east and south of Succoth. Etham was a habitable area with plenty of vegetation and water resources. But they were not going to stay there. From Etham, they would pass around Yam Suph's northern edge and down into Midian's Sinai range where the mountain of God thrust skyward.

They began their passage early in the morning and entered Ta Mefkat the very next day. For the next eighteen or so days, they would travel through large wadis or valleys with more traversable pathways than the surrounding rocky terrain. Though it was not a completely arid geography, it was nevertheless a difficult distance to travel.

Already, Moses was anxious with anticipation for his reunion with Zipporah in Midian. It had been so long. Months. He missed her so badly. And now with the real prospect of seeing her soon, it heightened the pain of separation—and the desire. He had so much he wanted to tell her, to relive with her the experiences he'd had with his new family and people, of Yahweh and his awesome power. He would tell her everything. Leave nothing out. Even the horrifying parts so she would not be so envious of having been absent.

Within days, thunderstorms broke out overhead. The rains seemed to follow the mile-long caravan winding its way through the wilderness highway. Another miracle that provided much-needed water for humans and animals alike. People would hold out vases and jugs to collect water.

Frequent rains had refreshed a small stream along their path. Moses knew that he was going to see plenty more miracles before they were settled in the Promised Land. They had to because otherwise these people would die in the wilderness.

The Angel of Yahweh leading them was one of those miracles. Moses employed a common nomad tradition of leading large numbers of travelers. A moving caravan can follow those in front of them well enough. But it was also easy to lose one's orientation in the midst of the masses, which could lead to the travelers' confusion.

So at the front of the caravan Moses placed a large mule-drawn cart called "The Messenger." In the brass-gilded cart, they would burn bitumen, a black, oily semi-hardened material that could burn for long hours and create a tall plume of smoke in the sky. During the day, anyone in the mile-long train of people could see that pillar as an anchor point for their direction. And the bright flames would remain a source of orientation in the dark of night.

Within the first week of travel, Joshua rode his horse up to Moses, who was on his cart leading the caravan, to tell him that the bitumen was burning without needing to be supplemented.

"It is a miracle!" cried Joshua. "We should have had to add more bitumen days ago, but it appears to have not lost a fraction of its original amount."

"Are you blind to miracles, my assistant?" chided Moses.

Joshua's face crinkled in confusion. "Did I not just say…?"

Moses interrupted him. "Have you not noticed that the plume of smoke retains the shape of a long pillar during the day without dispersing? And at night that the flames of the bitumen are three times their normal size? That is actually *three* miracles, not one. Get your count right, or I may have to reconsider your assistance to me."

Joshua looked at Moses and saw his impish smile. He returned it with one of his own.

Moses added, "The Angel of Yahweh resides in the pillar of smoke and fire as he did in the burning bush in Sinai. He goes before us to lead the way. *His* way."

"Excellent," exhaled a relieved Joshua. "For a moment there, I thought we were being led by you, and that surely would have resulted in decades of lost desert wandering."

They shared a laugh. Every moment of levity helped on this painful journey through an earthly Duat toward freedom.

CHAPTER 43

The Great Sea

The god Ra had lost all sense of time in the darkness of his prison at the bottom of the sea. Had he been here for days? Weeks? Months? It didn't matter. His bitterness had already compounded in his heart because all he had was time to burn in these infernal depths. So he burned with rage.

But somewhere in that timelessness, he felt an undersea current flow over him. Bu nothing moved down here. What could it be? An underwater volcano? He saw no burning magma.

No, wait. There it was. A flame coming toward him. But it wasn't volcanic. No, these were multiple flames. When they got close enough, Ra could see they were on multiple heads. Seven heads with seven sets of fiery eyes.

Apophis! The sea serpent of chaos had found him.

When the serpent circled near him again, Ra saw a rider on the main head. As the scales swished by him, he reached out his bindings to cut them on the preternaturally sharp scales of the creature. To anything on earth those scales were impenetrable. They alone could cut through cherubim hair.

Another pass, and he had successfully mounted the creature, cutting the rest of his bindings and climbing to the main head, where he recognized Set riding the thing like a steed.

He felt the cold deep fade away below him as they rose to the surface. The pressure of the depths lessened as he reached the surface. He felt strength return to his flesh.

"How did you do it?" asked Ra. "How did you secure Apophis's help?"

Apophis was not controlled by any force in heaven or on earth. As the bringer of chaos he swam where he willed. None of the gods could commandeer his lawless spirit.

Almost none.

"I have been with some of the gods of Canaan," answered Set. "You should meet Asherah, Lady of the Sea. She gave me primeval spells that could harness Apophis for a limited time and purpose. Up there they call him Leviathan. Oh, and Asherah is also a violent and degrading sexual partner. The perversions they have developed in Canaan will certainly gratify you. They perform child sacrifice on every high hill and under every green tree."

Ra was focused. "I am not interested in petty fetishes. I want to know if Apophis will help me fight Yahweh's hive of Hebrew sub-humans."

"He is especially willing to help in any fight with Yahweh *or* his hive. It is Apophis's purpose for being."

"Good, then help me hunt down the Israelites in the wilderness."

"No," said Set. "In light of the devastation Yahweh already wrought upon Egypt, your original plans for Canaanite allies have become even more necessary. I will return to the Negeb where I can be more useful."

Ra looked at Set. He did not trust the Watcher. Set had always been a loose arrow and a source of chaos. There was no reason why he would not remain so. It was his nature.

But Ra had special plans for his climactic battle with Yahweh. He didn't need Set for it. What he needed was the lector priest Jambres and Heka's magic to implement his plans.

Avaris

After fifteen or so days of mourning for Khonsu, Dudimose was still broken by the loss. But he was finally able to console himself again as he returned to frolicking with his child servants.

In another twenty days, the thirty-five days of cleansing would be over for Khonsu's drying body. The embalmers would then remove the corpse from the natron. It would be almost completely dried out by then. They would wash the body and internal cavities with wine and aromatic spices and stuff them with resin-soaked linen strips. As the resin hardened, the body would retain its full shape.

Next, the body would be anointed with cedar oil, frankincense, and myrrh as Jambres recited a spell wearing an Anubis mask. "May this anointing cleanse Khonsu to make him pure before the Great Hall of Osiris. May its sweet savor be like incense to the gods and provide for him an eternal rest."

Then it would be time for the wrapping. First, they would place gold, the metal of eternity, on Khonsu's toes and fingers. An amulet with the Eye of Horus to protect him in his Duat journey would be placed around his neck and over his heart.

The embalmers would then take long strips of linen and wrap Khonsu tightly to preserve his body until its resurrection.

When the mummification was complete and a proper sarcophagus made of Khonsu's visage, Dudimose would transport the body in a funerary barque much like Ra's solar barque to Thebes, several hundred miles upriver, where the necropolis of the Valley of Kings was located.

On his day of burial, an entourage of participants would engage in the "opening of the mouth" ceremony. Because Khonsu was crown prince, elect to the throne, Dudimose was determined that his son would receive the kingly ceremony. Actors would reenact Horus avenging his father Osiris's death, resulting in actual animal sacrifices for the apotheosis reserved for the elect-king to become the new Osiris.

Jambres would recite more prayers and touch the mouth of Khonsu's mummy with a tool, announcing, "With this instrument of Anubis, I open the eyes and mouth of Khonsuemwaset, son of Khaneferre Dudimose, king of Egypt. Your body shall walk and speak and be among the gods. You are young again. You will live again."

Only then would Khonsu's *ba*-spirit be free to leave his body and roam about. His *ka*-spirit would be empowered for its journey through Duat.

Khonsu's mummy would be placed in a coffin shaped as an ideal image of him as Lord of the Dead. It would be sealed and placed in the tomb beneath the necropolis of Thebes along with various furniture, jewelry of silver, gold, and precious stones, as well as other items for use in the afterlife. The sacramental goods in his resting place would ensure the continuing pleasures of this life in the paradise of the Field of Reeds.

On the tomb walls, engraved and painted spells from the Book of the Dead would aid Khonsu in his journey through Duat lest his heart forget them.

They were there as a permanent resource for him in the afterlife. A resource to help his *ka*-spirit as it journeyed to Osiris's Great Hall of Judgment to have his heart weighed on the scales of justice against the feather of Ma'at.

Final prayers would be implored, and the tomb would be sealed forever.

Dudimose wept again at the site of embalming across the river as if he had just lost his son for the first time. He wondered if the curses of that mountain demon Yahweh could reach into the Judgment Hall of Justice as easily as he had reached into the sacred and glorious Red and Black Land of Egypt with his plagues. Dudimose prayed he could not. Otherwise all was lost for both him and his son—for all eternity.

A dizziness came over him. He had not eaten in two days. When he looked up, he saw the hawk-headed gods Ra and Horus standing above him with glowing, angry eyes. Was he hallucinating? Both of them then pointed to the east with their hands.

He bowed his head to pray. But he felt his heart grow heavy again with hatred. He had let the Hebrews go, despite them being a significant labor force. His advisors had reminded him of this, but he hadn't listened because when he'd lost his son, he'd lost his mind over any final hope for his dynasty.

Now that sanity was returning to him, Dudimose realized that he had made a monumental mistake. He had lost most of Egypt's food and herds and livestock, a large portion of her populace, and some of her monuments and buildings. Egypt was devastated and needed to be rebuilt. But he had let go most of Egypt's slaves key to that rebuilding.

When Dudimose looked up, the gods were gone. He stood up from his knees. He kissed his hand and touched the pile of natron covering his son. Then he marched toward his boat to return to the palace. He had twenty days left before Khonsu's burial. Plenty of time to muster his army and hunt down the fleeing Hebrews in the wilderness to bring them back. If they refused, then he would torture and kill Moses and Aaron, then proceed to do the same to every single one of their elders until they obeyed.

He still preferred killing them all, but he needed them too badly.

As the boat docked back across the river, he barked to his vizier Harsekher, "Muster my army and all my chariots and horses. I am going after those Hebrew godlickers to bring them back."

"My king," said Harsekher, "you have six hundred chosen chariots and another thousand in waiting. Are you sure you want them all?"

"I said all, did I not?"

"Yes, my lord. And your entire army?"

"Yes. I want to strike such fear into their hearts with the power of my outstretched arm that they would hand over Moses themselves just to avoid the suffering I will inflict upon them."

"It will take several days to muster them."

"Then what are you standing around for, vizier? Every minute counts."

•••••

In the House of Life in Avaris, Ipuwer the scribe sat down to continue writing a lament for Egypt that described the judgments that they had just experienced and what it was leading to. It was not normal practice for kings to record their own defeats or failures. In fact, they would often employ fiction to record defeats *as* victories and failures *as* successes during their rule.

But Ipuwer was not about to share this with the king. He wanted a record that might one day survive as a lesson of true history for Egypt. Even as he wrote, he wondered if humanity ever learned from history. It seemed as if kingdoms rose and fell in similar patterns of arrogance and humility. Since human nature did not change, why would he think that anyone would ever learn from that fallen state of ignorance?

He wrote in Egyptian hieratic script.

> *What the ancestors foretold has happened.*
> *Crime is everywhere, there is no man of yesterday.*
> *The virtuous man goes in mourning because of what has happened*
>   *in the land.*
> *Foreigners have become Egyptians everywhere.*
> *Khnum does not create because of the condition of the land.*

He thought back to the beginning, when Moses had poured water to the ground and the Nile became blood:

> *Behold, Egypt has fallen to the pouring water.*
> *And he who poured water on the ground seizes the mighty in misery.*
> *The river is blood!*

Moses: Against the Gods of Egypt

As you drink of it, you lose your humanity and thirst for water.

Ipuwer considered the destruction of their crops and their livestock from swarms, pestilence, locusts, and hail:

Gone is the grain of abundance.
Food supplies are running short.
Lo, crocodiles gorge on their catch,
The nobles hunger and suffer.
Upper Egypt has become a wasteland.
Grain is lacking on every side.
The storehouse is bare.
Women say, "Oh that we had something to eat!"
What can we do about it? All is ruin!

Ipuwer remembered the terror of the three days darkness:

Those who had shelter are now in the dark of the storm.
The whole of the delta cannot be seen.
There is fire in their hearts!

Ipuwer thought of the solution to the "Hebrew Question" undertaken by Pharaoh Amenemhat III:

If only he had perceived the nature of his internal enemies in the
*   first generation!*
Then he would have smitten the evil
*   —stretched out his arm against it.*
He would have destroyed their seed and their heritage.

Ipuwer wrote of the ultimate abomination, the plague on the firstborn:

Behold, plague sweeps the land,
Blood is everywhere with no shortage of the dead.
Children are dashed against the walls.
The funeral shroud calls out to you before you come near.
Woe is me for the grief of this time.
He who buries his brother in the ground is everywhere.
Wailing is throughout the land mingled with lamentations.

Finally, Ipuwer wrote of the exodus of the cursed Habiru and the shadow of invading Hyksos on the horizon:

> *The slave takes what he finds.*
> *What belongs to the palace has been stripped.*
> *Gold, lapis lazuli, silver, and turquoise are strung on the necks of female slaves.*
> *See how the poor of the land have become rich whilst the man of property is a pauper.*
> *The districts are laid waste,*
> *Foreign tribes come into Egypt...*[3]

It brought shuddering chills upon Ipuwer to relive the terrors through which they had just survived. He prayed that these words would not be lost to history or destroyed for the benefit of Pharaoh's reputation. Despite all the many wars and famines and pestilence that had troubled Egypt's history, he was sure nothing like this had ever happened or would ever happen again.

• • • • •

Jambres entered a secret chamber in the temple of Ra known only to the high priests and walked down a tunnel of stairs to his destination. As far as he was concerned, he was alone. In fact, he was followed in the unseen realm by the gods Ra, Horus, and Heka.

Ra had appeared to Jambres and told him that it was time to call upon the forces of the underworld to aid Pharaoh Dudimose in his campaign against the fleeing Hebrews.

At the end of the tunnel, Jambres arrived at the entrance to a small subterranean cavern about the size of the sanctuary above him. He approached the shore of a small lagoon of black water. Egyptians understood this lagoon gave access to the underworld Duat. The Hebrews called it the Abyss.

The Abyss was the primordial waters of chaos that still encircled the cosmos, fed the river Wernes in the underworld, and was the abode of Apophis. The Abyss was a part of the underworld realm that intersected with

---

[3] "The Admonitions of Ipuwer," a document from the Second Intermediate Period, text translation provided by David Rohl, *Exodus: Myth or History?* (MN: Thinking Man Media, 2015), 150-153. Additional verse translation from the full text of the Admonitions of Ipuwer: William W. Hallo and K. Lawson Younger, *The Context of Scripture, Vol. 1* (Leiden; New York: Brill, 1997–), 93–104. Some verse has been altered for clarification of context.

the earthly waters and openings at various locations around the world. This allowed Apophis entrance to anywhere on earth in mere moments. To swim the waters of the Abyss was to enter a world where time and space had little meaning.

Therefore these netherworld waters served as a portal from which Jambres could call forth an army of evil spirits from any location on the earth.

Jambres set down a cage of ibis birds by the shoreline. He reached in and grabbed one, pulled out an obsidian blade, cut its throat, and placed it at the pool's edge to let the blood drain and mix with the water. He did the same with eleven other birds, placing them at various points around the pool.

He then performed incantations to call up the demons. In the unseen realm, Heka led the three gods in their own conjuring to call forth minions for their army.

The black waters began to swirl. The sounds of chaotic whispers filled the cavern. They were whispers of anger, hatred, and violence. The whispers turned to piercing shrieks and wails. Jambres had to cover his ears. These were the demons of war, and they would possess the bodies of Pharaoh's soldiers to crush the exodus of the Israelites.

CHAPTER 44

Etham

The Israelites had made it to the more habitable and fertile region of Etham at the edge of the wilderness near Yam Suph. It had taken them a couple of weeks to get there. Moses had allowed them to rest a day, gather up vegetation, water their herds and flocks, and enjoy the moderate climate before they would follow the downward slope around Yam Suph's northern edge and into Midian.

Then the Angel of Yahweh spoke to Moses from the pillar of fire at night, telling him to change course from his projected route east and veer immediately south into the mountainous region along Yam Suph's *western* coast. It didn't make sense to Moses. He knew that route would not lead them to Midian. It would lead them deeper into Ta Mefkat—*across the sea from Midian.*

He argued with Yahweh that night but in the morning told no one and obediently followed the pillar of smoke south through the wadi valley. No one was familiar with this land so no one realized how off-course they had gone.

Within a couple of days, the Israelites had come to the entrance of a deep valley with sheer walls of rock a hundred feet high and a small winding path barely wide enough to move their numbers. Moses called it Pi-Hahiroth because it looked like a canyon mouth. That entrance faced north toward Baal-Zaphon, the mountain of Ba'al in Syria that served Egyptians as a common compass reference. After camping there, they pressed on into the deep canyon.

•••••

Several days behind the Habiru caravan, Pharaoh Dudimose led his army into Etham. They had traveled double-time to catch up with the Hebrews, and Dudimose knew he was mere days away from falling upon his prey. It had been easy to follow their tracks, but Dudimose was confused to discover they had turned south into Ta Mefkat instead of pressing on into Midian. Thinking it might have been a trick, he sent scouts ahead toward Midian. But they returned with news that no large caravan had passed that way.

Dudimose's high priest Jambres was by his side as he stood in the chariot that his son Prince Khonsuemwaset had championed when he was alive. He wanted to use it in vengeance against the Hebrews, either as the means by which he would re-enslave them or massacre them if need be.

Dudimose signaled the chariot corps and his troops to follow the Habiru masses down the valley path. His chariots would lead with over a thousand vehicles. He knew he could subdue the Hebrews with his chariots alone and use the foot soldiers to guide their captives back to Egypt.

As they moved onward, Dudimose thought about the same thing he had thought about the entire week or so of their journey. Capturing, torturing, and destroying Moses, the Destroyer of Egypt.

Yam Suph

For the last few days, the Israelites had traversed about forty miles of the wadi canyon until they reached an opening that led to a large beach on the shore of Yam Suph.

It was a dead end. Before them was the vast, deep sea. To their backs was the steep mountain range Moses called Migdol because it rose over them like a tower.

And it blocked them from being able to go anywhere. They were trapped between the mountains and the sea.

The children didn't seem to mind. Screaming with delight, many of them ran to jump and play in the waters of the shoreline. Hundreds of them. They splashed and shouted, losing all sense of the danger they had just traveled through to get here and all sense of the danger that was lurking in the dark of the deep very near their little bodies.

Just offshore in the unseen realm not far from where the children splashed and played, Apophis, the seven-headed sea serpent of chaos, glided through the dark waters. He was prowling in preparation for the devastation riding down upon the Israelites. Ra had called upon the mighty creature with the spells Set provided.

Ra, Horus, and Heka were with Pharaoh and his demon-possessed army.

After they had pitched camp for the night, Moses called a meeting of the elders to pass on information to the clans. A couple hundred of them, they met past The Messenger, still burning its perpetual flames in the night. Grouped in their own tribes, the families were settled down for the evening, filling the beach.

Moses had Aaron and Miriam with him, trying to calm the elders' fear.

"Why have you taken us here?" questioned one of the elders.

"It is not I who has taken us here," replied Moses. "It is Yahweh."

"But you told us we were going to Midian," complained another. He pointed toward Yam Suph. "Midian is *across* the sea."

The elders grumbled in agreement.

They were interrupted by Joshua and Caleb, who walked up to Moses and whispered to him.

Moses announced, "No, tell us all."

Joshua and Caleb looked to Moses for a second assurance. Moses nodded.

Joshua spoke. "Caleb and I have returned from scouting the canyon." He hesitated. "Pharaoh and his chariots and horses have followed us from Egypt. They are in the canyon not far from here."

The elders erupted in horror. Men shouted and complained.

Moses calmed them down to speak one at a time.

One said, "But Pharaoh said we could freely leave!"

"I know," replied Moses.

Another shouted, "Why have you taken us all the way to this dead end with nowhere to go?"

A third accused furiously, "You have taken us from our lives in Egypt only to lose them in the wilderness!"

Another yelled out, "Let us go negotiate with Pharaoh. It would be better to serve the Egyptians than to die here!"

The crowd's opinion was split.

Taking out his sword, Joshua roared angrily, "Cowards and traitors! You would fornicate with false gods! I will stand and fight to the death for our god and our nation! Who is with me?"

Moses reached out and stopped Joshua. He made him sheath his sword. Joshua looked confused.

Moses said, "There will be no battle against the Egyptians this day. Yahweh is our banner of war. He will fight for us."

"But how?" called out another from the crowd.

"Do not fear," affirmed Moses. "Stand firm in your faith and see the salvation of Yahweh. After this day, you will never see the Egyptians again."

"How?!" shouted another. It was repeated like a refrain amongst the crowd. "How?! Yes, how?!"

Moses calmed them again. "Yahweh will fight for you. You need only be silent."

"He is telling us to shut up!" cried another.

Just then Moses realized that Joshua, Caleb, Miriam, and Aaron were all staring behind them in awe. Turning, he saw the pillar of fire and smoke that had been burning on The Messenger cart suddenly rise above the crowd and move on its own power across the beach back toward the canyon exit.

People encamped in its way screamed and moved as the pillar slowly made its way.

By the time it arrived by the opening of the canyon, the entire camp of Israelites had come out to watch it.

The pillar's flames now rose to the height of the canyon walls. It lit up the Israelites' entire camp so that it appeared almost as day. Meanwhile, they could see that the canyon beyond was still cloaked in darkness.

"Yahweh guards the beach entrance for us," Joshua said with open-mouthed wonder.

"That is not what I told you?" replied Moses.

"That would be three miracles in one," said Joshua with a smile. "The protection, the light, and the darkness."

"I am glad I kept you as my assistant," said Moses with a slightly upturned lip.

"But there is still nowhere to go, Moses," Miriam observed.

"You are wrong about that, Miriam. Yahweh has told me where to go."

The elders turned to watch Moses walk down into the surf and stretch out his hand and staff over the sea.

No sooner had he done so than a strong east wind from across the sea rushed upon them all. It was a cool roaring wind hovering over the waters.

Spotting in the distance a massive disturbance on the surface, the elders drew nearer to Moses on the shore.

At first the disturbance appeared to be a depression as if the wind was pushing the water down.

Then from the far side, the depression became a channel.

The waters were pulling back, creating a channel like a valley.

The elders were silent. They had finally shut up.

More Israelites began noticing what was happening and were congregating near the shore to watch the amazing sight.

The sea was parting before their very eyes.

Yahweh's hands were pushing back the waters to the right and to the left until a pathway several miles wide was laid bare on the seabed. It was an act of creation, bringing the dry land out of the waters.

The sea congealed into two walls of water, appearing to freeze as though cliffs of ice miles apart.

In the unseen realm, Apophis's body was caught frozen in the midst of those waters. It struggled to move, to break free from the prison of solidified water. It breathed out fire from its mouths to melt the ice. But it was too late. The hardening mass pressed in and crushed Apophis's many heads. Yahweh held the chaos at bay.

In the canyon, Yahweh also held Pharaoh's army at bay. The pillar of fire kept them from moving forward and exiting the canyon. The Angel of Yahweh's presence whipped into a frenzy the demons who had inhabited the soldiers for war.

The Angel's supernatural presence even immobilized Ra, Horus, and Heka.

No one was going anywhere—yet.

On the beach, the Israelites congregated before Moses. Before him, the wind had dried the seabed of all water. The several-mile-wide pathway dipped down at a steep incline, but it would still be traversable.

Yahweh had parted Yam Suph for the Israelites to walk through.

Moses ordered trumpets to announce that they were moving forward and must move quickly.

Some were frightened at first, but the ordered waters were at such a distance that they were able to trust stepping into what had previously been the chaotic sea. Yet another miracle was the fact that the sea floor had been dried up so that they would not get stuck in mud as they walked.

A mile-wide swath of Israelites descended the incline with their women, children, and elderly, as well as their livestock, flocks, and herds. They followed Moses through the deep, dark valley of the shadow of death with faith that Yahweh would get them to the other side. With their numbers, it would take them all night to cross. But they moved faster than they ever had before.

They ran for their lives.

By morning, Pharaoh had become impatient. They could not pass the pillar of fire blocking the exit of the canyon. His army had finally caught up with his chariots and horses.

Then without warning, the huge pillar of fire just lifted into the air and dissipated before their eyes, taking with it the darkness that had covered them.

Dudimose did not tarry. He charged forward with his thousand chariots and several thousand horsemen, racing onto the beach to attack the Hebrews.

But the Hebrews were gone.

Before Dudimose was a wide, dry path of the seabed where there should have been Yam Suph! Driving his chariot up to the incline's edge, he saw in the distance what appeared to be frozen walls of water held back to the right and to the left.

Before him were tracks the multitude must have made on their way across the seabed.

Well, whatever this Yahweh had done to provide for the Hebrews' passage, Dudimose figured he would use it to his advantage and hunt them down.

The sun god was starting to rise in the east. He imagined Ra shining upon the Egyptians, providing them the opening they needed.

He sounded his trumpets and all his chariots and horsemen raced down the incline to catch up with the slaves.

The army followed behind.

In the unseen realm, Horus and Heka went with Pharaoh, but Ra stayed behind on a rock overseeing the seabed.

Ra could see what was coming. Apophis was already frozen in the waters, his heads crushed. Ra had spent enough time bound in the deep. He was not going to allow that to happen to him again.

He knew what would happen next. Yahweh loved water and floods. This was the end of Pharaoh's Egypt and the end of Ra's own power because Hyksos kings were already amassing in preparation for invading the land.

With all of the Egyptian gods bound or destroyed, Ra would have no power to withstand a takeover by the Semitic gods. No, Ra would not be a fool and go down into Duat for this lost cause. He'd had a change of plans.

He was going to escape this cursed kingdom and flee to Canaan. His own exodus. He was going to shed his Egyptian identity and come out as who he really was: Mastema.

He turned and left the Egyptian gods and men behind to meet their fate.

When Pharaoh had nearly reached the other side of the seabed, he could see the last of the Israelites climbing the incline and onto the bank. The sun rose behind them in the east.

Thank Ra, he thought. The Hebrews had made it across, but he could catch them anyway. Ra would have his victory.

But the long incline to the bank was steep and slowed them down. Pharaoh whipped his horses madly to go faster, but it only seemed to slow them further. His frustration turned to fury. He was so close. He was within striking distance of his enemy. He saw Moses looking down upon the Egyptian army.

"Moses!" Dudimose screamed out. "Curse you and curse your god! I will send you to the underworld!"

"No, you will not!" Moses yelled back.

The pillar of fire came down from heaven, once again blocking Pharaoh's way. Thunder above struck fear into the pursuers' hearts. Horses whinnied and froze in fear. Some threw their riders to the ground. Chariots crashed into each other. Full-blown panic fell upon Pharaoh's forces. Then for some inexplicable reason, chariot wheels began to lock up.

They were so close! Pharaoh's fury turned to madness.

He saw Moses raise his staff over the seabed. Then he heard a distant rumbling. Turning to look at the walls of congealed water. About a mile away, he saw them begin to collapse as if Yahweh's hot breath melted them. The water came crashing down and rushing toward them.

From both sides.

The horsemen screamed. They'd seen it too.

Some of them got off their horses and made a break for the crest of the sea bank.

Pharaoh's infantry was only halfway through the valley. Dropping weapons and armor, they ran with all their might.

But it was hopeless. The coming waves were too swift. They rushed in like a flood. Pharaoh called out to Ra.

But Ra was not there.

Horus and Heka were, since they'd accompanied Pharaoh on his attack. But they could not help Egypt's king as giant walls of seawater crashed into each other from the right and the left, engulfing man and god alike in a great flood of judgment.

Before he even had a chance to drown, the weight of the waves crushed Pharaoh to death. His high priest Jambres, still riding loyally at his side and calling out incantations to gods no longer listening, suffered the same fate as his king. Dudimose would never have his revenge on Moses and this people. And he would never return to bury his son because the Sea of the End, Yam Suph, would bury Pharaoh first.

Within moments, the Egyptian military host ceased to exist, their infantry, their horsemen, and their chariot forces entombed in the deep with their Pharaoh.

And with them, four hundred years of Egyptian affliction.

Moses stood on the seashore with Joshua, Caleb, Aaron, Miriam, and the Israelite caravan, watching the sea swallow their enemies into oblivion. Screams of shock and horror from shoreside observers filled the air. Even though these were Yahweh's eternal enemies, even though they were guilty of enslaving the Israelites and treating them cruelly, the sheer power of Yahweh's wrath frightened a people with little understanding of this new Name who called them out of Egypt.

The swirling turmoil lessened as the waters found their equilibrium on the sea floor. When the foam and whitewater dissipated, countless Egyptian and equine corpses could be seen floating in the water. Some washed ashore, grotesquely crumpled and battered.

A dread silence weighed heavily over the Israelites as they contemplated this most powerful of all the signs and wonders they had ever seen or heard. Each of the plagues had increasingly demonstrated Yahweh's incomparable power and authority. But this? This would surely be remembered as history's greatest deliverance.

Picking up a tambourine, Miriam began to sing and dance. A host of other women dancers quickly joined her. Soon everyone was joining in as they sang a song of victory for Yahweh over Pharaoh and Egypt.

An inherently poetic people, they sang in responsive antiphony with spontaneous lyrics, caught up in the creative spirit of the moment. Moses would lead in verse, and the crowd would repeat it. Then another song leader would pick up where Moses left off.

> *I will sing to Yahweh, for he has triumphed gloriously;*
> *The horse and his rider he has thrown into the sea.*
> *Yahweh is my strength and my song,*
> *And he has become my salvation;*
> *This is my God, and I will praise him,*
> *My father's God, and I will exalt him.*
> *Yahweh is a man of war;*
> *Yahweh is his name.*
>
> *Who is like you, O Yahweh, among the gods?*
> *Who is like you, majestic in holiness,*
> *Awesome in glorious deeds, doing wonders?*

You stretched out your right hand;
The earth swallowed them.

You have led in your steadfast love the people whom you have redeemed.
You will bring them in and plant them on your own mountain,
The place, O Yahweh, which you have made for your abode,
The sanctuary, O Adonai, which your hands have established.
Yahweh will reign forever and ever.

As the people continued to raise their celebration of praise to Yahweh, Moses pulled Aaron and Joshua aside.

He spoke first to Aaron. "My brother, you have been an elder of highest standing in Israel during my absence. You have been my voice and my right arm in my confrontations with Pharaoh."

Aaron perked up with a proud, confident look. "I have shared your leadership, brother, and it is my honor to continue to do so."

Moses smiled. He knew his brother had always struggled with the idea of his younger sibling being chosen over him. But then Moses didn't think he was worthy of his calling either.

He said, "Now that we are free to worship Yahweh, we will need a high priest to guide us in worship. I would like you and your sons to take on that honorable task until Yahweh should reveal differently."

At first Aaron's countenance dropped from the news. But the more he thought about it, the more he appeared to resign himself. "I will lead our people in the worship of Yahweh, brother. Even as you lead us through the wilderness."

Moses slapped him on the back, and they embraced. Then Moses turned to Joshua.

"My assistant, you have obeyed my word to withhold from violence that Yahweh may prove his salvation. I am proud of you. Restraint and submission to authority is a sign of true leadership."

"I confess it has been difficult," admitted Joshua. "But Yahweh continues to prove his holy power and my need for holy trust."

"You have proven yourself," said Moses. "And now, on this side of Yam Suph, is a new journey. The land of Canaan, which Yahweh has promised us for an inheritance, is a land of great violence and evil. In Egypt, Yahweh fought for us. Now we are to fight for Yahweh. I need a holy army, and I want you to be my general."

Joshua's eyes teared up with gratitude. "My lord, it is an honor I do not deserve." He began to kneel but stopped himself with a smile. He straightened back up.

Moses said, "None of us deserve Yahweh's mercy. Yet he grants it."

"What are my orders?"

"Raise up men and prepare them for war."

CHAPTER 45

Rephidim

Moses walked toward the pillar of cloud that was outside the Israelite camp on Horeb's Hisma Plateau in the area called Rephidim. He knew this extremely arid region well from his forty years of sojourn in Midian.

The closer they got to Sinai, the more Moses ached longingly to see Zipporah, his sons, his father-in-law. But this moment shoved all hope aside. He was coming before Yahweh to plead for his life.

It was early morning, and the people were gathering their daily ration of manna to eat. Manna was a substance that appeared every morning on the desert floor after the dew evaporated. It was like coriander seed, white, flaky, and with a sweet honey flavor. The word *manna* meant "what is it?" because the Israelites hadn't understood what it was when they first encountered it. It was another miraculous provision from Yahweh in a series of miracles over the last couple of moons to bring them to this dry region. And it marked another instance of grumbling and complaining from the ungrateful masses of Israelites.

When they'd first crossed Yam Suph, they had traveled south through the Wilderness of Shur three days without water. When they came to a location with water, it turned out to be bitter water unsuitable for consumption. They'd called the place Marah, meaning *bitterness*. The Israelites had complained to Moses, at which time Yahweh revealed to Moses that throwing a log into the water would turn it into sweet, potable water.

Moses had tried to use this as an object lesson of faith. But after camping near Yam Suph, the Israelites entered the Wilderness of Sin and began grumbling again, this time for food. They complained that they'd had full meat pots in Egypt and made wild, scurrilous claims that Moses had brought them out to the wilderness to murder them with hunger. This had raised Moses's ire, but Yahweh responded first by providing a massive flock of quail in the evening to fill their bellies with meat. Then the next morning the miraculous manna began to appear after the morning dew. Yahweh had told Moses that this daily provision would continue until such time as the Israelites entered the Promised Land.

But Yahweh imposed restrictions. The people were supposed to only gather what they needed each day and store nothing. On the sixth day, they were to gather twice as much, then rest from gathering on the seventh day.

Once again, the Israelites could not follow Yahweh's simple commands. Some started hoarding manna, but it simply turned smelly and rancid and became worm-infested. Others attempted to gather on the seventh day instead of gathering double the amount the day before. But manna did not appear on that day.

Becoming angry, Moses yelled at the Israelites for their sinful disobedience to Yahweh's commands. Yahweh was trying to institute a weekly day of rest for the people, a *sabbath*, in preparation for what was to come. But the people could not follow even the simplest of rules. Instead, they griped and complained like spoiled children. They had tested Moses's patience because they were testing the very God in whom they were supposed to have faith.

This almighty God had destroyed Egypt and delivered the Israelites through the most spectacular display of his glory in all of human history. Yet within a couple of moons, they had seemingly forgotten that event and were grumbling and complaining to Moses as if Yahweh had never delivered them.

The latest situation was here in Rephidim, where they began to quarrel again with Moses. They accused him of wanting to kill them all with thirst. They refused to trust Yahweh and treated Moses as if *he* was their deliverer. When Moses lost his temper, he shouted at them that they all deserved the suffering they were experiencing because of their own faithlessness. He then accused them of being unfaithful harlots wanting to return to fornication with the gods of Egypt.

The outraged mob was on the verge of stoning Moses to death when Joshua arrived with a regiment of soldiers he had been building from the tribes. They protected Moses from the mob and dispersed the crowd as Moses made his way out to the pillar of cloud hovering outside the camp.

Kneeling now before the cloud, Moses pleaded with Yahweh. The pillar no longer used The Messenger cart as its connection point to earth. It now seemed to come down directly from the sky to lead them in the direction of their trek.

"What shall I do with this people?" Moses cried out. "They are almost ready to stone me."

In the camp of the Israelites, Joshua's soldiers now protected Aaron, Miriam, and the elders as the mob turned their anger against their leaders. They held back the pressing crowd with shields.

Cries rang out from the agitated mob. "Yahweh is not among us!"

"Would you kill us for demanding water?" someone yelled.

Joshua had ordered the soldiers not to use their weapons against the people unless he commanded it. But he would do it if the situation required. If they threatened Yahweh's appointed leaders, he would kill as many of this unruly crowd of apostates as necessary to maintain law and order. Mob resistance was rebellion and chaos. Yahweh was their law and order.

Suddenly, a shout from a large rock outcropping not far from the camp in the direction of the cloud caught everyone's attention.

It was Moses. He stood on a large rock, holding in his right hand the very wooden shepherd's crook he had used in Egypt to curse the Nile. But this time he held it high in his hand and struck the rock.

The boulder trembled. Moses almost lost his footing. Then an explosion of water emerged from a crevice in the large rock. Gushing out into a small, dried creek bed nearby, it flowed its way toward camp.

The crowd paused in silent awe. A voice cried out, "Water! We are saved!" The mob that just seconds before had been on the verge of anarchy stampeded desperately to the water to drink.

Moses stepped away from the rock to safety as Israelites launched themselves at the flowing water, gulping for their lives. The throngs pushed in like a frenzy of crocodiles. Many were trampled beneath the pressing masses. All thought for others was cast aside as individuals preferred their own survival.

Joshua was about to command his soldiers to restore order when a small, young scout interrupted him.

"General, a band of Amalekite nomads are approaching from the east. I believe they are aware of our presence."

"How many?" Joshua asked.

"By my count, several thousand. And they have giants."

CHAPTER 46

The Israelites filled their water jugs and packed up their tents to travel toward the Sinai Wilderness a week north of their current location in Rephidim. They were trying to distance themselves from the Amalekite tribe approaching from the south. And they moved as quickly as they could.

Unfortunately, any caravan made up of many thousands of men, women, children, and animals results in the slower travelers and stragglers ending up at the train's rear. These were the ones the Amalekites attacked first for their plunder of goods and victims.

The first strike came at midday en route to Sinai. A group of a hundred or so travelers with carts were separated from the main body of Israelites. The Amalekites swooped in and attacked them, killing some, saving the women and children for slaves, stealing their provision-laden carts and donkeys. The invaders made a distinct howling sound as they attacked. They sounded like unearthly desert animals and struck fear into the Hebrews.

By the time Joshua and his soldiers arrived, it was too late. The Amalekites had retreated to their hidden camp nearby with their spoils. Evidence left behind showed that the attackers rode camels and were well equipped to fight. They no doubt sought to draw the Israelite defenders into an ambush at the pass. Joshua would not fall for the trick, so his force returned to guard the column's rear.

Joshua prayed for the poor souls taken hostage. He didn't know which was worse: the sexual abuse and slavery they would face or the possible fate of being eaten by their captors.

That night, Joshua went to Moses's tent in their encampment.

"We must fight these jackals," said Joshua. "Otherwise they will continue to pick off our weak and run like cowards."

"They are no cowards," said Moses. "They are cunning Shasu nomads who save their strength and minimize their casualties. Do not underestimate them."

Moses was familiar with the Amalekites from his life in Midian.

"They are cannibals and possess a kind of madness from eating human flesh. They are particularly difficult to kill because they engage in occultic magic that possesses them in battle."

Joshua asked, "Is that the source of their disturbing howling sounds?"

"Yes. They worship Azazel of the desert, a satyr goat god, from whom comes the *siyyim* and *iyyim*—howling desert demons."

"Then how can we defeat them?"

"I have asked Yahweh, and he has told me how. But you must understand Yahweh is no longer our sole defender. He will be our help. But we must fight too."

"Thank Yahweh," said Joshua. "I have been waiting for this."

Moses cautioned him. "Never forget that all victory will be accompanied by real loss—of innocent blood and of good men. Nothing of value comes without suffering."

Joshua nodded. "I do understand. And I think I have an idea of how we can give these slippery Amalekites a taste of their own tactics."

• • • • •

In the morning, the Israelites continued their journey toward Sinai. The people were more desperate to keep up with the bulk of the caravan this time. But still there were stragglers, those too exhausted or burdened with extra weight in their wagons to keep up.

By late afternoon, a hundred or so stragglers began to drift behind. A handful of guards on horseback tried to hurry them along, but the travelers simply did not have the endurance to catch up.

One of the guards was Joshua himself, who had taken on the burden of protection of their weakest members. But with only a handful of soldiers more suited to sounding an alarm than taking on an entire Amalekite raiding party he was woefully unmanned.

Looking ahead, Joshua spotted Moses standing on one of the rocky buttes along the way. The old leader gazed out upon the expanse, his brother Aaron and Hur, a tribal leader of Judah, by his side. It was now the end of the day, and the sun was nearing the western horizon. They would set up camp soon. Would the Amalekites attack at night? It would be more difficult to capture any hostages and near impossible to judge strategy when you could not see victory or failure until the battle's aftermath.

It would be a foolhardy strategy for their enemies.

Suddenly from out of the deep shadows of the rocks, a horde of demonic warriors came racing toward them on camels. The Amalekites were back.

They had waited until the last moment to strike, at the end of the day when the Israelites were the most tired.

Caleb saw them first. He whistled to Joshua, who turned and saw the approaching host. They were like a swarm of locusts and frighteningly ugly as they had war paint of stark white with black thunderbolts across their bodies and faces. Thunderbolts of Ba'al.

But Joshua did not sound an alarm. Instead, he stopped the group of cowering travelers and waited for the Amalekites, five hundred strong, to descend upon them.

It would be an easy slaughter—if it were not for the five hundred Hebrew horsemen who bolted out from their hiding place behind rocky buttes.

Then the slow stragglers cast off their cloaks to reveal themselves as disguised Hebrew warriors. No innocent Hebrew blood would be shed today.

The two armies clashed. But Joshua had caught his enemies between two wings of horsemen and infantry.

Joshua had ambushed the ambushers in a pincer move. The Amalekites began their demonic howling. Their trumpeter called for help.

Up on the rock ledge, Moses raised his staff of God in the air and held it there. He could see Joshua's forces pounding the Amalekites despite the nomads' superior experience.

This was Yahweh's promised help. He had told Moses that as long as he could hold his staff in the air, Joshua would overcome Amalek. But if he lowered his staff, Amalek would prevail.

Unfortunately, the one thing Moses did not anticipate was how heavy the staff would become in his arms.

In the unseen realm behind the Amalekite lines, Ba'al and Set watched the Deliverer up on the rock—with Mikael the archangel standing behind him.

Down in the field, the other six archangels stood in the midst of the battle responding to Moses's raised staff with help for the Hebrew fighters.

"This is not going to be easy," said Set.

"This is not about winning," said Ba'al. "It is about learning the tactics, strengths, and weaknesses of my approaching enemy."

Ba'al was after all the Most High god of Canaan.

On the battlefield, Joshua sliced the head off one Amalekite and cut the sword arm off another. But it wasn't easy. Their camels were taller than the Hebrew horses, which gave the Amalekites an advantage.

Then he saw Amalekite reinforcements arrive. Several hundred of them. He called out to his herald, who called for their own help.

Then he saw a handful of enemy warriors who did not need rides running toward them. They were giants, seven to ten feet tall and fast as camels. Their huge size, long necks, and red hair identified them as the Anakim of which Moses had spoken.

And those Anakim began striking down Hebrew warriors with ease.

On the rocky ledge, Moses's arm trembled violently from holding up his staff for so long. He lowered his arm to rest. Then he saw the forces of Amalek prevailing over the Hebrews. He raised the staff again with both arms and growled for endurance. But he didn't know how long he could hold it this time.

Down in the valley, Joshua galloped straight at the first giant he could find. No desert dog was going to taunt the armies of the living God.

Instead of striking at Joshua, the red-haired monster struck his horse. Joshua went down. He rolled a distance to safety but realized his sword was stuck beneath his horse's body corpse.

The giant came at him, carrying a mace of bone and steel. He swung at Joshua, who dodged each wave. Because of its mammoth size at close to ten feet, the Anakite was slower than a normal-sized soldier. He had much more weight to carry, about six hundred pounds' worth, and a longer swing arc.

Joshua refused to counter the thing head on but stayed just out of its striking zone, frustrating the giant until it began to maneuver sloppily.

Then Joshua spotted a spear lying on the ground. He dived and rolled toward the weapon, picking it up to guard against the giant as it lunged at him.

What came next happened so quickly Joshua barely had time to think. As he raised the spear high, it caught the attacking giant below the jaw. When he rammed forward, the spear went up through the jaw and into the brain, dropping the monster at Joshua's feet.

Joshua noticed that his nemesis possessed a strange anatomy: six fingers on each hand. He moved to the giant's side and glanced quickly its sandaled feet: six toes each. He looked up to see another giant now fixing his sights on Joshua. This one looked like a leader. It bore special armor that looked metallic but didn't glitter in the light of the sun, thick sandals, and the largest mace he had ever seen.

"Lucky thrust, Habiru runt!" the monster shouted. "Now let's see if your luck holds out against the mighty Sheshai."

Joshua swallowed. This monster's reputation was well known even in Egypt. Joshua had never dreamed he'd face the hulking mass before reaching Canaan.

But here he was. And Joshua still had no sword.

Was the giant right? Was it just luck? Or would Yahweh help him? Joshua remembered what Moses had said. Victory would not be without the loss of good men. Joshua was not guaranteed to survive.

Sheshai attacked. He swung his mace at Joshua, who ducked and dodged like before. But Sheshai was faster than the other giant and more experienced. Within three missed strokes, he spun around and swatted Joshua to the ground with his free hand.

The blow severely disoriented Joshua. He tried to gather his wits before it was too late.

The giant raised his mace above his head to land a crushing death blow.

Moments before up on the rock, Moses's arms had collapsed again in weakness. He could see that the Amalekites below were once again beginning to prevail. Aaron spotted Joshua facing off against an Anakite giant. Thinking quickly, he came up with an idea.

"Moses, sit on this rock."

Moses did. He needed more rest.

"Now, Hur, get on his other side and hold up his arm. I will hold up this side."

"Wait," said Moses. "I don't think—"

But as soon as the other two men lifted Moses's arms, the Israelites began to turn the tide of battle.

Aaron said, "You see, Moses, Yahweh doesn't want you alone to carry the weight of responsibility."

Moses said, "Sometimes you are quite annoying, brother. And sometimes you are right."

Down in the valley, Sheshai lowered his mace upon his Habiru victim.

But he felt something wrap around the weapon from behind, stopping his swing.

His Habiru target rolled out of the way.

Sheshai looked up at the mace to see a metallic serpent wrapped around it. What was that?

Then the mace just snapped, cut in half. He realized it wasn't a serpent at all but a blade. The unearthly blade operated like a whip in the hands of an older bald Habiru warrior behind him. Sheshai instinctively backed away from the range of the weapon. It must have been ten feet or so.

The older warrior was very adept with the flexible sword like an experienced wrangler with a whip. Nothing Sheshai knew could have cut his metal mace in half like that. He was not about to face an unknown enemy with such an advantage.

So he bolted and ran, the ground shaking with every stride.

In the unseen realm, the gods Ba'al and Set continued to observe the battle from a place of safety. They were not going to fight today. There would be plenty of opportunity for that in the coming days. Ba'al was going to help Set create a Ba'al cult in the delta for the Hyksos, then return with his Anakim to Canaan in preparation for these invading Habiru. Watching the enemy's behavior today convinced him of what he had suspected all along. Egyptian hegemony was over. The War of the Seed was coming to Canaan.

Up on the rock, Aaron and Hur continued to keep Moses's arms raised until the sun went down in the west and the Amalekites faded back into the shadows, defeated and humiliated. They had lost three quarters of their forces. They would not be returning to harass the Israelites.

Joshua dragged an Amalekite hostage before Moses up on the rock. The prisoner was bloody, hands and feet bound. His white and black paint had been almost all rubbed off in the heat of battle. His eyes had that wide-eyed look of madness in them. But he was coherent.

"My lord," said Joshua to Moses. "This Amalekite says that word has spread through the Negeb about the fall of Egypt. The Shasu shepherd kings are amassing for an invasion."

Moses said, "That explains the presence of the Anakim. They are uniting for a bigger fight."

He spoke to the Amalekite. "What exactly do you know?"

Joshua kicked the hostage, who reluctantly offered, "Not much. Plagues, famine, and rebellion have crippled Egypt."

Moses nodded. "The Egyptian king and his entire army, including all his chariot forces, are dead."

The Amalekite's eyes went wide with surprise. "How is that possible?"

"You will not believe me when I tell you. But I will tell you anyway. We were escaping Egypt to come to Midian. Our god Yahweh parted Yam Suph for us to cross through on dry land. Then when Pharaoh and his army followed us, Yahweh closed the waters upon them and drowned them all."

The Amalekite was dumbfounded.

"We saw it with our own eyes," Moses added. "We would not be here if it were not true. Pharaoh would never of his own accord free the slaves who build his monuments."

The Amalekite considered the truth of his words.

Moses looked at Joshua. "Let him return to his camp."

Pulling the prisoner up to his feet, Joshua loosed his bindings.

Moses then said to the Amalekite, "Tell your leaders they can take the land of Egypt without a fight because Pharaoh and his armies are dead. The city of Avaris and nearby towns of Goshen are empty of residents. And tell them that the right arm of Yahweh delivered the people of Israel from Pharaoh and Egypt."

Cutting the Amalekite's wrist binding, Joshua pushed him off into the night. The nomad stumbled and scrambled away, looking back over his shoulder in fear of being chased. But no one chased him that night, and he quickly disappeared into the blackness.

The next morning, before returning to their march, Moses instructed the Israelites to build an altar right at that location. Aaron sacrificed a goat on it to Yahweh, and Moses announced to the elders of the congregation, "Yahweh has told me to write of this as a memorial in a book and to recite it in front of Joshua, our general, because it will be a charge to him in the future. Thus says Yahweh, 'I will have war with Amalek from generation to generation, and I will utterly blot out the memory of Amalek from heaven.'"

The people cheered. Moses saw that Joshua was a bit unnerved. If this was an example of the kind of enemies they would find in Canaan, they had a long, hard fight ahead of them.

Moses finished his blessing by raising his shepherd's staff, a symbol of what was weak in this world being used to shame the strong. The shepherd's staff had become a war standard.

He said, "I hereby name this altar, 'Yahweh is my standard! A hand upon the throne of Yahweh!'"

Once again, the masses cheered with joy.

And yet, Moses knew the masses were not to be trusted. For these were the same fickle children who had previously sought to stone him.

The mob was never to be trusted.

CHAPTER 47

Mount Sinai

It was midday when the Israelites arrived at their destination at the foot of Mount Sinai. Their journey here from Egypt had taken two full moons, but they had finally made it. Moses sighed with relief and looked up at the mountain with its black basalt rock top. He could not imagine what the god of this mountain had in store for the hungry, exhausted, broken people of Israel. After the miracle of Yam Suph, he was more assured of Yahweh's hand than ever before. But he much less sure of Yahweh's *people*.

"Moses!" The voice came from Miriam walking toward him with his father Amram. "Your Midianite family has arrived!"

Moses's demeanor lifted with joy. He walked as quickly as he could to the entrance of the camp, where he saw camels carrying his father-in-law, his wife, his sons, and extended family of dozens. Their herds and flocks were close behind.

It was summer, so it was time for the clan to move to the higher elevation of the Hisma as they did every year. Still, Moses had sent a messenger earlier in their journey to alert them of his coming. And finally, after a year of conflict, suffering, and death in Egypt, Moses was back safe with his Midianite family.

As patriarch, Jethro led the way. He was beaming and held his hands out. Moses met him with equal enthusiasm. First he bowed down, then they hugged and kissed one another as was the Midian custom.

They exchanged formal greetings. "It has been a year. How is your health and welfare?" asked Moses.

"I am fat, still grumpy, but mostly loved," said Jethro with a smile. Moses smiled at his father-in-law's sly wit.

Jethro asked in return, "And how is your health and welfare?"

"I am weary from travel, beaten by the elements, but with a story that will change the world."

"I cannot wait to hear it," said Jethro.

Next, Moses moved to his sons behind their grandfather. "Gershom." The forty-year-old seemed to have gotten more muscular in the year Moses had been gone.

"Eliezer." A few years younger than his brother and still as happy to see his father as a child would be. Their wives and children were close behind.

Moses hugged and kissed them both, but quickly moved them aside to see the one he most longed for.

And there before him was the most beautiful and precious woman on the face of the earth with her full figure, long braided hair, black ageless face, and deep, loving eyes.

"My precious Zipporah," he said with a smile so wide it threatened to split his cheeks. "You look younger than when I left you."

"My beloved Moses." She grinned back at him. "You look more handsome than the day we wed."

They embraced. He whispered into her ear, "I have counted the days until I would see you again."

"Yahweh has been true to his promise," she whispered back.

"I will never leave your side again."

"Yahweh willing," she added.

"Yahweh willing," he agreed.

They kissed as husband and wife. And he felt all his concerns lift from his heavy heart. He had missed her so desperately.

When he looked up, he saw that his father Amram had come forward and was staring at Jethro. Releasing Zipporah, Moses walked over to the two men.

They both appeared anxious.

Moses said, "My father Amram, I would like you to meet my father Jethro."

Everyone around them laughed. But it was a dual truth. Finding and reconciling with his lost birth father could not erase the love and training of his adoptive father. Moses had lived two separate lives. And now they were coming together in redemption.

All made possible by his heavenly father Yahweh.

Jethro opened his arms wide with Midian acceptance. Amram smiled, and they hugged one another.

Jethro then said, "Come now, my new friend Amram. Let you and our son tell me of your adventures in the Red and Black Land…"

Jethro stared with his mouth open in awe of what he had just heard from Moses. They were sitting alone with Amram in Jethro's tent.

Moses had told Jethro of his arrival in Goshen, of Pharaoh and his arrogant rebellion against Yahweh, of the plagues that had crippled the land, of the blood, the swarms, the darkness, and the death. He told of the lamb's blood of Passover, of their trek to Yam Suph, of Pharaoh's pursuit and ultimate destruction in the waves, and most of all, of Yahweh's deliverance. Yahweh was the living god for whom they were all searching. The true Creator and sustainer of all things. He was the God of all gods, incomparable to all. He was the same god of Mount Sinai and the burning bush. And he deserved total allegiance.

Jethro remained silent as he seemed to process everything Moses had told him. He trusted Moses deeply. He had loved Moses as a father, and Moses had returned the love as a son.

Now Moses looked into his father-in-law's eyes, searching for a sign of approval. Jethro was no longer a man of faith. Would he believe?

Jethro's awe turned into a deep frown, a disturbed look of revelation.

Then he looked back at Moses, and his frown turned into a grin.

"Blessed is Yahweh, who has delivered you out of the hand of Pharaoh and the Egyptians."

Moses and Amram sighed with relief.

Jethro continued, "When you first told me of Yahweh in the burning bush a year ago, I struggled within my soul to understand this alien deity. But I had already lost faith in Ba'al. His arrogance and the arrogance of all the gods against your people had persuaded me—as evil persuades one of what is good. And now I know that Yahweh is greater than all the gods."

Moses embraced Jethro. Amram joined them. Now the three fathers in their own right were truly united under God's fatherhood.

Jethro got up and opened a curtain, behind which were his priestly garments: a colorful blue robe, white undertunic, and Canaanite headdress.

"What are you doing?" Moses asked.

"What else, my son? I am giving my past to the flames."

The first thing Jethro burned in the fire on his portable altar was his priestly garments. Next he defaced his sacred instruments and buried them in the desert floor like the Egyptian ritual of red pots.

Finally, he brought a sacrificial lamb from the mobile pen and cut its throat, draining its blood on the ground.

Placing the lamb on the altar, Jethro prayed to heaven with uplifted hands. "Yahweh, please accept this sacrifice for the atonement of a life squandered on idolatry. I repent and will now serve you with all my heart, all my soul, and all my strength. I curse the gods and the temple of Ba'al forever."

When the holocaust was completed, Jethro put his arms around Moses and Amram, saying, "As old as we three are, we bring the future of Israel—of the world."

Amram replied, "I am up for a celebration. How about you two?"

But by the time the feast was set up and Jethro arrived with Amram, Aaron, and the elders, Moses was nowhere to be seen. Jethro and Amram shared a smile. They knew where their son was.

• • • • •

In their own tent, Moses and Zipporah lay naked and tenderly in each other's arms.

"My love," she said. "After forty years of marriage and at your age, you still surprise me."

He said, "Our times together are far fewer than in our youth, but our love is deeper and richer."

"Did you think of me often in Egypt?" she asked.

"Every day."

She snuggled in closer.

He added, "Every day, I would hear your voice in my head reminding me to watch my temper and pick up after myself."

She slapped him playfully. "Someone has to deliver the Deliverer from his own mess."

He sighed and turned serious. "Egypt was a world of extremes. I can barely describe the terror of each plague—and the majesty of Yahweh's signs and wonders."

"He *really* parted Yam Suph?"

"With the breath of his nostrils. It was walls of water on left and right. We walked through the seabed on dry ground, Zipporah. Dry ground. In all my life, I have never seen or heard anything that could compare to the majesty of that single act of Yahweh's hands. He was the true storm god who conquered the sea to start a new creation. To bring us out of chaos and into his order."

"And he really provided sustenance in the desert for all of you?"

"We ate the bread of angels. We still do. You will see that in the morning."

"I feel left out," she said. "Like I missed the glory of God while tending the herds and washing clothes in boring old Midian."

"Zipporah, there was much suffering too and death. Had you been there, I would have been too worried about your safety. But fear not, you will yet see the glory of God. Yahweh has told me to visit the mountain to receive instructions."

"Instructions for what?"

"For a covenant—of law and worship. A covenant establishing a new heaven and earth. Trust me, you will yet see his glory."

She kissed him. "I see his glory in you."

"What do you mean?"

"I see a glow in your eyes. You are a different man since you came back. How can you not be with all you have experienced?"

Moses stared up into the ceiling of the tent. She was right. She could always see into his soul. He had changed. He was a different man than that entitled elitist Egyptian or that broken Midianite shepherd. But would he become the man of God Yahweh called him to be?

She asked, "Will I be the wife of a king?"

"No. Yahweh is the king of Israel. He alone is our Deliverer. He alone is our salvation."

She hugged him tightly and whispered, "In your love, I feel like a queen."

"I'm afraid you will have to be satisfied with that," he teased.

They kissed again—as if they would never let go of each other.

CHAPTER 48

Moses awoke early in the morning and made his way up the mountain. He wasn't far along the path when he saw a burning bush like the one he had encountered a generation ago. This time he knew what to do. He took off his sandals and knelt in worship.

When he came down from the mountain a short time later, he called together the elders of Israel, several hundred of them, and told them what Yahweh had commanded.

"In three days' time, Yahweh is coming to the mountain in a thick cloud to deliver his covenant with Israel. All will hear his presence so that they will believe what I speak. Until then, the people must consecrate themselves by washing their garments and avoiding sexual intimacy. All must respect the mountain as sacred space for Yahweh. No one is to ascend the mountain or even touch it, for whoever does so shall be put to death by stoning.

"On the third day, Yahweh will come."

The elders agreed to spread the word to the people and made a vow with each other to do everything Yahweh commanded them to do.

Anticipation was high amongst the tribes. Many were speculating what the covenant might entail. Others were fearful because of the danger that holiness and sacred space could bring to bear. They had lived without their god's presence for hundreds of years. They had become Egyptianized in their culture. It was all they'd ever known. And many of them had worshipped Egyptian gods all their lives.

Now this god Yahweh had broken into their world, pulled them out of it, and was giving them an entirely new way of living and worshipping. Despite the display of majesty and power they had experienced, it would still be a difficult thing to make such dramatic changes. But how dramatic would they be?

Then again, they'd come so far and been shown so much mercy.

By the morning of the third day, the mountain of God had become wrapped in smoke with thunder and lightning all about. Yahweh had descended in fire, and the mountain quaked. It was both majestic and frightening.

When the sound of trumpet blasts echoed from the top, the people congregated near the base as Yahweh had instructed them. Moses took Aaron with him, and they ascended the pathway carrying parchment and writing materials, for Yahweh was to dictate his Book of the Covenant, and Moses was to write it down.

This time, the two brothers went all the way up to the peak. When they arrived, they sat to rest on a large, flat rock as dark clouds swirled above their heads. Though they could see the lightning and hear the thunder and wind, none of it was as loud or intense as it had been at the foot of the mountain. They were within the eye of the storm here. Even the pillar of fire that came down from heaven did not create a turbulence around them. It was a peaceful silence. It was *Shalom*.

Aaron helped Moses lay out his parchment and prepare his writing materials. "Maybe I should help you write it, Moses. I might be more capable."

"You are Yahweh's high priest," Moses reminded him. "I am Yahweh's prophet. It is not a matter of capability but of responsibility."

Aaron bowed in deference.

Then Yahweh spoke from the pillar of fire.

"Moses."

"I am here, Lord."

"Record these ten commandments of the covenant. They are the summary of the Law I am about to give you in full."

"I am ready, my lord."

Yahweh spoke. "I am Yahweh your God who brought you out of the land of Egypt, out of the house of slavery.

"You shall have no other gods before me.

"You shall not make for yourself a graven image or any likeness of anything that is in heaven above or that is in the earth beneath or that is in the water under the earth. You shall not bow down to them or serve them, for I Yahweh your God am a jealous god, visiting the iniquity of the fathers on the children to the third and the fourth generation of those who hate me but showing steadfast love to thousands of those who love me and keep my commandments.

"You shall not take the name of Yahweh your God in vain, for Yahweh will not hold him guiltless who takes his name in vain.

"Remember the Sabbath day to keep it holy. Six days you shall labor and do all your work, but the seventh day is a Sabbath to Yahweh your God. On it you shall not do any work, you, or your son, or your daughter, your male servant, or your female servant, or your livestock, or the sojourner who is within your gates. For in six days Yahweh made heaven and earth, the sea, and all that is in them, and rested on the seventh day.

"Honor your father and your mother that your days may be long in the land that Yahweh your God is giving you.

"You shall not murder.

"You shall not commit adultery.

"You shall not steal.

"You shall not bear false witness against your neighbor.

"You shall not covet your neighbor's house. You shall not covet your neighbor's wife, or his male servant, or his female servant, or his ox, or his donkey, or anything that is your neighbor's."[4]

And Yahweh did not stop there…

Moses and Aaron lost track of the time they spent on the mount. It could have been hours. It could have been days. As Moses wrote down the Book of the Covenant that Yahweh gave him, he noticed that it was structured similarly to other suzerain vassal treaties that he had read in his learning back in Egypt. The vassal treaty was an agreement between a sovereign and his subject peoples. It had five major points to its structure. First, there was a preamble that introduced the sovereign: "I am Yahweh your God."

Next, there was a prologue that described the historical events leading up to the making of the covenant: "who brought you out of the land of Egypt."

Then there were ethical stipulations with blessings and cursings based on obedience to those stipulations. The Book of the Covenant gave such rules

---

[4] *The Holy Bible: English Standard Version* (Wheaton, IL: Crossway Bibles, 2016), Ex 20:2–17.

related to slavery, capital offenses such as murder and kidnapping, and the value of human life in examples of personal injury.

Central to these ethics was the principle of *lex talionis*, or "eye for an eye." This was a unique ethical notion of fairness in punishment for crimes or offenses. If a man gouged another man's eye, it would not be just to punish the offender by taking out both his eyes or ending his life, as the desire for vengeance could lead to such excess. Instead, human nature should be restrained, and the punishment should fit the crime.

There were rules about sexual purity, idiolatry, perjury, theft, and restitution as well as the Sabbath and festivals. All ethical demands with blessings or punishments attached.

Lastly in this treaty paradigm was the invocation of a divine witness to the covenant. Yahweh would send the Angel of his very presence in which dwelt his Name to guard them and lead them to the territory that he had prepared for them: Canaan. He would lead the Israelites into the land and drive out all the cursed tribes who resided there. Yahweh would help them blot out the Hittites, Perizzites, Canaanites, Hivites, and Jebusites, among others. Most crucially, they were to devote to holy destruction all the men, women, children, and animals of the Anakim and Rephaim, the Seed of the Serpent.

Eventually, Yahweh would allow Israel to claim her borders from the shores of Yam Suph in the southeast to the Sea of the Philistines in the west and from the Negeb wilderness of the south all the way up to the Euphrates in the north.

Yahweh had promised Canaan as a land of inheritance to the Israelites so long as they did not serve or make covenants with the Canaanite gods. He pronounced, "And beware lest you raise your eyes to heaven, and when you see the sun and the moon and the stars, all the host of heaven, you be drawn away and bow down to them and serve them, things that Yahweh your God has allotted to all the peoples under the whole heaven. But Yahweh has taken you and brought you out of the iron furnace, out of Egypt, to be a people of his own inheritance, as you are this day."

When Moses and Aaron came back down the mountain, Aaron's sons and the seventy lead elders of Israel followed them. But they noticed that the people had retreated to a distance.

Moses asked Nadab and Abihu about it.

Nadab explained, "They are afraid. They heard the sound of Yahweh conversing with you as peals of deafening thunder and piercing trumpet sounds from the smoking mountain. They do not want Yahweh to speak to them directly because they fear he will smite them. They ask that you tell them what Yahweh says, and that will be good enough for them."

Moses sighed with discouragement. "That fear is not supposed to make them run away from God but to make them obey and avoid transgressing his commands."

Moses knew he had a long, hard road to travel with this ignorant and spoiled people. But he remembered that he too had been so himself, and his frustration with them was less out of concern for their holiness as it was his own impatient temper.

So he gathered the people and read the ten commandments or "Ten Words" and their just decrees, and they vowed an oath of loyalty as a people to the covenant. The elders represented their tribes and clans, and the people agreed.

Moses then had twelve pillars placed at the foot of the mountain according to the twelve tribes of Israel as the sign of their vow. He had an altar built of raw stone unhewn by human instruments. There Aaron and his sons performed burnt offerings and peace offerings of oxen to Yahweh.

Moses had half the blood of the sacrifices saved in a basin, which he then had carried before the crowd of assembled people. He dipped a hyssop branch in the basin and used it to throw the blood onto the crowd, saying, "Behold the blood of the covenant that Yahweh has made with you."

Then he continued, "I speak to you now as Yahweh's prophet. For you have sought an intermediary and were unwilling to listen directly to your God. Yahweh has told me that in latter days he will raise up a prophet like me from Israel's seed. Yahweh will put his words in the prophet's mouth, and the prophet shall speak to Israel all that Yahweh commands him. And whoever will not listen to his words, Yahweh himself will require it of them."

Moses saw that the people were not sure they understood his words. They whispered and murmured amongst themselves. But Moses was content to let the meaning remain a mystery, for he knew Yahweh had spoken of a future king, the scepter of Judah called Shiloh by his forefather Jacob.

These people could not even understand simple commands to obey. They could not begin to be understand the depth of mystery in the good news of this future prophet.

・・・・・

The next day, Moses called Aaron and his sons Nadab and Abihu along with seventy of the elders of Israel to accompany him to the summit. Moses assured them that Yahweh had allowed this exception. They followed their prophet up the mountain with fearful anticipation.

When they arrived at the clearing on the mountaintop, they were all overwhelmed by the sight. The clouds, the pillar of fire, the very presence of Yahweh. They fell prostrate and worshipped.

Moses said to them, "Yahweh has called you here to share in a vision. Lift now your heads."

They did so. Looking up, they saw the bright-blue lapis lazuli sky above them.

Though they were still on their mount, it appeared that the firmament of the sky was coming closer to them. Or rather, that the mountain they were on was rising to the heavens. They seemed to break through the clouds and arrive at the solid firmament that held back the waters above.

It dissolved, and their mountaintop kept growing upward through the dark waters of the abyss. The seventy elders stood up in awe as they watched the huge scaled body of Leviathan swim past them in its domain.

Then they broke through the waters to find themselves suddenly inside Yahweh's heavenly throne room. They all fell to their knees again in awe, mouths agape.

Moses knew this to be the Holy of Holies in Yahweh's heavenly temple. It was a square room of glimmering lapis lazuli.

Before them was a throne of lapis lazuli upon which sat the likeness of a man. He was bright like gleaming metal, so bright that they could not see his features. Behind him was a rainbow as after a storm. Above his throne were seraphim with six wings. Two covered their faces, two covered their feet, and with two they flew.

Below the throne were the cherubim. Unlike those of Eden, these were in the likeness of a man but with four faces, and they sparkled like burnished bronze. Each had four wings, two that covered their bodies and two with which they flew. They upheld the chariot throne of Yahweh with wheels of burning fire.

Beneath the throne was a stream of fire pouring out into the floor that absorbed it like water but without quenching it.

And suddenly, the foundations of the threshold shook with the voice of the seraphim and cherubim. They called out with voices that sounded like roaring waters, "Holy, holy, holy is Yahweh of hosts. The whole earth is full of his glory!"

Moses and all the rest were thrown to the floor at the shaking. They shielded their eyes and ears from the terrifying holiness that pierced their bodies and souls. They wept with dread in the presence of righteousness so pure, so beautiful, so true that their own hearts became heavy with the weight and ugliness of their own depravity.

It burned like fire, like the burning of dross from silver, a refiner's fire.

When they could bring themselves to look up again, they were back on the mountaintop, terra firma, surrounded by the rising walls of rock and a cool breeze that chilled their bodies underneath sweat-drenched clothes.

None of them could speak of the vision they had been allowed to see of the heavenly temple.

After living so long in a world of spiritual lies, they finally had a taste of the glory above and how unworthy they were to behold it. Later, they would try to describe what they had seen and heard that day, but no words could convey what their souls experienced. It was beyond words.

CHAPTER 49

Moses had a small tent set up for him just outside the camp near the foothill of the mountain. Large enough to contain his library of scrolls, it afforded him a solitary location from which he could spend time writing the history of his people that he had been planning to do for a long time.

But that was delayed when, after a number of days, Moses awoke from a dream and prepared to ascend the mountain again for more instructions from Yahweh. This time he took his assistant Joshua.

As Joshua followed Moses up the path, he asked, "My lord, why did you not choose Aaron to accompany you as before?"

"Because I need a strong young man to carry back some heavy stones."

Catching a look of confusion in Joshua's eyes, Moses chuckled. "Come along. You will soon understand."

Young warrior and aging prophet marched their way up into the cloudy top of the mountain of Yahweh's presence.

•••••

Because of Moses's age, the hike up the mountain took Moses and Joshua the better part of a day. When they reached the top, Joshua set up camp in a large clearing while Moses rested. The rocky walls of the ridges around them gave the feel of a fortress. They were safe and protected underneath Yahweh's banner. Moses fell asleep.

Joshua wakened him. "My lord, Yahweh is here."

Rubbing his eyes, Moses looked out to the clearing to see the pillar of fire and smoke restrained within its whirlwinds and rising heavenward.

The voice of Yahweh always gave Moses a chill. He and Joshua were before the holy and righteous Creator of all things who was now speaking to him. How was it they were both not struck dead? Moses was acutely aware of his own sin, and it shamed him. But there was something soothing in that holy fire that purified them, that forgave them. Yahweh was not like the gods of the nations who were themselves created by him. He was transcendent, wholly other, yet wholly present. His holiness burned painfully bright, but his love was everlasting like a father's or a shepherd's. Moses knew what it was to be a shepherd, and it left him even more in awe that such a mighty God would condescend to speak to a man. To speak to *him*!

"Moses," said Yahweh from the cloud. "Prepare your writing materials, for I am about to give you detailed instructions. I have already shown you a vision of my heavenly temple. Now you will build my earthly temple to match it."

Joshua readied quill and ink while Moses laid out his first animal skin parchment to begin. Moses wrote in Hebrew.

"Speak to the people of Israel and take for me a contribution. You will need important materials that they can offer to build me a sanctuary, a holy place that I may dwell in your midst. I will describe the pattern for a new tent of meeting, a tabernacle with all its furniture, and you shall follow exactly the pattern I give you because it is a reflection of my dwelling and throne in heaven.

"I have called by name Bezalel the son of Uri, son of Hur of the tribe of Judah, and I have filled him with the Spirit of God. I have given him skill and knowledge in craftsmanship and creativity. He will devise the artistic designs and work in metal, stone, wood, and in all materials needed for my tabernacle. I have gifted him and all the artistic craftsmen of Israel with the ability to make all that I command you."

Moses and Joshua knew Bezalel. He was a trustworthy man of God. He had a burly beard and a strong muscular frame like that of a blacksmith. But his soul was greatly sensitive to beauty. He always saw things from a different perspective that provided insight others had not considered. And he was a man who saw the beauty in Yahweh's works, even his judgments. When the people broke out in spontaneous song at the Yam Suph deliverance, Bezalel helped to express that terrifying incident in lyrics of beauty and grandeur.

> *Your right hand, O Yahweh, glorious in power,*
> *your right hand, O Yahweh, shatters the enemy.*
> *In the greatness of your majesty you overthrow your adversaries;*
> *you send out your fury; it consumes them like stubble.*
> *At the blast of your nostrils the waters piled up;*
> *the floods stood up in a heap;*
> *the deeps congealed in the heart of the sea.*

> *The enemy said, "I will pursue, I will overtake,*
> *I will divide the spoil, my desire shall have its fill of them.*
> *I will draw my sword; my hand shall destroy them."*
> *You blew with your wind; the sea covered them;*
> *they sank like lead in the mighty waters.*

Yes, thought Moses, *the artist Bezalel would be the perfect chosen vessel to build Yahweh's temple.* For that was what the tent of tabernacle was: a mobile temple for a God on the move with his people. And the artist was a reflection of the Creator.

But once built, a tabernacle would need priests to serve in it. So Yahweh told Moses, "Aaron your brother and his sons with him shall serve me as priests. Aaron, Nadab, Abihu, Eleazar, and Ithamar."

No longer would each father be the priest of his own household. A priesthood would be separated unto Yahweh. Israel would be a kingdom of priests to the world, but they too would need priests to atone for their sins and to do so regularly in the light of humanity's unchanging sinful nature.

Aaron already served as high priest in their midst, so that would not be a surprise to anyone, least of all Aaron, who treasured the position of authority. As in Egypt, so the priesthood would be especially sacred—set apart from the people to serve in their capacity as keepers of the holy. The high priest would wear a special ephod breastplate with twelve stones upon it that symbolized the twelve tribes of Israel.

He would have two special mysterious oracles hidden in that breastplate called the Urim and Thummim, or Lights and Perfections. These were special tools for the high priest alone to divine Yahweh's will in situations where it was not already clear. Moses would speak directly to Yahweh, but the high priest would have to use the Urim and Thummim in his absence. Though divination of any other kind was strictly forbidden, Yahweh would allow only the Urim and Thummim.

Aaron would also wear a special gold plate on his forehead attached to his turban and engraved with the words "Holy to Yahweh."

It had taken days to transcribe the details of the tabernacle. It was to be made of specific materials with exact dimensions. Moses had plenty of time to consider the symbolic meaning of everything this sacred space embodied.

The very notion of gods dwelling in tents on mountains was common enough around the world. And though this tent would begin on Mount Sinai and be brought along the way through the wilderness and into Canaan, Yahweh promised that his dwelling place in the land would ultimately be on a holy mountain as well. But he did not reveal which one.

The tabernacle, or temple, itself was an incarnation of the cosmic mountain, the original hillock that first emerged from the primeval waters of creation. Its placement in the center of the camp with all the tribes surrounding it was both a military layout as well as a statement that Yahweh's dwelling place of creation was the center of the earth. It was the link between heaven and earth where the people would go up and God would come down to meet with them. From his education about other nations like Babylonia, Moses knew of temples with names like "Temple of the Foundation of Heaven and Earth."

The tabernacle's shapes and functions would reflect the three-part structure of the cosmos as they understood it. First, there was a rectangular outer court defined by a fence of linen curtains one hundred-fifty feet long and seventy-five feet wide. This represented the visible earth. It was where the sacrifices of animals would take place for the purpose of preparing the people to enter Yahweh's sacred space.

Its furnishings would include a bronze altar that was considered the "altar of the earth." On this, the priests would offer grain and animals and other items for various sacrifices to make the people ritually purified for sacred encounters with their God. Nearby would be a large bronze laver for washing and symbolic cleansing, shaped to hold water like the seas.

That was the earth and the seas.

The tent of the tabernacle itself would be forty-five feet long, fifteen feet wide, and fifteen feet high. It would be covered with various animal skins and linens and symbolized the other two parts of the cosmos. First was the holy place where only priests could enter. The holy place represented the visible heavens as well as the Garden of Eden, Yahweh's original dwelling place on earth. This was where special furniture would used by the priests in their services as they cultivated and kept the sanctuary like the first man and woman cultivated and kept the Garden. But what garden could hold the Creator's presence? The whole earth was his. And what earthly dwelling would the God of heaven need?

Artistic decoration would reinforce garden imagery as columns with foliage carved in them would represent trees. Pomegranates on priests' garments and other artistic embellishments would represent that garden's fruit and foliage.

A large lampstand made of gold, the eternal metal of heaven, would have seven candles and would be specifically shaped as a tree, the Tree of Life, whose roots went down into the underworld and whose branches reached to the heavens. This tree was the "Light of the World," like Yahweh himself, in whom there is no darkness but is the light of life.

A gilded golden table of showbread would host bread for sacred meals to remind the people of manna, God's provision.

A gilded golden altar of incense would create a cloud of sweet fragrance that rose like prayers of intercession before Yahweh. On a specified Day of Atonement, blood from the sacrificial altar would be sprinkled on this to make atonement for the priests who served the people.

The altar of incense would stand before the final sacred space, the Holy of Holies, Yahweh's earthly throne room. This was symbolic of the third tier of the cosmos, the invisible heavens where God resided. It was so holy that only the high priest could enter it on just one day of the year, the Day of Atonement, when the sins of the people were cleansed. It would be separated off from the rest of the temple by a large, thick veil of purple, blue, and scarlet that was embroidered with images of the heavenly host.

The Holy of Holies would host Yahweh's throne. The room's dimensions were a perfect cube of fifteen feet to match the Holy of Holies in heaven. But whereas the nations would have an image of their god in their Holy of Holies, the Israelites would have no graven image because Yahweh was transcendent of creation and forbade images of himself.

The sanctuary did however have a most important piece of furniture that would function as Yahweh's real presence with the people and his throne on earth—the ark of the testimony.

Moses: Against the Gods of Egypt

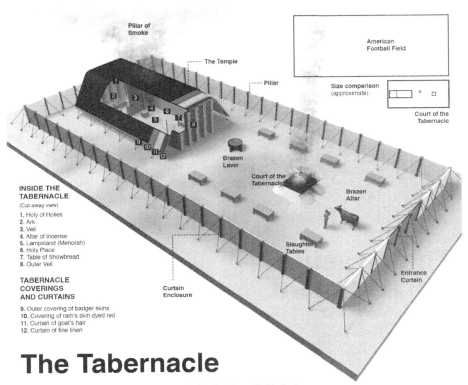

INSIDE THE TABERNACLE
(Cut-away view)
1. Holy of Holies
2. Ark
3. Veil
4. Altar of Incense
5. Lampstand (Menorah)
6. Holy Place
7. Table of Showbread
8. Outer Veil

TABERNACLE COVERINGS AND CURTAINS
9. Outer covering of badger skins
10. Covering of ram's skin dyed red
11. Curtain of goat's hair
12. Curtain of fine linen

The Tabernacle

This portable temple was built in the wilderness by the Israelites circa 1450 BC after they were freed from Egyptian slavery. The tabernacle was the first temple dedicated to God and the first resting place of the ark of the covenant. It served as a place of worship and sacrifices during the Israelites' 40 years in the desert while conquering the land of Canaan.

GRAPHIC BY KARBEL MULTIMEDIA, COPYRIGHT 2011 LOGOS BIBLE SOFTWARE

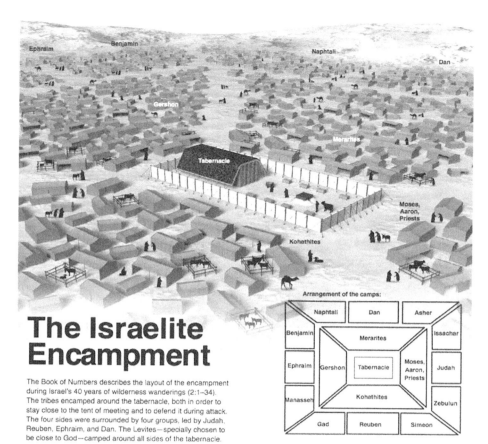

The Israelite Encampment

The Book of Numbers describes the layout of the encampment during Israel's 40 years of wilderness wanderings (2:1–34). The tribes encamped around the tabernacle, both in order to stay close to the tent of meeting and to defend it during attack. The four sides were surrounded by four groups, led by Judah, Reuben, Ephraim, and Dan. The Levites—specially chosen to be close to God—camped around all sides of the tabernacle.

GRAPHIC BY KARBEL MULTIMEDIA. COPYRIGHT 2011 LOGOS BIBLE SOFTWARE

CHAPTER 50

Twenty days had passed, and Moses had not yet come down the mountain. The people in the Israelite camp were restless and worried. Though the mountain was always covered by a cloud, they could see no lightning nor hear any thunder or trumpets as they had previously. Gossip was spreading like leprosy.

Aaron and his sons were cleaning up the altar of sacrifice that they had been using when Miriam arrived in a disturbed state.

"Aaron, may I speak with you?"

They went into his tent for privacy. Miriam spoke in a low voice, "Are you not worried?"

"About what?"

"About Moses's absence. We have heard *nothing* from Yahweh."

"The people pleaded with Moses not to hear Yahweh's voice."

"But we have not heard from Moses for twenty days. How do we know he is still alive?"

"Faith, I suppose."

Miriam looked toward the entrance of the tent to make sure no one was there. "Aaron, I want to talk to you about that. About our faith."

Aaron knew what she was going to raise. She had implied it in previous discussions.

She asked, "Who is our faith in? Moses?"

"No. It is in Yahweh. He is our deliverer and redeemer."

"Exactly. Moses is just an instrument of Yahweh's will. But our faith is in Yahweh. So is Moses the only one Yahweh uses for his purposes?"

"No. Yahweh has used me to support Moses."

"Why?"

"Because Moses was not up to the task. He was not as good an orator as I, nor did he have the boldness. Yahweh told him to take me with him to Pharaoh, and I even spoke for Yahweh on his behalf."

"Did you not perform some of the miracles yourself with your staff?" Miriam asked.

"Yes."

"Whose staff turned into a serpent before Pharaoh?"

"Mine."

"Whose outstretched arm and staff turned the waters to blood?"

"Mine."

"Whose staff brought forth the frogs and the gnats?

"Mine."

"Exactly," Miriam affirmed. "And without me watching over Moses as an infant floating down the Nile, he would have lost all contact with our mother and his people. He would never have survived."

"What are you trying to say, Miriam?"

"Only that Moses is not the only one through whom Yahweh has worked to deliver our people. You are the high priest, and I am a prophetess. Do we not also speak for Yahweh?"

Her points were all well taken. Aaron had sometimes considered those very same thoughts. Though the course of traumatic events they had just been through had not allowed him the time to reflect on them.

But she was right. Aaron had spoken for Yahweh as often if not more so than Moses had. When Moses did speak or perform a miracle, Aaron had to be there with his brother to make the impact that Yahweh wanted.

Aaron said, "He may have been a general in Egypt, but he does not really have the traits required to lead a nation like Israel boldly."

"Like your traits?" Miriam asked leadingly.

Aaron felt safe enough to share his other concerns. "I have more than once seen his temper get the better of him."

"As have I," his sister agreed. "Is Moses accountable, or is he a Pharaoh without limits?"

Aaron said, "His life as a royal Egyptian has certainly shaped him more than his Hebrew birth."

"Blood does not always determine loyalty."

"Which raises another concern," he said. "His Kushite woman. A foreign wife is not appropriate for the leader of a nation. Do we even know where her ultimate loyalty lies?"

"She has great influence on him," Miriam said. "I have heard that she dreaded becoming an Israelite. She felt herself of higher status than the rest of us slaves."

"Keep your eye on her," said Aaron, stroking his beard. "I will keep my eye on the people. We will see what they want—and who they want to lead them."

• • • • •

Zipporah had been going about her daily chores caring for the family household while Moses was gone. She had noticed something was going on in the camp, but she didn't know what. She'd first caught wind of it when she'd gone to the creek for water and the other women seemed to avoid her. She wasn't sure of it until she returned to her tent and found that someone had written the word "Kushite" in the sand at the entrance to the tent.

She used her foot to erase the word and continued about her duties. During dinner, the wife of Zipporah's younger son Eliezer spilled the poison that was spreading through gossip amongst the women.

Zipporah stood up from the table and marched out of the tent. Eliezer followed her to make sure she was safe.

She stomped over to Miriam's tent a few rows down, and yelled through the entrance flap, "Miriam! I want to have a word with you!"

Zipporah was righteously indignant. She was not going to allow gossip to ruin her reputation or that of her husband's.

Miriam pulled the flap back and stepped out, faking a surprised look. "Whatever could be so important as to interrupt my family meal?"

Aaron peeked his head out. "Is everything all right, Zipporah?"

"No, it is not."

Aaron saw Zipporah's angry face and retreated back into the tent like a rabbit.

She turned back to Miriam. "Do you know who is spreading these lies about me?"

"What lies?"

Oh, she is such a bad actor, thought Zipporah.

"Someone wrote 'Kushite' at my tent entrance. And now I hear women are gossiping behind my back that I control my husband."

"You do?" asked Miriam with a sarcastic edge to her words.

"No one controls Moses. Anyone who actually knows your brother knows that to be true."

Miriam flinched with offense. She said stiffly, "I heard it was subtle manipulation. Like a serpent's."

Zipporah felt ready to explode. "You heard this, did you? From whom?"

"Zipporah, I would not want to make the gossip any worse by accusing someone in particular. But I will be careful not to believe everything I hear about you."

Her look was so patronizing, so cunning, it made Zipporah think, *Serpent, indeed.*

"Well, then, please do me a favor, Miriam. The next time a woman tells you that lie, tell her that if she has any moral integrity at all, she can go ask Moses herself and see how he responds. Unless that woman is afraid of being struck with plague by Yahweh for false witness."

Giving Miriam a taste of her own fake smile, Zipporah turned her back and marched back to her own tent.

Her younger son Eliezer followed faithfully at her heels.

CHAPTER 51

It had now been over thirty days since Moses had left the Israelite camp for the mountaintop. And there was still no sign of his return. The elders called a meeting outside the camp to discuss their concern. All several hundred came. Aaron represented both his tribe and the priesthood. He led the meeting as the most respected among them, considered second only to Moses whose leadership Aaron shared.

The prophet Djehuty was there, accompanied by Miriam representing the female prophets in their midst. As firstborn, Gershom was asked to represent Moses in his father's absence. Gershom shocked everyone by bringing his mother Zipporah with him. He didn't explain his act but sat down and waited for anyone to challenge him—which was not about to happen.

Aaron glanced at Miriam. She had a look of clear disdain on her face for Zipporah. Women were not allowed in such leadership meetings, Miriam as prophetess being one of the few exceptions.

Aaron noticed Caleb standing silently alone in the crowd. He was grateful Caleb's usual comrade Joshua was not with him since the young warrior was up on the mountain with Moses. Joshua was a rabblerouser and would no doubt have caused trouble for them all.

Aaron led the assembly in quick prayer for Yahweh's wisdom, then got right to it. "We are having this meeting because of the reports from many of you of unrest that seems to be rising throughout the camp."

One of the elders rose to his feet. "My people are afraid. They think Moses and Yahweh have abandoned them."

Another elder rose to respond indignantly, "Moses has been absent one moon, and already our people are losing faith? It was not but a few moons before that we walked through the waters of Yam Suph. And before that, we were protected from the plagues on Egypt and her gods. What is wrong with these ingrates?"

Disagreement burst out in the crowd. Arguments had to be hushed by Aaron, who held his staff high with authority.

Aaron said to the lot of them, "Tell us, what is it that you think your people want?"

One respected elder named Rahotep said, "I do not think the tribes are ungrateful for all of Yahweh's deliverances. But we must remember that we have been born and bred in Egypt for over four hundred years. We are used to *seeing* our gods. It is the seeing of our eyes that confirms what we know in our hearts. But this god Yahweh is invisible. Like the wind."

Zipporah blurted out, "Like the wind that parted Yam Suph? Are we not supposed to be leaving behind Egyptian ways?"

Miriam jumped into the fray but attacked Zipporah instead. "Are you a prophetess, Zipporah?"

Zipporah looked like a chastened child. "No."

"Then I think you should be quiet and allow the *men* of *Israel* to lead the discussion." Miriam had clearly stressed the words *Israel* and *men* to marginalize Zipporah on both counts, seemingly oblivious to the fact that she wasn't the latter.

There was a mumbling of both agreement and disagreement in the crowd.

But Zipporah would not back down to the intimidation. "I am an Israelite as much as any of you. So says the law of the sojourner. I circumcised my own sons in obedience to Yahweh. And I am the wife for these forty years of Moses the Deliverer."

The crowd calmed in respect for her. The law of the sojourner allowed foreigners who converted to Israel the same rights as any natural-born Hebrew.

But Miriam would not stop. "And Moses the Deliverer is my *blood* brother." She pointed at Aaron. "And Aaron's blood brother as well. Foreigners are accepted into our midst, but as followers, not leaders of our nation."

Gershom glared at Miriam. "My father Moses is not here. And my mother knows my father's mind better than I do. She speaks for me as firstborn son of Moses."

Aaron did not want to let this battle sidetrack them. He chose a different tack. "Elders, I can see both sides of this dispute. So let us hold it in abeyance while we attend to the most significant issue before us: the people's faith in Yahweh."

An elder said, "I agree with elder Rahotep. The people need something tangible of Yahweh's presence. An image would accomplish this."

Caleb, the bald warrior of Judah, spoke up. "The second commandment Yahweh recently gave to us is clear: We are to make no graven images to worship them."

"But we would not worship the image," answered the elder. "It would merely be an aid to worship. It is a representation of his presence, not his actual being. We would worship the invisible Yahweh *through* the visible image."

The elder gestured with his hand horizontal to the earth, then lifted it up towards the heavens where Yahweh was.

"Think of our fathers on earth," Rahotep joined in. "When we are infants, we only know our father by seeing him. Yes, we hear his voice. But we do not understand him. We know him by his visage. Even as we mature, that physical body is not our true father. It is his *ka*, his spirit, that we know and love. But that spirit is in a body. Or consider the shepherd. If the sheep cannot see their protector, they wander and are eaten by predators."

Caleb replied again, "The sheep know their shepherd's voice."

"Indeed. But they follow his voice until they see him. Only then are they at peace."

"Yet Yahweh has commanded us to follow his voice, not a graven image."

Rahotep remained conciliatory. "Brothers, I do not deny the ideals to which we must aspire. Caleb is correct. We have our testimony from Yahweh in words on parchment. But we must also consider that the masses of people are not as literate as we are."

Someone shouted out, "More than the Egyptians!"

"Agreed," said Rahotep. "More than the Egyptians. But still like infants in their ability to understand. And we have the responsibility to help bring them along step by step into a new understanding. If we force alien prescriptions upon them too fast—and all of us here know this well—they will become restless. And restlessness leads to revolution. Why not accommodate their weakness as Yahweh accommodates ours?"

Caleb, Zipporah, Gershom, and others did not appear to accept this argument. But Aaron thought he would play it out to see where it led.

"If we consider Rahotep's wisdom, what kind of image would represent our invisible God?" he asked.

"A man!" shouted someone. "Man was made in his image!"

"We are in *his* image," Aaron responded. "He is not in ours. We would need something more symbolic, or we may end up worshipping our own humanity."

People shouted out options of animals that were predictable from an Egyptian background: scarab, canine, hippopotamus, crocodile, ibis.

Zipporah spoke up again. "Why is the pillar of cloud and fire not enough to see? Yahweh led us through the wilderness with it, and he will lead us to the Promised Land as well."

Miriam seemed to target Zipporah with her every comment. "Clouds, smoke, lightning, and thunder are powerful but not personal. Yahweh is a personal being, not a cloud or a fire."

"He is the great I Am Who I Am!" Zipporah replied. "As Caleb said, no image is worthy of him. I plead with you to wait until Moses returns from the mountain."

Miriam snapped back, "The reason we have this dilemma is because Moses has not returned in a timely manner. And he is not the only one who speaks for Yahweh." She gestured to Aaron. "Remember that Moses's brother Aaron is a prophet of Yahweh as well."

Miriam was not going to stop getting the last word. And now she was injecting an idea that was sure to cause controversy.

Aaron changed the subject. "Perhaps we have heard enough from the women tonight."

Miriam withdrew, scolded.

"It is time for the men to deliberate over what image we would use to depict Yahweh's presence." Aaron's mind went to the most common of Egyptian images of power and authority. "What about a bull-calf?"

This was the universal image of divine power. The Apis bull in Egypt was Ptah incarnate, the creator god. But the bull was also worshipped as Osiris. The high god Ra was depicted as the bull Mnevis in the city of On. In Canaan, the people of Israel's promised land, the high god El was called a bull and his most high Ba'al a bull-calf. The bull represented strength and virility. Its martial aspect was symbolic of Yahweh's military fight on Israel's behalf.

The assembly of elders took a vote, and the majority agreed to a bull-calf image. Depicting Yahweh as such would reinforce his power and provision while maintaining his transcendent identity as an invisible god. It would give the Israelites, accustomed to visual worship, something upon which to set their imaginations. It would help them visualize Yahweh's presence and nature in a more personal way than storm imagery. Eventually, the Israelites would become more accustomed to their new god, and they would rely more on Yahweh's words and less on his image.

And there was one material most fit for the eternal divine: gold. Gold did not rust or tarnish. It was indestructible. It was the flesh of the gods. Yahweh's image would have to be made of gold to express his divine immortal essence.

By now, Aaron was seeing their compromise as a helpful means to a good end. An image might not be ideal, but it would unite the masses and give them something to focus on until Moses returned. *If* he returned. Even Aaron was beginning to wonder if his brother was still alive up there on the mysterious mountain.

There was only one artist whom Aaron knew to be capable of delivering such a work of art.

He called out, "Bezalel! Where are you? Can you create a calf of gold for us?"

The burly Bezalel stepped forward from the crowd. Though he had the stature of a blacksmith, his attitude was that of a sophisticated scribe. He came to the very front of the crowd, but instead of addressing Aaron, he turned and addressed the elders as a group.

"I will never be a part of crafting your image of a golden calf. It is idolatry, and Yahweh forbids it!"

With that, he simply turned and left the crowd.

Aaron saw Caleb, Zipporah, and Gershom leave with him. Others followed in apparent agreement. But most stayed.

Aaron tried to draw attention away from the deserters. "Who shall make our golden calf of Yahweh?"

"You!" someone shouted. "You speak for Yahweh!"

Another shouted, "Make us a god to go before us! To lead us where we can see him!"

Voices of agreement drowned out the dissenters. They were virtually chanting Aaron's name as a call to craft their image.

"Please!" he shouted, using his outstretched hands to quiet them down. "I will fashion the image. But I will need gold—gold from every Israelite. Go and get me the rings and earrings of your wives, your daughters, and your sons and bring them back to me, and I will forge you an image of Yahweh that will display his glory!"

CHAPTER 52

On the mountain of Sinai, Moses had recorded all of Yahweh's instructions for building his tabernacle as well as the instruments and services to be performed in that transportable temple. But the purpose of that sacred space was to house the presence of Yahweh, who would leave the mountain and dwell with the people of Israel on their journey into Canaan.

Yahweh was not like other gods. He was not limited to earthly images. He forbade their use because images were believed to contain the deity for human convenience. But Yahweh did not serve human convenience or power. Nevertheless, he interacted with his human creation on earth. And Yahweh chose to use a portable throne called the Ark of the Testimony as an earthly connection with his heavenly throne. It would reside in the Holy of Holies and maintain a sacred distance from everything else. The ark was the sign of Yahweh dwelling with his people.

Yahweh instructed Moses to have the ark built as a wooden box gilded with gold in and out. It would be over three feet long and over two feet wide as well as tall. It would have rings on the ends of the ark through which wooden poles, also overlaid in gold, would be placed by priests by which to carry it.

Its lid would also be of gold with two images of winged cherubim on the cover. These were like the throne guardians of Eden: hybrid creatures with leonine bodies, human faces, and eagle wings that spread over the top of the ark. The ark was called the mercy seat because it represented in the Holy of Holies the very footstool of Yahweh's throne. Once it was made, Yahweh would speak to Moses there.

In Egypt, gods were carried symbolically in sacred barques like the solar boat of Ra. Their thrones would be in those barques on which sat the image of the deity. Over time, that concept evolved into palanquins, portable thrones for gods and kings carried on poles just like the ark. Such holy relics were even used to carry sacred elements into the tombs of the Pharaoh god-kings.

These were typically gold boxes with an image of Anubis on the cover to protect the contents.

Where this ark of Yahweh's testimony was different was in its meaning. Since Yahweh was transcendent and above his creation, he was not to be depicted in graven images. Heaven was his throne and the earth was his footstool. So the ark represented that footstool, not a throne. As kings would place treaties of their power beneath their throne's footstool, so the Ark of the Testimony would store Yahweh's covenant with Israel.

To Moses and Joshua's amazement, Yahweh had instructed them to cut two stone tablets from the rock. They should be small enough to carry. Then before their eyes, the figure of the Angel of Yahweh stepped out from the pillar of fire and approached them. He was the same terrifying son of man Moses had encountered in the burning bush and in his visions. He gleamed like bronze. His robe was as blinding white as fresh snow, and his eyes were flames of fire.

Moses and Joshua watched in stiffened fright as the Angel wrote all "Ten Words" of his covenant upon each of the two tablets with his very finger. He didn't even use engraving tools. He was God on earth. He used the written Hebrew language with which Moses had become familiar.

When he was finished, the Angel looked at them and said, "Place the tablets in the ark as a memorial for all generations." He returned to the pillar of fire, and the two men looked upon the tablets with awe.

Treaties were always two copies, one for the suzerain king and one for his vassal. In this case, Yahweh would safeguard both of them under his footstool.

Also inside that ark would be stored a single sample jar of manna from heaven. Whereas the daily manna would rot to make Israel trust in Yahweh for each day's provision, the manna placed in the ark of the covenant would never rot, as a sign of Yahweh's enduring trustworthiness.

And priests alone were allowed to carry the ark or touch it. Anyone else would be punished for violating that holiness. The ark would be located in the Holy of Holies, and Yahweh would display his presence by the pillar of cloud and fire in that sacred space alone.

Reproduction of the Ark of the Covenant without the carrying poles

CHAPTER 53

The process of making the golden calf began as quickly as possible. Because Bezalel and his cadre of artists were unavailable, Aaron found several others willing to help out who did not have their guildmaster's harsh judgments.

The first step in the process was to craft a wooden sculpture of the bull-calf, using hardened wood scavenged from the wilderness. The image was the size of a real calf, over three feet high and the same in length from muzzle to rump. The artists fastened carved legs to a torso and head that were carved from a single large piece. Though they made this structure in the rough shape of a calf, it functioned as only a foundation upon which gold gilding would engrave the final features and details.

Gold gilding was a process that the Egyptians had developed to a fine art over the millennia. And the Israelites were adept at it, having absorbed so many of their captor's ways. Using a simple forge, the golden earrings and rings of the Israelites were gathered and heated into a molten liquid state. The liquid was poured out onto a flat rock surface. Craftsmen then pounded out the cooling gold into a thin, flat surface called leaf.

The leaf was cut up into various thicknesses and sizes for use by the engravers, who layered the leaf onto the wooden sculpture and gently beat it into place. Once the calf was completely covered in the gold, engravers then used their tools to shape and carve out the fine details like muscles, hooves, eyes, and hair. The process took several days with multiple artists working around the sundial.

This was the same gilding process used on the pharaohs' sarcophagi. Their anthropoid-shaped wooden coffins were gilded with gold and shaped into the body and face of the god on earth.

Next was the Opening of the Mouth ceremony for the image, another familiar Egyptian ritual that allowed the breath of the deity to enter into the image as a representation of the god's presence. The ceremony consisted of a series of proceedings.

First, the image was placed on a heap of sand facing north toward the Promised Land. Second, the image was fumigated with incense from multiple censers. Third, Aaron took water and baptized the image with ritual sprinkling, announcing, "Thy purification is the purification of Yahweh."

The eyes of the bull-calf were painted with *kohl*, a black cosmetic widely used as eyeliner throughout Egypt. An engraver's instrument first touched the calf's mouth, and then Aaron's hand, which he had dipped in cow's milk. Aaron prayed to Yahweh, imploring him to breath his presence into the image in the same fashion that he had breathed his breath into humans, his images on earth.

Building a stone altar before the image of the bull-calf, Aaron sacrificed burnt offerings and peace offerings to Yahweh. He announced to the people, "Behold, this is your god, O Israel, who brought you up out of the land of Egypt!"

The sound of their cheers rose to heaven. Aaron could feel a unity amongst them he had not sensed for the last moon. The division, the petty grievances, the grumbling and complaining had all been set to rest with this single act of unifying the nation.

Aaron told himself that he had done the best thing. That he was a good leader who had compromised to successfully navigate a difficult situation.

Lastly, the entire camp was called to a celebration feast. Perhaps even one like the Passover the Israelites would commemorate throughout the generations, Aaron tried to convince himself. Sheep and goats were slaughtered all throughout the camp as families ate together, then joined the large gathering around the calf to sing and dance. And drink.

• • • • •

Writing down all the directions of Yahweh for the tabernacle and its elements, including the ark, had exhausted Moses. Joshua assisted him by replenishing his supplies and properly ordering the animal skin parchments.

After taking down the directions for the ark, Moses had gone to sleep for the evening. Joshua tended the fire to keep them warm before turning in. In the morning, they would return to the camp from their long absence. It had been forty days and nights.

But they were awakened by Yahweh's voice and the pillar of fire's presence. "Moses."

"I am awake, my lord. I listen."

"The people whom you brought up out of Egypt have corrupted themselves in the camp below. They have made for themselves a golden calf to worship. Go down now with your assistant Joshua to witness my wrath against this stiff-necked people. For I will consume them and make of you a great nation instead."

Moses and Joshua shared a shocked look over how quickly and easily Yahweh would destroy his own people. Would he truly take them all this way with miracles of deliverance only to wipe them out and start over with a single man? It seemed an extreme act of justice.

Then Moses remembered his own incident with the Angel of Yahweh. How he had almost been executed for failing to fulfill the covenant of circumcision—despite Moses's little knowledge of the ritual or its importance.

This was a holy god who allowed in his presence only those who were of perfect obedience and righteousness. Because of the nature of sin, it was not an extreme act of justice to destroy them all but rather an extreme act of mercy that he had not destroyed them already.

Pulling Joshua with him to their knees, Moses chose to appeal to that loving mercy he'd experienced so undeservedly in his own life. "O Yahweh, please reconsider. For if you destroy this people in your wrath, will your name not lose face before the world? Will not the Egyptians surely say that you brought the Israelites out of Egypt only to kill them in the wilderness with evil intent? Did you not swear to our forefathers Abraham, Isaac, and Israel that you would give their seed the Promised Land to inherit forever?"

Both men lay with their faces low to the ground, afraid to hear the response. They exhaled in relief as Yahweh spoke.

"Up on your feet. I will do as you ask. But go down now and stop this abomination, or I will not withhold my wrath."

· · · · ·

Down in the camp, the field of meeting was full. Miriam led the women in a procession of dance much like their joy at Yam Suph. They carried bells and tambourines, drums and percussive devices. Some of them waved long, flowing banners in an orchestrated manner to create a beautiful visual tapestry of movement like streams of water.

Aaron brought Miriam up to the platform before the golden calf. She was sweaty from the exertion and breathing heavily. She looked ecstatic as though she'd seen a vision.

"My brother," she announced. "I have been given a word from Yahweh."

Women did not have much involvement in leading Israel. Prophecy seemed to be the one place in which the people were willing to listen to their voice. It struck Aaron suddenly how many women Miriam was shepherding who were claiming to be prophetesses.

Miriam then announced to the people, "Children of Israel, Yahweh has given me a precious word. I have spent much time in his sweet presence in prayer. Our God is a caring, nurturing god like a loving mother who gave birth to this nation in the wilderness and now feeds her infants with milk from her very breasts."

The image that immediately came to Aaron's mind was of Hathor, the Egyptian Lady of Heaven. She was the golden goddess who helped women give birth, raise the dead, and renew the cosmos. She also had the head of a cow. Miriam's comparison felt odd to him. But he wasn't going to create dissension during such a blessed event.

Miriam continued, "And Yahweh has spoken to me much like he speaks to Moses. In words I could hear with my own ears."

The crowd applauded.

"And Yahweh said unto me, 'Miriam, I told Moses that another prophet would be raised up, one just like him, and I would put my words into his mouth. And everyone must listen to him.'"

More cheers from the people seemed to fill Miriam with more boldness.

"Did Moses not tell us all of this word from Yahweh? Now Moses is gone and I fear will never return. Yahweh has taken him to his sweet, sweet bosom."

The masses seemed to hang on her every word.

"Yahweh has told me that the prophet who would replace Moses is in our midst!" She turned and pointed to Aaron, who felt shocked with the revelation. But the people's encouragement seemed to fill him with energy as well.

Miriam kept going. "Aaron, the high priest of Yahweh, has crafted us this beautiful image of Yahweh. He was with Moses at every miracle, using his own staff as God's powerful instrument. He has even ascended God's very mountain!"

Aaron had become so caught up in Miriam's oration he didn't notice that a small group of people had walked up the platform to challenge her.

Gershom shouted, "No!"

Miriam stopped in surprise.

"This is not the word of Yahweh!"

Gershom was with his mother Zipporah, his younger brother Eliezer, grandfather Amram, Bezalel the artist, and Caleb the warrior.

"I say we wait!" Gershom continued. "It has been forty days since my father left us. But he was with Joshua. If anything had happened, Joshua would have returned to tell us!"

Zipporah spoke to Miriam without being heard by the crowd. "Miriam, why do you do this? Why do you grieve Yahweh's heart?"

Miriam ignored her.

Zipporah looked at Aaron. "Aaron, do you support this?"

All their eyes turned to him. He didn't know what to do. He had often desired to be Israel's leader and be Yahweh's spokesman. He had often been jealous of Yahweh's choice of Moses as his chosen one. But now that the opportunity stared him in the face, he suddenly felt inadequate.

He turned to the people and announced, "We will discuss this further with the elders. In the meantime, return to your festivities and let us worship the Lord together!"

The people turned back to their celebration.

CHAPTER 54

As Moses and Joshua approached the foot of the mountain, they could hear the noise from the camp. It sounded like women screaming and high-pitched wailing.

"It sounds like the noise of war," said Joshua.

"No. That is the sound of debauchery," said Moses.

Arriving at the mountain's foot by the tent of meeting, the two men saw the masses assembled before the platform with the golden calf.

The drinking and dancing had degenerated into an orgiastic frenzy. Many were passed out drunk on the desert floor. Others were half-conscious, waving their bodies around like drugged serpents. Yet others engaged in intimate acts openly. They were so engulfed in their depravity that no one noticed Moses and Joshua walk onto the platform.

When Moses blew a shofar trumpet, it seemed to break through the insanity. Everyone stopped to look for the sound's source. When they saw it was Moses with Joshua, some cried out in joy. Others were silenced in shame. But everyone seemed to wait for a word from their very-much-alive leader.

Moses was raging mad. He could not speak. He did not want to explain anything to these apostates. They didn't deserve it.

Joshua held the two tablets, one copy for the people, one copy for Yahweh.

Moses saw the people looking his way but not looking *at* him. He asked Joshua, "Why are they shielding their eyes?"

"Because you are shining."

"Shining?"

"The skin of your face is shining like that of the heavenly host. Like the Sons of God."

Moses pulled up his hand to see light reflecting off it. "By Yahweh, you are right!"

That must be why the heavenly host shone so brightly, Moses concluded. The more they were in Yahweh's presence, the more they reflected that glory in them.

"You may need a veil if you want people to look directly at you."

Moses was too caught up in his anger to concern himself with that right now. He grabbed the first tablet from Joshua. It was heavy, but he lifted it over his head and cast it to the ground. It hit a large rock and shattered into pieces. A silence came over the entire camp.

Moses shouted, "Since you have broken this covenant, may it break you!"

Grabbing the other stone from Joshua, he cast it down to the ground as well. It too broke into pieces.

He was so disgusted, so angry with the Israelites, that he thought he now knew how Yahweh must feel about idolatrous betrayal. And why Yahweh's wrath would be justified against these people.

Then he spotted Aaron and Miriam standing below the platform watching him with stunned looks. Without any more words, Moses walked off the platform, followed by Joshua. Aaron and Miriam fell into step behind as he walked right through the massive crowd that parted in front of him as Yam Suph had done.

He was eighty years old, no longer with the imposing physique of his youth. Yet the people were clearly afraid of him.

Afraid of me! he thought. *They have not yet learned to fear Yahweh.*

Moses walked all the way to the gates of the camp, and the people followed. The gates of a city were the location where the elders would make their judicial decisions regarding significant issues for the congregation as well as individual appeals for justice.

Tonight there will be justice.

Reaching the gates, Moses turned back to face the people.

He shouted simply, "Who is on Yahweh's side? Come to me! If you still want this golden calf, return to it."

The bulk of the people did not move. Crowds were like that. Most people waited to see what would happen. Only those most committed to their convictions would move.

Most in the crowd did not move.

But Moses saw individuals making their way toward him from various locations in the multitude.

As they gathered around him, others melted away to return to the calf where they had been celebrating. Many more just returned to their tents in shame.

Joshua leaned into Moses and said, "Levites."

He was right. Most of those coming to his side were from Aaron's tribe despite the high priest's clear lapse of judgment.

When a significant number had gathered around him, Moses announced to them, "Thus says Yahweh, the God of Israel, 'Today, this tribe of Levi has been ordained for the service of Yahweh.' Your first holy duty is to cleanse the congregation. Grab your swords, each of you, and go through the camp to kill all those still devoted to the bull-calf as their image of Yahweh. Do not spare your own family members. And Yahweh will bless you this day. For you have been consecrated unto the Lord."

The men looked at each other. Leaders moved first, drawing their swords, and the rest followed.

Moses ordered Joshua, "Burn the calf in the fire. And grind the broken tablets with it into dust. Scatter that dust on the water and make the people drink it. This will be their trial by ordeal."

Joshua nodded in obedience and took off to get the tablets. Trial by ordeal was one of the customs of jurisprudence Yahweh gave in the testimony. An accused adulterer's guilt or innocence was determined by the individual drinking water mixed with dust from the tabernacle floor. If nothing happened, the accused was declared innocent. If the accused became sick, they were judged guilty. The tabernacle had not been built yet, so the dust for this mass trial would be the very testimony itself pounded into dust. A fitting source of justice.

Moses pointed to Aaron and Miriam. "You two, come with me."

He turned and made his way back to the tent of meeting at the outside of the camp. On their right and left, they saw and heard Levites slicing and hacking Israelites to death, those who refused to repent of worshipping the graven image of Yahweh.

Women screamed in terror. Some men fought back. But the Levites carried Yahweh's very authority in their actions. Idolatry had to be cut out of their midst.

Moses led Aaron and Miriam into the small tent of meeting he had built outside the camp. Moses had stayed quiet the entire walk there. But when they entered the tent, he turned to face Aaron and said with a slow burn, holding back his mounting fury, "What did this people do to you that you have brought such a great sin upon them?"

Aaron squirmed in his presence. He looked at Miriam for support. She kept her fearful gaze on Moses. Finally, Aaron blurted out, "Let not your anger burn hot against your brother. You know these people. You know they are evil. Their hearts are set on evil."

"Then why did you make them a graven image in violation of Yahweh's command?"

"We thought you were dead, Moses. We all thought you were dead. Did we not, Miriam?"

Aaron looked to his sister. She said to Moses, "You were gone for forty days without sending a single message. We heard no word from you. What else could we conclude?"

Aaron was sweating now. His voice became more desperate. "The people said, 'Make us a god to go before us. An image that tells us Yahweh is surely with us.' You know well, my brother, that the people have possessed images for hundreds of years. It is no surprise they cannot conceive of a new god without them. It seemed like a legitimate accommodation."

Moses would not let him off. "You made for them a graven image."

"Wait," said Aaron. "I thought it was Yahweh himself who provided it. I just gathered the gold the people gave me! I threw it into the fire and out came the golden bull-calf!"

Moses stared incredulously at his lying sibling. He saw Aaron's eyes dart a look at Miriam with guilt.

Pathetic. Moses would not even dignify the desperate lie by addressing it. He looked straight at Miriam, knowing she was a strong influence on her brother. "How is it that the people just followed after Aaron?"

Miriam rose with her own anger. "You are not the only one through whom Yahweh speaks. Aaron was with you every step of the way."

Moses knew what else she was thinking. "And you are a prophetess."

She argued, "Moses, that Kushite wife of yours is not pure blood. Her loyalty is suspect. And you are acting like Pharaoh, as if everything is dependent on you, as if you are the god on earth for Yahweh in heaven."

Again, Moses could not believe his ears. He closed his eyes, trying to hold back his anger. When he opened them, he saw Aaron and Miriam frozen in terror, looking outside the tent.

Moses turned to see the pillar of cloud now resting down at the entrance, its plumes rising to the highest heaven like the smoke of a furnace.

Yahweh's voice spoke from the cloud. "Come out, you three."

They obeyed and came out of the tent. The three siblings stood in silent awe before the pillar. It swirled tightly into the night sky and disappeared into the darkness. All around the camp, people who a short time before had been celebrating a golden image now turned to stare with mouths agape at the presence of Yahweh in their midst.

"Hear my words." Yahweh's voice was thunder and trumpets and a rushing like the Nile at full flood. But every word could be heard clearly throughout the Israelite encampment. "I make myself known to prophets in visions and dreams. But not so with my servant Moses. He is faithful in all my house. With him, I speak mouth to mouth and not in riddles and unclear visions. He beholds me. Why then were you not afraid to speak against my servant Moses?"

Moses could sense the anger in Yahweh's words. He knew judgment was coming.

Aaron burst out like a crying infant and fell to his knees. Through his tears, he managed to pray, "Oh, my Lord, we have done foolishly and have sinned a great sin. We have acted with godless folly."

For the brief time Moses had known his brother, he knew Aaron to be quick to sin but also quick to repent. He couldn't conclude whether such a character trait was a strength or a weakness. Perhaps it was both.

As Aaron wept into his hands, Moses looked over to find Miriam standing still but with eyes wide with fear. Her entire body had turned leprous and white. She was covered with boils, and her skin began flaking off.

Groaning with pain, she raised an arm to look at her skin. None observing her could avoid comparisons with the hideous, painful plague of boils that had afflicted the Egyptians. An agonizing torment Yahweh's people had been spared. Nor could anyone question Yahweh's justice in bringing pestilence upon the woman who had usurped divine authority. Who had misled Yahweh's people with words she'd falsely claimed to be Yahweh's own.

Yahweh's judgment surprised Moses least of all. But it wasn't his siblings' betrayal that now gripped his heart. It was an anguished tidal wave of love. It was remembrance of all these two had been to him. Yes, they had just engaged in grevious sin, but Miriam had saved her brother's life from a mighty Pharaoh's wrath, and Aaron had been his staff of strength in the face of another Pharaoh's power. Without these two, Moses would not be here. It was a stark reminder of his own faithlessness, impatience, and disobedience. It simply proved that Yahweh was merciful in using fallible and broken vessels for his purposes of glory.

Falling to his knees before the cloud, Moses prayed fervently, "O Lord, have mercy on my brother and sister. They are fools, but so was I when you chose me."

Aaron looked more offended than grateful at the claim.

With desperation, Moses continued, "If you will not forgive their sin and the sin of your people this day, then please blot me out of your book that you have written. For have you not chosen this people out of all the other peoples on the face of the earth? O Lord, please may your Angel go with us in our midst. I know we are a stiff-necked people, but please pardon our iniquity and our sin and take us for your inheritance."

Aaron was now weeping with regret while Miriam trembled violently with the pain and fear of her curse.

Then Yahweh spoke from the cloud. "I have heard your words, Moses, and this very thing you ask I will do, for you have found favor in my sight. Those who have committed this grave sin I will blot out of my book. But I will not destroy the people for your sake. As for Aaron, whom I have chosen as my high priest, I will not relent. However, he will not enter the land of promise.

"As for Miriam, she will heal, but she remains unclean for seven days. Take her outside the camp to sit in her shame until the seven days are completed."

"Thank you, my Lord," cried Aaron. "Thank you!"

Miriam was so humbled in her diseased state that she said nothing. Only tremors of fear shook her.

Then Yahweh said, "As for you, Moses my servant, come back up the mountain where I will show you my glory. You will cut two new tablets of stone like the first, and I will write the Ten Words that I have written at first. I will renew this covenant, for I Am Who I Am, Yahweh. I am a God merciful and gracious, slow to anger and abounding in steadfast love and faithfulness, keeping steadfast love for thousands, forgiving iniquity and transgression and sin, but who will by no means clear the guilty, visiting the iniquity of the fathers on the children to the third and fourth generation.

"And now the time has come for you to depart this mountain and go up to the land that I swore to Abraham, Isaac, and Jacob, saying that to your seed I will give it. You will drive out all the cursed inhabitants of the land, the Canaanites, Amorites, Hittites, Perizzites, Hivites, and Jebusites. I will send an angel before you, but I will *not* go up among you lest I consume you, for you are a stiff-necked people."

The next day after the people of the camp had been given water to drink with the dust of the testimony in it, a plague broke out, and thousands became sick and died. Those who died had failed their trial by ordeal. An act of God had sealed their guilt. The people of Israel had been cleansed and were now prepared to receive the revelation of their covenant's tabernacle.

CHAPTER 55

Sitting in his small tent, Moses prepared his quill and ink for the parchment he had laid out. He had consulted his many scrolls from the library of Avaris and the Hebrew *toledoth* manuscripts of genealogies and stories from his forefathers.

This was a new beginning out of the chaos of four hundred years of oppression from Egypt. Now the people of Israel were finally starting over as if God himself were creating a new heavens and earth within which to dwell with his people. Praying for wisdom and guidance, Moses began to write the story of Israel.

Bezalel the artist had suggested to Moses that he begin the narrative with a creation story as an expression of Yahweh's covenant with Israel. It should be a dedication hymn used in the consecration of the tabernacle, Yahweh's itinerant temple. Since the tabernacle was a picture of the Garden of Eden, then the creation account Moses was writing should symbolically connect the building of the tabernacle with Yahweh's construction of Eden. Their Promised Land was, in effect, their Eden, so that one day in the near future, the dwelling of God would be in that new Eden.

It had been almost a year since the Israelites had left Egypt. The tabernacle's assembly and dedication would take place on the first day of the first moon of the coming new year. It would mark the beginning of their covenant's perpetual duties and privileges. Yahweh had given Moses detailed instructions describing the priests' duties and sacrificial and offertory system to maintain holiness in Yahweh's presence. He'd also laid out a feast calendar that the Israelites would observe to remember Yahweh's goodness to them.

Moses transcribed extended applications of the Ten Words for their society, a theocracy of Yahweh's rule. This was the heart and soul of law and justice. Upon it would be the foundation of their very civilization. It was an ordering of thei chaos, and it would be theirs forever until Shiloh came.

Moses had used the specialized writing he had learned from Aaron, a form of their Hebrew language. Ephraim and Manasseh had developed this form when the Israelites first arrived in Egypt. Hieroglyphics were too complex and bulky for Moses's purposes. The Israelites had simplified their language into what they called an *alphabet*. This new approach would use individual signs instead of pictures to represent all of their language's basic sounds. They had simplified it enough that Hebrews had a greater literacy rate than their Egyptian neighbors. Even slave miners in the turquoise mines of Ta Mefkat could read and write it.

Moses used that alphabet now to minimize the pages he would need to record all of Yahweh's revelations. Ipuwer had been right. Moses would be writing multiple volumes of books to tell this story and include the covenant Yahweh gave on the mountain.

For Israel, their covenant would be everything. It was their cosmos, their heaven and earth. When Yahweh had given his covenant to Israel, it was the creation of their particular heaven and earth. It was Yahweh establishing his order out of the wilderness chaos that was Egypt, Sinai, and—soon—Canaan. Yahweh had parted the chaos waters of Yam Suph and crushed the heads of Leviathan, its ruling denizen, only to deliver the orderly covenant of his kingdom.

The day of temple dedication for the tabernacle would be like the creation of heavens and earth. It was the cultic beginning of the covenant made by Yahweh. In one sense, the whole earth was Yahweh's temple. That was why the tabernacle served as an image of the entire cosmos. But in another sense, Yahweh was going to establish his holy residence with one particular people in one particular land to separate them from the evil that governed the rest of the world. That holy land and temple would be his starting point from which he would expand his kingdom to all the earth.

Moses had also taken the advice of Bezalel to write their creation story as a polemic against the gods of Egypt and their kingdoms, something Moses knew quite intimately, being learned in the literature of the surrounding kingdoms of Babylonia, Assyria, Syria, and Canaan. The Israelites were so conditioned to understand the world through their idolatrous Egyptian pantheon that they could barely understand the world through a new perspective of an exclusive God. Moses had to begin with imagery and concepts with which the Israelites would be familiar—and then subvert them. Separate Yahweh from these concepts as a sign of his holiness. In fact, true holiness was separation *unto* Yahweh.

Moses wrote the first words of his temple dedication hymn.:

In the beginning, God created the heavens and the earth.

The Egyptians conceived of their beginning creation involving the Ogdoad of four pairs of gods and goddesses who embodied the primeval forces. Hehu and Hehet were the formlessness and emptiness of original chaos. The darkness of Keku and Keket was upon the face of the deep of primeval waters, Nun and Nunet. But Amun and Amunet were the spirit winds that hovered over those waters.

Moses rejected this deification of nature. He knew that Yahweh was both creator and sustainer of all things from the earth and sea to the heavens and highest heavens. The actions of nature were his actions alone and not of the gods. Moses wrote on the parchment:

The land was formless and empty,
and darkness was over the face of the deep.
And the Spirit of God hovered over the face of the waters.

The sea was the symbol of chaos to everyone in this world. And Canaan was a wilderness wasteland without form and empty. But Yahweh was the one bringing his creative order to it, not the gods of Egypt, or for that matter of any other nation.

The creation stories of most other nations conceived of their world being created out of a cosmic battle of the gods. The gods would speak forth the purposes and functions of things in this world. In Egypt, it was the spoken word of Atum or Ptah. In Babylonia it was the decrees of the *MEs*.

But since Yahweh alone was creator and there were none beside him, he did not struggle with any other being when creating. He merely spoke forth each realm and spoke forth the functions of each inhabitant in that realm.

Let there be…and it was.

The temple's actual dedication would take seven days. As Moses set up the boundaries and tents and the instruments each day, he would establish their cultic functions. So he described Yahweh as establishing the functions of each inhabitant that filled each realm of creation on each day. He would do so by the act of separation.

The first act of separation was to be light and darkness.

> *For God said, "Let there be light," and there was light…*
> *and God separated the light from the darkness.*

God saw each of these acts as good and orderly each day just as Moses would perform his consecrating acts of the tabernacle each day and consider them good and orderly as well.

The second act was the separation of the waters of heaven and the waters of earth.

> *God said, "Let there be a firmament in the midst of the waters,*
> *and let it separate the waters below, seas,*
> *from the waters above in heaven…"*

Yahweh spread out the firmament above just as Moses spread out the tent of the tabernacle over its holy place.

The third was the separation and rising of the land from the waters, like the Egyptian primeval hillock—and its filling. Except Yahweh's land was not Egypt but Canaan.

> *Let the waters under the heavens be gathered together,*
> *and let the dry land appear.*
> *Let the land sprout forth vegetation…*

The fourth separation was separation of day and night by purposing the greater and lesser lights.

> *Let there be lights in the firmament of the heavens…*
> *The greater light to rule the day and the lesser light to rule the*
> *night—and the stars.*

Other creation stories would give names of deity to the sun and moon and stars. But in Yahweh's creation, these were mere objects for his purpose. The sun god Ra did not bring light to this world. Yahweh had proved that definitively when he blotted out the sun for three days in Egypt. So the golden lampstand would give light to the holy place of the tabernacle. And the stars on the roof of the tent and on the holy veil represented that expanse above as well.

The fifth act of purposeful separation was of creatures in the sky from those in the sea.

> *Let the waters swarm with living creatures,*
> *and let birds fly above the land across the face of the firmament.*

The sixth separation was the highest of all divisions. For in it, Yahweh gave the purpose of land and animals to be ruled over by humans, Yahweh's apex of creation.

> *Let us make Man in our image, after our likeness.*
> *And let him have dominion...*
> *So God created Man in his own image,*
> *in the image of God he created him;*
> *male and female he created them.*

With the advice of his own divine council, Yahweh created Man and separated the female from the male to establish as his images on land. They were to represent Yahweh by reigning over everything. Like an image of deity that received its breath from the Opening of the Mouth ceremony, so humans received the very breath of God to be his imagers on the land.

In this way, Adam—both male and female—was a symbol of Israel being placed in the Promised Land.

> *Yahweh Elohim took Adam and put him in the garden of Eden to cultivate and keep it...*

...just as the priests were ordered to cultivate and keep the tabernacle holy in their service.

> *Be fruitful and multiply and fill the land and subdue it and have dominion...*

...just as Israel was to be fruitful and multiply and subdue and take dominion of the land of Canaan, a land that was a wilderness without form and empty, ready to be filled with God's order and purpose.

Adam *was* Israel.

If they obeyed Yahweh's commands, the man and woman would live forever in the paradise of God. But if they disobeyed, they would be cursed by death and cast out of the garden, just as Israel would be cursed and cast out of the land for disobeying Yahweh's covenant. It was a perfect theological picture of the creation of the covenant of heaven and earth and the consequences of disobedience.

The last and most important separation of all was the seventh. For on the seventh day of the tabernacle's consecration, Moses and the people were commanded to rest from their labors because on the seventh day of Yahweh's covenant creation, God finished his work and sat down on his throne in his heavenly temple.

Sitting down in rest on a throne was symbolic of a king settled in his accomplished reign over his kingdom. Yahweh would be seated on his throne in heaven with the ark of the covenant in the tabernacle as his footstool on earth. A throne between heaven and earth.

On this seventh day of consecration, the pillar of cloud would come down from the mountain and take its new residence in the Holy of Holies over the ark of the covenant. From there, Yahweh would lead Israel by the movement of his cloud and fire through the wilderness and into God's rest in their land of inheritance. The Israelites would be both kings and priests.

These ten times of God speaking in this genesis of heavens and earth matched the ten times God spoke to Moses in the consecration of the chosen priests in preparation for their service in the tabernacle. The seven days of dedication of that mobile temple would be followed by twelve days of offering, one by one, of each of the twelve tribes of Israel for dedication of the altar where their sacrifices would be made.

But Moses knew that the stiff-necked Israelites would nevertheless turn eventually from Yahweh in the Promised Land and whore after the forbidden gods Yahweh allotted to the other nations. He knew this because Yahweh had told him. The Garden serpent Nachash was that false god who had tempted the couple, and they had fallen by eating the fruit of the forbidden tree of the knowledge of good and evil.

Yahweh had then exiled them from the Garden to work and toil in pain, just as Israel would be exiled from her land in painful slavery. Yahweh had cursed the couple with suffering and death and endless strife embodied in the pronouncement upon the serpent:

> *I will put enmity between you and the woman,*
> *and between your seed and her seed;*
> *He shall crush your head,*
> *and you shall crush his heel.*

As Moses wrote the words, he knew the nature of the people of Israel, and he knew how long it had taken Yahweh just to get them to this very place. He knew the power of the enemy that had been seeking their destruction for so long. He knew the long and brutal war ahead to take dominion of the Promised Land.

He knew the War of the Seed was about to turn gigantic.

•••••

For the next book in this storied timeline get Joshua Valiant. Though it is in the Chronicles of the Nephilim series, it is the next one you want to get. This is because Chronicles of the Watchers is interwoven with Chronicles of the Nephilim to fill in the gaps of the storyline of the Nephilim series.

Sign up for Godawa Chronicles Updates at Godawa.com to be the first to hear about new releases, special deals and articles on strange things in the Bible.

If you liked this book, then please help me out by writing a positive review of it on Amazon. That is one of the best ways to say thank you to me as an author. It really does help my sales and status. Thanks! – *Brian Godawa*

More Books by Brian Godawa

See www.godawa.com for more information on other books by Brian Godawa. Check out his other series below:

Chronicles of the Nephilim

Chronicles of the Nephilim is a saga that charts the rise and fall of the Nephilim giants of Genesis 6 and their place in the evil plans of the fallen angelic Sons of God called "The Watchers." The story starts in the days of Enoch and continues on through the Bible until the arrival of the Messiah, Jesus. The prelude to Chronicles of the Apocalypse. ChroniclesOfTheNephilim.com. (affiliate link)

Chronicles of the Apocalypse

Chronicles of the Apocalypse is an origin story of the most controversial book of the Bible: Revelation. A historical conspiracy thriller quadrilogy in first century Rome set against the backdrop of explosive spiritual warfare of Satan and his demonic Watchers. ChroniclesOfTheApocalypse.com. (affiliate link)

Chronicles of the Watchers

Chronicles of the Watchers is a series that charts the influence of spiritual principalities and powers over the course of human history. The kingdoms of man in service to the gods of the nations at war. Interwoven with Chronicles of the Nephilim. ChroniclesOfTheWatchers.com. (affiliate link)

Get the Book of the Biblical & Historical Research Behind This Novel.

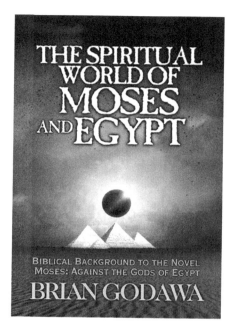

Explore the Spiritual World of the Land of the Exodus.
If you like the novel *Moses: Against the Gods of Egypt*, you'll love discovering the biblical and historical basis for the fascinating, mind-bending story.

Also available for purchase in paperback.

https://godawa.com/get-spirit-moses/
(*affiliate link*)

GREAT OFFERS BY BRIAN GODAWA

Get More Biblical Imagination

Sign up Online For The Godawa Chronicles

www.Godawa.com

Updates and Freebies
of the Books of Brian Godawa
Special Discounts,
Fascinating Bible Facts!

ABOUT THE AUTHOR

Brian Godawa is the screenwriter for the award-winning feature film *To End All Wars*, starring Kiefer Sutherland. It was awarded the Commander in Chief Medal of Service, Honor, and Pride by the Veterans of Foreign Wars, won the first Heartland Film Festival by storm, and showcased the Cannes Film Festival Cinema for Peace.

He previously adapted to film the best-selling supernatural thriller novel *The Visitation* by author Frank Peretti for Ralph Winter (*X-Men, Wolverine*), and wrote and directed *Wall of Separation*, a PBS documentary, and *Lines That Divide*, a documentary on stem cell research.

Mr. Godawa's articles on movies and philosophy have been published around the world. He has traveled around the United States teaching on movies, worldviews, and culture to colleges and churches.

His popular book *Hollywood Worldviews: Watching Films with Wisdom and Discernment* (InterVarsity Press) is used as a film textbook in schools around the country.

In the top ten of biblical fiction on Amazon, his first novel series *Chronicles of the Nephilim* is an imaginative retelling of biblical stories of the Nephilim giants, the secret plan of the fallen Watchers, and the War of the Seed of the Serpent with the Seed of Eve. The sequel series *Chronicles of the Apocalypse* tells the story of the apostle John's book of Revelation, while *Chronicles of the Watchers* recounts true history through the Watcher paradigm interwoven with the other two series.

Find out more about his other books, online digital lectures, and DVDs for sale at his website, www.godawa.com.

Made in the USA
Middletown, DE
05 July 2023

34562983R00225